MW01136771

PENNIES FOR HER EYES

PENNIES FOR HER EYES

A Surf City Mystery

James R. Preston

authorHOUSE®

AuthorHouse™
1663 Liberty Drive
Bloomington, IN 47403
www.authorhouse.com
Phone: 1-800-839-8640

Published by AuthorHouse   09/19/2012

ISBN: 978-1-4772-6926-8 (sc)
ISBN: 978-1-4772-6925-1 (hc)
ISBN: 978-1-4772-6924-4 (e)

Library of Congress Control Number: 2012917066

For Lillian Preston

Wife, Mother, Grandmother, Great-grandmother, Friend.

Inspiration to us all.

Thanks, Lillian. This one's for you.

Author's Note

This book wouldn't exist without: Billie & Bruce, Dildette, Ernie & Ethel, The Half, Ennaman, Ragman, Claudia & My Bruce, Snake, Carol, Ace & Louise, Bob, and Bob & Susan, Pete, and Hosehead & Janet.

And, of course, always and forever—her name was McGill, and she called herself Lil, but everyone knew her as Nancy.

It's late; dinner's been over a long time, and I've got a paper due tomorrow.

Well, okay. One more cup of coffee, and a story . . .

Table of Contents

White petals

drift to the floor

There is no blood.

Mary

From the Journal of Mary Shaw.

Dear Diary—Once again I have shamefully neglected you.

Kandi—Screw that. Pat yourself when you write in this, and when you don't, who cares? Geez! Which one of us is the shrink?

I seem to slip into the Kandi persona that I created more and more easily.

I have been totally involved in the latter stages of my dissertation. When that is complete, certainly my employment, but possibly my relationships, will change. I must prevent at least the latter. At all costs? Perhaps.

Why did I write "perhaps?" I meant "Of course."

Let's see, what else? Today T. R. and I went out on an enormous boat, an actual yacht, I presume, with some friends of Walter Darlymple.

They are interesting people, and the boat was magnificent, but I was not entirely at ease.

A pleasant afternoon although I had to take a nap below because I did not feel well.

I must go now. A few more details to check on the dissertation.

From Kandi's iPhone Calendar, same date:

```
Boat ride with Berkeley geezers. Mary almost puked,
had to get rid of her. Awesome Cosmos.
```

Chapter One   Invasion

Text from Alys Winters to T. R. Macdonald

`Mac Rgr wnts 2 email U. OK 2 give him yr address?`

T. R. Macdonald to Alys Winters

`I'd rather have a colonoscopy. No.`

I was folding Kandi's underwear when the home invasion began. It was around nine in the evening of a chilly December day in Huntington Beach—Surf City, USA.

I know what you're thinking: I have this reputation of being sort of a tough guy, at least when I had my slightly-less-than fifteen minutes of fame on the web and in various blogs that's what they said: that I was a tough guy. So why was I folding underwear? I lost a bet, and I should have known better.

My Significant Other knows less about sports than your average housecat but she can pick hockey winners. Kandi, who is known as Mary Shaw when she is teaching at UCLA, wanted to do some work on her dissertation after working a two-hour fill-in shift across the channel at Fred's Fine Mexican Food, so we came back to my house. A great cruise off the coast of Long Beach, a plate of shrimp enchiladas and black beans at Fred's, and now hockey. Life was good. You'd think I'd learn, wouldn't you? I turned on the Kings and in the third period she looked up from her iPad and said, "they're going to win." My boys were down 3-zip and struggling to survive yet another power play. I said, "Name your stakes."

She was in the family room, sitting on my new couch with her feet tucked up under her. I smiled, because looking at Kandi always makes me smile. She's tall, with thick, lustrous, blonde hair pulled back in a ponytail while she worked, and hazel eyes that could stop traffic on the 405 freeway. Her legs are great in part because she does more serious running than I do; the other part of the reason is that they are simply great legs. She had on a faded yellow chenille bathrobe that looked good on her. Like I said, I enjoy looking at her. When she didn't answer my challenge I made highly-realistic chicken noises and danced around flapping my arms. Without looking up, she said, "Laundry. And if that was supposed to be a chicken, it was awful." That led to a pile of what my grandmother would have called "Unmentionables."

Tell me about your adventures.

Well, I once was shoved down a flight of stairs at the house next door and the people I thought were paramedics helping me instead threw me in the channel to drown. That was an adventure all right, but not one I want to talk about. I would have drowned if a teenage girl named Alys Winters hadn't jumped in and pulled me to safety.

Walking into the garage, two-car, connected to the house through a door into the right side of the entryway, those words went through my head again.

We'd spent the early afternoon off the coast of Long Beach on the *Waiting for the Sun II*. The *Sun* was a Grand Banks 65 RP, and it was one of the most amazing yachts I've ever been on, a four-million-dollar floating palace. My friend the Snake and three of his Berkeley college friends had invited us out. The *Waiting For the Sun II's* owner, a sixty-something named Brad Zucco, a striking blonde named Lisa June Culhane, and a tall, gray-haired woman in her sixties named Henrietta Graveline, plus Kandi, me and the Snake, made up the party. Snake's wife Cheryl was reading poetry somewhere, so she missed the party—just as well since we don't exactly get along. Henrietta had asked me about my adventures. It's not that unusual a request; like I said, I had my fifteen minutes. It turned chilly so we moved from the outside deck to the yacht's main cabin. She was sitting in the dinette, staring at me intently with wide-set gray eyes peering over the top of a wine glass, while I stood behind the ship's owner and watched Brad steer us deftly through the traffic—a few sailboats barely under way in the light wind, and the usual kayakers and kids on jet skis. We cleared the mouth of the harbor and began to roll a little in the mild swell.

Tell me about your adventures.

She'd Googled my name and wanted to know about the supertanker and the serious craziness that Kandi and I had gone through. She wanted to know about Roger Winters, and the man in the desert; like Mary, she wanted to know how I felt about it. About death, up close and personal, since I'd killed the man in the desert. And I had no answer, other than a shrug. So I talked about the silly parts, like barging into a party wet and bleeding, holding the hostess at gunpoint and how it was all right because it was a costume party and the host was dressed as Elvis. I left out the part where I had to shoot a kid.

The fact that the party's hostess, Allison Winters, had been in her underwear—black fifties costume garter belt and stockings—at the time pulled me out of memory lane and back to the present and my work. The washer and dryer, a candy-apple red pair that my wife Diana had purchased on line one night after some serious partying (I'm sure she was surprised when the delivery truck showed up and the workmen brought out the dolly and the paperwork and the products) are located at the back of our garage, close to the door to the house. We have a gray strip of carpet over the cement floor in front of the appliances, a puke-green cabinet above for supplies, and a green Formica counter for folding. Before I left Surf City for Wall Street and a promotion I'd sent my shirts out; since my return I was learning new skills, like basic plumbing (I'd been forced to replace the toilet that somebody had shot a hole in) and laundry, and was working my way up to doing something about the basketball-sized burned place on the deck out back. It's good to learn new things, keeps you from stagnating. Also, I could no longer afford the services of a dry cleaner. Okay, full disclosure—I also didn't need them.

On the way home after cruising we talked a little about the people we'd met, then the conversation had almost turned to one of those Serious Relationship Talks, but I dodged the SRT bullet when Kandi got a text about some guy questioning part of her dissertation research.

Tell me about your adventures. Henrietta Graveline was tall, with short gray hair and she looked like—

From the family room Kandi called, "That's who she reminds me of—Jamie Lee Curtis."

"Yeah, only a few years older, maybe. Same short gray hair." Then it dawned on me. "I hate it when you do that."

"Do what?"

"Read my mind. And you knew I was going to say that."

Kandi stood in the doorway to the garage, holding her iPhone. "Of course I did. Wow, this is lucky. Kandi said she'd cover for Josie tomorrow for lunch. Good thing I looked at my calendar, because I'd forgotten completely." She slipped the phone into the robe's pocket. "So, returning to our conversation—"

"What? Right." Although I was pretty sure I knew what she was talking about.

"Mac . . ."

There were two types of underwear—plain, practical cotton, always white, and Victoria's Secret in a wonderful variety of colors and styles. Kandi wore the underwear appropriate to whatever job she was doing. I dragged it out of the dryer, dumped it on the Formica counter and stuffed in a load of jeans. I started sorting the underwear into two piles—and why on earth does she have so *much*?—practical white and hot damn! Maybe if I pretended to be really involved in laundry she'd go back to her dissertation. Hey, it could happen. "Mac, what about my doctorate? I'll need to do an internship somewhere." She took a breath. "You do not have to answer this immediately, but, will you come with me if, as is likely, my internship is out of state?"

I'd had a good job, a wife I loved, and a future that had been planned since grade school, only the details subject to change. It was all gone. I folded a green pair of panties, making certain to line the seams up perfectly.

"Mac, I understand, I really do. You are not in a position to make life decisions; that's natural, completely natural, but I'm moving toward something, and you're, well, I'm afraid it's inevitable that you will be impacted by my actions. We are not at a point where decisions have to be made, but that point is approaching."

I kept on folding. Eventually it worked and she went back to the family room and her dissertation. When I'd earned my living as a stock market broker-analyst I'd learned to listen. She'd said, ". . . you will be impacted." Not, ". . . *we'll* be impacted."

Our cars, Kandi's fully-restored 1962 MGA and my Porsche Carrera, both black, were behind me. To my right there was a door leading out to the side of the house, where a cement walk ran from the front gate to the tiny back yard and boat dock. The outside lights were on, but the garage was dim. I was folding in the light that spilled in from the open door to my left, so the light from the small vent at the bottom of the outside door was relatively bright.

Tell me about your adventures.

Did Henrietta really want to know about a crazy guy who sat and stared for hours at his collection of Golden Books and who died horribly? Seated on the couch in the main cabin of the *Waiting For The Sun II*, she had looked at me like she meant it, but I didn't think so. For most people, violence is something best contained on TV or stories. Sanitized. In real life it's different. It can get out of hand. It leaves scars.

From the corner of my eye I saw the light coming from the vent in the door eclipsed twice—blink-blink—and all at once I realized I had seen that a minute ago. There was somebody in the side yard.

Now, your average homeowner might throw open the door and yell "Who's out there?" but I am no longer your average homeowner. The door is a brand-new steel fire door and the house is protected by serious electronic security installed by Kandi's cousin, my friend Chet Shaw. Recent events, the adventures Henrietta Graveline wanted to know about, have taught me a degree of caution.

I set the next pair of folded panties—red, if you must know—on the stack of other folded lingerie, stepped out of my sandals and slipped into the shadows between the cars. Once there I dropped to my knees and crawled over to the door where I peered through the small wire-mesh grating. I was wearing the Huntington Beach uniform of board shorts and t-shirt. Fortunately, the t-shirt was black. I saw booted feet, topped by dark gray pants, moving toward the back yard. As I started to get up, the dryer launched into one of its cycles and something in it, maybe the fastener on a pair of jeans, banged against the metal drum as it tumbled. Bang-bang. Pause. Bang-bang. The feet stopped, turned, and headed back toward me. They came all the way to the door. There was no rattle, no attempt to turn the knob and open the door; they just stood there. Afraid of what was coming next, I slid back into what I hoped was deeper shadow. My knees were cold from pressing against the cement, and my toes were folded uncomfortably under me. Something dark was placed on the cement next to the boots. It was easy to identify. The stock of a rifle. The figure bent and a face hidden by a dark ski mask appeared in the grating.

Well, I didn't really think it was our local SWAT team practicing stealth maneuvers.

Tell me about your adventures.

Hey, Henrietta, I seem to be having one right now, and I don't like it much, and Kandi's in the family room checking citations, the family room at the back of the house with sliding glass doors leading out to the back yard, and to the dock where there might be more people with guns.

I didn't move. Didn't breathe. After a moment the masked face went away, and then the boots. I peeked out and saw them turn the corner into the back.

Part of what I have learned, in addition to a degree of caution about things like opening your doors late at night, is that I need weapons. I own a Colt .45 automatic and a sawed-off shotgun, and I regularly carry a truncated pool cue handle that I have gone upside a few heads with, with the expected results. Unfortunately, all of my arsenal was upstairs. I mean, really, who packs heat to do laundry? I got up and ran for the door to the house, pausing only to snatch up a can of Raid from the cabinet as I passed. Up close, if I got very lucky, a shot to the eyes might slow down an opponent. And it was all I had.

Kandi was curled on the couch in the family room, in that pose that seems to be possible only to women, where your legs are folded under you and your feet are jammed up under your butt, iPad next to her, working on her dissertation. The vertical blinds covering the windows were open. I didn't look out back, just strolled over, plopped down next to her, pushed a strand of hair back over her ear and kissed her neck lightly. I whispered, "Heads up. The game is afoot and we're on the clock."

Her hand squeezed a little tighter on my forearm. She nuzzled back. "Where?"

"Side of the house, back yard, at least two, military outfits, armed, probably assault rifles." Her hand dipped into her purse and came out with the Raven .25 that she's never without. It's a tiny black automatic, six rounds in the magazine, one in the chamber, so small it was almost completely covered by her hand. With her free hand she set the iPad aside, then looked at me. Her breathing was slow and regular, her lips slightly parted, and her eyes were wide, bright with anticipation. Mary was gone. Kandi smiled at me. Deadly Kandi.

I set down the can of insecticide and pulled my phone out of my hip pocket, pushed the little button on the top, and saw the dreaded, "No service." When she tried it, hers said the same thing.

We sat for a minute. "Well, let's look," I said, stood up and looked out back.

I live in a part of Huntington Beach called Huntington Harbour, a community made up of large houses built on islands dredged out of a mud flat in the sixties. Channels connect the islands to Alamitos Bay and the Pacific. My wife's parents bought the place brand new; we moved in when they went into assisted living. I inherited it when she was killed.

All the good houses in the Harbour back up to the water and have docks and mine was a good one. At the moment the dock only held my Boston Whaler since I had found it necessary to set fire to and sink my sailboat during one of those adventures. I didn't much like that, but at least Kandi and I had been rescued. There are big windows that look out from the family room and kitchen toward the dock and channel behind it and late at night you can sometimes hear the surf from the state beach across the highway.

Tonight a black inflatable was tied up behind my little dinghy. Two people dressed in dark gray, wearing ski masks and holding automatic weapons, stood in plain view in front of it. They looked at us; we looked at them. The rifles were pointed skyward, which I took to be a good thing.

Kandi moved a step to my left to put more distance between us and whispered, "Say something witty." We both edged to the side, presenting smaller targets. The people on the dock didn't move.

"We have armed, crazed Ninjas standing in my back yard."

"There are no indications that they are suffering any type of mental issues, and Ninjas don't wear boots, they wear little sock-like things called tabi, with split toes."

"Okay, you can be witty. Why are we whispering?"

"Our cell phones don't work and I can only conclude they have somehow done that. What do they want?"

I shook my head, then said, "There's someone upstairs."

"This is where you say, 'Stay here,' and I say, 'No way.'" Kandi didn't take her eyes off the figures on the dock.

"We go on three." She looked at me curiously. "If they wanted us dead, we'd be dead. One, two . . . ," I bolted for the stairs, Kandi matching me stride for stride. No hail of bullets shattered the windows.

At the top she said, "Sometimes you are *so* obvious." She was flushed, breathing hard and grinning.

And, no, I'm not a total sexist pig who says to the heroine, "You stay here while I go see if that really is a big drooly guy with a machete in the basement." Kandi had just spent some time in the hospital, recovering from a gunshot wound. That's why she was breathing hard. So, okay, call me a sexist pig, but anyway, I don't have a basement.

She said, "You were going to draw their fire."

The house is five-bedroom, three and a half bath. At the top of the stairs there's a landing, open on one side to the living room below. Double doors to the master suite, located on the water side, are at the end to the left, the other bedrooms, bath, and my office take up the rest of the hall.

I looked into my office just in time to see a gloved hand vanish over the windowsill. By the time I got there the gray-clad figure had pulled some kind of release and a rope ladder dropped to his feet. He picked it up and trotted for the backyard, coiling the ladder as he ran, coiling it clumsily with one hand because he was carrying a laptop computer in the other. I put one hand on the windowsill and vaulted over.

Like most kids, when I was growing up we used to jump off the garage roof onto the driveway. Sure, it stung a little when you landed but for moment you were *flying*. And there is a technique for jumping off high places, which we practiced. The key is to keep your knees loose, never lock them. On the way down, you get your hands up, over your shoulders, land on your toes and throw your hands forward to hit the ground—the idea of course is that that's better than your head. Your arms take the impact and then you roll. Piece of cake. Well, my feet must have gotten tender or something, because it did more than sting—it hurt like hell when I landed, my teeth clicked together, and it felt like all of my internal organs sort of sloshed around, jumping up and bumping into each other. I planted my hands, rolled forward and finished upside down in a heap against my neighbors' fence. My insides sloshed some more, then settled down. The crazed Ninja turned and looked back at me, maybe because he recognized a fellow crazy, before continuing on. I rolled to my left, struggled to my feet and limped after him. He tossed the rope ladder over his shoulder, dipped his hand into a small pouch at his belt, and scattered small objects behind him as he ran. When I stepped on one pain lanced through my foot. Stumbling, trying to pull it out, I went down and felt another one jab me in the knee. I pulled them out and went on, watching where I put my feet.

Of course the invasion crew was making their escape by the boat tied to my dock, and of course I missed it, but I did get to see the one with my laptop jump in and cast off the bow line just before it pulled away. It was a mid-size inflatable, black, with a hard bottom. The outboard was very quiet. They didn't even bother to look back, just motored toward the main channel that ran parallel to Pacific Coast Highway, behind Peter's Landing and which connected to the sea after passing through the Seal Beach Naval Weapons Depot. The engine cover on my Boston Whaler was open so I had a pretty good idea that it wouldn't start. It didn't.

Kandi ran out to stand on the dock next to me. We stood and watched the little black boat vanish into the dark.

Our cell phones worked again, so I called the police. The Harbor Patrol was on the lookout for the inflatable in a matter of minutes but there was no trace of it. The police came, we talked, and talked, and talked. After a couple of hours they had done the paperwork, the Crime Scene Investigation people were finished, and Kandi and I were left alone. We sat out back, on the deck with a Dos Equis for me and a long-stemmed glass of Kendall Jackson for Kandi. A paramedic named Mike, who I'd met before, had smeared Betadine on the punctures on my foot and knee and covered them with small dressings. They both still hurt. Around us the Harbour was silent. A helicopter thrashed up the coast, probably carrying workers from the oil field to the south out to one of the offshore drilling rigs. The lights belonging to my neighbors that had been turned on to see what all the commotion was had been turned off, their owners back in bed, perhaps muttering sleepily about the new excitement at that crazy guy's house.

Kandi was asking about Diana, what it had been like right before I left her for New York, something she'd been showing interest in lately, and I didn't like it. Her phone buzzed. She showed me the text. I didn't like it, either.

```
CHET SHAW
    K tell M don't use his cell. Call me. Use the phone
I gave him in Vegas. Go back outside. Call from the
dock.
    Tex
```

Chet Shaw is Kandi's cousin, and he's a genius. While he was getting his doctorate in Computer Science at Cal Tech he created a game called—I'm not making this up—Attack of the Space Floozies that made him moderately wealthy. Now he owns Space Floozy Enterprises, but they don't do games; they provide security for casinos and that business allows him to live on a ranch outside Las Vegas where he raises ostriches and has a purebred angora goat named Gerald who hates me. He's "Tex" because he's seen every Western ever made.

I leaned over and nuzzled Kandi. "Chet thinks the house is bugged." I could feel her nod against my cheek. I slid my hand up under her shirt, causing her to sigh and move against me.

She whispered, "We must keep this authentic, right?"

"Well, the bugging is probably audio only. But I don't like to let an opportunity slip by."

I am made of stern stuff. After only a moment I pulled my hand out from under her shirt, went inside and got the disposable cell out of my sock drawer. To my surprise the battery was still charged. Back downstairs on the dock I called Chet.

"Tex, how did you know?"

"About the home invasion? I've got a web spider trolling for any mention of you or Kandi. Based on what I saw, I thought I should warn you. I don't like that part about your cell phones not working."

"That seems a little paranoid. I think we have to let the police handle this." I looked out at the still water for a moment. I looked at my tiny back yard. Nobody jumped out of the bushes with a gun. No crazed ninjas threw spiky things at me. After assuring Chet that we were okay and taking precautions, we went back inside and locked the door.

I'm a semi-unemployed broker-analyst for a boutique investment firm called Fields, Smith, and Barkman. A few months ago my wife Diana, who had stayed behind when I moved east to work on Wall Street, had some pretty serious problems so I left the exciting world of moving averages and candlestick charts and returned to SoCal to try and help. In the course of trying to help I involved the police on more than one occasion.

I'm T. R. Macdonald, and this sort of thing—home invasion—really doesn't happen to me very often Of course, I guess it doesn't happen to most people ever.

Chapter Two   Help From My Friends

The morning after the ninjas stole my laptop the plan was for me to drive Kandi to work the lunch shift at Fred's and then take her car in for servicing. The MGA is a fine machine, but at its age it requires a certain amount of care and feeding. Before dealing with the cars I replaced the outboard's missing spark plugs and confirmed that my Whaler would start, then we headed for the restaurant in her car, with me driving.

We were in the middle of the narrow bridge connecting my island to Algonquin Street and the mainland when a red Mustang convertible lunged out ahead of us and slid to a stop across both lanes. Behind us another identical red convertible blocked the other end of the bridge. A man in a clown mask—white face, giant red lips, tufts of green hair sticking out—jumped out of the front vehicle and trotted toward us. He had a shiny chrome revolver held low at his side. I yelled, "Down!" and pushed Kandi's head down, shoved the MGA into first and popped the clutch. The little car responded gallantly, lunging forward as if it weren't half a century old. They had intended to block the entire bridge, but hadn't done a very good job—there was a small space between the red car ahead of us and the railing, enough for us to slip through if I took the right wheels of the MGA up on the sidewalk. I aimed the car at the guy with the gun to discourage him from shooting me, and when he jumped aside I swerved, bounced up the curb and slipped the little sports car through the gap. The clown stood in the middle of the street shaking his fist and shouting, "Come back here!"

Five minutes later I pulled off Pacific Coast Highway into the Peter's Landing parking lot and looked at Kandi. She was staring at me, dazed. "Did that really happen?"

"Yeah, I think it did." I was watching the rear-view mirror for signs of red Mustangs, and saw none. Two kids carrying surfboards trotted across the street to their battered van, carefully leaned their boards against the car and peeled their wetsuits down before taking out gallon jugs of water that they dumped over their heads.

"Mac, what in the world is going on?"

"They're getting cleaned up. Probably late for an afternoon class at Long Beach."

The kids had wrapped beach towels around their waists and were pulling their wetsuits off. They tugged board shorts up under the towels, unwrapped them and tossed the towels in the back of the van, pulled on t-shirts, and got in. Morning toilet complete, time for school. "Mac, what in the world is going on?" Kandi said again.

No red Mustangs.

"First ninjas, now clowns. I'm afraid it's time for Tex to saddle up." I walked her around back and into the restaurant through the kitchen. Instead of leaving, I stayed at Fred's, making some calls. My first was to the police, to brighten their morning by reporting the marauding clowns. If worst came to worst, and it looked like it might, I wanted a record. After they quit laughing and determined that I meant it, they said they would keep an eye out for Bozo and Ronald.

Chet picked up on the first ring. I said, "Fred's kitchen. Tomorrow afternoon."

With no hesitation he said, "Done. Can I stay at your place?"

"Hell no. You snore loud enough to bother the fish."

"Good." Then he was gone.

Fred's Fine Mexican Food is in Peter's Landing, an upscale shopping/dining/office complex sandwiched between the water of the Huntington Harbour main channel and Pacific Coast Highway. They have floating boat docks in back, so the next day

I motored across and tied up my Boston Whaler at Fred's dock and went in through the kitchen.

Carnitas was cooking in a huge copper pot, a wide variety of peppers and onions were being sliced, sauces were boiling, cooks were slamming pans down, flipping strips of beef, chicken or carnitas onto the grill, stirring pots of rice and beans, and sliding steaming platters of food out for pickup. The serving staff rushed madly trying to keep up, balancing plates of enchiladas, fish tacos, chiliqueles, and burritos as they hustled the food out. There were conversations in rapid-fire Spanish and English, and the two Vietnamese servers yelled at each other in some obscure dialect of what we believed was Hmung. There was the warmth the cheerful noise and controlled chaos of a kitchen in full swing in a place where the people who worked there liked each other and their jobs.

It's a classy place—all dark wood and glass looking out at the water, no fake adobe peeled back to reveal fake brick. The waitresses wear French maid costumes—short black dresses with little white aprons and lots of frilly white slips underneath, sort of odd for a place whose specialty is shrimp tacos and squid burritos. They used to wear real, seamed stockings but the cost of replacing snagged ones got out of hand so Jesus, the owner, dropped them.

As I made my way through the crowd Josie slipped by expertly balancing a tray full of drinks, giving me a friendly hip check as she did. When Kandi is not at UCLA she works at Fred's serving cocktails. However, for the shy, bookish Mary Shaw dealing with the bar crowd was difficult, so she developed the persona named "Kandi," and, trust me on this, Kandi had no trouble at all handling lecherous drunks.

About a month ago Jesus had responded to requests from some of his regulars for private dining. He knocked out a wall and converted a storage area into a small dining room that was separated from the kitchen proper by a glass wall. The new dining room seats eight in high-backed wooden chairs around a circular yellow table, and the ambience is great—all the smells of Mexican food being prepared.

A few minutes after I sat down they were all there. Seated at the table were the people I cared most about in the world—Chet Shaw, Alys Winters, the young woman who had pulled me out of the channel after her brother Roger and his pals threw me in, and of course, Kandi. My friend the Snake had asked to be part of it, but since he had to work at the CSULB Library, he was looking at us from the camera in one of Chet's laptops in the middle of the table. I had a Dos Equis, Chet a Mountain Dew, and Kandi an iced tea. Alys Winters had tried for a Budweiser and been carded, so she had a Diet Coke.

"Walter I understand—he saw the news and wanted to listen in. But why involve Alys, unless—" Kandi's eyes widened as she got it. "Her brother? Roger?"

Alys brushed her hair back and just looked at me. I said, "I hope not."

The table was crowded with computers and samples from the kitchen—plates of enchiladas, shrimp in spicy green sauce, and miniature tacos with a variety of fillings. Jesus rushed in, cradling an enormous steel bowl of salad. He was dressed in his uniform of black pants, white short-sleeved shirt, black skinny tie with silver tie clip and as always he had a white towel draped over his shoulder. He has black hair parted in the middle, a thirties-style narrow black mustache, and is rail-thin, and how he runs a restaurant and stays so skinny would be a mystery if you didn't watch how hard he works. The man never sits still. "Try this, try this. My new chef Mario just created it." He set the bowl down, pulled the towel off his shoulder and wiped an imaginary spot on the table, and began passing out small plates, thick ochre Mexican stoneware. "And I want honest opinions, really, tell me the truth, honestly. It's spinach, arugula, papaya, hazelnuts, avocado, with a spicy chipotle dressing. We plan on adding grilled chicken on request. You will either love it or hate it. Try it, try it." Jesus can be a little intense. "Remember, honest opinions." He flipped the towel back over his shoulder and looked at us expectantly.

I used the tongs to put a sample of salad on to my plate, tasted it and said, "Too bad you didn't bring enough for the others," as I grabbed the whole bowl. Jesus twitched his mouth, the closest he comes to a smile, clapped his hands, and hurried away. Kandi threatened me with a butter knife so I reluctantly shared.

We were secure. When Chet flew in from Vegas he brought Bryant and a Space Floozies team with him. The tall Asian in the black suit came into the kitchen and looked around carefully before coming into the dining room. I stood and walked over to him. He gripped my hand warmly. "Man, I owe you." Bryant had been our driver on a Vegas trip, and his skill and coolness under literal fire had kept us from being carjacked. I told Bermann, the head of Bromeliad Security, about him, and now instead of driving a limo he wore an ear bug, had a tiny microphone clipped to his lapel, and carried a 13-shot Glock. "Chet's got a van in the back, watching the parking lot, the dock area, and the back entrance to the kitchen. I'll be in the restaurant where I can see the dining room, bar, and main entrance to the kitchen. And there's something else I need to tell you." He moved closer, spoke softly. "Herr Bermann wants you to know that he got a call about you."

"When?"

"This morning, before we flew out. Somebody said they were checking references, like you'd applied for a job."

"What did he tell them?"

"Bro, this is Herr Director of Security Bermann we're talking about. He didn't know these people and you hadn't told him to expect a call. I don't think he even told them *his* name. But he definitely wanted you to know about it. He says to tell you if you need some uh, help, of any kind, just call. We can keep the hotel jet for two days, then it's got to go to Denver."

"I only get the G5 for two days?"

He held out his fist for the obligatory bump and grinned. "I'll be in the restaurant. Josie wants to see my weapon." I nodded, then turned to survey the room.

Everybody was sampling food, sipping drinks, talking, laughing at one thing or another. For a moment I paused, and just watched, just enjoyed it. Kandi's salad plate was empty, and so was the bowl; without a pause in her conversation she switched her salad plate with my full one. Chet, dumping green Tabasco on his enchilada, was in his usual jeans, pressed with a razor crease, blue-and-tan Tony Lama ostrich boots, and plaid western shirt with "2012 Million-Dollar Calf Auction" stitched on the pocket. His white ten-gallon hat was hanging on a chair in the corner where it was safely out of range of flying salsa. To his right was Alys Winters, seventeen, with bangs down to her eyelashes, straight black hair parted on the left and falling down just past her ears, black t-shirt with the sleeves hacked off, yellow-and-black striped micro-miniskirt over snagged and ripped black tights, black Goth lipstick and lots of silver bracelets on both arms. This fetching outfit was completed by green high-top Converse tennies with pink laces, and a black leather motorcycle jacket draped over the back of her chair. She had ear buds jammed in and, her iPod in front of her, and was bopping to thrash metal. Kandi was in her French maid outfit since she had to work later. In my jeans, black Polo shirt, and blue Topsiders I felt like a seagull at a peacock convention.

I stood and rapped a spoon on a glass for attention, causing them to look at me, laugh, and go back to talking. Undaunted, I started anyway. "Okay, the first order of business is to make my home more secure. Last night can't happen again."

Chet had his smart phone, two laptops, a plate of salad (how did he get more?) and his burrito in front of him but was able to tear his attention away. "We're on it, Pard" he said, "but understand that it ain't never gonna be perfect. Them rustlers was pros. Now, we can make it harder with better fences—installing us a bunch of alarms, but remember, the more secure you are, the less convenient your life is and the less privacy you have. What about your cop friend? Tony Genucci? Can we get some help from him?"

"At this moment he is in the Loire Valley in the south of France, tasting wine and visiting castles. I want to think about the privacy thing. Anyway, are we set here?"

He ate some of his salad. "Yep. My guys swept the room and it's clean."

From the laptop in the center of the table, Snake said, "Okay, look, I just want to know what really happened since I didn't get a call and only read about it. But I'm not complaining. So, talk."

I went through the break-in and then the attack of the clowns, ending with "So after the guys tried to carjack us on the bridge, I used the burner cell, called all of you and set this up."

Alys said, "They really yelled, 'Come back here'?" and giggled.

On the laptop screen Snake stroked his full gray beard. Behind him I could see his office at the library. "You called Alys because—?"

She bristled. "Hey, why is everybody—"

I cut her off. "We'll get to that."

He leaned back, laced his fingers behind his head. "You said the cops are dealing with the break-in and the carjack. Your reason for this meeting is, what? Besides your normal reaction to anything, which is to call a meeting."

"An old client called me two days ago, says he wants to meet, face time, no email, no videoconference, and he says it's not about his portfolio. I haven't spoken to him since I came back from New York. He's also a neighbor, different island, but he lives in the Harbour, but says we need to meet someplace else, and he'll send a car for me. I said no." I stood up and limped around. My foot hurt from the spiky thing I'd stepped on. "And according to Bryant someone's been asking about me at the Bromeliad."

"The little critter you stepped on is called a caltrop. It's sort of like a kid's jack, but with sharp spikes. You throw it and no matter how it lands one of the spikes is facing up. Goes back to the middle ages, and they—great big suckers, of course—have been used successfully against tanks. You're lucky, Pard, sometimes them spikes got poison on 'em."

"Sailor, it looks like you think there's a connection between all this." Kandi said. She cautiously took a taco. Kandi has a healthy appetite, but is not an adventurous eater. "I don't get it."

I sat back down, had a bite of shrimp taco. "Neither do I."

"You know somethin's happenin' but you don't know what it is, do you Mr. Jones?" Snake muttered. "Listen, Mac, I gotta go in a minute, I'm due on the Information Desk, but I wondered if there was anything else?"

"More? You want *more*?" Kandi was the only one that didn't look blank. "That's from a classic, you know. I got it free on my Kindle. Kandi's getting me to read books." They looked at me like I'd lost my mind. I sighed. "Just trying to bring you people some culture. Yes, there is more and I'm afraid it's the scariest. It's what made me think we should have some face time."

The new cook Mario slipped in, deposited a plate of steaming Bonita tacos in the center of the table, said, "Hot plate," and left.

I said, "Alys, you're on."

She had pushed her plate aside, and didn't look up from the pack of Salems she was idly spinning on the tabletop. "Yeah, right, me. Um, my brother, Roger, he's like, nuts." Mary—Kandi was Mary Shaw when she was in counseling mode—pressed her lips together at that. Alys looked up and saw her. She jerked out her ear buds "Well, he *is*. Batshit. Totally. And he's locked up."

"He's being treated at a secure facility, from all indications with remarkable success."

"Yeah, right, Mary. Okay, it's my fucking psycho brother."

"Alys—"

She threw the pack of cigarettes into her purse. "I *hate* him, I fucking hate him and I wish he was dead. I wish Mac had let him die when he had the chance." She grinned viciously. "See, I'm *so* in touch with my feelings." I kept my mouth shut. There were times I felt that way, too. Not that I felt like I was in touch with my feelings, I wasn't even sure what that meant. No, there were times when I felt like I should have let Roger Winters suffocate in the yellow cloud of sulfur gas he had released part of one of the 'adventures' Henrietta Graveline had wanted to know about.

Mary said, "Alys, you obviously have a great deal of resentment toward your brother, and we have talked about this at length, and certainly much of that resentment is justified—"

"Like the part where he beat the shit out of me and put me in the fucking hospital? Yeah, I fucking resent that."

"You need to get past this anger. Carrying it around is potentially very detrimental."

"Oh, wow, did I forget to mention the part where he painted 'doper' on my stomach?"

Mary threw up her hands.

I put my hand over Alys', gave it a gentle squeeze. Hers was trembling and she wouldn't look up. "And I bet it was just *weeks* before you could wear a bikini."

She sucked in her breath sharply, glared at me, then exhaled and smiled and squeezed my hand back. "You are such an asshole." She looked around the table. "I love all you guys, you know? But I don't know why." She swiped at her eyes, smearing her thick black eye shadow but truthfully it didn't make much difference, and pushed her hair out of her face. "Gimme those fuckin' little tacos."

I said, "And now Roger's in the Biggin Hill Recovery Home, inland from here, right? Temescal Canyon?" I said. Alys nodded. "And you've had no contact with him until, what? A week ago?"

In the kitchen one of the servers dropped a plate and all the rest of the staff applauded. He bowed and started picking it up. Alys took a tentative bite of the taco, smiled hugely, and jammed the rest of it in her mouth, pushed her hair back again and talked while she reached for another one. "Yeah, okay, he tried, you know, like texting me and stuff after the trial, but I never answered, and after a while he quit. I guess their messaging is pretty limited."

Roger Winters, the one Mary says Alys has issues with, didn't even approach the remotest boundaries of 'normal,' but he is also very, very smart and that, combined with wealthy parents supplying very expensive legal help, had enabled him to convince a court that he was nuts (true) and not a threat anymore (most definitely not true) and now he was doing whatever it is you do when they lock you up to try to get your head screwed on right.

Alys mumbled around more taco, "So, I haven't heard from him in months, ok, and then he sends me this text that says he wants Mac's email. He said it was really important so I asked Mac."

"When did you get this text?" Chet asked.

"A week ago."

"And I hadn't answered," I said.

"Yeah, so I got another text from Roger and this time he said it was really important."

"But, when Alys asked me I said I was not interested in becoming a pen pal with Mr. Chock-Full-O-Nuts. Then my client calls, we had Snake's party on the yacht and then the break-in was that night."

On the monitor, Snake nodded. "Right. Brad, Henrietta, and Lisa June. College friends of mine."

I said, "Some of your radical pals?"

"These guys? No way. Pure capitalists. Brad was a business major, they all made a bunch of money."

"What about Cheryl? Anything out of the ordinary?" Cheryl is Snake's hippie wife. We do not get along very well. She likes casting runes, blank verse, whatever that is, vegetables, and communing with Gaia the Earth Mother by smoking a lot of dope and lying face-down in her garden. She also believes I am corrupting her husband, leading him to eat meat, doughnuts, fries, and to drink beer, and smoke cigarettes, all of which he does to excess. They've been married almost forty years and are the happiest couple I know.

"Nope, just the usual readings. *Geranium Joy* is doing well, for a book of poetry. No, nothing weird here, and I'm out of time. Too hip, gotta go." He broke the connection.

"So Roger wants to talk, and right after that you have a break-in?" Chet said.

"Right. And the clowns."

He said, "We've got some video I pulled from a traffic cam, but it doesn't give us anything new. I want to hear about this old client."

"Elijah Eddington the third. He was one of my first clients, when I was just getting started."

"Whoa, whoa, I know that name," Chet's fingers flew over the laptop keyboard, "Yeah, sure, here he is. Known as Big E, or just E. Basketball player."

"That's him. UCLA, then the Clippers, then a few other teams. Had a good career. He's retired now, and a multimillionaire, thanks in part to excellent portfolio management by yours truly."

"*So* modest," Kandi murmured.

"As I was saying, I advised Eddington about some investments and we've stayed in touch in a loose sort of way."

"Hmmm. Owns something called Slam Dunk Management. What does he want now?" Chet said, after skimming the information on Big E.

"He won't tell me, except that it's not investment advice. He's sending a car for me tomorrow morning." They all looked at me. "Yeah, I know. Very mysterious. I'm not sure where we're going."

Kandi said, "I thought you said no." I shrugged.

Mama, the cranky sixty-something bartender, yelled in about an order for the bar. Chet drummed his fingers on the table. "Chronologic order. Roger wants to talk, somebody asks Bermann for a reference, and Eddington wants something and won't say what it is. Then crazed ninjas break in and steal your laptop, clowns try to carjack you. All out of nowhere. All with no explanation. I say again, 'Whoa.'"

I took a deep breath. "There's a connection. At least some of these events are related. So I called Eddington back and said I'd changed my mind."

Chet said, "Okay, here's what I've got to bring to the party. First, we have been fielding calls on your old cell since last night. You have a message from a woman named Al-Thani, she wants you to come to a party, and two from Bernice, who first said she was just checking in, then she called back and said she'd heard about the home invasion and wanted to make sure you were all right."

"Bernice is the executive assistant to my boss at Fields, Smith, and Barkman. She's my friend, so I'll have to call her. Harriet is a major player in the FSB Los Angeles office"

"If you have to call them, go ahead. But use your old phone, and don't say anything you don't want overheard."

"Great."

"Assume you are being monitored at all times. These people, at least the ones who broke in, are serious. If you stop using your cell they'll get suspicious. They had to have a vehicle out front with some pretty sophisticated equipment to block your cell phones. That means at least one more person."

Kandi took a piece of quesadilla, looked at a tiny tentacle dangling out, hastily put it back and said, "They turned off the alarm and got around the sensors at the windows and doors. And because they disabled the cameras we have no video of them. Yes, I would say that 'serious' adequately describes them."

I took Kandi's quesadilla. Spooning green sauce on it, I looked at Chet. "You want to tell them or shall I?"

He swallowed. "How did you guess?"

"I know you, Tex, you are Mr. Redundant Backup. And I never guess. Shocking habit."

Alys pushed her hair back, said, "Sherlock Holmes. Saw the movies. Awesome."

I said, "And you knew we were on the dock last night."

Chet turned white, swallowed again. "You're not going to like it."

I reached out, flicked a bit of taco shell out of Alys' hair. "I already don't like it."

He couldn't meet my eyes. "Remember when your neighbors, the Applegates, had that cable problem?"

"No. Wait, wait, don't tell me you bugged their house?"

"Um, no, well, more like the area around the docks, out back. When they had their cable problem, the guy who showed up was one of mine, and when he was on the roof he sort of put some cameras up there."

I was stunned. "You set a camera on my neighbors' roof and didn't tell me? Or them?"

"I knew you wouldn't like it." He still couldn't look up. "It's only pointed at your back yard."

"It's still there?"

"Yeah. Well, uh, actually, they're still there. Three cameras on one mount, motion-activated."

"Pull them."

"Mac—"

"Pull them today."

He looked up at last. "How about the video?"

"Let's see it."

We gathered around his laptop. Now that he was back on familiar ground, his voice lost its quaver, but the cowboy jargon was gone. "Okay, this is really straightforward. It's low-light, low-power, and like I said, motion activated. You got your basic date-and-time stamp in the lower right corner. The Applegates are not home right now—"

"You know because you saw them leave, right?"

"Yes, Mac, they took the boat out two days ago. And, no, I have no idea where they went. There's no audio." The 'Joy of Troy' was Beth and Myron's forty-foot Chris Craft. Beth was University of Southern California to the core; her most prized possession was the tiny gold megaphone on a chain that she got for being a Varsity cheerleader. Hence, the boat name and truthfully, it wasn't as goofy as a lot of boat names.

We watched the two gray-clad figures stand on the dock, the third trot up, they all waved at the house, then they jumped in the boat, pushed off and motored away. On the little screen a barefoot figure that looked at lot like me hobbled out on the dock and watched, Kandi came out and stood next to me; then we went inside. "Go back," I said, "and freeze on their boat." I whistled softly. "Now zoom. Okay." I studied the image carefully, whistled again. "I thought so. That's not an ordinary dinghy, it's a rigid-hull inflatable, RHIB, developed in the nineties for the military and built for very special operations. *Not* a cheap toy."

"So, Sailor, what are you going to do?"

"Meet Elijah Eddington the Third tomorrow, see what he wants. Try to figure out the next step, basically say 'Yes' and see what happens."

She stared at me. "That plan sucks."

"My guess is we won't have long to wait."

I was right.

Chapter Three   Mr. Baines Wants to Know

There was a discreet beep. Chet looked at his phone, read the text message. "Uh-oh. Mac, you have company." He tapped some keys and turned the laptop so we could all see the screen. Two men stood on my front porch, dressed in identical gray jackets with some kind of logo on the front breast, dark pants, and baseball caps. As we watched they rang the bell again. "My guys are in back of the restaurant. They want to know if you want them to go see what this is about."

I looked at Chet and he could not meet my eyes. "Yes, your cameras are connected to my network."

"But no sound?"

He tapped some keys, "Well, yes, in this case there is. Through your home intercom."

"Okay, I'll talk to them."

"Sure." He tapped some keys. "Ready?"

"May I help you?" My voice came out of the speaker mounted next to the doorbell.

"Yes, sir. We're from Interagency Insurance Investigations. We're looking for Mr. T. R. Macdonald.

"This is T. R. Macdonald."

"Good afternoon, Sir. I'm George and my partner Rodney and I would like to talk to you briefly about last night's break-in. We represent a group employed by a consortium of insurance companies. The owner of our group, Mr. Baines, wanted us to get some information and see if there is anything we can do to help. It won't take long, I promise."

"I've already told the police everything."

"Please, Mr. Baines wants us to speak with you and we don't want to disappoint him." He laughed nervously. "Hey, you know how it is when your bosses' boss wants something."

I remembered my plan, such as it was. "Yes, if I can help I'd be glad to. How about later this afternoon? Wait a moment while I check my schedule." I motioned to Chet to cut the audio.

"Mac, are you nuts? You don't know who those guys are." Kandi sounded a little tense.

Chet had been tapping keys on his laptop while the conversation went on. "Mac, she's right. I show no activity by your insurance company, like calling in help."

"So they're fakes. Good, maybe I'll learn something. Okay, Chet, here's what I need. They're going to come to my house. I'll get them to come out back, we'll talk on the deck, it's nice out, blah, blah. Leave your camera in place."

Chet stopped poking at his smart phone, reached out and tapped a key on the laptop. "I get no Interagency Insurance."

"No web page?"

"Very basic. Blank screen, fields for log-in."

I gestured and he turned the sound back on. "Now is not convenient. Can you come back this afternoon, around five?"

"Yes, sir, we'd be glad to. It won't take long."

"I'll be out back. The gate will be open." They said thanks and we watched as they stood for a moment, then moved out of camera range.

"Are you mad?" Chet swallowed hard.

"You planted cameras around my house without telling me. Those cameras are accessible to your network. What do you think?"

"Only the back yard, honest."

"And to do that one of your employees pretended to be a cable repairman and trespassed on my neighbor's property." He nodded miserably. "My neighbors, Chet! I have to live next to these people!"

"I'm sorry. He really did fix their cable, and we did get a look at the boat."

"Are there any other cameras I am not aware of?"

"No. None."

"I want your word you will never plant surveillance at my home without telling me."

"I promise."

"All right."

Kandi said, "So, what now?"

"I say, 'yes,' to everything and see what happens, starting with the Interagency Insurance guys this afternoon. I answer Roger's text and find out what he wants, and tomorrow morning at six Eddington's car picks me up and I go off to wherever. In the meantime, Chet's guys go over the house and try to make it more secure." He looked wounded. "Chet, you were not planning on a military operation. This is new, and off the scale."

He grinned, tentatively. "I'm on it, Pard. Um, are we still friends?"

I pointed at the exit.

After they all were gone Kandi sat down next to me. "You were a little hard on him."

Alys muttered, "Oh, puh-leaze," then said, "I'm going out back for a cancer stick. You can smoke on the dock, right?" Without waiting for an answer she left.

Kandi said, "You know how much he looks up to you."

"He set a camera spying on the back yard! What if we'd been doing something personal?"

"Like having wild Kama Sutra sex in the Jacuzzi?"

"That would count."

"Mac, Chet lives in Las Vegas. His significant other is the star of a topless rollerskating show. We'd have to bring a goat and a boa constrictor with us to get his attention."

We sat for a moment.

I sighed. "It would be a cute goat, right?"

Then I had an idea. "Well, let's stir the pot." I picked up my cell and called Henrietta Graveline, keeping the phone on the table so we both could hear the conversation.

"Mac, honey, good to hear from you, and how fortuitous! We need your help!" Her sexy, smooth voice belonged to a woman thirty years her junior. It made me smile despite myself. And I was 'Honey' after one meeting.

I looked at Kandi and pumped my fist. All right, maybe we were getting somewhere at last. Somebody needed help. Now we'd find out something.

"Sure, Henrietta, what can I do for you?"

"Shopping!"

Okay, I admit it—my face fell. I looked at Kandi, who shrugged. I said, "Um did you say, 'shopping?'"

"Yes! I need advice *desperately*. I'm buying a present for my friend's son, he's *so cute*, he's fourteen and he rides this thing called a skimboard and I thought I should buy him something at that place in Huntington Beach, a surf shop, it's famous—"

"Jack's."

"Yes! That's it. Oh, this is wonderful. We're on our way down there, right now, Brad and I. Could you possibly meet us there this afternoon? Please say yes!"

I sighed. "Henrietta, I'd like to help but there's sort of a lot going on right now, and—"

"We're just leaving my house in Belmont Shore. I dragged Brad away from that boat of his for a while, but it won't last. Good, wonderful. I'll buy you a beer at that bar on Main Street, Perqs I believe it's called."

I could fit it in before the people from Interagency Insurance showed up. "Um, Henrietta, Perq's is not exactly upscale. We could find someplace a little nicer."

"Oh, I'm sure with you and Brad to protect me I'll be just fine. I drove by the other day and it looked so interesting, all those shiny choppers out front. I read on the internet it's the oldest rock and roll blues place in Orange County."

Perq's, 'interesting?' Well, the oldest part might be true; my dad talked of going there years ago to hear local bands on Sunday nights. Nowadays, although most of the Harleys parked out front belonged to dentists and lawyers, Perqs still had the occasional drunken fight or customers lurching out front to upchuck in the gutter. It's been nominated for "Best Dive Bar" in Orange County and that says it all. "All right. Say half an hour in Jack's. Then we'll take a look at Perqs. It's early so we probably won't get knifed." We all listened to her throaty laugh and I disconnected.

"Kandi, would you see if Chet's outside?"

"And if he's speaking to you?"

"That, too."

She stood up, then whirled and glared at me. "Why don't you just paint a damn target on your back?"

"I thought you were all right with this. If you have a better idea I'm willing to listen."

"Kandi was all right with it, I'm not." For a moment she looked confused, then her face cleared. "Hell, Sailor, go for it. Okay, gotta go sling some margaritas."

The answer to both questions about Chet was yes. I told him what I needed and he grudgingly agreed.

After Henrietta bought three Ezekiel shirts at Jack's we walked a half-block, pushed open the door to Perqs and stood waiting for our eyes to adjust. The long oak bar along the left wall was mostly empty this early in the afternoon. Several big screen monitors were mounted on the walls, all but one with sports on, the lone standout showing a music video of some hair band jumping around. The tables in the front—the ones with a view of the twenty-thousand-dollar Harleys—were all full, but we got one in the back by the stage. I'd been here before so I didn't need to pick out exits, and the door to the alley was propped open. Henrietta handed me a twenty and asked for whatever Brad and I were having, so I dutifully went to the bar and got us schooners of draft Bud. It took me two trips to bring the three goldfish-bowl sized beers to our table.

Brad hoisted his, said, "Cheers," and gulped down a hearty portion.

Henrietta matched him with a gulp of her own, wiped foam from her lip. I paid more attention to her than I had on the yacht. She had on tight dark gray jeans, a long-sleeved purple shirt worn unbuttoned over a lavender tank top, and enormous hoop earrings that matched her top. Her silver-gray hair was cut short; it looked like a feathery cap that a woman swimming in one of those 40's water-follies movies might wear. Esther Williams? Somebody. I'd watched a lot of late-night TV waiting up for Diana. Henrietta said, "Whew, that's good shit." She paused, looked at Brad. "Hey, Mac, on the boat when I said to tell me about your adventures I didn't think you'd be having one so soon." She leaned forward on the stool, elbows on the table, completely at home in the dark bar. She poked me with her elbow. "Pretty wild. So, tell us, tell us. Brad and I want *all* the details. What was the home invasion all about?"

"No idea."

Brad—blending in by wearing plaid board shorts, Corona tank top, brown goatee, shaved head and Birkenstocks—dragged his eyes off of three girls all in cut-offs and bikini tops—yeah, it was December and if you don't live in SoCal eat your heart out. Their concession to the possibility of a chilly afternoon was sweatshirts tied around their waists. He looked at me intently. "All they took was your laptop?"

"That's it."

He looked at Henrietta, and said, "Mere coincidence? Or . . ."

She finished, ". . . proof of ancient astronauts. Remember when everybody was reading that and—"

My radar went *ping!* "So, where's your friend, Lisa June?"

They looked at each other again. Brad said, "Henrietta—" .

"We're doing this, Brad."

He shrugged and said, "She's the reason we're here."

"All right. Look, when we met on the boat it was not *entirely* by accident," Henrietta drank more beer. "We need your help. We're worried about Lisa June."

Brad snorted. "It's all in her head. God knows there's plenty of room in there for stuff to rattle around."

"Brad, please." He went back to staring at the girls. I am made of stern stuff, and I was working, so I only stared a little. All three had bikini bottom ties showing above their shorts. Aha! A clue! "Mac, Lisa June has been acting strangely lately. She thought someone was watching her."

Brad had finished his schooner. "And now she doesn't. End of story."

"We were hoping you could help."

"Me? How?"

Henrietta leaned forward. "Tail her." Yeah she said, "Tail her." Too much TV when she was a kid. "Follow her and see where she goes when she goes out, and find out if someone else is following her. C'mon, honey, you can do things like that, you have before and we want to hire you. We can pay."

"That kind of surveillance is difficult, and not cheap, and no, I've never done it. You need a detective, really more than one if you want to follow her around all the time."

Henrietta frowned at Brad. "I told you we'd have to tell him the whole thing. Mac, honey, we want you because, well, Lisa June lost her iPad about a week ago—"

"What does that—" I stopped.

"And then Brad's office was broken into and the hard drives were stolen out of his computers."

Oh, boy, at last a connection. "What about you?"

"I got a virus and my PC is being cleaned so I don't have it right now."

Zucco sighed. "On the off chance that there is something to this, yeah, we'll pay. Cash." He took out his wallet and counted out ten one-hundred dollar bills on the table.

I said, "I'll see what I can do," and picked up the money.

Promptly at five the investigators were at my front door. I buzzed the gate open and they came around back to my dock. This time there were three. I was standing next to my battered lawn chair. I'd put on a loose black sweatshirt, to hide the fact that my .45 was tucked in the small of my back. My sawed-off pool cue handle was up my left sleeve, taped to my forearm.

"Sir, thank you for taking the time," the first one said. "As I said I'm George and this is Rodney. This is our supervisor, Ms. Valentine."

"And Mr. Baines is—"

"The owner." He grinned. "Call me Chooch. Everybody does." Chooch was the taller of the two, with a fading case of post-adolescent acne scattered across his prominent cheekbones. He was football-player big, I'd guess 6'3" and probably 220 pounds and not much of it was fat. A big tough guy who knew he was big and tough. His partner Rodney was shorter, but pumped from a lot of time lifting weights. Neither one had any visible tattoos.

The woman was the one that made an impression. "Hello. I'm Faith Valentine." She held out her hand. She smiled, but her voice was, 'odd' was the only word I could think of, like she knew a joke that nobody else did.

She was in her forties, shoulder-length black hair parted on the side, short bangs. The hair was asymmetrical—curving just under her jaw on the left side, hanging down almost to her shoulder before curving in on the right. There was an inch-wide streak of pure white running down the long side behind her bangs. Full, sensual lips, painted deep red. Dark glasses hid her eyes. She was wearing black stilettos, and a black-and-white Donna Karan skirt and jacket that must have set her back at least three thousand dollars. You work around rich people you learn about clothes.

"T. R. Macdonald."

One thing I hadn't noticed when they were on camera—both of the men had long hair, worn like the Fab Four in the "I Wanna Hold Your Hand" days. If that meant something it was lost on me.

We shook hands all around, and settled onto the benches attached to my new redwood picnic table. They handed me business cards, I pulled my card case out of my jeans and reciprocated, and they asked me to review the events of the night before. Chooch and Rodney opened bags and took out laptops. Faith Valentine sat perfectly still, spine straight, probably looking at me behind the shades, with her hands motionless on the redwood table.

"We really appreciate this," Chooch said.

Rodney went on, "We have, of course, read the police report, but we'd like you to tell us about what happened in your own words."

So I went through it again. It didn't take long—I'd had a lot of practice. I saw someone in the side yard, they broke in, I jumped out the window, they got away. Blah, blah, blah. I ended with, "There were no damages beyond the theft of my laptop, so I'm not sure why you're interested."

"Other than your computer, did they seem to be looking for anything in particular?"

"No, just the laptop. If I had to guess I'd say that was the whole reason for the break-in."

"And they both wore black ski masks."

"More dark gray than black."

Faith spoke for the first time. "Dark gray is actually harder to see at night than black. Shows they knew what they were doing. Mr. Macdonald, has anything unusual come into your possession lately?"

"Like what?"

"Strange packages?"

Chooch grinned. "Right, like a present from somebody you don't know."

"What does that have to do with the break-in?"

Rod leaned forward. "Just answer the question, man."

Faith looked at Chooch who immediately put his hand on his partner's arm. "Be cool, bro."

"Dude could be more cooperative."

Faith's full lips twisted into a smile, revealing teeth that were contained in adult braces. "It's probably nothing. Just a standard question we like to ask. Like I said, this is part of an ongoing investigation. One more question. Can you think of any reason someone would want your laptop? We are aware that you have been involved in some pretty, shall we say, exciting, escapades. Is there anything going on now?"

I grinned. "That's two questions, but what the hell. Nope, nothing's going on. If you want, I can walk you through how it went down. In fact, that might help me remember more, too."

Faith said, "Chooch, take Rod and stand on the dock. I want to see where the men with guns were." Rod started to say something, thought better of it. I positioned them; she ordered, "Wait there."

So she dropped her glasses in her purse, we went into the house and I showed her the washer and dryer, the vent where the light going "blink-blink" had started all of this, the stairs, and where I jumped out the window. They watched and nodded. I watched them, but learned nothing.

When I told them about the holes that the little spiky things had punched in my foot and knee, Faith nodded and said, "Caltrop."

Not to be outdone, I came back with, "Medieval weapon, modernized and used against tanks. Sometimes coated with poison."

We went upstairs and I showed her where the ninja had escaped. "And you just jumped out the window?"

"Not one of my better ideas."

"What a rush." Her blue eyes were bright. "You must have really felt it."

"Felt it?"

"Alive. So alive. So rambling."

Back on the deck I said, "Well, that's what I remember."

I pushed their cards around on the table with my index finger and said, "Funny thing, after we talked I tried to look up Interagency Insurance and got nothing."

Chooch smiled. "We're under the radar, man."

Rod said, "The deal is, there's this group of big insurance companies, and when the problem's important enough, when there's, like, multiple companies involved, and multiple incidents, they bring us in."

Faith said, "Nice job, genius. All right, Mr. Baines probably wouldn't want us divulging this, but, since my talkative assistant has already started, yes, it's important." Rod turned pale and swallowed hard. "More than just a break-in. Possibly. You're a broker; you handle a lot of money."

"All of my secure client information lives on the company server. I couldn't store it locally if I wanted to because the company wouldn't permit it and FSB has some of the best database security there is."

She nodded. "How about the days leading up to the break-in? Anything strange?"

"You mean before the masked ninjas climbed around my house, waving automatic weapons and stealing my computer? Nope, just the same old routine."

She shrugged. "I admit I am at a loss. Anything. People watching the house?"

"This is suburbia. Anybody sits in a parked car for long, a neighbor calls the cops or our private security, Harbour Protection. You could talk to them."

"We will. If you think of anything—" Faith sighed.

"Sure."

On that note we all shook hands, and left. After I closed the gate behind them I gave Chet's cameras the finger and went inside.

Upstairs, I took my new laptop out from where it was hidden in my closet and reviewed the video. Chet sent me a text saying he still had nothing on Interagency and the license plate of their car was obscured by mud.

That night Kandi and I had dinner at Tantalum in Long Beach, sitting at the bar, looking out over the water and going through an assortment of appetizers. I had eaten five sliders and was debating one more order. No contest. I sipped my Sapporo and said, "I had an interesting voicemail when I got out of the shower."

"Are you going to eat that last shrimp?"

"Nope. I'm saving myself for the next round of little Kobe burgers. Planning like that is important when one is doing serious eating. Or, well, maybe I'll have it—" I reached out. Too late. He who hesitates gets his shrimp eaten. "Anyway, about my message." Kandi delicately patted her lips with a napkin and nodded. "So, there's this voice, kind of scratchy like a walkie-talkie, and it says, quote, 'Okay, this is the part where I say you have something we want and you say you don't know what I'm talking about and I say you better come up with it or else. So we're gonna skip all that. You either have it or you will soon. We'll call again to arrange pick-up. We're asking nice this time.' Click. They hung up." The sliders arrived and we each ate one. "So, what do you think?"

"I like the pulled pork better."

"Don't make me spank you in public."

Kandi is not a giggler. She has a low, throaty laugh that means she is happy and she laughed now. "Sailor, when you set me up like that it's difficult to ignore." Then she cleared her throat the way she does before she gets serious. "I want to give it some thought. *Mary* wants to give it some thought. Come by Fred's when I get off?"

"I planned on it. We need to stay close till we figure this out."

She twisted my arm so I ate the last Kobe slider, to save her from it. Sometimes you make sacrifices for those you care about.

At 10:00 that night I was seated in the bar at Fred's Fine Mexican Food, admiring Kandi in her black-and-white French maid outfit as she glided between the closely-spaced tables, balancing a full tray of drinks. Watching Kandi do anything is a treat, but her grace and poise at work never failed to please me. Her shift ended at midnight, but it was slow—fortunately a rare event for Fred's—so she got off early. She changed into tight white jeans, a sheer black long-sleeved blouse over a lacy white camisole, and a black-and-white knit scarf wrapped around her throat. We held hands like kids as we strolled along the cement walkway that runs between the rear of the shopping complex and the channel. To our right sport fishers gently nudged against their bumpers. As we passed Fred's dock I automatically checked the lines on my Boston Whaler.

"All right," she said briskly and in the blink of an eye Kandi was gone and I was talking to Mary Shaw, brilliant PhD candidate at UCLA. "Two conclusions come to mind. First, it's obviously a script."

"You mean my mystery caller was reading lines? Like telephone sales in a stock boiler room?"

"No. This is a life script that the caller is living up to."

"I'm lost."

"You shouldn't be. The two German guys were living up to a script that might be named Las Vegas Thug."

"Dieter and Franz." I'd been forced to kill Dieter. And it wasn't the thought of what I'd done—I felt no guilt—and it wasn't the way he looked that occasionally woke me in the dark of the night. It was the sound. It was the sound as I hit his head with that rock. I shivered, but it was, after all, December. A cabin cruiser, small, maybe thirty feet, rumbled by, probably on its way to the offshore kelp banks, timing their departure to bag early-morning Bonita. "Go on." It was so late we'd missed the Christmas Parade of Lights, where owners decorate their boats and motor up and down the channel.

"We all have life scripts, patterns of behavior with which we are imprinted and which tell us how to behave. It's a necessity; we can't just figure out everything every time we need to. In this case, the caller is playing the role of criminal, call it Mafia Soldier. And it is likely that they are *not* associated with the people who broke in."

I glanced over my shoulder. Nobody back there, lurking in the shadows. The truth is, I'm not all that good at spotting surveillance, so they could be there. But I had the .45. "They would have said something like, 'Give it to us or you'll never see your laptop again.'"

"Precisely. Therefore they are not the ones with your laptop."

"And? You said two conclusions."

"And this is what you've been looking for."

"Go with that thought."

With her free hand she absently played with the scarf, pulling the end up so she could comb the fringe with her fingers as we strolled. The only sound was the occasional soft squeak as a boat rubbed against its bumper. We passed The Happy Fish Chinese Food restaurant and turned back. "You called all of us together in Fred's kitchen ostensibly to analyze the things that had been happening to you. In reality that was a secondary purpose—you wanted to alert us to possible danger. However, as an operating hypothesis, you assumed there was a connection between at least some of these events. She dropped the scarf end and looked up at me. "This, my darling, is that connection. Not one but two groups think you have, or can get, something."

"Whoever broke in wanted whatever it is the caller is looking for. The ninjas thought they could find something about it on my laptop, maybe in an email. The callers want me to get it for them. But what is it they want?"

"No idea, but perhaps a better question is: do you have it?"

"No, well, make that I don't think so."

"And?" She casually flipped the scarf over her shoulder, turning as she did. She was watching behind us, too.

"And Roger tried to contact me, practically begged Alys. But these people, whoever they are, wouldn't know that."

"And we come back, again, to what is it these people think you have or can obtain?" She slipped her hand free, rooted in her purse for a stick of watermelon gum, skinned it, popped it in her mouth and after two chomps Mary was gone and Kandi was back. "So, Sailor, where do we go from here?"

"Well, I go surfing."

When we got home I had another message on my land line. It said, "We can get to the bimbo whenever we want." I did a perimeter check, testing all the doors and windows, set the house alarms, put my .45 on the nightstand and we went to bed.

Chapter Four   Breakfast at Fred's

The next morning, as I was carrying mugs of Kona coffee up the stairs to the master bedroom, I could hear Kandi yelling. "Rat bastard! Lazy, stupid, plagiarist!" She was sitting tailor-fashion on the bed, chenille robe pulled tight around her, staring at her iPad and pounding her fist into a pillow. She looked at me slitty-eyed. "He does sloppy research. He can't get away with this."

"You're right. I've never liked him." I took a step back. "So, maybe this is not a good time for you to have coffee. I'll just—"

"Give it here. Give it here *right now!*"

"Sure thing. Here it is." I handed her the mug and stepped back. "Should I ask?"

"There's this guy. Bernard Sigmund."

"That's a name?"

"Are you going to listen or am I going to kill you?"

"I could brew some decaf . . ."

"Siggy—his name is Sigmund and he hates being called Siggy so naturally everybody does—is in the PhD program with me. He's a candidate. Two quarters ago he did some sloppy work and I called him on it. Then there was a Teaching Assistant spot and we both went for it. I got it and as a result he hates me."

"Hates you?"

"Are you kidding? What, you think we're all colleagues, we put on raccoon coats and go to pep rallies? Mac, academia is ruthless, cutthroat, and a zero-sum game. When I got that TA job, it meant that Siggy didn't. Yes he hates me and he's been waiting to get back at me and now he thinks he's caught me using somebody else's work."

"If he's not too big I'll beat the crap out of him."

"Will you please take this seriously? If he wins I'll be out of the running for Chicago."

I can honestly say that, at that moment, my heart did not skip a beat, but it should have. I just leaned against the chest-of-drawers and sipped some coffee. I didn't get it. "Chicago?"

She looked up from the iPad, startled. "Oh, my. Well, heh-heh, can you spell 'Freudian?' I didn't mean to say anything until I knew more. I guess the old subconscious didn't agree. Look, I have to go to school. Right now." She handed me the cup and was up, off the bed and jamming notes and computer into her backpack. "Do I have a clean blouse here?"

"Yes. Hanging downstairs to dry. Chicago."

"My blouse is in Chicago? That's a joke." She stopped, looked at me, looked toward the bathroom as if debating whether or not to make a break for it, then sighed. "All right. There's a University of Chicago internship, very high-profile, a real prize."

When I finally got it, it was like being sucker-punched. For a moment I was frozen and all the air went out of my lungs, hell, out of the whole room. When I could speak I said, "How long? If you get it?"

"There are at least a dozen applicants. It's not likely that I'll get it."

"How long?"

"Six quarters."

"What does that mean?"

She took a deep breath. "A little under two years."

Sitting out back, looking at the water, I heard the garage door go up, her MGA start and pull out. The door went down.

It was an overcast morning, hazy and dull with a dirty gray-white sky. Also the way I felt so it was perfect. Fortunately, I was hungry and the thought of food cheered me up.

Fred's doesn't officially open until 11:00 but I motored over in my Boston whaler anyway. I could smell the cooking from the dock. I went in through the kitchen. and threaded my way through the activity, waved to Mario, and went out to the restaurant proper and sat at the bar. Mama, the tiny bartender of indeterminate age who has been my friend ever since I gave her some stock advice, brought me coffee and set a tiny pitcher of real cream next to it. She was constantly glancing over her shoulder at one of the bar TVs tuned to the stock channel. The Last of the Day Traders said, "Mario already has it cooking." The breakfast burritos at Fred's are one of my favorite foods, along with just about anything else that I don't have to cook. They aren't on the menu but if you ask nice and they aren't busy they'll make one. Thin strips of tender steak, scrambled eggs, cheese, onions, roasted chilies, all wrapped in a warm corn tortilla with a side of homemade green sauce over chiliqueles.

"What's this?" Mama asked. "A deliveryman came to the back, said you'd be here and it was for you." She handed me a package.

It was a FedEx envelope, the kind that they hand out in kiosks. This one had no return address, no address, just my name written in black marker on the front. It was very light. I didn't like it.

When I sliced open the envelope with my Swiss Army knife, a small white box tumbled out on to the bar. I closed the knife, slipped it back into my pocket, drank some coffee and looked at the little box. Cardboard, about four inches long, closed with masking tape. Finally I decided to open it. It was so light that I didn't see how it could contain anything like a bomb, still, I waited until Mama was at the other end of the bar stocking green olives before I tried to get the lid off. Unfortunately, the lid was stuck on with a lot of tape and she was back, wiping her hands on the bar rag, before I finally got it loose and the box slipped out of my hand, bounced twice on the counter and the lid came off.

A toe plopped out. A human toe, probably male since it was pretty good-sized as toes go and had no polish on the closely trimmed nail. A large pin that had a fake pearl head was pushed through the toe, into a little plastic surfboard. My mind, obviously looking for something, anything, to think of other than a toe, whispered, 'hatpin.' Because the tiny little surfboard came complete with a tiny little fin, the whole thing sat on the bar tilted at an angle. Hatpin, toe, surfboard. On the bar in front of me. A toe.

There was a moment when everything sort of went away—the cheerful noise from the kitchen, the traffic from Pacific Coast Highway—and the world centered on the box and its contents. Eyes wide, wider, widest, Mama stood, frozen, gawking at the toe. Her mouth dropped open. I was pretty much frozen, and I suppose my mouth dropped open, too. Suddenly she flipped the bar rag over the whole collection—surfboard, box, toe. The hatpin made a bump in the center of the rag. She cleared her throat, drummed her fingers on the bar. "Tell me it's not a real toe."

"Um—"

I lifted the corner of the rag, peeked under. The toe had been severed just behind the joint, and the chopped part was facing me. White bone in the center, surrounded by gray flesh. Little ragged flaps of gray skin around the circumference. No blood. Hatpin pushed through the flesh, passing beside the bone.

"Um—" I said again. Well, *you* try to think of something clever when a severed human toe jumps out at you before breakfast.

"Oh, shit, oh shit, oh shit, it's real. It's real." Mama was hopping from one foot to the other, backing away, with her hands in front of her as if to ward off the toe. "You brought a real toe into my bar! You brought a real toe into my bar! I can't believe you did that!"

"Calm down, now—"

"Calm down? It's a toe! A *toe*! I'm freakin' out here! I'm allowed to freak out when a freakin' toe jumps out onto my freakin' bar and we're not even open yet!"

Hard to argue with that. And okay, I was a little freaked out, too. I lifted the corner of the bar rag and looked again. Still there. Little white circles in the cross-section of skin, flesh, and bone, with something darker in the center of the bone that I supposed was marrow.

"Tell Mario to put my burrito into a to go container. Then bring me a baggie, and ask Jesus if I can use the kitchen dining room again. I need to make some calls." I looked under the rag again. Tucked into the box lid was a little note with, "Hang one, dude, from your friends at the New 521" printed on it.

The cop on the desk when I phoned it in wanted to know if I was the guy who'd been chased by clowns.

"Forensics guy took one look at the toe and said it was removed post-mortem."

It was late afternoon and Fred's was starting to get crowded. We were gathered in the kitchen dining room again, in an effort to make some sense of this. We gathered again, not because I thought we would come up with answers, but because my business background dictates that response—when in doubt, call a meeting.

"Sure! Sure! I bet there was no epidermal bruising." Alys was so excited she could hardly sit still. This would be major props back at school. We all stared at her. "What? What? I watch all the police procedurals. Did the forensics guy say what kind of tool they used? Or—they didn't *bite* it off, did they? That would be so totally *awesome*. Do you still have it? You took pictures, right?"

Kandi and I stared at each other for a moment. I said, "You take this one."

"Not on your life."

"What? What? I need to know; I've got people waiting for my Tweet." Alys nervously spun her lighter on the table. "Pictures! You took pictures, right?" She asked again.

"Yeah." I passed my cell phone over to her. She looked and her eyes widened.

Without looking up from his laptop Chet said, "Human bite? Naw, ain't likely. Jaw don't exert enough pounds per square inch. Horse could do it if'n he really wanted to."

Everybody was there except Snake, who was on the reference desk at the library. As usual, they all had laptops, including me. I had a new MacBook Air courtesy of Space Floozy Enterprises. Next to me, Alys was sending the toe pictures from my cell to her laptop. Kandi had a psychology journal open on hers. Nobody had much to say. Mario brought food and we ate. I don't really remember what it was.

My old cell phone, the one Chet was sure was tapped, chirped and vibrated on the table.

"Opened it yet?" Same scratchy voice.

"Opened what?" When in doubt, play dumb, right?

There was a crackle of static. "It's the sample."

"The sample?"

"Yeah. You're gonna get it for us. You weren't taking this seriously enough so we sent you that little surprise." I said nothing. "Okay, how long will it take for you to get what we're looking for?"

"At least two weeks."

"You're still not taking this seriously."

"Sure I am. What is this a sample of? And why do you think I have it?"

"Listen, you know Carnegie?"

"Pro surfer? Moved to Tahiti last year?

"Listen—"

"I've got it! CEO of a big trading firm, now serving three-to-five for wire fraud."

"Andrew Carnegie, you asshole. He did a lot of good, you know, libraries and shit like that."

"How long ago did you stop taking your medication?"

"I'm gonna do shit like that, good shit."

"And the only thing you lack is billions of dollars."

"Quit playing dumb. And you want to watch your back. Somebody you know is not what you think they are."

The line went dead. I looked at my phone and said, "Who's playing?"

Chet said, "Give me that, quick." He cabled the cell to his laptop and started typing. "Let's see what we can find out about these people."

Kandi said, "What was that all about?"

"The psycho who sent the toe wants to build libraries." For some reason they all stared at me.

Pacing from the glass wall separating us from the kitchen to the other side of the room, I said, "Okay, what have we got here? Somebody breaks into my house and steals my laptop."

Kandi said, "Wait a minute. Am I the only one who heard you promise these people whatever it is in two weeks? Are you out of your mind?"

"It was time to roll the dice. I bought some time."

"I give up. Chronologic. Do it in the order it happened, not the order in which it came to your attention," Kandi said and threw up her hands.

"Right. Good." Jesus had a white board and dry markers on an easel in the corner. I moved it next to the table and started listing events as we knew them. "First, Roger wants to talk. He emails and texts Alys. She asks me and I say no. Then somebody breaks in to my house and steals my laptop. Then somebody tries to carjack us."

Kandi said, "We go out on the boat with Walter's friends. Then the break-in followed by the attempted carjack. Then you call us and decide the best way to get more information is to bumble around, say 'yes' to things people ask you to do and see what happens. And have I mentioned I thought that was insane? You do it anyway and that leads to an encounter with so-called investigators from something called Interagency Investigations, followed by an attempted carjack. And then there's Elijah Eddington III, and don't forget the toe."

"And somebody thinks I either have something or can get it. And now they say it's a sample."

Chet closed his laptop. "Nada. Disposable phone. What's next?"

I had ideas but I couldn't act on them till tomorrow so we all went to my house and I ordered dinner.

I said if Alys promised to do her homework she could stay. Dinner was two giant buckets of spicy Popeye's fried chicken, plus a large mashed potatoes and a large coleslaw. It was way more than the four of us could eat, but Kandi would be at UCLA for the next couple of days, Chet might go back to Vegas to check on his ostriches, and I like to be prepared with leftovers. As I unpacked the food Kandi said, "How's Jesus dealing with all this?"

I said, "Loves it. At first he was freaked, you know, Board of Health issues and so on, but those got taken care of and he only opened an hour late. Now the free publicity has people lining up."

My blonde Significant Other shook her head, setting out a Dos Equis, a Diet Coke, a Mountain Dew and a glass of Kendall Jackson for herself. "I guess Kandi will have to work tomorrow after all." I had not mentioned Chicago, and neither had she. I guess I was what Mary would call 'conflicted.' I wanted her to be successful in her chosen profession, but I didn't want her to move to Chicago for two years. So I did and said nothing and neither did she.

We sat around the table in the kitchen with paper plates, plastic utensils, and dug in.

Chet answered emails as he gnawed on what was probably a thigh. Alys carefully pulled most of the batter off her chicken part before examining it closely and finally eating it. Kandi said, "Alys, I'm glad to see you trying to eat healthy."

She shook her head. "I keep thinking about the toe."

"Eeuw!" Kandi dropped her chicken part. I snatched it off her plate and popped it in my mouth.

"More for me." She glared at me, pushed her plate away. I said, "You could make a salad. I have lettuce."

"Mac, I saw that lettuce a few days ago when I opened the refrigerator. It had fur, and it made a break for it. I think it's living under your dock."

Chapter Five   The Titanium Redhead

The Huntington Cliffs is the name of the surf spot south of Huntington Harbour, across Pacific Coast Highway from the Aminoil field; in my father's day they had real cliffs of dirt and sand that you had to scramble down dragging your board with you. Today, there are cement walks leading down to the sand, it's been renamed Dog Beach, and it's much more civilized. Particularly in the winter, the surf can be good, and today it was huge.

That's where we went.

Promptly at six am two shiny pearl white Cadillac Escalades with dark tinted windows and "Slam Dunk Management" painted discretely on the doors arrived at my house. One pulled into the driveway, the other stopped at the curb. Both kept their engines running. The one in the driveway was driven by a seven-foot-tall black man dressed in a gray business suit, who stepped out and opened the passenger door for me. We crossed the bridge from the island to the mainland, (no carjacking clowns this time), took Warner to Pacific Coast Highway, turned south, and a few minutes later I was escorted to meet my client, who was sitting on a cement bench watching the dawn patrol shred some overhead surf.

The sky was overcast and gray, haze blending with the water, obscuring Catalina. The surf was big, big enough that only a dozen surfers, all in black ankle-to-wrist full suits, were outside the break line, scratching to hold position against the current that was pulling them to the south. And it had brought out media—several camera crews were set up on the cliff as well as down on the sand with tripods and cameras. The rest of the beach was devoted to dogs running madly, chasing Frisbees, splashing into the water and in general having a great time.

Two hopefuls swept metal detectors side-to-side over the sand, prospecting for who knew what; behind us runners, skaters, and cyclists dominated the bike path. Just a typical December day in Surf City.

Eddington stood and towered over me as we shook. He had on a gray Armani, unstuffed white Polo shirt, aviator mirror shades, and was sporting a trendy goatee and close-cropped hair showing a small amount of gray at the temples. He sat and nervously drummed his fingers on his knee. Me? I watched the surf and was glad I hadn't gone. It was big, all of the sets overhead and with a goodly number of double overheads, big thick winter waves that built up, pitched out and went *krump* as they broke. Before New York I could have handled it, maybe not easily but I could have gone out, in fact I would have loved it, but I was just getting back into shape and this was more than I wanted to take on. Just paddling out though nasty beach break like this was a real challenge, which is why tow-in surfing was invented. As I watched an Asian thirty-something trudged up the ramp to the parking lot, limping and carrying the two halves of his board.

"That's her," Eddington said, pointing at the line-up "Only girl outside." He handed me binoculars, and I focused on a girl with long hair that was probably red when it was dry, wearing a black full suit. As I watched she scratched hard and caught a wave, a double-overhead monster that looked like it would close out and crush her. My throat caught at the lateness of her takeoff but she handled it like a pro—a smooth drop, cut to the right, three quick slashes up and down the face and back over the top with a nice kick-out that had her airborne. Then I noticed the largest of the film crews jumping and hooting and I wondered just what was going on.

"Her name is Nadzia Kamnik and she's been living with me—"

"Whoa, dude—"

"—while she finishes high school. She's nineteen, graduated in June."

"Let me say again, 'Whoa, Dude.' You want me to manage your money while you're in prison?"

He looked pained. "I come to you for help and ya'll ain't taking it seriously. It's not like that. Look, ya'll want to hear this story or not?"

I punched him on the shoulder. "Yes, E, I want to hear the story."

"Well," he paused, looked at me. "Well, okay." He gestured and one of his assistants brought a chrome thermos of coffee, white ceramic mugs that had "Slam Dunk" on the side and poured us cups. I sipped cautiously and recognized Starbuck's Breakfast Blend. "She's been living at my place for almost a year and I'm just a little sensitive, so lay off the humor, all right? My wife Mildred travels a lot and yes, the neighbors have talked. Do you remember Pyotr Kamnik?"

"No, I—Wait a minute, he played with you in college."

"UCLA, then two years with the Clippers. That's his daughter. Pyotr and Fiona lost a big chunk of money in 2000 in the tech crash, then decided to recoup their fortune by getting into real estate, flipping houses."

"Uh-oh."

"That's it, bro. That time they lost it all, everything. They sort of freaked out, decided the world was ending. They'd always been Jehovah's Witnesses, but after the real estate crash they got serious, really into this End of Days stuff, joined a fringe branch of the Witnesses, and moved to Idaho. Nadzia wanted to finish up at Marina High, all her friends are there, so she asked if she could stay with me. I hired a full-time, live-in housekeeper. Like I said the neighbors talked, but what the hell."

"And what do you need from me?"

"I'm gettin' to that, man, ya'll gotta give me time here."

As he talked I was watching the surf. The girl, Nadzia, took off again, big wave, and lost it. She came off the board at the top of one of her slashes, tumbled down the face with her board on top of her and it buried her, the sound clear even where we sat—a loud thud. I held up my hand for Eddington to stop talking for a minute and focused the binoculars on where I thought she was. The board popped up, she came up after it, yanked angrily on the leash to drag the board to her, slid on and paddled back out. I let out the breath I'd been holding. "She's tough."

"Understatement. A year ago she was in a bad situation with a couple of guys and got out. That girl's been on a skateboard since she could walk. She's good, real good, she's got a following, and about a year ago she started getting some pretty good endorsements. Now she surfs, too. First a question: is she good on a surfboard?"

"Surfing? Hell, yes. She's very good. Good wave sense, good timing, flashy kick-out, pretty much fearless if today is any indication. If she's thinking of turning pro I think she'd stand a chance."

"Problems?"

"She wants to go for it. Late take-offs like that last one can mess you up. But she's good."

"Damn. Man, oh, man, was I ever afraid of that? Yessir, I was afraid and I am afraid. She wants to surf Maverick's."

I put down the binoculars and turned to look at Eddington. "She's out of her mind. Obviously you know something about Maverick's."

"Damn right I do. Never been there but I've seen pictures and YouTube clips."

The surf spot known as Maverick's is at Half-Moon Bay, south of San Francisco and, despite the fact that people have known about it since the early days, it's only been ridden in the last twenty years, for good reason. The waves break a half-mile offshore, the paddle-out the long way is 45 minutes to an hour and the short way is nuts, the waves break over a reef, and if you fall there are rocks, lots of rocks and the wave holds you down till you think you're about to die. A double hold-down, where you surface and another wave breaks on top of you, is much worse. Then you can die.

"E, Maverick's kills people, better surfers than her. Just trying to paddle out when it's big is something I don't even like to think about, and dangerous in itself."

"She says the endorsements will make her rich, and set her up to snowboard the X-Games. She says she'll be a triple threat—skateboard, surfboard, snowboard. She wants to surf Maverick's and then enter that Huntington Beach surf contest next year."

"The boards have footstraps because it's impossible to stay on a surfboard going that fast without them."

"She's ridden Waimea and Todos Santos. Last winter, and again few weeks ago."

I shook my head. "One winter when I was in college some guys from Long Beach and I drove up the coast on a surf trip and Maverick's was so huge, none of us went out, never even considered it. We just sat on the cliff and watched. Okay. I'll try to talk her out of it."

"Do I wish that was it? Hell, yes, I wish that's what I wanted but that ain't it. She had this guy lined up but it didn't work out and now she wants you."

"Wants me for what?"

"She wants you to drive the jet ski." My jaw must have dropped. When Maverick's gets really big, so big it's impossible to paddle out, then on rare occasions it becomes a tow-in spot where the surfer is pulled into the wave behind a PWC—Personal Watercraft to the uninitiated. Pulled in front of a wave about the size of a three-story building, tons and tons of churning water slamming down onto rocks, with another wave right behind it. It made today's double-overhead sets look easy. In comparison they *were* easy.

I stared at him for a moment. Then, because I couldn't think of anything else to do, I reverted to talking about something I understood while my brain processed the information. "Okay, E, before we go any farther here, where's the money coming from?"

"What do you mean, bro? Ya'll helped me make it."

"Yeah, I was there when you sold your first large block and cleared a million. You're rich, E, but *this*?" I gestured behind us at the parking lot. "Bodyguards? SUV convoys?"

He flapped a hand casually. "Man, don't worry about it. I got me some rich friends, you know what I'm sayin'? Look, if you want to know if I can afford to pay for all this, bro, I can, no problem."

"Okay, how about this? Surfing Maverick's is dangerous, really dangerous, not fake danger like bungee-jumping or riding a roller coaster."

"Man, all you gotta do is drive the damn jet ski. I'll pay you a grand a day and cover all the expenses. You buy one of these jet skis, hell, when this is all over you keep it, okay?"

In the back of my mind I could hear myself at our strategy meeting saying, 'Why, I'll just say yes until we figure this out. That's the best way to find out what's going on.' It looked like Kandi was going to be right about yet another of my plans. To my friend I said, "If I can talk her out of it, would that be a good answer?"

"Oh, hell, yes. My man, ya'll do that and you will have my undying gratitude, and I will pay, oh, yeah. But it ain't gonna be happening. This girl is, uh, single-minded."

The wind was coming up; the surf was blowing out, and people were coming in. The camera crews were capping lenses and folding tripods. I watched as Nadzia took one last wave, let it close out behind her, dropped to her stomach and proned out to the beach. She picked up her board, tossed her long hair over her shoulder, and started trotting across the sand. She saw us up at the street level and her face lit up. Two steps later and she was surrounded by a crowd. She broke out and came up the path to our bench. Cameras snapped as she unzipped the wetsuit and a skinny dark-haired kid put down his clipboard and helped her pull it down to her waist, revealing a red-and-white tiger-striped bikini top. More cameras snapped. She wrung water out of her hair, the same kid handed her towels for her hands and face. She dried off, tossed the towels back to him and put her hands on her hips, cocking her head to the side and looking me over. I was looking her over, too, and she was worth a look.

She was stunning. Tall, about 5' 11." Long red hair that looked like it might be wavy when it was dry, brilliant, slightly slanted green eyes in a square, strong face with just a hint of freckles across her nose, cupid's bow mouth, of course bare of lipstick and not needing it, and a figure that the fullsuit couldn't hide even before she pulled it down to her waist. If she was looking for sponsors, hell, I'd sign up just to hang out at the photo shoots. Two things hit me: first, I'd been staring at a beautiful young woman in a bikini, and second, that about a dozen people, mostly kids, were snapping pictures with everything from cell phones to iPads to professional SLRs. I cleared my throat and smiled.

Eddington stood up and said, "T. R. Macdonald, meet my adopted daughter, Nadzia Kamnik, also known as The Titanium Redhead."

She stuck out her hand and we shook. "Hey. I recognize you from your pictures. I'm Nadzia." A fresh towel appeared and she snatched it without taking her eyes off me. She grasped my arm and guided us a little way apart from the crowd. They tried to follow but she signaled a short blonde to her side and said,

"Kaylee, where's Luke?" The blonde waved and the dark-haired Kid popped up. He was wearing black stovepipe jeans, an oversized white t-shirt with things printed on it in Magic Marker, and was trying manfully to grow an "iron jaw" beard. Nadzia said, "Luke, do your job. Get on this." He bobbed his head and spread his arms, moving the mob back out of earshot.

Nadzia grasped the blonde's elbow and pulled her forward. "Mr. Macdonald, this is my BFF, Kaylee Miraflores."

"Hey."

"Hey, Kaylee." She was young, maybe fourteen, a little chubby, with a round face and thin blonde hair that her ears stuck out through. She was wearing fur-topped pink Ugg boots, pink short shorts and a black sweatshirt with "TTR" lettered on the front in Old English script. She mumbled something I didn't catch and turned away.

When we had a bit of privacy, Nadzia said, "Kaylee's shy. Please say you'll do it."

"Nadzia, that was a spectacular session. That next-to-last kick out where you got so much air—awesome. You're good."

"I know. And, thanks. I blew the landing on that one but they'll cut it from the video." She was tall enough to look me in the eye. "That's not an answer."

"You should leave the landing in, it adds realism. And it's not supposed to be an answer. We're talking. Tell me something—why me?"

She glanced back at Eddington. "My dad will pay you."

"That's not an answer, either."

"I saw you on YouTube, okay? And dad talked about you a lot especially when all that stuff was going on. I trust you."

"Why?"

"I'm going to rinse off. And I need to condition my hair." She snatched another fresh towel from the ever-present Luke, threw it over her shoulder and stalked away. Her back was proud and straight and her hair showed red highlights as it began to dry. Kaylee was trotting behind her with a bag presumably full of soap, shampoo, and conditioner.

"Mac, please." Eddington had come up behind me.

"Call me tomorrow. We'll talk."

When the Escalade dropped me at my house Kandi was in the family room, dissertation notes spread around her, iPad and laptop open and running. She had on white pants, a pale red silk blouse with the top three buttons undone, and big dangly silver earrings that looked like tiny champagne glasses. Her crimped blonde hair was pulled back into a ponytail. All in all, I had to restrain my natural impulses, a lot, because I knew she was squeezing in a little dissertation work before her shift started at Fred's. I settled for burying my face in her neck and then working south to the land of awesome cleavage. In minutes my restraint was slipping so I quit unstuffing her blouse, settled in next to her on the couch and told her what I'd been doing, what Eddington had wanted. I am made of stern stuff.

She put her hands on my shoulders and firmly pushed me back. Okay, maybe I was still doing a little unstuffing. I'm stern, not perfect. "Another young woman in jeopardy. Mac, you *do* realize that you are saving Diana over and over, and that you simply cannot do it?"

I said, "I need a nap." A couple of hours of sleep and I was back downstairs. Kandi was still at work.

As if there had been no interruption, she said, "Another young—"

"Woman in jeopardy. I get it." I groaned dramatically, watching from the corner of my eye to see if I had a chance of diverting her and, when it was obvious I didn't, went into the kitchen and ground some Tilawa, a new coffee I was trying that was from a small producer in Costa Rica. The grinder noise kept Kandi from talking and gave me time to think. Unfortunately I didn't think of much of anything except that maybe I'd go surfing tomorrow, see if I could still handle the big stuff.

She called out, "It won't work. You will be forced to come back in here sooner or later."

"You think I can still handle overhead surf?"

"I'm serious."

"So am I. The report says it will still be big tomorrow and low tide's at 6:34 am." The water started to drip slowly into the pot. I watched it for a while as if it were interesting, but it really wasn't. "It's the paddle-out that worries me."

"Mac—"

"Look, I know you worry about me. About us. And I know we have decisions to make. And—" We looked at each other for a moment. "And she's not really in jeopardy. Yet." I finished. Lame. Lame.

"You're trying to dodge the issue I am referring to. I know you'll be all right doing the surfing thing."

"Frankly, the thought of Maverick's scares the hell out of me. And it's tow-in where I'm supposed to drive the wet bike. But the odds are against it happening, for a lot of reasons, like tow-in is very restricted in that area. It's a marine sanctuary and—"

"Whatever. It's your mental state I am concerned about."

"I am, too, for even considering Maverick's. And before you ask, no, I see no connection between Eddington and the ninjas or the clowns or the toe." I could see the charming wit was lost on her. I looked back at the dripping coffee but it still was pretty boring, except that there seemed to be a little more of it. "Kandi, has it occurred to you that you may be predisposed to worry about my mental state because that's what you do? Counsel people?"

She nodded. "Give a kid a hammer and everything looks like a nail. Yes, I understand that and I try to temper what I say with that knowledge."

"Well, I haven't said yes to Maverick's, and I have a plan."

She smiled and lightened up. Picking up a thick three-ring binder full of with papers, all organized and divided by tabs, she said, "Sailor, I've had some experience with your plans and, forgive me for saying so, but some of them have been less than optimum."

"Har de har har, Alice. This is a good plan."

"Been watching *The Honeymooners* again, have we? You really think this will somehow lead to some kind of information about the break-in?"

"Well, yeah that's the idea, sure. Thrash around and see what turns up. It could work." I pulled out my cell phone. "I didn't really get a chance to talk to her at Dog Beach, because she had this gang of kids that came up as soon as she rinsed off . . ."

"Her posse."

"Yeah, exactly. Well, one of them, a blonde kid named Kaylee, had a webcam and was uploading video, and anyway, it was too public to really talk."

"If you get into this you better get used to that."

"I know, I know. Anyway, when she came back Nadzia wasn't mad anymore, hugged me, said how she appreciated my help. Blah, blah, blah. By the way, she's called The Titanium Redhead. It's on towels, sweatshirts, tattoos, everywhere. And I've got an idea." I turned away so I wouldn't have to see Kandi roll her eyes.

I called The Titanium Redhead. She answered the phone with, "Hey. Dude, you gonna do this?"

I'm old enough to remember when people actually said, "Hello."

"Frankly, I doubt it. But while I decide, there's someone I want you to meet. When can we get together?"

"Shit. Hey, you board?"

"Skateboard? Uh, yeah, I used to."

"At least talk to me about it, please? I really, really need you to do this."

"I'll talk. I'm not saying yes or no, but there's a friend of mine I want you to meet. What does me riding a skateboard have to do with this?"

"Thank you, thank you. You know Toilet Bowl?"

"The skate park? Off Gothard?"

"Right. My crew's gonna film me there, uh, wait, let me check." I could hear her yell, "Luke or Kaylee! Who's here? Toilet Bowl shoot, when?" I couldn't hear the answer, but Nadzia came back on and said, "Day after tomorrow. It's a shoot but it's not like, huge or anything, so we can talk and I can meet this person. You should ride with us. I got a board you can use."

I hadn't been on a skateboard in—what?—five years? Could it be that long? All at once it sounded better than good, it sounded great, absolutely great. Maybe jumping out of that window had jarred my brain loose. If it had I didn't care. "Got my own board."

"Whoa, I'm impressed. Okay, we'll roll up in the afternoon around four. Meet you there. So, who's this friend you're bringing? Is it Kandi the waitress, 'cause I'd really like to meet her."

Some of the time, no, make that all of the time, I wish my life and my friends' lives had not become so public. "No, it's somebody else. Her name's Alys."

"Whatever. See you there."

I remember when people said, "Goodbye."

Kandi said, "And your plan is . . . ?"

"Talk to somebody I probably should have killed."

That night I dug my old skateboard out of the garage, cleaned the dust off of it, did some minor maintenance on the trucks—the metal part on the underside of the board that supports the wheels—listened to the bearings click as I spun the wheels, took a deep breath and pushed off down my driveway, grinning like a loon. I stepped down too hard on the rear kick plate, the front of the board went up, followed by my feet zooming up over my head, and I sat down on the cement, hard, as the board took off, looking like it was headed for low-earth orbit.

On my next attempt I was suddenly lying in the middle of the street, fortunately not in front of a car, while the board went off for more adventures on its own.

An hour later I'd ripped one knee out of my jeans, shredded the skin off my left palm, and decided that I still had it. I could board. But I promised myself I'd skip the dry swimming pools.

I was still grinning like a loon. Life was good.

Chapter Six   Sociopath

"I want out, Roger Winters said.

"Yeah? I want a pony and that's not going to happen, either."

Two days after watching The Titanium Redhead shred Dog Beach, Alys Winters' brother and I were walking down a flagstone path that wound through the grounds of the Biggin Hill Recovery Home, an island of landscaping in a wilderness canyon in eastern Orange County. I had driven out to see what was on his twisted mind, other than blowing up stuff and killing pushers. Getting permission to see him had been remarkably easy. One call yesterday to Dr. Quentin Roll, the guy who ran the place, and it was set up. Roll told me on the phone that Roger had made "remarkable progress" and was a "changed man." I felt like telling Roll that Winters was really good at fooling people, had in fact fooled me and I'm naturally suspicious, but refrained. Roger might have something interesting to say. And since nobody had broken into my house, tried to carjack me, or sent me a severed human toe, it was the only thing available.

"Just a day pass, not out as in released. As an interested party, if you signed for me I could spend a few hours, a day maybe, outside. Maybe talk to my dad. It would mean a lot to me."

Roger's father, "Happy" Winters, owned a chain of auto dealerships and bought almost as much TV ad time as that guy who yelled a lot and sold magic cleaning solutions. I bought some of his stuff—from the cleaning guy, not from Roger's father—for my living room carpet and ending up throwing it out—both the carpet and the magic solution.

"I'd put that in the same class as me getting a pony." I stopped walking. The two burly, white-jacketed orderlies who were about ten yards behind us stopped too. They watched us. Somewhere birds chirped enthusiastically, discussing important bird issues.

A breeze stirred the low bushes and sycamore trees on the other side of the wall. Roger was wearing what might pass for street clothes until you noticed that the orange sweatpants had no cord around the waist, and his white tennis shoes had no laces. The white t-shirt had "Biggin Hill" stenciled in large letters on the front and back.

Biggin Hill is located in inland Orange County, in a wooded area at the end of Temescal Canyon. Less than an hour from the shopping palace of South Coast Plaza/Crystal Court/Metro Pointe, Temescal Canyon and others like it were undeveloped and wild—scrub brush, trees, and animals, with the occasional fire, mudslide, or flood to liven things up. The main building, visible from the road only through the gate, is three-story white Colonial, with a large portico across the entire front, stately white columns, and black shutters. The whole complex—there are cinderblock treatment buildings hidden behind the original structure—is surrounded by a cement wall. That, in turn, is surrounded by twelve-foot chain-link fence topped by concertina wire. Tara meets Alcatraz. You wait in your car outside the black iron gate in the fence on a gravel turnaround. If they're expecting you the guard opens the gate and you drive to the wall, go through another gate, park, and then walk up the gravel drive and climb the steps to the solid mahogany double doors, where you pass yet another visual inspection, followed by a metal detector, and sign in.

Mary tells me there are at least seven different kinds of intelligence, whatever "intelligence" really is. Alys' brother Roger is a genius in at least three of them, but he's off the low end of the scale in others. He's not quite as tall as I am, with brown hair worn barely long enough to part and brown eyes. He likes things that make very loud noises when they explode, and martial arts. He's lean and solid muscle; probably about 4% body fat. When he was on the outside he dressed in black t-shirts that looked like they'd been painted on and black jeans. If he really wanted to he could snap my neck before the guards could cover the distance between us; he was that fast. I knew it was useless but never stood within reach anyway.

"Roger, you know I'm not going to get you out of here, so tell me what you really want or this conversation is over."

He hooked his thumbs inside the waistband of the sweatpants and tugged them up. Looked at me intently. "There are times when you wish you had let me die, when we were on the boat and the sulfur gas was all around us." He smiled. "Help me get out and you might be able to rectify that mistake." Somewhere someone, presumably an inmate, was sobbing. The sound of their misery carried in the still air, silencing the birds. Then it stopped. After a moment the birds started again.

"If I wanted you dead, you'd be dead."

His eyes are what tips you off that this guy is—what? I wasn't sure. Dangerous, yes, certainly. But then, so was I. The difference was that his eyes held nothing, no fear, no regret, no thought about the things he had done. "Ah, but you were tempted, right? For a moment there you thought, 'If he was outside I could kill this asshole, make it look like an accident.' I could see it in your eyes." Did I mention that he was perceptive?

I said nothing, because of course he was right. That thought had surfaced in my mind like a bubble of noxious gas rising out of an evil, haunted swamp. "Good-bye, Roger." I turned my back on him and started back down the path. A blue jay fluttered down on the path, cocked his head and said insulting things about me. He was too smart to stay inside with the loonies, so he was probably right about me. If Roger was going to jump me, this would be the time.

"It's more than the break-in, isn't it? The odd things happening around you." I stopped, turned and looked at him, and waited till he came to me and we started back toward Tara.

"I got some emails—if you're a good boy and the doctor agrees you can have limited Internet—from people I didn't know and they were asking about my dad, was I still in touch, had he been to visit, that sort of thing. Then they got to what they really wanted."

"Which was?"

"Names. People he knew at Berkeley. Radicals, especially."

"And you told them, what?"

"Nothing. I wanted to see what they would do next. So, a week ago these two clowns show up with credentials and Doctor Roll says okay and allows them in to see me. They let us walk outside, like we are now. These people know I'm good with, uh—"

"Explosives." Roger had built the handheld missiles he had used to attack a ship off the coast of Orange County. That had led to the blazing tanker, poison gas, and my missed opportunity to let him die. Yeah, he knew a lot about substances that made loud noises when ignited.

"Solid propellants are really my specialty. Although before I came here I was exploring binary liquids."

I could play the game, too. "You mix the liquids and they explode."

We walked off the path, found a couple of rocks to sit on. I made sure mine was as far from him as possible. The two orderlies stopped behind us. In front of us the ground dropped away and the wall and fence followed the contour of the land, so both wall and fence were hidden from where we sat. We looked down the canyon, over trees and scrub toward the city. "I like this spot," he said. "The illusion of freedom is apparent. You think you're free outside?"

"I suppose you're going to tell me I'm not."

"Correct. There are players who really run the show, people you see but never recognize for what they are."

"I saw *Conspiracy Theory*, too. What do you know about my home invasion?"

"The people who came to visit me didn't want a bomb. I'm sure of that. I'm not sure exactly what they wanted, but I think they wanted to know how to find a particular supplier for a weapon. Nothing they said directly, they were being oh-so-clever. Nothing I could take to the authorities."

"The home invasion? You think it's the same people?"

"Maybe, but from what I read it was very slick. My visitors were pretty clumsy. Except for the fake credentials."

"So these two guys show up, you get interested and decide you want a day pass. You write to your sister because, for good reason, you don't have my email."

"It was a man and a woman."

"What did they look like?"

He shook his head. "Freedom," he said again, looking out over the scrub brush of the canyon. "I've thought about it a lot. In here you have time to think."

"Stop, stop, I'm getting all choked up here."

"Freedom? No, I guess we're not free. But that doesn't mean there's more freedom out there."

"Roger—"

"Here the reality is just closer to the surface. You can actually see the fences and guards. I like that. Out there, you can't see either one, but they're there. Like sitting here, where we can't see the fence, you understand?"

I stood up. "Call me when you're not crazy."

"They had guns."

Uh-oh. I had a feeling that I didn't want to ask the next question, but of course I did it anyway. And I sat back down. "The two people who came to visit you. They had guns?"

"Automatics. The man's was in an ankle holster. She kept hers in the small of her back." Two people getting by the security with weapons? I doubted it.

"How do you know?"

"Please, remember who you're talking to. I'm good with stuff like that."

"Right."

I looked at the damn blue jay and that's all it took.

Roger was sitting next to me, one leg stretched out in front of him, the other pulled up so his knee was at chin level. And the side of his shoe pressed against my knee. I didn't move.

"The birds always distract me. I took a chance, thought they'd do the same to you. Lateral tear of the anterior meniscus. You'll walk with crutches for a few weeks, but the damage won't be permanent."

"What do you want?"

"I don't want to hurt you. I believe I'm proving that right now."

"Hey, works for me, Roger. You've turned over a new leaf; you're completely harmless, except if I say no to a day pass, you tear up my knee. Well, this will give you something to think about when you're in solitary."

"Biggin Hill is much too progressive for that. And it would be very hard to prove. You stumbled, you see. Uneven path, happens every now and then."

"Okay, you win. Where do I sign?"

"Why don't I believe you?"

"Possibly because I'm lying. What I think I'll do is sell some bonds that I'm tired of, donate the money and ask them to let me watch your electroshock therapy."

"*Way* too progressive for that."

"Let's find out." I stood up. He didn't lash out with his foot and cripple me.

Roger laughed. "I like you, Mac, I really do and I want to help you. Please."

"Why you? Why did they pick you to ask about weapons, if that's what they wanted?"

"Who knows?"

I was several paces along the path when something clicked. My last question resonated with another thought and it made sort of sense. "You wanted to change the world. They do, too. That's why they came to you, isn't it?"

"Will you get me a day pass?"

"Sorry, dude. Gotta skate."

Chapter Seven   "Skateboarding . . ."

Skateboarding can best be described by three words: *go for it*. A rough translation is "Try this stupid, dangerous trick and see if you get seriously injured."

Two hours after leaving Roger Winters to contemplate the illusion and reality of freedom I had followed Jamboree Boulevard out to Newport Beach, picked up his sister Alys at school and we were back in Huntington Beach, pulling into the cracked asphalt parking lot in front of the Toilet Bowl Skate Park.

Kaylee stood watching us and tapping out texts on her cell phone as I pulled my battered skateboard out of the trunk. We walked up to her and I said, "This is my friend Alys Winters." Seeing them standing, staring at each other presented a contrast in teen styles. Alys had fashionably outfitted herself for the occasion in red high-top Converse tennies with green laces, cut-off denim short-shorts over patterned black tights, an oversized black t-shirt, and a black hoodie with a smoking skull on the back. This was topped off with giant hoop earrings—one red and one green—and a black knit cap. Kaylee was wearing black cigarette pants, a white gauze blouse over a white tank top, and a slim black vest.

She slipped the phone into her hip pocket and said, "Hi, I'm Kaylee Miraflores."

Alys was staring at Kaylee, open-mouthed. "Kaylee *Miraflores*? KayleeTalks?"

Kaylee blushed, looked down at her shoes. "Um, yeah, that's me."

"Ohmygod! Ohmygod!" That's the way it came out of Alys' mouth, all one word. "I read you all the time, all the time. You're the shit, girl, you really are and I just *love* your stuff, like when you told Ferretgurl she had to tell somebody about her friend and how the friend's boyfriend wanted her to get into sexting and she didn't want to. That was the shit. I'm MemorialGirl."

Kaylee's face lit up. "Hey, yeah, wow, sure, I really like your posts 'cause I never have to edit them, they just go, you know? Awesome to meet you in person." They touched fists and then hugged. She jerked her chin in my direction. "You're with him?"

Alys nodded. "Girl, he saved my life. I was in this totally *awful* place."

Kaylee was bobbing her head, her hair alternately covering and exposing her ears. "I can relate. Cool." They hugged again, then remembered that I was standing there, holding a beat-up skateboard and feeling as old as my skateboard looked. Alys turned to me.

"Mac, this is so awesome. Why didn't you tell me it was her? Kaylee's blog, KayleeTalks is really great, totally huge."

"Um, thanks." Kaylee beamed.

"Really, it's awesome."

I said, "One more awesome and you're grounded." Alys giggled. "To keep the record straight, Alys saved my life first. Kaylee, where's Nadzia?" Kaylee held out her fist and I awkwardly bumped it with mine.

She frowned. Maybe I'd done the fist-bump wrong. "Z's my BFF, has been for a year."

I looked at Alys, who rolled her eyes and whispered, "Best Friend Forever."

"I knew that."

"She took care of me when I was the new and I want to help her. You know, I just—" She bit her lip. "My blogs helped Nadzia get her first sponsors, but this surfing thing, this Maverick's, I don't like it."

"Join the club."

"And you, you're going to drive the thing, the wet bike, for her." She made it sound like an accusation. Maybe it was.

"That's not decided yet, not by a long shot. I want Alys to meet her."

"Hmmph. Well, anyway, the girl sent me a text and said the last part of her morning photo shoot ran over. She'll be here in a few minutes." She grinned. "Hey, check this out." She handed me an issue of *Thrasher* magazine. "Page 47." It was a two-page spread headlined "The Titanium Redhead SHREDZZZ." It was all pictures of Nadzia, getting huge air, grabbing the skateboard's rail as she flew out of dry swimming pools. There was a series of her jumping the board up onto a railing that ran down the center of cement stairs, sliding down the railing, and jumping the board off the end to a successful landing. It looked impossible. There was one shot of her standing with her board, looking back over her shoulder, winking, with her sweatshirt slipped down to show a tattoo that said "TTR" in old English, and several close-ups of other tats, one in the small of her back that I recognized as the creature from *Alien*.

I nodded, started to hand the magazine back, but Kaylee said, "It's for you," so I rolled it up and stuffed it into my hip pocket, which turned out to be a good thing. Dropped my board, planted my left foot and pushed off. A few easy bowls would be a good warm-up.

Skate parks, if you haven't been to one lately, grew up because so many places decided that, despite the bumper sticker, skateboarding really is a crime. Toilet Bowl was typical—about 20,000 square feet of graffiti-covered cement molded into a huge full pipe, thimbles, ramps, spines, stairs with and without rails, steep drops into bowls and of course, half pipes. A half-pipe is a cylinder, just like you see snowboarders sliding up and down on TV, only it's cement. You drop in, swoop down to the middle, up the other side and—if you're good—crouch and grab big air as you go flying into space before you drop in and do it again up the other side. Spines are ridges that you jump your board up on and slide along on the bottom of the plank, doing what is called a grinder. Bowls are just what they sound like—dry swimming pools. Skateable planters with long-suffering palm trees surrounded by ice plant broke up the cement grayness.

All in all there are a wide variety of ways to mess yourself up. Since there were no easy bowls, I dropped into the first one I came to, came up the far side, stepped down hard on the rear kick plate, rotated the nose and made the turn. No air, but a clean 180. That loony grin came back and I did it again, up the far side, another 180 and back down. I jumped it out of the bowl, stuck the landing took a half-dozen hard pushes, pushed down on the raised front and rear lips, flexed my board and jumped it up onto a spine. Ah, the benefits of a misspent youth. I did a respectable grinder, sliding along about half the length before I lost my balance and stepped off. More loony grin. Kaylee and Alys stared, open-mouthed, then both gave me fist pumps and hoots.

I was saved from injury or embarrassment because at that moment a thirty year old Ford Econoline van covered with graffiti pulled in, followed by a beat-up hearse with pink flames painted on the hood. They both parked next to my Porsche.

Doors opened, tooth-rattling base thumped, kids with skateboards poured out of both vehicles, so many that it looked like the circus where a dozen clowns pile out of a tiny car. Professional-looking tripods, silver with black rubber tips, and one compact monopod were dragged out and carried off into the skate park, with the skinny bearded kid called Luke carrying a clipboard, pointing and yelling about where to put the equipment. "Tempus fugit! Let's go, people, let's go. We'll start to lose the light in an hour." Two kids with the obligatory knit caps and hoodies on twin lime green BMX bikes powered up out of a half-pipe, grabbing major air, twisting the handlebars, and lifting their feet off the pedals before landing to swoop up to the cars, where they locked their rear brakes and skidded to a stop in classic brodies. They raised tiny minicams and on cue, Nadzia opened the passenger door of the pink-flamed hearse, tossed her board out and jumped on to it. Cell phone cameras popped, everybody cheered and hooted, fist-taps were exchanged and the bikes zoomed away.

Luke Cunningham hurried up with clipboard in hand, saying, "Okay, it's not a really long sequence but we need three different t-shirts and four different boards so time is tight here."

Nadzia saw me and her face lit up. She ignored Luke and skated over to where I was standing. "You came! I'm so glad! Thank you, thank you!" She hugged me, took both shoulders and said "I like you, you know. You're okay. No matter how this works out. Really."

"I just hope my insurance covers the medical bills. Nadzia, this is my friend Alys Winters."

"Hey"

"Hey."

They looked at each other. There was no fist bump. Nadzia finally said, "So, where's your board?"

"I'm not a skater."

"No?" Nadzia looked Alys up and down. Alys shrugged. "Luke, get her a couple shirts. Black." The redhead turned away and was immediately surrounded by kids, holding out skateboards, shirts, body parts, anything for her to sign. Without looking she held out a hand, Kaylee slapped a Sharpie into it with the precision of an OR nurse and she got to work.

Alys looked at her new shirts, said, "Bitchin'."

"That went well."

"Skate bitch and I know the type, trust me. We can go if you want."

"I want to grab a few more bowls first; okay with you?"

"Sure. I gotta send some texts, tell people I met KayleeTalks." Alys pulled out her Zippo and lit up a Salem before she started texting.

"You're gonna take care of her, right?"

I turned and Luke Cunningham, the emaciated-looking boy who had been directing the placement of cameras confronted me. He had a pencil over his ear, a clipboard in one hand and a mini-cam in the other. He had on a sleeveless white t-shirt covered with 'The Titanium Redhead' hand-lettered over and over with multi-colored Magic Markers, black pipestem jeans tucked into plaid high-tops and about a dozen chrome bracelets on each arm. Spiked black hair, 'TTR' tattooed on his left bicep. In uniform. Totally.

I was saved from responding—Alys had plugged in her Skull Candy ear buds, was absorbed in her texts and I was at a loss—by the arrival of a shiny silver Lincoln Navigator. It parked about twenty yards away, in the lot close to the end of one of the larger half-pipes. The two insurance investigators, Chooch and Rodney, got out of the front and stood looking at us. Then they looked around the area carefully before Chooch, the tall one, spoke into a cell phone and a moment later a black limo pulled in between the Navigator and the half-pipe.

Chooch and Rodney walked over to me. Chooch said, "Mr. Baines would like to speak with you."

"There's nothing I can add to what I've told you."

Rod said, "Hey, bro, just get in the limo, okay?" He put his hand on my elbow to encourage me to move along.

I pulled my arm free. "No." He looked at me for a minute, deciding. Me, I'd already decided. He took a cell phone out and made another call.

A moment later, the driver's door opened and Faith Valentine got out of the limo, wearing a short black leather skirt and white long-sleeved silk blouse unbuttoned to display a lacy camisole and some very respectable cleavage. She looked around before she opened the rear door and a shorter guy got out. He had black Pat Riley hair—slicked down and combed straight back. He looked solid, like possibly lots of serious hours at the gym. She reached in and pulled out a hanger with a sharkskin suit coat on it that he slipped over a white shirt with a red power tie.

Chooch and Rod hurried over to them and there was a brief conversation. Chooch shrugging and gesturing, palms-up like, "I tried," and the barrel-shaped guy looking disgusted. Then he adjusted his Ray-Bans and all four of them walked over to where we were standing, the stocky guy in front, Faith one step behind and the other two trailing. Chooch stepped up and spoke to the guy in the sharkskin coat. "Mr. Baines, this is the man we told you about. His name is T. R. Macdonald. Mr. Macdonald, this is Mr. Baines. You've met his assistant, Ms Valentine. Mr. Baines has a few questions for you."

When I looked at Baines my first thought was, "He looks like a department store mannequin." He had a fresh, open face, smiling, but there were no wrinkles, no laugh lines, no lines of any sort, and no expression. His face was a blank. His eyes were blanks. Still holding his meaningless smile, he stuck out a meaty paw. "Blondell Baines. Pleased to meet you, Mr. Macdonald. Aw, hell, the questions could have waited, but this got me out from behind a desk, you know? Is there someplace we can talk?"

"This is my friend, Alys Winters, and I've told Chooch, Rodney, and Ms Valentine all I know about the break-in."

"Hi, there, little lady."

I don't think the grinding noise I heard was really Alys' teeth, but it might have been. She dropped her cigarette, mashed it with her tennie and smiled sweetly. "So nice to meet you, Mr. Baines. I really like your suit."

"Why, thank you, sweetie. I got it in Singapore last month."

"I'm Chooch." Chooch was even bigger than I remembered, at least 6' 4" and built solid.

"And I'm Rodney." He leered at Alys, hooked his thumbs in his belt. "They call me The Rod."

Alys stared at him for a moment. "Why?" One of the kids watching snickered. The Rod was apparently stuck for an answer.

I said, "And this is—"

"Luke. I'm Luke and we're gonna be filming in a minute. Are you here to see TTR? Are you new sponsors? Nobody told me about new sponsors at the shoot today, but it's cool, no problem at all; you won't be in the way. Come with me and I can show you a good place to stand."

Baines said, "Chooch."

Chooch stepped in front of Luke, towering over the kid. "Mr. Baines doesn't want to talk to you."

Nadzia rolled up on her board, followed by Kaylee trotting behind her on foot, carrying hangars with half a dozen t-shirts on them. While Nadzia posed with two fans, standing between them and pulling up her shirt to show a bleeding heart tat, Kaylee said, "What's the hold-up? We're ready, Luke." Nadzia saw Baines and a look—surprise, something—passed across her face. Kaylee waved and another girl ran up lugging a make-up kit covered with skate stickers and started powdering off Nadzia's forehead. Another kid held up a silver reflector to balance the shadows and cameras snapped.

I grinned at Baines. "Sorry, dude, gotta skate."

Luke said, "All right, enough with the static shots, let's go! Positions! Okay, you guys in the suits need to move over—"

After that things happened fast. Luke stepped forward around Chooch and Baines straight-armed him in the chest, hard. Chooch kicked his feet out from under him and he landed on his butt, sliding back a foot or two on the cement, with a ridiculous surprised expression, but still holding his mini-cam safely up off the cement. Kaylee yelled, "Hey, quit that," and rushed at Baines. He slapped her, and since he outweighed her by close to a hundred pounds the blow was hard enough to spin her around in a full 360, dropping her phone and clutching at her cheek. Alys said something I didn't catch and he grabbed her. Chooch was next to me. He reached under his coat and before he could pull his hand out I had him in a half-nelson, my elbow up under his armpit and my hand behind his head, bending his shoulder back painfully (I hoped) and pressing the rolled-up *Thrasher* against his left eye with my other hand. Baines had balled a fist, ready to hit somebody. The black-haired woman, Faith, had her feet spread and her hands behind her back. The black coat she had put on after handing Baines his was unbuttoned.

"Pull a weapon out of there and Chooch's new nickname will be 'Patch.'" A little hokey, but I thought it sounded tough. She smiled and showed me empty hands. I ground the magazine into Chooch's face, pushing hard and twisting. When you roll a magazine tight like that and press hard enough it will slice into skin. I pressed hard enough. A thin trickle of blood ran down the side of Chooch's face. He squirmed and tried to hit me with his free arm, so I applied more pressure to the rolled-up *Thrasher*, really digging in. He made a rabbit noise and settled down nicely. The thought of losing an eye will do that to you.

Rodney moved quickly, getting a forearm around Kaylee's throat, pulling her up and dragging her back, almost lifting her off her feet. Nadzia stepped up next to him, seemed to touch his neck and all at once he went limp, his eyes rolled back in his head and he went down, twitching. Kaylee staggered away, tripped and went to her knees. Then those of us on our feet stood just looking at each other.

I had no clue how all this had happened. One minute we were talking, then people were getting shoved, slapped, zapped with a stun gun (I was guessing on that last one, but I thought it was a good guess), and I was threatening to poke a man's eye out. I wondered if I meant it. Several of the things that have happened to me recently have led me to think about violence, and controlling it, and if, once started, it *can* be controlled. I had no conclusions, only questions. For most people they would be academic, but I was inflicting severe paper cuts into Chooch's face and I meant it. I said, "Your move, Baines."

He shoved Alys away, snatched off his glasses, nostrils flaring, eyes narrowed, flat mannequin face distorted by anger. "My move? My move? I'm calling the authorities, that's my move. You attacked us. This is assault, yes, assault, and who will the police believe—licensed investigators or a bunch of skate punks?"

"Cave, cave, Deus, videt." Luke was on his feet with his clipboard tucked under his arm, rubbing his elbow. He nodded toward the lip of the nearest half-pipe, where the two BMX kids sat straddling their bikes and pointing mini-cams in our direction. The taller one flipped Baines the bird.

"What the hell?" Baines shaded his eyes and looked at the kids on the bikes.

I said, "It's Latin. Means, 'Beware, beware, God sees.'" And all at once I was back in Art Appreciation 101 at CSULB, with the professor droning on and Diana next to me, dozing with her chin propped in her hand, the doors of the lecture hall standing open in the warm September afternoon. The coffee machines were around the corner from the lecture hall and every now and then we'd hear a cup drop and the trickle as it filled. Hieronymus Bosch? That was it. I shook my head to clear it, but Diana stayed with me for a moment, waking, tossing her silky, thick brown hair back and taking my hand. I could feel it, feel her touch and the comforting squeeze instead of the tightly-rolled issue of *Thrasher*. After class we'd met the Snake in the cafeteria for coffee. He'd talked about his undergraduate years at Berkeley, the demonstrations, the bombings. Diana nodded vigorously, urgently. Then she was gone and I was alone, again. "It's from a painting called 'The Seven Deadly Sins and the Four Last Things.' In the painting Jesus sees sinners, but in this case I think Luke means, 'Smile, you're going to be on YouTube.'"

Baines looked at the cameras again, took a deep breath, then another, put his glasses back on and straightened his coat. His face smoothed. The rage vanished and it returned to mannequin blankness. "Okay." He tugged at his coat again. "Perhaps my staff overreacted. I apologize for them; sometimes they don't listen. This all got out of hand, hell yes, out of hand, and I'm sorry. It is extremely important that we learn all we can about your home invasion. We gotta talk to you."

I let go of Chooch, stepped back and waited for him to decide. He had four inches and probably twenty pounds on me; in a fair fight he could hand me my head. Fortunately there is no such thing as a fair fight. He glared at me and wiped at the blood running down his face, smearing it, before wiping his hand on his black Dockers. Faith had not moved through all of this, and still stood quietly, with her hands once again behind her back, in sort of a parade-rest position. She stared at me, smiling, then winked.

Chooch said, "Any time, tough guy. Any time at all."

"Meet you behind the swing set at recess." He looked confused, but I seem to do that to people.

Rodney struggled to his feet and stood, swaying, head down. He belched, drooled a little, and said, "Oh, man, I feel like shit. Think I'm gonna be sick." Everybody sort of moved away from him.

"Hold it, sir," Kaylee said. "Old Mr. Griffith gets upset if kids make a mess."

Alys said, "You mean like when guys blow big greasy chunks in the parking lot?"

Luke grinned and his silver bracelets jingled as he brought his mini cam up and pointed it at the unfortunate Rodney.

It must have been Alys' description, the "big greasy chunks," that tipped The Rod over the edge. He staggered over to Chooch, who tried vainly to push him away, clutched his shoulder weakly, and upchucked on his friend's black wingtips. The steaming pile of barf looked like everything he'd eaten for the last week. Naturally, the skate kids who had rolled up to see what was going on thought it was the funniest thing they'd seen all day. Chooch did not seem to share their amusement; couldn't tell about The Rod since his head was down in the neighborhood of his knees.

Baines sighed, shook his head and signaled Faith. They started back toward the limo.

From the corner of my eye I could see Kaylee angrily brushing at tears and picking up small objects off the asphalt. I said, "Hold it. Pay for her cell phone." Baines pursed his lips and I could almost hear him counting to ten. The he nodded to Faith who took a wallet out of her purse and handed me two fifties. I shook my head and she added two more to it. She raised her penciled black eyebrows and, when I nodded, she and Chooch took The Rod's elbows and the three of them backed slowly toward their cars.

Faith checked her makeup, dropped the compact into her purse and asked, "Would you really have poked his eye out?"

I looked her in the eye and smiled.

She laughed and clapped. "Wonderful. Oh, very good." She turned and strode after the others.

Luke said, "Guess they're not sponsors." Naturally he was filming them as they backed away. Now that it was over, Kaylee was sniffling and picking up the little dolphins she'd had glued on to her cell phone. The rest of the crowd went back to what was most important—those bowls and spines and stairs.

I gave Baines and company a minute, then tossed the bloody magazine aside, snatched up my board, jumped on and dropped into the half-pipe that led to where they had parked. Instead of coming up and trying for air, I stayed close to the bottom of the trough until I was close, then rode up the side and grabbed the edge of cement, letting the board roll back down. I wanted to make sure they left, and if possible I wanted to hear what they had to say. I pulled my head up and could see everything that was going on, and their voices carried. Baines was glaring at Faith. "You let that happen."

"Your stair is in the car. I'm ready to ramble if you are."

It sounded like she said, "Stair," but how could he have a stair in the car?

She said, "And you were never in any danger. Really, and Rodney and—"

He slapped her hard, a loud smack that carried above the sounds of skating behind me. The dark-haired woman didn't raise her hand to her reddening cheek, just stood there. "That's for disputing my word." His voice softened. "Faith, Faith, you know I only want the best for you; I'm trying to help. You *do* know that, don't you, darling? Darling?" She nodded dumbly. "You know how much you mean to me. You and me, right?" She nodded again. He patted her shoulder, turned and walked toward the limo. I had a clear view of her face after his back was turned. It wasn't anger I saw there.

It was gratitude.

Chooch finished wiping his shoes off and threw the rag aside. They eased The Rod into the Navigator, powered all the windows down, and drove away.

Faith hurried to open the limo door for Baines, but he paused, said, "Wait a minute. I want to have a word with Mr. Macdonald." He turned and walked quickly back toward the site of the confrontation, striding along with his chin down on his chest and his hands at his sides.

I muttered, "Oh, shit" and quickly slid back down the curve of the half-pipe to my board. I got it up to speed with three quick leg swings, came out of the end of the pipe and into the neighboring bowl in time to jump the board out and meet Baines.

"Heard you got a little present." He took off his dark glasses and polished them with a silk handkerchief from his coat pocket. "Getting rough out there, isn't it?" I just looked at him. "All right, I'm gonna make you an offer. There's people who think you can get something they want, and I want it too, so you're gonna help me. In return I'll keep you from getting hurt."

"No."

"Mr. Macdonald, I can make you do it."

"No, you can't." Our Mr. Baines was apparently not used to the word, "No." He stared at me for a moment, then turned and marched back to the limo. This time I stood and watched from a distance.

He carefully took off his jacket and handed it to Faith to hang up. Then he took a cell phone out of his pants pocket and started dialing. She took care of her chore, closed the passenger door, hurried around the car, slid into the driver's seat and followed the SUV. Turning to the others I saw that they were all staring at something on the ground.

Alys said, "Could be worse. The tall dickhead with the zits carried a lot of it with him on his shoes."

Luke chuckled, "But I sure wouldn't want to ride in that car," and we all laughed and the tension was broken.

Nadzia took Kaylee's shoulders. "Are you okay?"

The cherubic blonde brushed away tears and nodded. "Sure. I'm fine, really."

"You know you're my BFF. I'd kill anybody who tried to hurt you." Kaylee nodded and hugged her. "He hit you and I just freaked, you know?" Kaylee nodded again, lower lip trembling.

I said, "Stun gun?"

Kaylee whispered, "Nobody's ever hit me before. Not like that."

Nadzia looked closely at her BFF, then nodded. "It won't happen again. Okay. Hey, let's skate. Luke, let's go." He was there instantly with his clipboard and minicam, pointing and getting the crew into position as the makeup girl passed supplies so Kaylee could power off Nadzia's forehead. Another day at the office.

Alys grinned, fired up a Salem, said, "The toe, now a fight in a skate park, man, this is so fuckin' cool," and started sending texts to all her friends.

Here's the strange thing: Skating seemed like a fine idea, perfectly reasonable.

Just as I planted my front foot and pushed off, I felt my old phone, the one with the number that everybody knew and that Chet said was probably tapped, vibrate. *Private number* showed on the display.

"Pardon me, am I speaking to Mr. Macdonald? T. R. Macdonald?"

"Who's this?"

"My name is Harker. Blondell Baines is my assistant."

"You need to revise your hiring practices."

"Please. I spoke with Mr. Baines a moment ago and he feels very badly about the incident at this uh, this skate park place." I said nothing. "Mr. Macdonald? Are you there?"

"All right. Baines feels bad."

There was another pause while Harker—whoever he was—waited for me to say something. Finally he sighed. "I'd like to meet. We can ameliorate this unfortunate situation."

"Your pet shark Baines slapped a young girl and he choked another girl who is a friend of mine."

"I know, I know. Please, let's talk about this. Your friend, Mr. Eddington, Elijah Eddington the Third, will vouch for me, he had a business relationship with my employers. At least see what he has to say."

Big E, the client from my past who wanted me to drive the wet bike at Maverick's, will vouch for the guy who employs the guy who slapped around Kaylee and who wants whatever it is. Oh, boy. Coincidence? "How do you feel about ancient astronauts?"

"Pardon me?"

"Never mind. Eddington. How do you know him?"

"I am not at liberty to discuss it but we have mutual friends, and—"

"Sorry, dude, gotta skate. Call my office." I jammed my phone in my front pocket, kicked my board up, took three running steps, threw it down on the cement and jumped on.

At the end of an hour my legs were like jelly, and the hardcore skaters were just getting warmed up, but I'd had a great time, only falling twice, the first time sliding down the wall of a half-pipe on my ass, the second going down and skinning a knee. After a close call where I jumped my board off a curb and almost blew the landing because my trucks had loosened up, I pulled up, stomped the end of my board to flip it up, caught the nose, and said, "I'm done." And I was grinning like a fool.

Zia did a perfect grinder, sliding the underside of her board along the curb of the half-pipe, and stopped next to me. Three members of her posse, plus Kaylee and Luke with clipboard, gathered around us. Somebody held out the next hoodie she was supposed to model, another assistant held a reflector to balance the light and shutters clicked.

I said, "Today is Tuesday. Be at my house at 6:00 am Friday morning."

Kaylee shook her head, started to say something and thought better of it. Nadzia's face lit up. "You'll do it! You'll do it! Oh, thank you." The Titanium Redhead hugged me, board in one hand, and kissed me, hard. She pulled back, smiled, and kissed me again.

I disengaged. "I'll train you. We'll see how that goes. Then I'll decide." She nodded, hugged me one more time, held out her arms for the next hoodie to be slipped on and stood patiently while one girl fluffed her hair and another touched up her lip gloss.

Kaylee Miraflores followed me and Alys to the Porsche. Her cheek was red where she'd been slapped, she was frowning and a line showed between her pale eyebrows. She pursed her lips and handed me a tissue, gesturing to my mouth. I scrubbed off Nadzia's lipstick. Looking down at her shoe tops she said, "Hey, thanks for getting me the money for my phone. My folks would be ballistic, you know? My Dad really doesn't like it when people mess with me." She paused, then looked me in the eye. "So you're going to do it? Um drive this jet ski?" She had that teenage girl speech pattern: quick, clipped words, every sentence ending with a rising inflection, like a question.

"And I only said I'd train her. Then we'll see. She may figure out what's involved and come to her senses."

"No way. Not The Titanium Redhead. She's *totally* into this and she won't change her mind. Don't do it. Don't train her. Don't drive the, the bike at this Maverick's place. Please."

I pushed the button and the Carrera unlocked. Alys hugged Kaylee, then walked around to the passenger side and stood looking across the roof at us. I said, "I know why I think it's a bad idea. What about you?"

"Well, duh! It's so, like, *dangerous*, you know."

"Kaylee, if I don't do it she'll just get somebody else."

"No, no, that's just it, don't you understand? She only wants you. Nobody else."

"That's crazy. Why? Why me?"

"I don't know, I don't know and she won't tell me and she's my BFF and I'm scared."

Luke jogged up. "She wants you. Hates the lip gloss, needs your input. And tempus fugit."

"Um, *oooh!*" Kaylee glared at me and fled.

"She talk to you? Kaylee?"

"She doesn't think Nadzia should do it, or that I should help."

"Yes. Look, the girl's smokin' hot, mad skills."

"And if she gets hurt a lot of people are out of work."

He looked at me a moment, then at the crowd fussing over Nadzia. "Mr. Macdonald, you helped out today, with those thugs, so I'll cut you some slack. This time next year I'll be a business major at Georgetown. I do this because it's fun and good experience, but primarily because Nadzia is my friend. I care about her." He turned and walked away.

Not exactly my day for making good impressions.

Chapter Eight   The Zebra Top

Early the next morning the three of us gathered at my kitchen table, over doughnuts and coffee and went over what we knew so far, which wasn't much. I told them about the slap and what I'd heard Baines say to Faith.

"Their relationship, while unhealthy, is not that unusual." Kandi said. "And what did she say was in the car?"

"Stair. She said, 'Your stair is in the car. I'm ready to ramble if you are.'"

She worked at her iPad for a moment. "Thought so. It's a homonym. S-t-e-y-r. Steyr is a machine pistol that Kandi heard about in a weapons class."

We all looked at each other. Chet said it. "Pard, what is this all about?"

I said, "Baines sent the toe."

Kandi said, "Maybe you should have talked to this Harker person."

"He'll call back."

Chet's people picked him up for an early flight out of John Wayne to supervise a security installation in Vegas. Kandi went to UCLA. I made some notes about the events so far, but finally gave up and went surfing. After an hour the wind came up and I went home.

About noon I got a text from The Titanium Redhead herself.

```
TitaniumRed
Mac U home? I want to stop by.


TRMacdonald
Sure.
```

A few minutes later she showed up on my new security display, a wall-mounted 17-inch screen that divided into six small squares, one for each camera. She was on the front porch, pushing back the hood on her green sweatshirt, grinning at the obvious camera, the one people were supposed to see, and hoisting two giant white paper shopping bags so they filled half the screen. I let her in, locked the door behind her and led her through my empty living room to the family room. She put the bags down in front of the couch and stood with her hands on her hips looking out at the water in the channel and my empty dock. "Hey."

I said, "Hey." Oh, boy, conversation.

"Nice view."

"Thanks. So, Nadzia, look, I think I know why you're here and I'm glad you came. We need to talk."

She smiled slowly. Her spectacular green eyes lit up the whole room. "No posse, right? I know it takes some getting used to."

"Yeah, I bet. Look, some practice sessions does not equal a promise to actually help you surf Maverick's."

"I know."

"First, you may come to your senses and change your mind when you figure out what's involved. Second, we may not see a big enough break this winter, or it may come before you're ready."

"Yeah, whatever. I brought—"

"Finally, and believe me when I say this is the most likely, I may decide you can't do it. On top of all that, personal watercraft are really restricted in that area because it's a marine sanctuary. So, even if everything else works out, we may not get permission."

The bags were at her feet. She held up both hands, palms out. "Whoa, okay, okay, I get it. I know, I know all of that stuff. I just came to say thanks, you know, for what you did at Toilet Bowl when those guys jumped us."

"Attack of the rolled-up magazine."

Entertaining is not my strong suit, in fact it's hardly a suit at all. We stood in my family room awkwardly before I realized we were standing in the family room, awkwardly. Outside in the channel a guy swam by, apparently oblivious to the cold water since he was wearing a cap but did not have on a wetsuit. Better him than me, despite the fact that I wasn't having a lot of fun at the moment. Finally inspiration struck and I said, "Um, sit down, please. Can I get you a Coke or something?" As I said it I hoped I had a soft drink of any kind. Maybe in the garage. There were some supplies left over from Diana's parties. Grocery shopping is not my strong suit either, but Kandi was exaggerating about the lettuce. I think.

Nadzia looked down at the bags as if she expected somebody to unload them. Then she blurted, "I brought you a present," hauled a brand-new skateboard out of the larger of the bags, held it up, and spun the wheels. "Your old board, the one you rode at the Bowl, is okay, you know, I know you like it and all but, shit, I could hear the bearings and it sucks, all right? It's *old*, man, so I got you one from Cranial Fracture, that's this skate shop that sponsors me." The wheels were white, the deck was covered in black sure-grip, and the underside was airbrushed with a good likeness of The Titanium Redhead wearing a tight green tank top, holding her board and snarling.

"Nadzia, thanks, but—"

"Hey, no strings, man, honest. It's not some kind of bribe. And I've got it all set up for you. Check it out and if the trucks are too tight let me know. I set 'em for somebody who's just getting back into it." She held it out and looked up at me and she looked so young, tentative and hopeful, what could I do? I took the board, spun one of the wheels—they were larger and smoother than the ones on my board—and listened to bearings that were quieter than my old ones.

"It's a great board. Really sick."

She clapped her hands and laughed, bobbed her head and in one fluid motion unzipped her hoodie and shrugged out of it. The sweatshirt probably fell to the floor behind her but I didn't notice; I was busy staring at Nadzia. *Way* too busy. I think I almost dropped my new skateboard.

She had on tight, bright pink pants that ended at her calves, but saying "tight" doesn't do those pants justice, but maybe, "tight, tight, tight," tight cubed. Yeah, that was closer. Her feet were squeezed into black four-inch spike heels. Then there were the pink pants. The rest of her was covered—mostly—by a zebra-striped bandeau top that could have been airbrushed on, and, paint or fabric, gentleman zebras would have reared up on their hind legs, pawed at the sky and whinnied or whatever it is zebras do. I stared. She grinned. I stared some more.

"Whinny? You said 'Whinny?' Wow, you are one weird dude, but I like you. You know that, right? That I like you?" She cocked her head and looked at me intently, hands on hips.

"What, uh, why, sure, I like you, too, sure I do. You bet. Totally sick."

"Awesome." She pulled a large can of Red Bull and a pint of 100-proof Smirnoff out of the other bag and said, "I turned twenty-one today and I thought we could celebrate."

"You're nineteen. I read your web page."

She rolled her eyes. "Okay, so I have friends. A girl's gotta have friends."

She was in the kitchen with glasses out on the counter, dropping in ice cubes and mixing drinks before I could open my mouth. A moment later she came back and handed me a glass full of some murky greenish-yellow stuff that looked like a fish tank that really needed cleaning. I tasted it. About as good as it sounds. No, not quite that good. The tip of my tongue went numb. Probably a good thing. She tossed her thick red hair, put her hand to my chest and pushed me down on the couch, then settled gracefully next to me. No, that doesn't do it justice, either—any more of next to me and she'd be in my lap. I thought about the morality of the situation. I thought about Nadzia curled up in my lap, looking up at me with those amazing emerald eyes. I thought about hockey scores. I thought about surfing, but that led to a vision of Nadzia in a white bikini so I quit that line of thought and went back to hockey. Yes, sir, how about them Ducks? Think they'll make the playoffs? She'd be in high heels, wearing a white bikini and holding a striped beach ball—yellow, red, green—over her head and posing like one of those fifties pin-ups . . . "How about them Ducks?" I muttered.

"You know, you really have a pretty good grinder for somebody who's, uh, I mean for somebody who hasn't skated for a while." She slugged down half of her concoction, stood up and stretched. "You did it again, made that funny horsie noise." Then she crossed her arms, grasped the bottom of the top and proved it wasn't airbrush by peeling herself right out of it. Yessiree, right out of that thing. Must have been too hot in the room, or the zebra top was too tight, too confining and she was having trouble breathing. One toss of her head and her hair was back in place, flaming red, flowing down over her smooth white shoulders. The Ducks went out the door, down the drain, run over by the Zamboni, whatever, along with my brain.

I had visions of dinner with Kandi. "So, Sailor, what did you do today?" We'd be in my kitchen, working our way through a large Numero Uno thick crust pizza, half pepperoni and black olives, half cheese.

"Oh, not much. Nadzia came by to tell me I had a nice grinder. Then she took her clothes off. Then I made zebra noises."

Since my vision of that conversation ended with me saying, "Put down the knife." I snatched my glass off the coffee table and gulped down as much of the fish tank stuff as I could without gagging. She had her thumbs inside her waistband. I decided gagging wasn't so bad and drank some more. I noticed that she had great abs, yes, I really noticed because I was trying hard. Have I mentioned that I am made of stern stuff?

He reddish brows drew together slightly. "Hey, oh, geez, I'm sorry, I'm sorry. Are you one of those guys that likes to make the first move? I'm down with that, totally. Look, I'll just stretch out here and close my eyes, okay?" She sat primly on the couch, stretched out, raised her arms over her head and kind of squirmed around a little, putting her legs across my lap—she still had her pants on—and kicking off her high heels. I noticed two more tattoos peeking out between her navel and the waistband of the pants. That's right, now I was checking out her tats, the ones on the several inches of pure white skin that showed between her waistband and her cute little navel, not ogling her remarkable breasts that had, at last, quit squirming. They squirmed longer than she did. Her eyes closed, dark lashes fanning out across her pale cheeks, and her lips, done in retro pink to match those pants, parted slightly. She sighed deeply. Parts of her squirmed some more. My drink seemed to be gone, must have gotten spilled, so I gulped down the rest of hers. It really wasn't bad once you got past the involuntary "I'm going to vomit" reflex, and anyway my tongue was now completely numb.

"Nadzia, I may kick myself later, but I'm spoken for. Hell, let me up so I can kick myself right now. No sense in procrastination."

She smiled, answered without opening her remarkable eyes. "Kandi? Your waitress friend? Aw, man, she'd be down with it. And she's at work. I checked. Really, she won't mind."

I grasped her ankles, put her feet on the floor. "I mind."

"She's gonna want you to commit, you know."

"How do you know that?"

"Girls know. Honest, she won't mind."

In my mind I said, and she may be in Chicago anyway. "One more time. I mind."

"Hey, it's not like some kind of bribe, you know, we do it so you'll drive for me at Maverick's, really, I just like you and we were here and I thought it would be nice, and . . ." Here eyes opened. "Still not interested huh?"

"Of *course* I'm interested, I'm human, despite the horsie noises. Shimmy back into your shirt. We need to talk."

She stuck out her tongue, then sat up, picked it off the floor and pulled it over her head. "You'll be *so* sorry. *Playboy's* talking about a feature called 'Hotties Who Skate.' I'm gonna be in it."

"Hell, I'm sorry already. Look, back to business."

"Whatever." She shrugged. It was a great shrug, even with her shirt on. "What?"

"What?"

"You said 'Back to business' like you had something to say."

"Oh, yeah. Right. Business. Got it! Can I get you a Coke?"

"No, I'm good."

"Yes, you are. You betcha." She laced her fingers behind her head and leaned back. "I have a question. I know I do. Ah! Why me to drive the bike?"

"You're famous."

"Not good enough."

She stuck out her tongue

The thought of a beer crossed my mind, but on top of two of those whatever they're called—Lower Tract Torpedoes, maybe—I wasn't sure of the results so I got up and put on a pot of coffee. As I measured out filtered water and ground some Tilawa, I said, "Nadzia, pay attention, because this is for real. You told Elijah that you read about me and he bought it, but I don't. If, against my better judgment, we actually try to tow you in at Maverick's, we need to trust each other. So, one more time, why me?" When she didn't answer I picked up my new board and dropped it back in the bag.

"Okay, okay look, I got in with this group, kind of a club, well, more than that, really, but anyway, they said I should use you and I knew about you already and I knew that E knew you and they said it was really important for me to ask you to do it, so please say yes. Please."

"Tell me about this more-than-a-club."

"I can't, I mean there's like levels and I'm pretty low, and anyway we're not supposed to talk about it with outsiders."

"Nadzia—"

"Really, I don't know any more. Please. Look, you said we had to trust each other, so okay, I know I'm pretty—"

"Understatement. You're beautiful."

"Thanks, but I'm not model material and I know it. And I'm not really smart like Kaylee, but I've got a good set of boobs and I can ride any plank made. This is my shot, Mr. Macdonald. Maverick's, then a surf contest, then the next Winter X Games. I've got a life to figure out, and I don't want to run Keno in Vegas or serve drinks—oh, shit. I didn't mean anything, honest."

I came back from the kitchen with two mugs of coffee, handed her one. "Kandi likes the job. Okay, at the skate park for a minute there it looked like you knew the guy in the suit, Blondell Baines. Do you?"

"Who?"

"Baines."

"I'm sure your girlfriend's really nice, honest. I really think she must be. Oh, I've messed this up, I know I have. I've messed it all up. Now you won't help." She tentatively sipped some coffee, found it too hot and carefully set it on a coaster on the coffee table. Staring down at it, she blurted, "Look, I have abandonment issues, I mean my parents leaving me and all and our school doesn't have counselors but I blogged about it and some people on Kaylee's site say it can lead to inappropriate behavior. Was this inappropriate? I didn't mean any harm."

"Coming to a man's house, a man you've just met, and taking your top off? Well, in some circles, yes, that would be considered inappropriate."

"Can I talk to you about all this?"

"Who, me? About this? Talk?" I stared at her. "Nadzia, up until a few months ago I moved money around to make it make more money for rich people. Now, well, now it seems like I beat people up for money. What I'm trying to say is I'm not the best person to talk to about this sort of thing. My answer to most problems is to go surfing."

"For me it's boarding. Hey, how about your girlfriend?"

"Well, considering that I'm the guy you did the zebra dance for, maybe we should find somebody else."

She giggled. "I did, didn't I? I, uh, and you, uh . . ." Suddenly she smiled and her face lit up. Then, she blushed and said softly, "Hey."

I pulled my board out of the bag. "You say the trucks are set tight?"

She stood up and waved at the bottle and cans on the table. "That stuff tastes like ass. What's next?"

I stuck a leg out, blocking her. "Baines."

"Oh, him. I've seen him before."

"Where?"

She giggled. "Would you believe a poetry reading? I had this assignment last summer—I had to go to summer school to graduate—and I had to go to this reading and he was there. I don't think he remembered me. And that woman was with him—the bride of Frankenstein—geez! What a freak."

"He's looking for something and thinks I can get it for him."

"Oh."

"Nadzia, you get one chance here. I think you know something." It wasn't that wild a guess. She knew Baines and she didn't acknowledge him at Toilet Bowl.

She licked her pink lips. "Well, this club, you know, they want to make the world a better place."

"And?"

"People have to know how dangerous these science things are. They're going to reveal the truth, prove it."

"Change the world. Right. Baines is looking for something, he says a sample."

"I think it might be some kind of germ." I waited. "That's all I know, really. The club has like, levels, you know, just a few people at the top and a bunch of others who want to move up. I'm low-level."

After years of talking to business executives I can usually tell when people are lying. But sometimes that makes me overly-suspicious; Mary seems to think I have trust issues, but in my line of work that's a good thing. I wasn't sure that was the whole story but I let it go and stood up. "Be here at six in the morning on Friday. I suggest not wearing the zebra top."

Slam Dunk Management, Elijah Eddington's sports merchandising company, was located in Newport Beach next to the Fashion Island shopping center, on the water side in a red brick four-story office building, top floor looking out over Newport Harbor. It looked like Elijah was doing well advising sports stars which shoes to endorse. The drive out Warner to PCH and the cruise south to Newport was pleasant; the windows were down and Chumbawumba was singing about getting back up after you got knocked down. It was about 6:30 in the evening after Nadzia had dropped in with my new skateboard and the zebra top when I slid the Carrera into an end space in the underground parking, after business hours, but it never hurts to be careful about door dings.

The seven-footer who had driven the Escalade to Dog Beach was waiting for me when I got out of the elevator on the top floor. He led me down a short hall and through a door he opened with a key card and into the Slam Dunk offices. One wall of the reception area featured a life-size mural of Eddington in the Clippers red road uniform, impossibly far off the hardwood floor, doing a behind-the-back dunk. Black leather couches, granite counter with phone and computer, dark gray carpet, pale gray walls with walnut crown molding, photos, trophies and memorabilia everywhere. All of the doorways had been raised to accommodate his height. The seven-footer knocked once, opened a door and we went into E's office. One wall looked seaward at the lights of Newport, with the mushroom-shaped Pacific Life building off on the right. There was no desk, just a glass table with a laptop and cell phone on it and comfortable-looking chairs positioned around it so that each looked out the window. Eddington jumped to his feet, grinning, and greeted me warmly, one of those guys that can't just shake your hand, but who has to grip your elbow so you don't get away. He still moved with the grace of a natural athlete, honed with a lifetime of serious workouts.

I gestured at the walls, full of more memorabilia, trophies from the glory days of his basketball career. "Impressive."

He let go of my elbow and grinned. "Do clients just eat up that shit? Hell, yes. And, to tell you the truth, hell, I like looking at it, too. Had me a whole lot of fun back then." For a moment he looked at the cases full of memories and I was afraid he would launch into a basketball story. He shook his head, reached behind himself to close the laptop and said, "But ya'll look like you could use a beer. Hey, Tucker, bring us—" The tall guy appeared in the door balancing a tray with glasses and carrying a silver bucket with bottles of Dos Equis dark sticking out of

the ice. Eddington rolled his eyes. "Hate it when he does that."
Tucker did an obsequious, mocking bow before softly closing the
door behind him. We settled in with beers. Eddington killed the
overhead lights and the only illumination came from recessed
spotlights inside the trophy cases. The lights of Newport blazed
close beneath the windows, then the dark of the Pacific, broken
only by the lights of an oil island with a helicopter approaching
it, probably to switch crews out. "Mac, I'm impressed. You can
handle yourself. And you can still board. I thought you would
have given that shit up years ago."

"You heard?"

"Heard? Man, I saw it all. Bro, you're all over YouTube. Most
of the clips are called 'Skate Park Rumble,' and I think you better
look at it if you haven't."

"You must be kidding, I—"

But he was already clicking keys in a moment he picked
up a remote and pushed a couple of buttons. Two memorabilia
cases slid aside and an enormous flat screen lit up. We watched
conversation, Luke stepping forward, Kaylee rushing at Baines
and getting slapped. E paused the video and said softly, "Don't
believe I like that boy." Faith Valentine was at the edge of the
image, hands behind her back, holding something. "What's that
in her hand? Under her coat."

Eddington said, "You tell me."

"E, it looks like a gun. And I have reason to believe Baines
had one in his limo. What's going on here?"

"Same answer. You tell me, bro, you tell me. These folks are
real interested in you."

"To quote a young friend of Nadzia's, 'Awesome.' All right.
You talk to her?"

"Sure. She's real happy, and I am, too. But I was pretty sure
you'd do it." He stroked his goatee and smiled.

I had to remember who I was talking to. Elijah Eddington the Third was not like other people. He was used to getting what he wanted, just because he wanted it. Since the eighth grade people had been telling him how special he was, how with his talent if he worked he could make the pros and be rich, and before he got out of high school colleges were lining up to offer free rides, his parents took out an insurance policy to cover him for lost income if he blew out a knee, and the first shoe contract wasn't far behind. And his posse was right there the whole time—carrying his gym bag, driving the car, saying yes. They *always* said yes. Yeah, he expected me to do it. He couldn't help it; he just didn't know any better.

"No. I said I'd train her and believe me, it won't be fun. After that I'll decide. What she wants to do is not easy, and it is every bit as dangerous as people say. And it won't be cheap. We're talking modern professional big-wave surfing here and mounting a team will be very expensive."

He waved a hand. "Whatever ya'll need, just go out and buy it."

"For starters, a couple of skis, wet bikes, I haven't decided on the model yet, probably Sea Doo, and a trailer to haul them."

"Done."

"A big vehicle to tow the bikes."

"Take one of the Escalades." He took an envelope out of his coat pocket, slapped it down on the glass table. "Okay, son, let's speed this up so we can drink us some beer. This is a corporate debit card from Slam Dunk Management. Use this sucker for everything. We'll start you with a hundred grand, replenish as needed. Will that do for equipment?"

I drained my beer. "Yeah."

He pulled another bottle out of the ice and handed it to me. "Don't be cuttin' no corners. I mean it, Mac, I want that girl to have the best, whatever she needs. As for you, for tax purposes—yours, not ours—we're gonna add you as an employee. Pay you a thousand a day."

I decided to test him. "I want to include my day at the skate park."

"Already done. We'll send over some papers for you to sign, temporary employee stuff. Anything else?"

"Nope, for now. Just remember—"

"Ya'll ain't made no promises. I get it."

After knocking off the Dos Equis, I stood up, we shook again so he could do the elbow-grab, and I headed for the door. When I got there I pulled a Colombo, minus the raincoat—turned and said, "Oh, one more thing. I got a call from a man named Harker. He said he was the boss of the people who pushed us around at Toilet Bowl. And he said you would vouch for him." Eddington was silhouetted by the windows behind him, but I think his face changed. "Before you answer, E, this one's a deal-breaker."

He licked his lips. "Hey, okay, sure, sure. Y'all called it, you know, there's more money in Slam Dunk than we started with, lots more, and well, Harker works for the people it came from."

"And?"

"That's it, bro. Can't tell you what I don't know."

"What about this guy, Blondell Baines?"

"Beats the shit out of me. I think Harker's a personal assistant, a gopher, for some folks that lent me money, and no, they ain't Mob. The one I think he works for is this old lady with a big family and a whole lot of cash. Owns a winery up in Central California. I didn't know Harker had anybody working for him. And that's it, 'cept I don't like that Baines boy. No, I don't believe I do."

"Make a call. Find out about him and the woman, Faith Valentine."

"Sure, sure, glad to do it."

It was all too easy. Maybe I'm just naturally suspicious—you would be too if you knew the executives I did—but it was all way too easy. Eddington said he would learn what he could and call me. Then, when I had the door open, he returned the Colombo favor.

"Mac. Let it go."

"What?"

"All of it. Leave the invasion alone. Go surfing. Train my girl."

I could have told him about this sample everybody wanted, that his girl knew about. "Thanks for the beer."

All the way up the coast, rowing along in the traffic—first gear, second gear, repeat till you're crazed—all I could think about was more money, lots more money, in Slam Dunk Management. And an old lady with a big family.

That night Kandi pulled the blanket up to her chin—it was December and I keep the window in the bath open all year long—and said drowsily, "That peculiar noise you made when I came in from work" (she'd been wearing the black French Maid costume, complete with white apron and frilly white slips), "was that a whinny?"

Chapter Nine   Training

"Timing! Timing! Watch the float as it comes toward you. Don't think about the board." I yelled into my bullhorn.

We were in the Long Beach Outer Harbor and Nadzia Kamnik was practicing swimming for the watercraft while dragging a surfboard attached to her ankle by a leash. She was not having a good time.

Between 1899 and the end of World War II eight and a half miles of breakwater were constructed, creating the Long Beach Outer harbor. There are four small artificial islands in the harbor, home to oil drilling rigs, all named after astronauts killed in accidents—Theodore Freeman, Virgil Grissom, Ed White, and Roger Chaffee. We were just south of Oil Island Chaffee. There was a brisk breeze so there were a dozen or more small catamarans out, flying by with a pontoon raised and the passenger hiked out over the water. Windsurfers leaned back for head dips, seagulls cruised, pelicans flapped by, looking ungainly until they spotted some hapless sardine and folded their wings to plummet into the water like feathered missiles. In the distance the once-proud *Queen Mary* sat grounded, next to the dome that used to house the Spruce Goose. Long Beach's white elephant collection, except the Queen had a great restaurant. There's talk of removing the breakwater to improve water circulation through the harbor, but if it ever happens it will be quite a ways down the road, as Chet might say. All in all, it was a fine winter day, clear and crisp.

I was starting Nadzia in the harbor where there was calm water, but soon we'd move offshore where it was rough, the rougher the better. I was straddling my new SeaDoo Wake Pro 215, looking back at Zia. My new toy was black and white with red trim, could carry three people, had a rack for surfboards and came with five acceleration profiles that I was still trying to master. At just under fourteen grand MSRP, I thought the price might put Eddington off and get me out of this, but he didn't bat an eye. I bought two. If we got to actually challenging Maverick's I didn't want to fail because of mechanical issues.

She flailed, thrashing toward the bright orange float I was towing. She was wallowing side-to-side, kicking weakly, her breathing was irregular, and she showed every sign of extreme fatigue.

"Not bad, but you need to learn to watch for oncoming waves. We'll do that seriously later, but it won't hurt to think about it now. *Always* watch out to sea."

"I need a break," she gasped, looping one arm over the stern rack.

Kaylee and Luke putted over on the hard-bottom inflatable I'd bought for the team. Slam Dunk's debit card had taken a major hit in the last couple of days. Kaylee was driving; Luke was holding a tiny video camera. "Hey, girl, are you okay?" Kaylee called. She had on a pink sweatshirt and matching sweatpants; Luke, impervious to the cold, was in his uniform of tight black jeans and white sleeveless t-shirt with slogans scrawled on it.

Nadzia waved. "Yeah, yeah. I just need a break."

I hadn't wanted an audience for the training, but since the whole point of this was publicity I could hardly say no.

"No, no break. If you're in the water at Maverick's that means you fell, and, trust me, you'll feel a hell of a lot worse than you do now, and you won't get a break." I put my foot on her shoulder and pushed her off the watercraft. "Twenty more catches. We'll do fifty today, seventy-five tomorrow, then a hundred." She gave me the finger, but when the Wake Pro came by the next time she caught it. And she made the fifty catches.

It was our third day of training, and, though I'd never tell her, I was impressed. The first morning she'd shown up at my place, on time and by herself, as instructed. She had a bag with wetsuit and fins that I told her to leave in the car. I had on my

O'Neill fullsuit. "First thing we're going to do is swim around the pier."

"The Pier? The *Huntington* Pier?"

"Are there any others?"

"I'll get my wetsuit."

"Don't bother."

"You've got one on."

"I know. The guy who makes these says it's better to be warm than cold and he's right. You, however, are going to be cold."

"Hey, listen, I . . ." Then she stuck out her tongue. "Asshole. Right. Let's do it."

The Huntington Beach Junior Lifeguards start their training with a round-the-pier swim, and it's a no-joke feat. Since the last rebuild after a storm it's 1,800 feet long and by the time you make the turn at the seaward end it looks like the beach is as far away as Catalina. I had a sneaking hope that maybe the red-headed skate bitch would not make it, and I could call this whole thing off. Unfortunately the surf was small, maybe two to three feet, so getting outside wasn't a problem, but as we cleared the break line and the few surfers sitting patiently, the red roof of Ruby's at the end of the pier looked like it was a long way off, and it was. It was a cold, windy December day, overcast with the lead-colored sky blending perfectly with the dull, lead-colored sea. I settled into a steady crawl, breathing on every stroke, keeping an eye on my trainee as she tried to match my pace. It had been a long time since I'd done this particular swim; frankly I hoped I could make it. It was long and I was starting to tire—too much time behind a desk talking on the phone—before we pulled even with Ruby's. As we rounded the end it got windy and choppy, spray blowing off the swells as they slid indifferently under us toward shore. After the turn they were behind us, pushing us along. When we were close to the beach I caught a wave and bodysurfed the last fifty yards. Nadzia tried and missed and had to swim until at last her feet touched bottom. When we waded ashore she sank to her knees on the firm wet sand close to the water, hung her head and panted, but she didn't throw up, and she didn't say a word about quitting.

The next day we were practicing in the Long Beach Outer Harbor.

An hour after I shooed Kaylee and Luke back, requesting more space, Nadzia had made her last catch and was draped across the WakePro's stern. A hundred yards to starboard the blue-and white Catalina Express cleared the harbor mouth and got up on a plane as it sped on its way. A few seconds later the wake got to us and the bike rocked back and forth. "Okay," I pointed at the beach where we had launched. "Swim in."

She brushed her bangs back off her forehead. "You're getting even for the Zebra top, aren't you?"

I raised my bare foot as if to push her away. "I'd start swimming if I were you." She looked at the inflatable with her friends, looked at me and let go of the wet bike. Suddenly she swept her arm and sent a wave of cold water over me before she laughed, put her head down and started for the beach. I waved the boat in, handed the SeaDoo over to Luke to return the launching ramp and swam in after her. Not being exhausted from fifty surfboard catches I caught her easily and paced her in.

After she dragged herself out of the water she flopped face-down, throwing out little puffs of sand as she panted. "Give me a minute to catch my breath. Then I'm going to kill your ass."

I sat next to her. "Go to bed early. Seventy-five catches tomorrow."

She made seventy-five, then a hundred. She swam in from Island Chaffee, then Island Grissom. She waded underwater carrying a cinderblock until she could do it holding her breath for two minutes. At the same time I learned the quirks of the wet bike, mastering the acceleration profiles, and getting a feel for how sharply you could turn and how to shift my weight while doing it. I had bought two of the WakePro 215 top-of-the-line SeaDoos, both with the big engine, figuring that if we needed the acceleration, we would *really* need it. And it wasn't my money.

A week later we swam the Pier again. I deliberately chose late afternoon so it would be windy and cold, with choppy, blown-out surf. Wading into the 57-degree surf we encountered the notorious Huntington Trench. Three steps in, you're knee deep, one more and you're up to your neck in frigid water. Then it's knee deep again. She laughed, dove under a wave and started swimming. I think that's when I started believing she might really do it.

Later, wrapped in towels, sitting on the sand just north of the Pier and looking out at the sun setting behind the offshore drilling rigs, she started talking.

"You do this with your girlfriend?"

"Mary? No, she doesn't swim. And right now she's pretty involved with her dissertation." All at once I found myself saying, "And she may take an internship in Chicago."

"Oh. Sucks, man." Then, all at once, "They ditched me, you know?" I didn't need to ask who. "They said, 'We're moving to Idaho and I said, 'It's my Senior year, I don't want to go.' And you know what? They said, 'Okay.' My own fucking parents! They just said 'okay' like it was no big deal." There's nothing anybody can say to that, so I kept quiet. She brushed at some sand on her cheek and trotted into the water to rinse it off. I pretended not to notice the tear tracks. She came back and sat, not looking at me. "That night, my Dad comes into my room and goes, 'Daughter, these are the Last Days.' You could hear that he said it like that, capital letters, you know? And he starts going on about signs and portents and I'd heard it all before, right? So I go 'Dad, I got a book report due tomorrow' and the next week they emancipated me. Just flippin' cut me loose, took Job—my brother, he's five—and left."

"You hear from them?"

She nodded. "Yeah, I get a letter once a week. Only it's always the same: Daughter, it is the End of Days. Get on a bus, come to Idaho."

"They write. Maybe they're doing the best they can." She nodded. We walked back to my car.

And we surfed. Every day, any place surfline.com said was big. The only day we took off was one day after a heavy rain when the bacteria count was off the scale as a result of run-off. A big storm flushes a lot of shit—literal bird excrement—into the sea and it can cause a nasty infection, particularly if you've got an open cut. In our spare time we skated and my grinder improved.

Kandi was either hustling drinks at Fred's, teaching at UCLA, or revising her dissertation.

Nobody broke into my house. No severed toes were delivered, gift-wrapped or otherwise. In this way a quiet week went by.

The final day in the Long Beach Harbor she waved and started to swim in. I stopped her and said, "Wear this," handing her a weighted backpack that I'd stashed in the Wake Pro's storage compartment. She didn't say a word, just pulled the straps over her shoulders. Then she grabbed my arm and yanked me into the water, said "Race you," put her head down and started toward shore in a smooth, powerful crawl. I almost didn't catch her.

On the beach I pulled the six-pack out of the pack and popped a can of beer. Then I extracted a plastic bottle of orange juice and handed it to her. "As much as anything, big wave surfing is about confidence, knowing what your body can do if you push it. By the time somebody's got their nerve up to attempt Pipeline or Sunset or—"

"Or Maverick's."

"Yes, or Maverick's. By the time they've got the nerve to get into the lineup, they've got the technical ability. To succeed, what they have to have is the mindset that says, 'I can do this.'"

She looked down. Damp red hair fell forward, hiding her face. She let it hang there, dribbled sand through her fingers, played with the quick-release on the leash. Four girls in bright bikinis carried a Hobie 14 catamaran past us to the water's edge and started attaching the jib. I drank some beer. "You think this is stupid, don't you? Nobody's really behind me, except you, and you think it's stupid, too, but you're doing it. They think it's for the money, the X-Games. You think I'm trying to get famous just to show my parents, prove to my Dad, I don't even know what, but prove it." The posse had taken a day off, having recorded plenty of training video. The buzz was building. Kaylee had set up one site devoted exclusively to the Maverick's effort. "You're not doing it for the money, are you?"

"No."

"You're watching out for me."

"I have reasons."

Nadzia said an odd, wistful thing then. "I wish this was just about the surfing."

"Nadzia—"

"Hey, call me Z, okay?"

"Sure, Z. Listen, I thought you'd choke and quit the first time we swam the Pier. I *hoped* you'd quit. But you didn't."

"You think I can do it?"

I drank some more beer. Here was my chance to talk her out of it, keep her from taking the risk.

"Yeah. You can ride Maverick's."

On my part I watched and waited for my unknown adversary's next move.

That night, after our last day of training, we all had dinner at Duke's, the outstanding Hawaiian-themed restaurant on the south side of the Huntington Pier. Good food, awesome view out over the bike path, then volleyball courts, then sand to the Pacific, oil rigs and Catalina.

Here's how dinner works when you know there are people after you. Duke's was alerted a day in advance by somebody from Eddington's office. Two hours before we arrived two of his staff—read bodyguards—completed a perimeter check. An hour later one of Chet's Space Floozy vans took up station in the lower, beach level lot and started electronic surveillance.

Just your basic friendly dinner.

I pulled into the upper lot and Trevor opened the passenger door and handed Kandi out. Trevor is in his early twenties and for him all of life's problems were solved when he landed the job parking cars at Duke's. He works nights, surfs days, and is living proof that utter contentment is attainable. Of course, the endless supply of bikini-clad hotties parading by all year long doesn't hurt. He parked my Porsche and Eddington's dark blue Bentley convertible. Part Two of Eddington's support staff pulled their Escalade into the upper lot and stood next to it. Trevor recognized Nadzia at once and they did the fist-bump thing, but he looked blank but polite when I introduced Eddington. As the young brunette in the official Duke's Aloha shirt showed us to our table I murmured, "How quickly they forget," and he laughed. I asked the former star, "Do you miss it?"

"Honestly? Sure, every now and then. But it's life under a microscope, as you're finding out."

"To a much lesser degree than you. My fifteen minutes will be gone soon."

"See Kaylee with her cell phone?"

"She's going to post pictures on her blog?"

He looked at me pityingly. "They're videos and they're already posted. We're dining in real time, bro. Try to use the right fork."

"And people will spend time watching." I shook my head. "Why? Who cares?"

"Sorta replaced hanging out on the corner. Ya'll should talk to Kaylee about it. Broaden your horizons."

"Chet calls it 'screenworld.'" Kandi had vanished as we stood in the lobby. She came back, caught my eye and gave a tiny nod. She'd checked the restaurant, too. We were as secure as possible.

We made a jolly group—me, Kandi, Nadzia, Kaylee Miraflores, Elijah Eddington and his wife Mildred, just returned from Fiji. Kandi was stunning in a knee-length pale blue sheath dress and a string of pearls. Her hair was done simply, hanging loosely to her shoulders.

As always, I had the seared ahi and, as always, it was wonderful. Wafer-thin strips of fish, cooked on the edges, red and raw in the middle, arranged artfully on a bed of greens. Eddington kept us laughing with hilarious, improbable tales of basketball road trips. I believed the one about the underwear tree, created by decorating a flowering peach tree after a midnight run through the girls' dorm, but not about the four-foot iguana. Kaylee ordered a jalapeno burger, carefully cut it in quarters and took a small bite out of one corner. She kept her smart phone on the table next to her plate, but mostly she ignored it when it flashed and watched me attack my seared ahi.

Small talk is not my strong suit. "How's the burger?" I finally asked.

"Um, good, yeah, it's really good." She looked down at her phone. The ear that stuck out through her thin hair turned bright red.

Nadzia poked her in the ribs. "Kaylee, tell Mac about your blog." Kaylee shook her head. "C'mon, don't be a dweeb." More staring at the cell phone. Nadzia started chanting, "Dweeb, dweeb, dweeb."

Kandi kicked my ankle under the table. I gave her a dirty look, then growled. "All right, kid, talk or I'll put the leeches on you."

Kandi kicked me again, harder, but Kaylee said. "Do you really have leeches?"

"Well, I'd have to go get them. They're home, resting, after a big day of—"

She giggled, "Sucking on people."

I growled, "So talk, blondie, or else."

She looked down at her plate, fiddled with her burger, carefully pushing an escaped pepper back under the bun. "Um, okay, well, I started this blog, you know, and I write stuff, and kids write in and we talk and stuff."

"Sounds cool. I mean, totally sick." For some reason Kandi covered her face.

Nadzia rolled her eyes. "Tell Mac how many hits you get."

She put down the quarter burger and said proudly, "We're peaking at a hundred an hour when school's not in session."

I started to say something polite, but then the numbers clicked. I like numbers. "Wait, wait a minute, you get a *thousand* hits a day? That many people look at your blog?"

She pulled the pepper out and ate it, followed by a handful of fries. I waved Izzy, our server, over and ordered her a side of jalapenos. Kaylee nodded. "Seven days a week."

My jaw dropped. Eddington grinned at me. 'Told you, bro."

"And they're kids?" She nodded. I whistled. "What a demographic. This is an advertiser's dream."

Nadzia said proudly, "Our Ms Miraflores is a star. Blonde, blue-eyed, Hispanic surname, oh, yeah, after I ride Maverick's and score at the X-Games, with her fan base there's no limit to what we can do."

"Now that you mention it, if it's not too personal a question—"

"I'm adopted, of course. Oh, I didn't mean for it to come out that way. I'm sorry, I'm sorry." She looked at me uncertainly, then looked down at her plate again. "My, um, my biologic father ran away when I was three and my mother fell in love and when I was five she got remarried and my new father is this wonderful man and I love him so much. So one day—I was seven—we were moving down to Huntington and I asked him if I could tell the kids at school my name was Miraflores instead of Keene and he started crying and said he wanted to adopt me but he didn't know how to ask me so now I'm Kaylee Miraflores." She stopped for breath, looked up, then quickly looked back down at her burger. Izzy set a plate with sliced peppers on it down next to her and grinned.

I said, "Watch it, punk, she's with me." Everybody laughed, and Kandi didn't kick me under the table, which was a good thing since my ankle hurt like hell. Kaylee looked up at me wide-eyed. "Look, it's Miley Cyrus," I said and pointed at the front door. When Kaylee turned to look I snitched a slice of pepper and popped it in my mouth.

I like spicy food but this was off the scale. Sweat broke out on my forehead before I choked it down. It felt like I was holding Alys' Zippo against my lip. It was like one of those peppers that come with Asian food that are there to provide flavor and color, but are not meant to be eaten.

Kaylee saw my expression, giggled, and said, "My Dad cooks with them. I grew up eating peppers."

It's a myth that water helps in situations like this. I suppose it's better than nothing, but what you really need is oil or grease. Butter is best, so I grabbed a pat from the roll tray, skinned it and smeared it on my flaming tongue and lip. Kaylee said, "You should wash your hands, in case you touch your eyes." I gulped down the rest of my Dos Equis and signaled a laughing Izzy for another before I got up.

Two of Eddington's ex-basketball players, dressed in identical gray suits, were standing in the lobby, watching everything. I nodded to them on my way to the Men's.

The rest of dinner was uneventful, after everybody poked fun at me and dared me to eat another pepper, a dare I refused, claiming that they were really for Kaylee. When we got up the guys from Slam Dunk started to check outside. I beat them, coat unbuttoned for access to my gun. The tall black men checked, too, and Kandi brought up the rear, purse open for access to her Raven .25. Then Trevor pulled the cars up.

Inside the house after I locked up I saw the message light was flashing on my answering machine. I was surprised because the machine is connected to my land line and hardly anybody calls that. I pushed *Play*. "Uh, yes, Mr. Macdonald? This is Mrs. Struan. I'm calling for Dr. Roll at the Biggin Hill Recovery Home. The doctor just wanted me to check in and make sure everything was going all right with Roger Winters. Please give us a call when you get this message."

There were two hang-ups, then, "Mr. Macdonald, this is Dr. Quentin Roll. I am the Director of the Biggin Hill Recovery Home. I'd like to check on our patient Roger Winters. Please return my call at your earliest convenience."

It was late and I was tired, not to mention stuffed full of ahi and salad and the last half of Megan's jalapeno burger, minus peppers. Biggin Hill would keep till morning. I perimeter-checked all the doors and windows, double-checked the alarm system, kissed Kandi goodnight as she settled in to do some dissertation work, and went to bed.

It was a mistake.

Chapter Ten   Alys Winters

One of the benefits of being a broker on the left coast is you learn to get up early, and that pays off when you're surfing, not selling. At five a.m. surfline.com showed 17th Street, a part of what used to be known as the Huntington Cliffs just south of Dog Beach, was breaking in glassy shoulder-high left and rights.

Nadzia was spending the morning at an inland skate park signing autographs. Kandi was asleep. I looked at Kandi sprawled across my new bed. Looking at Kandi always makes me smile and this morning was no exception. She'd be up and gone before I was back, on her way to an early class at UCLA. There's no surf on Lake Michigan. Why did that pop into my head?

I didn't exactly forget that I was supposed to call Dr. Quentin Roll, the Director of the Biggin Hill Recovery Home, but I have my priorities, and anyway he probably wouldn't be at work that early. On top of that, cell phones don't do well in extreme heat—like the inside of a car parked in the sun at the beach even in December—so I didn't get the new voicemails, three of them, the last near-hysterical, from Alys Winters until I got home a little after ten. I rinsed off using the outside shower and draped my wetsuit over the back of a lawn chair to dry. Then I looked at the blinking light on my cell and dialed voicemail. All the messages were from Alys. They all said basically the same thing: call me. As I punched Alys' speed dial with my thumb I shut the door to the patio and dropped the metal rod into the track. Chet calls it crude but effective. I waited for the connection while I trotted up the stairs to the master bedroom, feeling in the pit of my stomach that bad things were happening. I was right.

Alys answered on the first ring. "Mac, oh, man, am I glad to hear your voice. Shit, oh, shit. Look, I'm trying not to freak out here."

"Deep breath." I waited a moment. "Now tell me what's wrong."

After another breath she said, "Okay, okay, yeah, I'm okay. Mac, what are you doing with my brother?"

All at once the calls from Biggin Hill seemed more important, maybe a lot more important. The wording of the message clicked into place. That feeling in the pit of my stomach got worse. First things first. "Alys, where are you right now?" It sounded like kids in the background.

"Outside the gym, walking to my French class."

"Okay, good. Now, about your brother, what do you mean 'doing with him?' The answer is nothing. I visited him a week ago. Why?"

"You didn't check him out yesterday morning on a day pass to do some tests down in Irvine?"

"No, of course not. I—wait a minute, wait a minute here. He's out? Roger is *out*?"

"Oh, shit. Mac, I got a call this morning from a doctor named Roll—"

"At Biggin Hill."

"Yeah." She took another deep breath. "He said you and another man arranged a furlough for Roger, for some tests at some Irvine clinic. Dr. Roll said he'd tried to call you and you hadn't returned his calls. He said you picked up Roger yesterday morning and they haven't heard from you since." Explaining that the surf was up, while true, seemed lame. "Oh, god. I knew it couldn't be true. How did this happen? How did he do this? How did—"

"Deep breath, Alys, deep breath. Later. We'll figure all of this out later. Okay, right now you're at school. Inside the building?" Roger had beaten Alys seriously enough to put her in the hospital before I caught him. Now he was loose.

"No, they'd bust me for using a cell phone. I'm still outside the gym. Oh, man, now the AP's spotted me. I'm tardy and I'm on a cell phone. I am *so screwed.*"

"All right, Here's what I want you to do." As I talked I stepped out of my Kanvas by Katin surf trunks and pulled open a drawer looking for underwear. "When the Assistant Principal busts you tell him—"

"Her."

"Tell her everything. But, and this is important, do it inside. Go to her office. Give her my cell number and tell her to call me for confirmation. Above all, do not go outside. You go to class if the AP thinks it's safe, but do not leave the building."

"Oh, Mac, can't you come get me right now, please? I'm scared, I'm so scared."

It tore my heart. I wanted to jump in the Porsche and jam down to Newport, with my .45 on the seat next to me. I couldn't do it. I should have let him die. "Honey, right now you're safer there. He's probably on the run, out of the state already." Neither of us believed that. "Really. I'll pick you up after school. Alys, I—" I heard a voice in the background and I was talking to a dial tone.

Tell me about your adventures.

Forty-five minutes later I was seated in his oak-paneled office on the ground floor of Biggin Hill, talking to a very nervous Dr. Quentin Roll. He looked like a movie version of what a shrink should look like: comfortably plump, gray beard, full head of tousled gray hair, beige turtleneck and chocolate slacks. Brown eyes that under normal circumstances probably radiated warmth and understanding; now they jerked from one part of the room to another, anywhere but looking directly at me. A camel's-hair coat hung on a rack in the corner, complete with leather elbow patches. The walls had the usual framed diplomas; the window looked out over brush-covered hills to the brown haze of Orange

County. "I'd never met you," he said for the second time, "and one of them looked somewhat like you, and he had a baseball cap on," he was saying, "perhaps a bit younger. Very clean-cut. I spoke with both he and his associate here in my office and then with all of them in my consultation room. As I said before, he had all of the necessary documentation. The signature matched yours from two days ago. And, after all, I had never seen you in person."

I guess I was glad to hear I was considered clean-cut. "And Roger didn't object?"

"No, no."

"I'd like to see the consultation room."

"Of course, of course." He pushed a button and said, "Mrs. Struan, can you come in here?" She was in her sixties, thin, with a slash of red lips, steel-gray hair done in rows of curls, a black mid-calf skirt, rose-colored blouse buttoned to the throat and a pinched expression that said she was not having a good day and fully expected it to get worse. "Please show Mr. Macdonald the consultation room we used yesterday for Roger Winters' visitors."

She looked at him and said, "Dr. Roll, I would be more comfortable if you came along," then she turned to me. "You understand nothing like this has ever happened before? And that I'm—"

I said, "Certainly. I'd like the Doctor along, too."

Roll hesitated, then said, "Yes, of course, if you insist."

Mrs. Struan said, "This way, please."

After Roll put on his coat we went out of the office down a short hallway and into another room with cream-colored walls, soothing abstract paintings, two comfortable chairs, a coffee table complete with box of tissues, and—I swear—a beige leather couch against one wall. Struan said, "There's this door and another private exit in case there are people in the hall."

Roll nodded, back on comfortable ground. "Even in this setting we believe it is important to protect the privacy of the analysand."

I looked around. No clues jumped out at me.

Back in Dr. Roll's office I said, "I want to see the video."

"Oh, we don't record here, we—"

"Respect the privacy of the analysand. Yeah. Now let's look at the recording."

He gave me a dirty look but he shooed Struan out, turned his laptop so I could see the screen and we looked at the video. There wasn't much. It showed two men, both about my age, both wearing baseball caps, smiling, chatting with the receptionist, shaking hands, grasping Roger Winters' arm and guiding him out, accompanied by a white-coated assistant. We watched it twice. The second time something nagged at me. "Mr. Macdonald, at what point do you think I should notify the authorities?"

"Now, Dr. Roll. Call them right now." I had the ever-helpful Mrs. Struan burn me a copy of the video, and got out of there.

That afternoon they found no trace of Roger Winters. I didn't really expect them to. I called Vegas, left a message for Chet and borrowed Bryant to watch Alys. I alerted the private security that patrolled Huntington Harbour. We were in lockdown mode, even more severe than before. And I knew it was useless. If Roger wanted one of us, he'd get past it all. Our precautions might make it harder for the clowns.

I watched the video again and I got it. Roger paused on his way out, looked directly at the hidden camera, and shook his head. He was sending me a message. But what?

That afternoon Chet showed up at my house. He arrived in a rental car that he parked across the street; after I let him in he closed the drapes in the front room and peered out cautiously for several minutes.

"Do I need to get my gun?"

"Brought my own," he said, lifting his unstuffed cowboy shirt to show the butt of a revolver sticking out of his hip pocket. "So, nope. We need to talk."

"You get my message?"

"Roger Winters? Yep. Ain't done nothin' on finding him yet."

"I'm making the assumption you have good reasons for changing priorities."

"Background on your pals Baines and Valentine and their muscle, and, before you say, 'What took you so long,' let me answer by saying it didn't."

"Tell me."

We moved into the kitchen. I got him a beer while he pulled his laptop out of his backpack and set it up.

"Okay, bottom to top," he said, sipping the beer. "Chooch and The Rod. Real names George Joseph Reese and Rodney Hamilton Deery. Both have AA degrees from Orange Coast College, where they met. Both have records for minor stuff—pot, speeding—and Rod has assault charges that were dropped. Faith Valentine. First named in a divorce proceeding when she was nineteen; the young lady made friends easily. Went into the Army after high school, served two tours. Marksman, marksperson, whatever. First alternate for the '94 Olympic team. Weapon of choice a Ruger 25 caliber target pistol. Baines is a college graduate, for the last five years has owned Interagency Insurance Investigations, which is a real company."

"Before that?"

"Ah, the good part. Before that he lived in Newport Beach, picked up spot work as a helicopter pilot, no other visible means of support except the gratitude of wealthy ladies. Faith was his, uh, 'roommate.'"

"They were working the circuit. Entertaining wealthy folks of either sex looking for a plaything."

"When they got a little long in the tooth for that, they started this investigations company, with one client."

"A winery in central California."

"Whoa, pard, not bad. Yeah. Okay, now ask me why it took so long."

"You said it didn't."

"Oh. Yeah, well, when I was looking, of course using a completely untraceable laptop, somebody started looking back."

"Baines figured out you were researching him and Faith?"

"Sure looks that way. And I think I was followed this morning."

I went upstairs and got my gun. We waited and watched. Nobody came.

Two days later surfline.com reported a storm brewing off the Aleutians. The word went out and within an hour around the world the pro crews started hustling, loading up, from France, Costa Rica, Australia, and the US, packing quivers of boards, booking flights. Maverick's was going to be firing.

Chapter Eleven   Maverick's

It's the sound that gets you first. Most surf sound is so relaxing that people load it on their iPods for stress relief and to help them sleep. Maverick's isn't like that. Some big-wave spots, Pipeline in Hawaii for example, the waves are beautiful, scary, but beautiful. Maverick's isn't like that. Sleep? If you understood what the sound meant you'd have nightmares. Big waves that pitch out as they break, sound like a bomb going off—a solid booming noise that on a still day can be heard a mile inland.

Maverick's is in a spot called Half Moon Bay, about an hour by car south of San Francisco. To get to it from Orange County if you have a lot of stuff to take, you drive up the 5 freeway, cut across to the coast on the 152, to the 101, to the 280 and the 92 and then continue north on Route 1. We made quite a caravan—we took one of Eddington's white Escalades, Luke drove up in another, towing the trailer with our twin Wake Pro 215's, and Nadzia's film crew followed in the flamed hearse with still more loads of equipment. Kaylee's parents gave permission for her to miss a couple of days of school; Luke just ditched. Kandi said this was something she had to see and swapped work schedules around to get time off from work. Henrietta Graveline, the queen of my micro-posse, had convinced Brad Zucco to bring the Waiting For The Sun II up the coast and now she, Brad, and Lisa June were on the cliff with binoculars.

On the drive we got several hundred texts and posts wishing us well. Many were from girls who said they wanted to be just like Nadzia, more were from guys who wanted to date her; none were from her parents. She didn't say anything about that but Kaylee told me. I had several from co-workers, some wishing me well, some saying, "If you die can I have the Porsche?" Traders. To my amazement one was from Blondell Baines wishing me luck and one was from Faith Valentine. The latter was one word—"Ramble." Proof of what the Snake says, "The universe is stranger than we know, maybe stranger than we *can* know." I put all of the messages out of my mind.

Half Moon Bay is a small community, devoted to agriculture, floriculture, and a quiet lifestyle. Until the winter surf gets huge. Somehow Eddington had pulled strings and we had rooms, but the town was filling up fast with surf crews from all over, and more crews to film them.

At seven in the morning Nadzia Kamnik and I were sitting alone on the bluff overlooking the bay and the surf, watching huge, ugly waves build, crest, pitch out and smash down against the reef as if they wanted to destroy it. We both had on black fullsuits, unzipped, and rubber booties. The water temperature at Maverick's can get down into the forties, and water that cold is nothing to fool around with. I'd made her crew wait a quarter-mile down the shore on the boat that would take us out. I didn't say anything stupid like, 'There's still time to back out.' We watched for almost an hour as the waves built, commenting on take-offs and kick-outs and studying the break. Finally it got too big and even the most hardcore paddle-in surfers called it a day. It had been a good session; six falls, six successful rescues. One broken nose, one dislocated shoulder. And now that the really big sets were starting to roll in the tow-in crews were moving into position.

Most people think of surfing as tanned, healthy young people dashing across the sand carrying boards down to the sea while Dick Dale wails on his Fender in the background. Big wave tow-in isn't like that. It's more like an assault on Everest, with a dedicated team managing serious, complex equipment. It takes a boat, multiple wet bikes, and often a helicopter in case things really go south. We had all that waiting.

I reached around behind her and tugged on the long cord to zip up her suit. I said, "Let's go surfing."

In the lineup, with the Wake Pro idling under me and Nadzia close behind, straddling her board and clutching the coils of line, I was always watching out to sea because a rogue wave, while rare, could swamp us and then not only would we be tumbling through the freezing water, we'd be doing it in the company of an 800-pound machine. This was not like the Long Beach Outer Harbor, it was not like offshore at Huntington where we'd gone on several stormy days for rough-water training. It was like nothing I'd ever experienced. The gray-green hills rolled in and you slid up the side, up, and up and then up some more until you were almost at eye level with the top of the cliff and the bay spread out beneath you as if you were in a low-level plane. And those gray-green hills weren't smooth; they were bumpy and choppy and came complete with their own whitecaps.

I said, "Rule Number One."

"Don't pick the first wave of a set."

"Why?"

"Because if you fall you've got five or six more waves to contend with." She didn't let go of the line. "Mac, listen, if, uh, if—"

"Don't tell me the hardcore skate bitch with the monster from 'Alien' tattooed on her butt is going to get all mushy on me. Screw that. You're The Titanium Redhead."

"Fuck you. Listen—"

"Say it. Who are you?"

She swallowed, took a deep breath. "I'm The Titanium Redhead."

"Yes, you are." We bumped fists.

"Take care of Kaylee."

It was not at all what I expected. "What? Kaylee?"

"She's just a kid, okay, and she's totally famous, and she's got this following. She thinks she can do anything and she always wants to help, but she's just a kid. She's just a kid and there are bad people out there, really bad people."

Mental note: when this is over, make her tell me about these 'bad people.' Use force if necessary. "You got it. Now, you gonna show 'em something or not?"

A green Yamaha covered with sponsor logos buzzed by us, going airborn as it powered over the shoulder of a wave after the surfer released the line. A moment later we heard the solid *ka-rump* as the wave broke and cold spray blew back into our faces, but the helicopter didn't swoop in so it must have been a good ride. Faint cheers reached us from the crowd on the cliff top.

Our eyes met. I said, "Go for it, Z." The Titanium Redhead swallowed and nodded. Took a deep breath. "Let's rock." Reached up and we bumped fists. I waved to the boat. Luke waved back and moved it a little farther off. The skinny kid had turned into a good boat handler, and Nadzia trusted him. She trusted me, too.

It's the sound. I heard one crash on the reef and my mouth went dry. What I hadn't talked about with Nadzia were the problems that come up if the driver of the wet bike loses it and finds him (or her) self sucked under and thrashing around with the ski. I didn't discuss it much with myself, either. I reached down, splashed salty frigid water on my face, and it was all right. Everything—the home invasion, the carjack, the severed toe, the missing Roger Winters—everything went away and the world narrowed to the machine under me, the next set, and the girl on the end of the line. I felt great. I yelled, "Rock and roll!" at the top of my lungs, the skaters on the boat hooted. The Titanium Redhead dropped the loops of line, straddled the board, slid back to the handle and it was on. I maneuvered us into the take-off zone. The idea is that when she selects a wave I pull her in front of it till she's going fast enough to catch it, she drops the line and if all goes well I power up the face and out of the way. Another big swell lifted SeaDoo and surfer skyward, up, *up*, then up some more until once again we looked down on the beach and the cliff, covered with tiny figures looking back at us. The rescue helicopter buzzed us. I heard a bike winding up the revs and watched as another rider was towed, released the line, dropped in and made it.

It's the sound. The set ended and we got a moment of quiet. We sat, her on one end of the line straddling the board just behind the foot straps. Modern boards are so small they float the rider but are themselves under the surface so the rider is in water up their waist, and I knew the cold was starting to work its way through the neoprene of her wetsuit. Above us the helicopter buzzed again. Then—total cliché—somebody yelled, "Outside," and on the horizon we could see the next group of waves marching toward us.

No one took the first wave, three took the second. Zia, never looking away from the developing set, waved, signaling for the third wave. I put the WakePro in gear and drove in between the waves directly in front of the one she'd picked. I turned, accelerated, felt the line get tight as she got up to speed, watching over my shoulder to time it, staying down low as it lifted me, thinking, come on, come on, now, do it.

And she did.

She was a tiny bit late releasing the line, but was athlete enough to make up for it and start the drop. I saw this part as I rode ahead of the swell, glancing back over my shoulder. Then I lost track since I had my hands very full trying to get up the face and over the shoulder before it broke. I was carrying too much speed as I came over the face of the wave and for a moment the bike and I were airborne. Calling on my limited experience with offroad motorcycles I rose to a crouch and made the landing, flexing my legs to cushion the impact. Barely. I sat down hard, my hand slipped off the handlebars and I smacked my cheek on the dash, but didn't fall off.

Nadzia did a nice kickout, slid down the back of the wave, stepped out of the foot straps and into the water, pumping her fist as she did. I raced over, she caught the shelf, climbed on. We could hear cheers from the boat and I could see Luke and Kaylee jumping up and down. Kandi was waving both arms and cheering as loud as anybody. Sensible people would have called it quits, after a completely successful ride. She looked at me and grinned. I took us back into the line-up and we did it again.

Half an hour later I could sense Nadzia tiring and was ready to reel her in and head for the boat, but she waved for one more and I nodded. Go for it.

This third wave was a disaster from the beginning. She was late releasing the tow line which made her later dropping in, and that meant that she had less time to make it down the face of the wave before being swallowed by the white water. It's the drop, that moment of stepping off a three-story building with a plank strapped to your feet, that makes or breaks most rides. Experts like Laird Hamilton can recover from mistakes, but Nadzia wasn't an expert. Athlete that she was, she'd been able to recover from a late take-off on her first wave, but fatigue and over an hour in the frigid water had robbed her of some of her skill.

The face of a really huge wave has texture, smooth areas, rough spots complete with whitecaps and chop; think of a rough, churned-up sea standing practically on edge. When you catch a rail it's because the edge of the surfboard hits one of those rough spots, slowing that side of the board, messing up your balance. What happens is, you twist and pitch forward; if you've ever caught an edge skiing a black diamond you know just what it feels like, including the impact, because at those speeds water feels solid and hard.

She was halfway down the face when she snagged the right rail. It was a good fall, as good as any fall like that can be. She couldn't save it. She got her feet out of the straps and dove off the board headfirst, fell through the air about ten feet, slammed into the face of the wave, skipped like a stone on a pond, hit the surface again, this time flat on her back, and was engulfed by an avalanche of churning white water.

Of course, I got most of this from the video. I saw the take-off and the beginning of the fall before I realized that I had been distracted watching her and had made a very basic mistake—I'd looked away from incoming surf and was out of position for the next wave. It was the sound as it started to break saved me. I looked out to sea and saw a wall of water, white on my right, still gray-green in front of me, bearing down fast. I opened the throttle all the way, ran toward the wave, up the face and over the top. It was close, so close we actually punched through the lip as it curled over, but the bike and I made it—airborne again, with me hanging on, slipping to the side and landing her, only to get thrown off when we hit the surface and rebounded. I landed on my back, and it knocked the wind out of me. For a moment I couldn't move and I didn't really feel much of anything. Then my head hurt, the shoulder that I'd sprained my senior year of high school wrestling in the CIF semi-finals *really* hurt and that arm didn't work too well, and the bike was ten yards off. I rolled over on to my stomach, actually glad the water was so cold because it revived me, thrashed over to it one-handed, grabbed the handlebars with my good arm, got one leg over the saddle, hit the throttle, and headed back to find Zia with the sound of the next wave in my ears.

At first I didn't see her. The rescue helicopter dove low over me, flattening the water with prop wash, then pulled up. Finally there she was—I saw hair, floating dark against the froth, and an arm moving weakly. She'd survived a two-wave hold-down. I opened up the throttle and raced the next wave. I pulled in next to her, her arm came up and caught the back of the bike but she was too weak to hold on so she missed the grab and slid off, vanishing beneath the surface. The next wave was closer, roaring toward us as I skidded around in a 180 and came back. Her hand reached up, she tried for the grab again, missed, and sank and our time was up. It was the sound. I could hear the next wave and I could hear somebody in the helicopter with a bullhorn yelling some useless information, but I had no idea what and didn't care. I was counting seconds because I couldn't take my eyes off the spot I'd last seen Nadzia. Counting, looking for her, and trying to judge when the next wave would be on us.

I wheeled the ski around to where I thought—hoped—she was. Nothing. Suddenly there was a hand, then a wide-eyed pale face just under the surface. Her mouth opened, a large bubble erupted and she started to sink.

Grabbing the collar of her wetsuit my left hand, opening the throttle up to max with the other, I tried to get us out of there. I'd lost count of the seconds, but it didn't matter anyway. The Wake Pro responded gallantly, but we weren't going to make it running for the shoulder, so I turned and raced the wave, heading straight for the rocks. At the very last second I savagely yanked the handlebars to the right. The rocks flashed by on our left, I had a moment of relief, then the whitewater had us. She'd had the presence of mind to hit the quick release on her leash so her board was not thrashing around with us, but the bike was.

Think of a washing machine the size of an office building and you're in it on the Extra-soiled Spindle-Mutilate-Thrash Cycle only it's freezing cold and there's this eight-hundred-pound rock flopping around with you. One hand locked in her collar, the other gripping the handlebars, bouncing, bouncing, turning over, smacking my face into the dash once, twice. If the bike's engine had died we probably would have died, too, because we were so close to the rocks, but it didn't. We popped out, into sunlight, the engine pushed water out of the jet and took us to safety. Then I saw the blood on Zia's face.

As the rescue boat moved in I shook her. "Zia! Zia!"

Her eyes, which had been open and staring, focused and her eyelids fluttered. "Where's your fucking white horse?" Then she passed out.

The boat got there. They took her away from me. She had a three-inch cut above one eye where one of her board's fins had clipped her, a mild concussion, and a dislocated shoulder, but she was otherwise okay.

Video of the event flashed around the globe in real time. She was famous; The Titanium Redhead had conquered Maverick's

Two days later someone killed her.

Chapter Twelve It's Her Party

We were upstairs at my house, in the master bedroom getting ready for the gala celebration. The sun was going down, shadowing the still water of the channel. Kandi was sitting in the easy chair, one of the pieces of furniture that had survived Diana's parties, reading an email with pursed lips; I was kicked back on the bed. She zipped her iPad into its case, stood and focused those amazing hazel eyes on me. "I don't like it," she said.

Nadzia had originally wanted to hire the entire Toilet Bowl Skate Park, but saner heads had prevailed and, thinking of sponsors beyond t-shirts, skateboard trucks and wheels, she agreed to Duke's. They don't usually do private parties, but if you have enough money, and are friends with enough important people, it can be arranged. To my knowledge Elijah Eddington had neither—he had money, yeah, but not that kind—and his contacts weren't that good, but it happened anyway.

Eddington told us to go shopping, his way of saying thanks, and I'd taken him at his word and put another hole in the long-suffering Slam Dunk debit card. Kandi was in a periwinkle blue floor-length sequined gown with a scoop neck and no back whatsoever; her blonde hair was up, pulled back in a sleek knot—not a schoolteacher bun, think sexy tango dancer—her earrings were blue-and-silver mermaids, dangly works of art by Lunch at the Ritz, her shoes black enamel patent leather pumps with four-inch cigarette heels from Jimmy Choo. I had warned her that she might cause heart failure in some of the older male sponsors. Inside the gown there was nothing but Kandi, and a holster strapped around her thigh holding the tiny Raven .25. I wore a black three-thousand-dollar Armani tux that was the souvenir of a recent Vegas stay.

"I don't like it," she said again.

"I do. I could watch you doing that for hours."

She had gone back to practicing whipping the skirt up and drawing the tiny pistol. "You *have* watched me do it for hours."

I leaned back against the pillows. "I know. Life is good."

The doorbell rang. I went downstairs, stood to the side of the door and checked the peephole—more low-tech but easy to use—let Chet in and marveled at his Western tux, black with gray piping around the lapels and pockets, black ostrich-hide boots, and black Stetson that he took off as he crossed the threshold. We went upstairs where Kandi did two more practice draws while I got out my cannon, the 1912 Colt .45 that my friend the Snake had given me. I checked the clip, verified the safety was on before I put it in the shoulder holster and slid the whole rig on over my ruffled white shirt. I rolled up my sleeve and strapped my sawed-off pool cue handle to my forearm, thinking, hoping, that all of this was unnecessary. Technically our job was done. Nadzia had challenged Maverick's and won, and whatever threat had existed (Eddington didn't bother denying it anymore) was presumably gone. No severed body parts had been delivered and no one had called up ordering me to find "the sample." But it didn't feel right. It felt worse. Chet watched our preparations, raised his eyebrows and whistled softly.

"That's right," I said. "If some of the rich folk run amok, we're ready."

By the time we got to the restaurant clouds were moving in and it looked like rain. Duke's sits at the top of the cliff on the south side of the Pier, about one story above the beach level. Wide stairs, divided by a steel pipe railing, lead from the street level down to the sand. The area adjoining the turnaround directly in front of the restaurant had been almost filled with an enormous white tent from which Nadzia would make her grand entrance, which meant that most of the guests' cars had to be parked on the lower, beach level. Only four spots were available on the upper level. Trevor, feeling the pressures of management as he supervised the crew of extra parking lot attendants laid on for the event, handed Kandi out of the Porsche and hurried around to take the keys and give me a stub. He was decked out for the evening in what I assumed to be some advertising geek's idea of surf wear—enormous straw sombrero, hot pink puka-shell necklace, pink-and-green plaid board shorts, and a really hideous mostly-orange aloha shirt with "The Titanium Redhead Rides Maverick's" stitched on the pocket and printed across the back in Old English script. All of this was topped off with matching pink goo smeared across his nose and under his eyes like athletes wear to reduce glare. He glanced down at his shirt and said, "This is *not* my idea of a good time and if you laugh I can promise you a door ding. I mean it, man. And I'm keeping the shirt and selling it on eBay. Already got a lot of interest."

I slipped him a twenty, fully intending to add it to my bill to Slam Dunk Management, and said, "Two questions. One, can you keep it handy, up here?"

The twenty vanished, he looked at what was left of the turnaround, with a Rolls Royce, a Bentley, and one impossibly-low yellow Maserati, grinned and said, "No problem, man. It's like, equal opportunity or something."

"Or something."

"What's the other question?"

"Does that stuff on your beak glow in the dark?"

Kandi slipped her arm though mine and we headed up the steps. We went through the greeting line, shaking hands with Eddington and his wife Mildred, and got to the doors before I snapped my fingers and trotted back down the steps to the turnaround.

"Trevor, just leave the keys in it, okay? Don't keep them at the desk." He looked at me strangely, started to speak, but then nodded as a chauffeured silver Bentley pulled up.

Back at the doors, Mary was not exactly tapping her foot, but she was close. "I *so* enjoy standing around in an evening gown in front of a bar."

"If you shoot me you'll never find out about the nice surprise I have for you." Of course, I didn't have one, but I had a couple of hours to come up with something.

"A nice older gentleman offered to escort me. He seemed to enjoy cleavage."

"If he's really old and feeble I could beat him up."

She poked me, and Kandi said, "So, all right, Sailor, what was that all about?"

"Being prepared."

"Oh, geez, I'm sorry I asked." She took my arm, looking totally at ease, but I noticed that she made sure her gun hand was free. We went in.

As we walked through the waiting area and into the main room, I was checking exits and Kandi was doing the same.

Sponsors, media, and some wealthy folks had gathered to celebrate Nadzia's victory, and to eat, drink, cut deals, pick up hotties of either gender, and stab the occasional back. Mary was uncomfortable with the business elite, and Kandi felt like she should be serving drinks instead of taking them. For me it was old home week.

There were about a hundred guests who would be served dinner, and twenty or so members of the press (who would have to be satisfied with a buffet outside), ranging from the *LA Times* to *Thrasher Magazine*. Kaylee's posse from KayleeTalks was there, too, taking pictures of her as she took pictures and talked to people, many of whom were also taking pictures of each other. Last but not least, the skate crowd was there, not in force but enough to keep Nadzia happy and to give the press some real skaters to badger for outrageous quotes. Finding black in the skaters' wardrobes had not been a problem; formal was more of a stretch. I waved to Luke, who had the inevitable mini-cam. He pumped a fist back at me. The kids were watching the videos, trying to get drinks with alcohol and getting carded. College students in white jackets inexpertly circulated with trays crowded with champagne flutes, while the tables in front of the windows held silver buckets filled with Diet Snapple and Mountain Dew. Chet came in, checked the exits and moved through the room, whispering into his cell phone. I knew there was one of his vans somewhere close.

After the usual small talk—with people paying so little attention that you could respond to "How are you?" with "My spleen ruptured on the way here," and they'd say, "How nice"—the first level of guests, sponsors other rich types, gathered on the steps in front of the restaurant, waiting for Nadzia to make her entrance. On either side of the tent twelve-foot flat screens showed video of the Maverick's ride, followed by clips of her skateboarding, and finally—a word from our sponsor—some of her modeling sweats and tees and tennis shoes.

The announcer, sounding properly awestruck, intoned, "And now, and now, *and now*, from Surf City, USA, ladies and gentlemen, the young lady who conquered Maverick's, The Titanium Redhead herself, the fabulous, the one and only, Nadzia Kamnik!" The tent curtains parted, the flat screens switched to a live feed, and she made her entrance, striding down the red carpet while flashes strobed and the crowd ooohed and aahhed. She was resplendent. Her white off-the-shoulder gown fitted her perfectly, molding to every curve. Her flaming hair was up in a French roll, held in place with emerald clips that matched her eyes and the dangling earrings brushing her pure white shoulders. A white gauze dressing covered the stitches on her forehead where the surfboard fin had clipped her. A badge of honor. Everybody applauded, the older business crowd politely, the skate kids wildly, backing up their claps with fist pumps, whistles, hoots and the occasional full-on yelp. Full disclosure—I did some fist-pumping and hooting myself. Those Maverick's rides were something special.

Nadzia moved up the stairs gracefully, smiling, shaking hands and greeting people like royalty, as if she did it every day of her life, as if she knew each person and was really glad they were there. I was proud of her. She saw me, her eyes lit up, and she swerved over, and stood for a moment, just looking at me. She started to speak, couldn't, so she hugged me fiercely, and we raised our arms over our heads as strobes popped. Eddington handed me a box with a corsage; I took it out and slipped it around her wrist, gently because it will still tender from the Maverick's fall. Strong gardenia smell filled the air.

Inside, we mingled and sampled hors d'oeurves and talked. I saw a society matron talking to a rail-thin skater girl in a black coat. The girl turned and pulled up the coat to show a tattoo on the small of her back; the matron smiled and slipped down the waistband of her red silk pants show a slightly age-blurred Zig Zag Man on her hip.

I was standing next to Elijah Eddington, who was stylin' in a white suit and white snap-brim hat, when the crowd parted and I saw who was standing at the bar, grinning and drinking. I gripped Eddington's arm. "What the hell are they doing here?"

"Now, Mac, don't get excited."

Blondell Baines and Faith Valentine stood casually chatting with Henrietta Graveline and Brad Zucco.

"Mac, don't get excited," Eddington said again. "Blondell and Faith are on the guest list and you added Brad, Henrietta, and Lisa June."

"You put those two on the list?"

He looked down at me in surprise and frowned. "I know Baines' boss, Harker, sure, in fact ya'll have spoken with him. Like I told you, he works for a very wealthy old lady. But, no, I didn't invite him. No, he's a friend of Nadzia's and represents a potential sponsor."

I can't say that it was one of those moments when puzzle pieces fall into place, but I knew for sure I had another piece.

Something in my face must have given my tall friend pause, because he pulled away from me. "Mac, now, listen, what are you going to do?"

I grinned and he looked even more nervous. "Why, I'm going to buy Mr. Baines a drink."

"It's an open bar."

"I know. That's why I'm willing to buy." Across the room I caught Kandi's eye. In three long strides she was at my side, not looking at me, watching the crowd. "Tick-tock," she whispered.

"At the bar. Black suit, black silk t-shirt. Woman next to him in another Donna Karan original skirt and jacket."

Kandi tensed. "Be careful around her. Very careful." She looked at me, impressed. "You can tell Donna Karan from across the room?"

"I am a man of many talents, and I made it my business to study wealthy people. That's probably a three-thousand dollar outfit and it's the second one I've seen her wearing."

"Plus shoes. And they are great." Women and shoes—something I'll never understand.

We didn't have to go to them. Baines turned away from Brad and Henrietta as Lisa June walked up and he came to us, marching purposefully with his chin pressed down on his chest, gripping a glass half-full of what looked like dirty dishwater, while Faith moved off to talk to somebody. Kandi followed her. He grinned, showing fine white teeth in his smooth mannequin face, and said, "Mr. Macdonald, I want to buy you a drink." He wore black-rimmed Buddy Holly glasses, something I hadn't noticed before. That made the shades at the skate park prescription, or he wore contacts some of the time.

"Funny, I just said that about you."

"Hey, great minds, right?" He slurped down the rest of his dishwater and we moved to the closest bar. "Great! Listen, I want to apologize for my people the other day. At the skate park."

"It's so hard to get good help."

As so often happens, my wit was wasted. "You better believe it, pal." Frowning, he muttered, "Gotta watch them every minute." Then he seemed to remember I was there. "Okay," he slapped the bar, hard enough to make empty glasses jump around. "It's done. Over. Glad you understand that my people just got a little carried away. So, you work with a lot of rich people, right? What are they like? I bet they all have secrets, see, I have this theory that all great dynasties are founded on a crime. You know, somebody back there pulled a fast one. Now, tell me, did your father fight in the war?"

"What?" Hard to keep up was only the beginning of describing talking with this guy.

"Viet Nam. Did he go over there?"

"Yes. Why do you ask?"

"Defining moment in modern history. Yes. Both sides, you know. Personally, my sympathies are with the protestors. They had it. Moral certitude. Look, have you found your laptop?"

This guy liked to jump around. On the other hand, he didn't seem to care if you participated or not. "No."

"Right. We need to talk about that. It's part of something bigger. People are looking for something, something you know about. Heard you almost got carjacked."

Two could play his game of jumping from topic to topic. "So, what are you drinking?"

"Bullshot."

"No, I mean it. I'll get you a drink."

He waved his glass in my general direction. "A bullshot. Very old school. Classic."

"Ummm, I don't think I know that one."

"A shot of Stoly in beef bouillon with salt, pepper, lemon juice, Tabasco, and Worcestershire. You oughta try it." He waved at the bartender, who apparently was willing to serve this concoction. Personally, I'd rather gargle prune juice laced with barium, but I chose not to share that with Baines and instead got a club soda with a twist of lime.

"What is it they're after? And who are they?"

"Get it with Clamato juice and it's called a Bloody Clam, but I'm partial to this one."

"Baines—"

He took a swig, set the glass down. "Don't play games with me, Macdonald. This is serious. I know she told you."

"I got a new laptop. Got most of my data back."

Kandi came up and touched my shoulder. "Dinner's starting." Baines put his hand on my arm, stopping me from leaving. I looked at his hand. He moved it. Faith stepped up next to him, grasped my shoulders, hugged me and kissed me on both cheeks. Not to be outdone, I took her hand and shook it formally. "Ms. Valentine, how nice to see you. This is my friend Kandi Shaw." They looked at each other. "Love your—" "—dress." "—shoes." And they smiled, showing teeth.

"The carjack," I said. "What about it?"

"Second-stringers. You want to watch out that whoever it is doesn't send the pros next time." I said nothing. We all smiled at each other, he shrugged, and they left to find their seats.

Kandi whispered, "Gun."

"On her right hip, under the jacket."

"How do you, oh, never mind. What happened to Walter and Cheryl? I haven't seen them."

I said, "You're right, where are they?" Snake's cell and land line gave me voicemail, so I assumed they had been held up and were on the way. I looked back and Baines was talking to a white-jacketed server.

The Counters restaurant had set up a temporary burger grill and deep-fry station to help Duke's handle the crowd. It offered singles, doubles, and two kinds of thick-cut fries. The wine served with dinner was a dry Pinot blanc from Babbling Brook, a California winery I'd never heard of. We were seated at the head table, on the ocean side of the room. Behind us windows looked out at the beach, wave sound buried under the talk, and sunset. Nadzia was in the center of the table, flanked by Eddington, his wife, and the Vans shoe representative. Kaylee Miraflores was on my left, Kandi on my right. Kandi rolled her eyes when I got jalapeno fries from Counters to go with my grilled salmon, but then ate half of them. Kaylee actually put away her cell phone and talked. She talked about Nadzia, and how she'd been bullied until Nadzia had put a stop to it. I had always thought of bullying in terms of guys, pushing and shoving, taking lunch money from little kids, but it seemed I had a lot to learn.

After dinner the tables were whisked away and there was dancing.

All at once, when I turned to Kandi, Nadzia was standing there and the crowd was watching expectantly. A flash of blue across the room—Kandi next to Chet, both of them looking at me and grinning. I held my arm out. Nadzia took it, flowed smoothly into my arms, and we danced, moving around the otherwise-empty floor to something soft and classical. She raised her head and looked up at me reached up to touch my cheek, brushing it with the petals of her corsage. I started to speak but she shook her head and rested it on my shoulder again. We finished on the beat, I bowed and Nadzia curtseyed. Everybody applauded and other couples moved out.

I found Kandi and if I do say so myself, we acquitted ourselves well. My Junior High dance lessons came back to me with reasonable accuracy, allowing me to perform the box step flawlessly. Kandi's bare back was silky and warm under my palm, and she responded to the slightest fingertip pressure, as if we had actually done this before. She snuggled against me and the strap holding the small automatic around her thigh pressed against my leg. I ignored all it represented and focused on guiding my blonde companion around the floor without counting steps any more than I really had to. I'm made of stern stuff. The song ended, and I was ready for a cold Dos Equis, but prepared to settle for club soda when Kandi whispered, "Ask Kaylee to dance."

"It's totally beneath you to get even this way. You should be ashamed." She made chicken noises.

"She's what? Fifteen?"

"Fourteen. She skipped a grade. And she's by herself on the sidelines, wearing what is probably her very first adult party dress, and she has a crush on you. You remember what that was like." She looked at me. "No, I guess you don't."

Does anybody ever get over High School? Sure. I think the real trick is realizing that you're over it. And that's as profound as us broker-types get. I couldn't have a beer anyway until all this was over and the guns were secured, so I muttered, "I made the chicken noises first and mine were better."

The cherubic blonde was at the edge of the dance floor, watching us and talking on her cell phone. She had on four-inch heels, a strapless pink dress with a ruffled skirt and a matching pearl choker. A prom dress on steroids. As I strolled up she was saying, "No, Mr. Eddington asked me about it so I don't think he knows where she was, either. And another thing—" She stopped in mid-sentence and looked up at me.

I clicked my heels together, bowed from the waist and said, "Ms. Miraflores, may I have the honor of the next dance?"

Her eyes widened. She said, "Gotta go."

To be honest, Kaylee was a pleasant armful, warm and cuddly, only giggling once or twice as we moved around the floor and her posse snapped pictures for her site. I was pretty sure she didn't expect it, and I figured, "What the hell," so I kept her out for a second dance. There was a pause while the recorded codger music was replaced by DJ Unit, Eddington's concession to Nadzia. It was timed so a good portion of the money crowd would be gone, and Mr. Unit immediately put on something by the Black-Eyed Peas. This meant that the dancing was mostly hopping around and waving your arms in the air, so I did just fine. A lot of the black t-shirt crowd stared at me open-mouthed, so I know they were impressed. Totally.

After the waving and hopping stopped I offered my flushed and smiling companion my arm. For a second she looked at it blankly; then she slipped her hand around it. I said, "Looking good, kid." She dimpled and did a little half-curtsey, holding my arm for balance, but only a little. Then she pushed a strand of hair back, leaned close and whispered, "Can I talk to you? It's important."

"Well, sure. Let's find Kandi first."

"No, no, she doesn't like me and no, I want to talk to just you." Perfect. Something else to hold against Kandi. Now I wasn't sorry I didn't have a nice surprise for her. So there.

"Hey, we're working, remember?"

"Oh, sure, just blow me off 'cause I'm a kid. I want to help and I can help and, and I'll put the leeches on you." Everybody steals my lines. I turned back to her. "I'm scared, I'm scared for Nadzia. She's into something really bad and she was gone, nobody knows where and she won't tell me and I'm her BFF and she's supposed to tell me everything, and she was gone for a whole day and I think those awful people from the skate park are her new friends and I don't like them, they're here tonight, and she won't let me help and I *can* help." She had to stop for breath.

"I heard she met Baines at a poetry reading."

"She told me she was going to fix things and then she was gone for a day, only when she came back last night she didn't act like it was fixed. She's scared of something."

"Do you know anything about some kind of sample? A germ?"

She shook her head. "You'll think of something." And she looked up at me, believing it. Believing in me. Now what?

We found my date by the windows, talking to an elderly couple, both of whom looked acutely uncomfortable. As soon as we joined them the man muttered an excuse and they hurried off. Kaylee said, "Whoa, what bit the old dudes?"

"Mary, were you talking about your dissertation?"

"Well, he asked." She turned to Kaylee. "It's about clinical responses to media depictions of violence against women. The title is 'C'mon, Baby, You Know You Want It.'"

"*Cool.*"

"That's it," I said. "You dudettes are both *so* grounded. *Totally.*"

Chapter Thirteen   Teen Angel

It happened after DJ Unit had packed up and gone on to another gig. The crowd had started to thin, and Nadzia had taken a position by the main entrance, giving out handshakes and hugs to people as they left. During a lull she sank into a chair under the framed black-and-white of Huntington surfers in the 60's, stuck out her lower lip and exhaled. Her red bangs fluttered and she brushed at them idly before kicking off her electric blue high heels and wiggling her toes gratefully. She saw us standing next to the information desk and winked.

One of the temporary servers brought in to help with the large crowd stopped to talk to her. I turned and looked at Kandi for a moment, because I always like looking at Kandi, and saw her eyes narrow as she glanced over my shoulder. When I turned back Nadzia's face was contorted in anger. Kandi and I were moving as Nadzia started to get to her feet, running as he pushed her back down. She had something in her hand as she grabbed his wrist; he turned, blocking my view and when he moved—we were almost there, so close, so close—he was not running but walking quickly, heading for the front doors and Nadzia was slumped back in the chair as if she were sleeping and we were close, so close. Her wrist slipped off the arm of the chair, the back of her hand brushed the floor and five white petals were knocked off her corsage. They fluttered in the breeze as the door opened. Funny how your mind takes these snapshots, instants of time preserved in amber that stay with you always. Those five soft, white petals fluttering gently to the floor are one of mine. Kandi slid to a stop next to Nadzia, shoved me at the door and shouted, "Go!" before bending over the girl. I never even broke stride.

I straight-armed the door open in time to see the kid in the white jacket jump on the back of a Yamaha dirt bike that was idling in the turnaround. The rain had started. As I took the stairs three at a time, he wrapped his arms around the driver's waist and they took off, swerving around the chain separating the parking area from the cobblestone area in front of the stairs down to the beach. Trevor had backed the Carrera in so the nose was pointing the wrong way. I slid down behind the wheel and turned the keys, thankful that Trevor had followed my instructions and left them in the ignition, started the car and slammed it into reverse and popped the clutch. The ends of the chain scraped across the roof as the Porsche snapped it and I was thankful I traded my convertible for a hardtop. I jumped the curb with no problem, and I slid the car around in a reverse K-turn in time to see the bike bump its way down the stairs to the beach. The space might or might not be wide enough for a car but I didn't hesitate, just pointed the nose down, sliding down the first set of stairs, scraping both walls as I did—the space was not as wide as I'd thought—bounced across the landing and down the next set of stairs. The car bottomed out on the lower level with a tooth-jarring smash, then the tires dug in. The driver of the bike looked over his shoulder, the chase was on and there was a soundtrack. Earlier in the afternoon Kaylee had been riding around with me, getting an interview for her blog, and fiddling in the glove box while mumbling about upgrading my iPod song collection. Now Miley Cyrus was yelling about a fly on the wall as I hit second gear and roared after the dirt bike. The Yamaha crossed the bike path and churned through the sand down almost to the water's edge.

The bike was built for off road work and my sports car definitely wasn't; for one thing the rear engine made the weight distribution all wrong, beyond the ability of the onboard computer to compensate for. I could keep them in sight but I wasn't gaining as we slid around a lifeguard station, heading toward Long Beach. Miley told me I didn't understand and she was right—I couldn't figure it, what the driver had in mind. In a matter of minutes the police helicopter would be overhead, police would be in cars on PCH, and probably on 4-wheel-drive ATVs. An All Terrain Vehicle would run them down easily. Basically I had no reason to chase them because they were as good as caught. I never thought about stopping. Not once.

The back end kept slipping side-to-side as clouds of sand obscured everything. "Fly on the Wall" ended and something by Justin Bieber started. Twice I went airborne, jumping over the ridges of sand built up in winter to keep storm surge from coming in too far. The second landing snapped my head back and the shocks bottomed out with a solid *thunk*! I mashed the gas pedal all the way down and hung on. Hysterical laughter bubbled up as I noticed the little seat belt logo blinking on the dash; Justin and Miley had drowned out the insistent "bong bong." As we swerved down to the hard-pack sand at the water's edge I reached over my shoulder, jerked the harness out and snapped it in place. Seemed like a good idea. Water sprayed behind the bike, covering my windshield and momentarily blinding me. I twisted the wheel and moved up the beach out of the spray.

There was a ridge of sand that would have bogged me down if hadn't been going so fast; instead I went airborne for the third time. There was a loud pop, then the engine redlined, and there was a muffled thud and a burst of heat from behind me. Ahead of me the Yamaha was also flying and I was glad to see that first the passenger, then the driver, were launched into the air. Then I landed, slamming into the shoulder harness—later I would have a belt-shaped bruise—the front and knee air bags deployed with loud bangs, the car did a 360, and settled into the sand. All at once it got very quiet. A moment later I could hear sirens and in the distance a helicopter that I figured was police.

In the movies the stalwart Dan Strongheart jumps right out of the car and races after the bad guy. The reality for me is that you sit there for a minute thinking, "Huh? What happened? Am

I dead?" Then there is a moment when you wonder if you're hurt. After that passed and I decided that I would live, I fumbled with the release, got the shoulder harness unlatched, and found that the door was jammed. I pushed again, harder and it still wouldn't move. Trevor had rolled the windows up and they were frozen, too. That was when I noticed that the seat back was hot and saw the flickering lights in the windshield—the reflection of flames from the engine compartment. I slammed my shoulder into the door and at last it gave a little. I forced it open—it squealed like it was badly twisted—and promptly fell out onto the sand flat on my back. My legs were still in the burning car, spread across the seat, one foot tangled in the shoulder harness, and with deflated air bags draped across them. The impact of falling out and landing on my back snapped my jaw shut and I tasted blood.

I got my legs free, losing both shoes in the process, and lurched to my feet. Thank god for Velcro. My .45 was still in its holster under my tux jacket. I pulled it out and stumbled up the embankment to see that the motorcycle driver and passenger had both survived the crash.

The driver was half-carrying, half-dragging the waiter. They weren't moving very quickly, but then, neither was I. We slogged through the rain, over sand and kelp that had been washed up at high tide, with me gaining slowly. There was just enough light to see by, but not enough to keep me from tripping and falling forward again, this time jamming my face into the sand. The driver, still wearing his helmet, looked back, saw me, and with his free hand pulled out a small pistol and snapped off a shot. I wasn't afraid enough to even duck. At that distance in poor light Annie Oakley would have found it a tough shot. I kept after them.

A minute later he dropped his friend and ran for it.

I sank to my knees next to the guy lying in the sand, carefully staying out of his reach and pointing the gun at him, trying to watch and listen in case his pal decided to circle back and shoot me. He was a kid, early twenties at most, hair puffed in a Caucasian version of what my Dad called an Afro. He was spread on the sand on his back, with one arm at an impossible angle.

"I'm dead. Oh, shit, I'm dead," he mumbled weakly. I pulled his coat aside and saw the white end of a bone sticking out of his arm. Compound fracture. There was a fair amount of blood, but it wasn't spurting, so I thought he'd missed any major blood vessels.

He tried to get up, I put my hand on his chest and said, "Your arm's broken, yeah, but you'll be okay. Why did you try to hurt Nadzia?"

"I'm dead," he said again. "Bitch got me. Bitch got me good."

"Nadzia? How did she get you?"

"But I got her back." His eyes rolled, his hand scrabbled in the sand, then waved in the air as if he were batting at bugs, bugs only he could see; he was suddenly drenched with sweat that ran in little rivers from his forehead down to his ears. His bloody tongue shot out over and over. The bugs came back; he swatted at them with his good arm, but weakly.

"Tell me what you're talking about."

He reared up and clutched at my lapels with surprising strength. "Ask your friend. Ask the Snake. Ask him about five to one." His head lolled back, his legs started to twitch and he let go of my coat. He said, "It doesn't hurt." The spasms spread to his good arm, which waved like he was trying to make half of a snow angel in the sand. Then it all stopped. His back arched. He coughed twice, expelling clumps of frothy pink foam, and died. Just like that, he exhaled, and he didn't inhale. His eyes closed and his mouth sagged open. I probed under his jaw for a pulse and got none. It started to rain again, a steady drizzle soaking into the sand and my jacket and the waiter's body. I closed his mouth. It seemed wrong to leave it open, filling with the relentless rain.

Then I left him laying there on the beach. On the highway above I could see police lights. Above me the helicopter moved toward us from the south, flashing its spotlight. I dove and hid. Called the Snake, cell and land line, got recordings, and remembered I hadn't been able to get him earlier. Called Kandi. "Are you all right?"

"Yes, but—" She didn't sound right. Not right at all.

"One guy's dead. The other got away. How's Nadzia?"

She didn't answer. Instead I got Eddington. "She's dead, Mac. Nadzia's dead. They—" He choked; there were muffled voices. Kandi came back on.

"They pronounced her dead at the scene. No idea yet what killed her. Are you all right?" It took me a minute to process the information. Dead? But she'd surfed Maverick's. How could she be dead?

Adventure? Adventure sucks.

"Mac?"

"Yeah." I literally shook myself. "I'm okay. Put Eddington back on."

"Mac, he—yes, I will."

He came back and mumbled something. I said, "Elijah, listen to me. I know this is terrible, I know you're in pain, in shock, but it's not over. Do you understand? It's not over and I need your help. Please."

People who fold under pressure don't wear championship rings. There was a minute or two when all I could hear was him breathing and faint, urgent conversations in the background. I knew at that moment he was probably hating me a little. Couldn't blame him if he did. "Tell me what you need."

I told him what the killer had said about "Ask the Snake," finishing with, "and he's not answering voicemails. I need to get to Long Beach as fast as possible. I need you to get the police to wait to talk to me about this until I get back."

"I'll deal with the police. Tucker will pick you up." He told me what to do and five minutes later a white Escalade slid to a stop on the northbound side of PCH, with the seven-footer behind the wheel. I stepped out of the shadows and got in and saw that Kaylee Miraflores was in the back seat, clutching her purse and her cell phone. Her first adult party dress was rumpled and wet, her eye shadow smeared down her cheeks.

Tucker said, "I'm sorry, man. She was hiding in the back, I didn't even know she was there till I was almost here. I figured you was in a hurry."

"Kaylee, this is not a good time. Really."

"No shit, Sherlock. She was my BFF." Her lower lip trembled, but she held it together, determined to be a big girl, determined not to cry in front of me. "Go, will you? Drive. Cops will be here." Tucker looked at me. Kaylee said, "Am I talking to myself here? Cops are coming." I nodded to Tucker and the Escalade pulled into traffic, already slowing to gawk at the lights on the beach and the helicopter. She said, "I heard Mr. Eddington talking to you and I want to help."

"Good. Talk to Luke and the others, because all of her friends are going to be upset. We'll drop you at the restaurant." We made a U-turn at 17th Street and headed south. "Where are we going?"

Tucker said, "Cops are setting up roadblocks going north and south, looking for the motorcycle driver, and Big E says they probably would like a word with you, too. We got us a helicopter waiting on the roof of the Hyatt."

Under normal circumstances my jaw would have dropped. I would have had a lot of questions starting with, "Helicopter?"

You know what? At that point I was on overload and just went with it.

The Hyatt Regency Huntington Beach is probably our finest hotel. It's a large, Spanish-Style complex on the inland side of PCH, just south of the Pier, with its own bridge across the highway to the beach. To my knowledge they didn't have a heliport, but like I said, my brain was on overload. We pulled into the Reserved section of underground parking; Tucker nodded to the uniformed hotel security standing by the elevator door, who whispered into his lapel microphone and opened the doors. With Kaylee trailing along, we took a private, express elevator from the parking garage to the roof, where it was windy and about ten degrees colder than it had been on the beach. Sure enough, there was a small executive helicopter waiting with the rotor turning slowly.

Her hair flying in the breeze, Kaylee clung to my arm and said, "Please, take me with you."

"Kaylee, I just can't. See that she gets back." I pushed her at Tucker, who caught her arm, and I ran for the chopper.

"Please, don't leave me here alone. I'm scared and they stole my laptop, too."

That stopped me, made me turn. "What? Like they stole mine?"

"No, what are you talking about? Like they stole Nadzia's."

I grabbed her hand and we sprinted across the roof to the helicopter. "If your father blows my head off with a shotgun it will be your fault."

"How did you know he has a shotgun?" I climbed in, turned and lifted her in after me.

"Lucky guess." I reached across her and cinched her seatbelt down tight. "I don't suppose anybody knows you're here with me?"

"Are you kidding? I sent four texts while we were driving. *Everybody* knows I'm here." Well, that was probably a good thing—maybe "kidnapping" wouldn't be added to "reckless driving," "leaving the scene of a crime," and "material witness."

"Somebody stole your laptop?" She bobbed her head twice while snuffling and smearing her make-up some more. "Any idea who?" Head shake. "Have you told your parents?" Nod. "Okay, I'll make sure you get home. Tell them I said this is as bad as it sounds and they need to take precautions. Give them my cell number."

Seal Beach is north of Huntington, and south of Long Beach, so it seemed like we took off, gawked at all the flashing lights along the coast, and then immediately landed on the roof of one of the aerospace buildings on Seal Beach Boulevard. We took the elevator down to street level, where a black sedan with driver was waiting. Tucker waved the driver off and folded himself behind the wheel.

I caught up with Snake at his small, ridiculously expensive bungalow. About three blocks from the beach, it was built in the forties, and is normal for that time—large lot, small house—white stucco with blue shutters, two bedroom, about a thousand square feet, with a front door that opens directly into the living room. I was able to persuade Kaylee to wait in the car with Tucker keeping an eye on her.

Walter Darlymple, aka The Snake, is my best friend. He's got a degree in physics from Berkeley, but he makes his living as a librarian at CSULB. When we met he was clean-cut and dressed conservatively, long sleeves hiding the "Che Lives" tattoo on his forearm. Then he got tenure, and immediately grew his hair and beard. He's in his sixties, pear-shaped, having successfully avoided all of the exercise programs offered by the university. I walked up the cement path to his front door. It was open and he was inside, sitting on the couch with an unlit joint and a Corona.

After two tries he struck a match and got the joint going. "It was on the web," he mumbled. "Tragic incident at local beachfront restaurant. Film at 11:00."

"Nadzia Kamnik is dead."

He nodded, took a big hit and held the joint out to me. I shook my head. After a long moment he exhaled. "Fuzz say they'll be questioning a 'person of interest.'"

"That would be me."

"Who else? You need a place to stay? Cheryl's gone for a few days."

"No. I need you to explain something." I repeated what Nadzia's killer had said.

"Whoa. Man, he, uh, he actually said my name? He said, 'Ask the Snake?'"

I was watching him carefully now. "Yes. He said, 'Ask him about five to one.'"

My friend didn't miss a beat. "Five two one? What is it, odds on something? Or the combination to a safe?"

"Something about Nadzia is my guess."

He shook his head, drank some beer, took a big hit. "I have no idea what he was talking about. Saw her picture on the news, but I never met her. He probably read articles about you, saw my name and just wanted to mess with your head." He carefully pinched out his joint and put the roach in a metal Altoids tin. "The girl must have gotten mixed up in something nasty and it got out of hand, and then it got her killed."

"Seems that way."

He finished his beer. "Listen, you sure you don't want to crash here, Mr. Person of Interest?"

I stood. "No, I better get back. I'm surprised Eddington's been able to hold off the cops this long."

Snake stood and hugged me. "I'm sorry about the girl, man, that sucks, big-time." He paused. "Listen, if you find out anything about this five two one thing, let me know, will you?"

"Sure."

I spent almost a decade in business, moving large amounts of electronic capital from one place to another, looking for the best return for my wealthy clients. Fields, Smith, and Barkman gave me the Porsche 911 Carrera—my poor Porsche, now sitting on the beach probably waiting to be winched up onto a flatbed—because I was very, very good at a very tough game, and one reason I was good was I had a feel for truth. Nadzia's murderer had been telling the truth, at least as he knew it.

And my friend the Snake was lying. And he knew I knew and he did it anyway.

Chapter Fourteen   Agatha Plumlee

The moment I got outside Snake's house my cell phone vibrated in my pocket. "Elijah."

"I'm at the restaurant and there's someone here who needs to talk to you. And ya'll need to do what she says."

A woman came on. "Mr. Macdonald? This is FBI Special Agent Irene Morse speaking. First, how are you? Were you injured in the car crash?"

"No, I'm okay, thanks."

"There are people who need to talk to you."

"Not surprised at that. Wait, you said, FBI? Why are you involved?"

She said, "Apparently I was unclear. 'Talk to you' is a euphemism for question you. We ask, you answer. Clear now?"

"Show me some ID."

"At present I'm attached to Homeland Security, and the answer to your question is that we have assumed jurisdiction. Local authorities are being very cooperative." She paused. "So, you do not require medical attention?"

"Right. I'm okay." Actually that was an exaggeration. I felt pretty bad, every muscle stiffening up, joints aching.

"All right. Mr. Macdonald, what I need you to do is very simple. Mr. Eddington has a car waiting. Get in it. It will take you back to the helicopter, which will take you to your meeting. The driver will bring Ms. Miraflores home."

"No. I'm responsible for Kaylee. I need to take her home."

"I know how unusual this is, that's why I had Mr. Eddington place the call. If necesary we can force you."

"That might have a higher price than you're willing to pay." I paused, looked around at the quiet neighborhood. "Kaylee first."

"Wait one." There was a pause while she talked to somebody. "Kaylee's father is presently en route and can meet you. Will that do?"

"Where's Kandi?"

"At her request Ms. Shaw was taken to your place of residence after she supplied her statement. And that's it, Mr. Macdonald."

"I'm going to call Kandi and confirm that. And I think I want to do that before I get in the car."

All at once she laughed. "I like your style, Macdonald. You know we really could make you."

"You can try."

She laughed again. "What about the girl?" I said nothing. "Make the call."

Kandi confirmed everything the woman from the FBI said. I called Special Agent Morse back. "I need to see Kaylee and her father together."

"Pacific Coast Highway and Seal Beach Boulevard."

"I'll tell the driver."

"Please. He knows. And, Mr. Macdonald," she paused. "My superiors insist I say this, I don't feel it's necessary. Don't try to do anything foolish."

"You couldn't get rid of me if you tried. Once Kaylee's father picks her up, I'll get in the helicopter." In the back of the car, Kaylee clung to my arm, blue eyes large and staring. That's how I got to meet Mr. Miraflores. I don't think he liked me very much. Given the things I'd gotten his daughter into, I couldn't blame him at all.

I got a few hours of sleep at the Long Beach airport. I could have gone home and slept in my own bed, except I was pretty sure that my new friends didn't want to let me out of their sight. The private terminal actually had small, comfortable bedrooms complete with electric razor, toothbrush and other essentials. A short, fussy, white-jacketed, very British butler showed me to the room and clucked at my clothes. ""Ow do you feel, sir? They told me you was all right, but if I may say so, you appear a bit liverish."

"Where am I?"

"Private terminal, for the swells, mostly. No offense intended, sir."

"None taken. I'm all right, thanks."

"That you are, sir, that you are. You was on the news, wasn't you? Chasin' them people on the beach."

"Yeah. And now after all the rushing around now I'm supposed to rest."

"She don't like to stay up late, she don't."

"Who?" He shook his head. "And she can just tell the police and Homeland Security to wait while she takes a nap?"

He leaned close, spoke very softly. "That and more, sir, that and more." I started to ask another question but he went on briskly. "Just put yer pocket things 'ere on the dresser. I'll do what I can with that tuxedo, but it's seen better days, now hasn't it?" He didn't bat an eye at the Swiss Army knife, the shoulder holster, the .45, or the pool cue handle strapped to my forearm. Beige silk pajamas were laid out on the bed. I called Kandi despite the late hour and found her awake and glad to hear from me. I told her about my unsatisfactory conversation with The Snake, and she had no insights.

"Mac, what are you doing now? Going with these people? I mean—"

"If it was just Homeland or FBI I'd be in their office. It's time we got some answers. Wherever I'm going they have them."

"What makes you think they will answer your questions."

"They want something."

"What about the phone? This one."

"Yeah. They know what I want. Good."

She said the silk pajamas sounded nice, and that I should swipe them. My head was churning when we reluctantly hung up, and I was sure sleep would be a long time coming. I was unconscious in minutes.

Before dawn the phone next to my bed buzzed discreetly. I'd like to say that there was a moment when I felt okay, before I remembered, but I knew everything that had happened the moment I opened my eyes. When I fumbled the handset up to my ear the butler said, "Sir, the pilot says you'll be taking off in a 'mo. I put new clothes and a cuppa outside the door. Them clothes you come in was pretty much ruined."

"Thank you, uh—"

"All part of the service, sir, innit? They says that lunch will be served where you're going but I put some rolls out."

"Thanks."

I shaved, showered, had two cups of excellent dark roast from a silver thermos, three little biscuit-like thingies that might have been crumpets. Whatever they were, they were great. I could have eaten a dozen. While finishing the last biscuit thingie I dressed—black slacks, black loafers with tassels, a black Polo shirt of some silky material, and a gray suede sport coat that was tailored not to show a bulge over my shoulder holster. I wasn't sure if that was a good thing or not.

The butler showed me the way across the tarmac out to the waiting helicopter.

After an hour in the air we were landing in the center of miles and miles of precise rows of grapes. About a half-mile away I could see three buildings, one that appeared to be a mansion, a smaller wooden structure with "Babbling Brook Winery" painted on the roof, and the other a low industrial rectangle. Next to the helicopter a limousine waited, but what a limo! No silly stretch HumVee with chaser lights around the wheel wells, this was a totally mint black 1950's Cadillac with a uniformed driver standing next to the open rear door. The pilot was doing pilot things in the cockpit, and I'd drunk all the coffee. What else was there to do except get in the car?

We drove up to the mansion, where the door was opened before I could knock. A uniformed butler nodded and said, "Good morning, sir. Welcome to Babbling Brook. I am Clark. If you will follow me?"

I don't think I'd ever seen anybody actually wearing an ascot before, at least I think it was an ascot, sort of scarf wrapped around the neck and fluffed out under the chin, but the guy who rose from a deep easy chair to greet me when the butler opened the door to the library had one on, and it had the cutest little pink-and-gray flowers on it. He also had on a burgundy belted smoking jacket with three points of a perfectly-folded white handkerchief showing above the pocket, and dark gray pleated slacks. He had a pipe with a silver band around the bowl in one hand. Very thin light brown hair was parted on the left and combed across a lot of pink scalp. In his late thirties or early forties he looked like a young man training hard to be an old codger.

He stuck the hand without the pipe out at me. "Ah, Mr. Macdonald, so good of you to come."

I expected a limp, moist grip, but his was firm and brisk. "I thought about jumping out of the helicopter, but decided not to. The coffee was good."

"Ha, ha. Yes, yes, I know you must have many questions. My name is Harker. We spoke on the phone."

"That's your pet shark Baines who likes to push around little girls."

"Indeed. His recent conduct is one of the items we need to discuss. On the agenda, so to speak. If you will follow me, please."

He laid the pipe in an ashtray and we went through the great room, which was much lighter and cheerier than I had expected, down a short hall lined with framed posters about various kinds of wine, and out the back door. To the right there was a car barn with room for six vehicles and what were probably servants' quarters above, and directly in front of us on a gravel path a golf cart with driver waiting. He drove us maybe a quarter mile into the vineyard, arriving in a large clearing at the top of a hill. The clearing held a small single story white frame house. Close-cropped lawn, flowerbeds bordering the walk, three steps leading up to a porch complete with swing.

The front door of the storybook house opened directly onto the living room, and when Mr. Ascot ushered me in I was not entirely surprised to see Elijah Eddington III sitting on a green couch with a bird-of-paradise print and white doilies on the arms, long legs stuck out in front of him. He was wearing the same tuxedo he's worn to Nadzia's party, now looking rumpled and creased.

He looked worse than the tux, drawn and tired, with red-rimmed eyes and a day's worth of gray stubble above his goatee. He got to his feet, came to me, tried to shake my hand, but ended up hugging me, sagging, and if you think supporting a 6'7' ex-pro-basketball player is easy, just try it. I walked him back to the couch and let him sink down. For a long moment he buried his face in his hands. Then he looked up, took a deep breath, and said, "Mac, thank you. Thank you. Am I glad you got him? Hell, yes." He gripped my arm and looked up at me and his face was terrible Full of grief and pain and anger. And gratitude. "I don't think I could stand it if he'd gotten away. It's, it's just too much, she rides Maverick's and then this. I'm glad you did it. We'll fix it all. Don't you worry, no. Well take care of everything."

"Elijah, I—"

"I know you must have a lot of questions. I'll tell you everything I know, all of it."

"I didn't kill him."

"Right. Of course."

I sat down next to him. "Elijah, I really didn't. He fell off the bike, laid on the sand with a broken arm, then just looked at me and died. I have no idea why, because his arm didn't look that bad."

"Of course I bel—" then he frowned. "Ya'll *really* didn't?"

"I really didn't."

"But, well, okay, bro, if you say so." He scrubbed fiercely at his eyes and stood. Somehow he looked smaller, older. He looked at Harker, said, "She's in the garden. Tell her he's here." After Mr. Ascot obediently went out the back, Eddington said, "Long flight. Bathroom's that way." I availed myself of the facilities, noting the tiny white octagonal tiles that covered the floor, the pedestal sink with white propeller white hot and cold handles. It didn't look retro and cute; it looked real. I wondered who lived here.

When I came back Eddington was sitting with his face buried again, his shoulders shaking silently. I went back out and came in again, whistling before I entered the room. This time he was on his feet and looked as good as he had before, which was not too good. I said, "How?"

"A stiff wire, we think from a coat hanger, pushed through her ear into her brain. Killed instantly."

"And now the guy who killed her is dead, too."

"And you say you didn't—" I just looked at him. "Okay, yeah. Do you know what a Borgia ring is?" I had an idea, but shook my head 'no' anyway, to see what he would say. "A Borgia ring has a small barb on the inside, with poison on it. The method of delivery is a handshake. The victim feels a tiny scratch, if they feel anything at all."

"Poison?" The death of the waiter began to make sense.

He nodded. "The method of delivery wasn't a ring in this case. It was a flat disk designed to be held in the palm of the hand."

I sat for a moment, digesting the information. "It was Nadzia who had the disk with the poison." Eddington nodded. I sighed. "He tried to show me. He had a scratch on his wrist. Nadzia had the poison?"

A large black man in a gaudy floral sport coat stepped into the room from the back door, followed by a black woman almost as big as he was. They didn't speak, just looked around, then took up positions by the doors and stood quietly, arms loose at their sides. He watched out the windows. She watched us. Eddington said, "Ray-Ray, Edna, this is Mr. Macdonald." They nodded. I nodded back.

Ray-Ray said, "Your gun." I reached under my coat, slid the .45 out of the shoulder holster, made sure the safety was on and handed it to him butt-first. After all, I was there to talk. He double-checked the safety and put it in his pants pocket. I sat down on the couch.

"Well, my goodness, here you are at last." An elderly woman bustled in, pulling off a blue-checked bonnet as she did. Edna stepped forward, took it and placed it on a small table next to a china closet. "Even though it's winter the garden needs attention. I got some nice seeds for next year's flowers, and some gladiolus bulbs."

Harker was right behind her, but I didn't realize that until later. When the old lady entered Eddington stood, and I did too. That much presence radiated from her. She was, quite simply, the most impressive person I'd ever met. Sharp, intelligent blue eyes peered out of a face that was a mass of wrinkles. Her gray hair was pulled back into a braid that hung halfway down her back. She wore a simple gray dress with bits of lace at the cuffs and throat.

She held out her hand. I held it carefully. It felt like a small bird in my grasp. She said, "My name is Agatha Plumlee."

"T. R. Macdonald." I released her hand.

"You boys sit, sit. Take off your coats, just give them to Harker."

We handed our coats to Harker but remained standing. "We'll have a nice chat and then I'll fix us toasted cheese sandwiches." She cocked her head to one side and looked up at me with her clear blue eyes. "Would you like that Mr. Macdonald? I like mine with tomato. I grow my own but this time of year I'm afraid they'll have to be store bought."

I realized that except for the crumpet-thingies I hadn't eaten since last night. "Yes, Ma'am, I'd love a sandwich. Thank you."

She sat in a chair facing the couch. Once she was settled we sat, too. She indicated that I should sit across from her and when I did she patted my knee. "My goodness, a big fellow like you, why, I believe you could eat at least two. However, as my father always said, business before pleasure. Mr. Macdonald—"

"Please, call me Mac, or T. R."

"And you must call me Agatha. T. R., we have been keeping an eye on you for some time."

"I'd like my laptop back, Agatha, that is, if you're finished with it."

She smiled. Her papery skin wrinkled from the corners of her eyes back to her ears, but her sharp blue eyes never left my face, not for a moment. "My goodness, they told me you were quick." Without taking her eyes off me she said, "Of course. Harker, if you would?"

"But, Mrs. Plumlee—"

"Thank you."

He hurried out the front door without another word, almost trotting. Agatha nodded at Ray-Ray. He vanished into the kitchen and came back in a moment carrying a tray laden with cups and saucers in that famous old apple pattern, and a shiny chrome percolator, vintage 1957. When we all were balancing cups and saucers, Agatha said, "Young man, how do you think the world works?"

Okay, not what I expected. I said something really clever like, "Excuse me?"

"Come, come, we know you're a bright young fellow. Who runs the show? Governments?"

"Ma'am, I don't want to be rude but a young woman I care about has been killed."

She sipped coffee. "On a day-to-day basis, yes, of course governments do run things. However, T. R., have you ever considered who runs the governments?" I started to speak but she met my eyes and I found I didn't want to. "We do, at least in the western world. A group of two hundred and thirty-nine families."

All at once it seemed to get colder. You ever have a moment where someone tells you something you don't want to believe, but you instinctively know it's true? Yeah, it was like that. I swallowed. "And these families run the world?"

She smiled gently. "If you mean a secret headquarters buried under the Rockies, lands sakes, no. No, running the world as it's portrayed in silly movies is impossible. Take my word for it. Our mathematicians say there are far, far too many unintended consequences."

"Well, I feel better," and I meant it. "So, what is it you do?"

The smile again. Her bright blue eyes twinkled as she said, "As little as possible, T. R., as little as possible."

"Fascinating. So these families could rule the world, but it's just too much trouble."

Eddington, who had been perched next to me with his long legs pulled up under his chin, and who had contributed nothing to the conversation so far, muttered, "He's got you, Agatha. That's it, isn't it? Just too damn much trouble."

"Elijah, please. I know you have many questions, T. R., and of course we will answer as many as we are able to. However, I believe the simplest approach is for us to tell you what we know, what we suspect, and what we need to ascertain. Afterwards, if you still have questions, like I said, I will try to answer them."

I said, "Yes, Ma'am." She was that kind of woman. I had a brief thought that fifty, sixty years ago she must have really been something. Tailored suits by Coco Chanel, dominating a room simply by walking in. Sipping a Sazerac with the Rat Pack at The Sands.

"It has come to our attention that a weapon is being offered for sale, a weapon that is believed by some to be of great destructive power."

I kept my mouth shut. Nadzia was right.

"I will get to the details at the appropriate time."

"Yes, ma'am." There it was again. Agatha Plumlee simply elicited that kind of response.

"We found out because Roger Winters, despite being incarcerated, was approached for assistance in either finding a buyer or establishing the bona fides of a potential buyer." With difficulty, I restrained myself, merely gritting my teeth and nodding. This got a thin smiled from the old lady. She patted my knee again. "I know, I know, it's difficult for you. When Roger began rather urgent attempts to contact you, it was decided to examine your laptop computer. Ray-Ray and Edna led the team that broke into your home."

They all looked at me expectantly, except for Eddington, who had slumped down and closed his eyes. I drank some coffee. After another smile, she went on. "The path of our inquiries led to some surprising individuals."

It was time to show off a little. "Like Nadzia Kamnik and Kaylee Miraflores."

Eddington lurched forward, resting his elbows on the knees of his rumpled slacks, Agatha Plumlee pursed her lips. Ray-Ray looked out the windows; Edna never took her eyes off me. Harker chose that moment to bustle in with a laptop case hanging off his shoulder.

The silence was broken by my stomach rumbling. We moved to the kitchen and sat around a yellow Formica table. Agatha cooked while we talked. I ate half of my toasted-cheese-and-tomato sandwich in three bites, looked down at my plate and realized someone had eaten the other half. I patted my lips delicately. Agatha set a tray—more apple pattern—with another stack of sandwiches on the table, used a spatula to slide one onto my plate. I took a bite. "By the way, these are delicious."

"Thank you. It's nice to see a young man with a good appetite. Go on, please."

"Well, okay, so you find out about somebody offering this weapon for sale, and Roger's involved because they've gone to him for help. It's a pretty big jump from there to breaking into my house."

Harker started to speak, "I ordered—"

I cut him off. He didn't elicit the kind of respect Agatha did. "No, you didn't."

"I-I don't know what you mean."

"Baines did it. Used your name to get Ray-Ray and Edna to cooperate."

Agatha Plumlee had focused her blue eyes on him and they were no longer warm. He fiddled with his ascot. "It, it was precipitous on his part."

"Precipitous. Ah, yes, one could say that, couldn't one?" Somebody had eaten all of the sandwiches but one. It was time to quit fooling around. "All right, I've had a helicopter ride, coffee, and food. Agatha, lunch was wonderful. Thank you. Now, why am I here? You can't be after information because I don't have any. I have a new laptop, so I don't care too much about the old one, but you know that already. You want me to do something. What?"

Agatha sat across from me and used the spatula to slide half of the last sandwich onto her plate. With a knife and fork she cut off tiny bites, dissecting the half sandwich into pieces which she studied critically before picking up one in her fingers and eating it. "First, you should eat the rest of this sandwich. I will only eat half."

"I don't want to be a pig."

She smiled and slid the remaining half onto my plate. "As I am sure you have surmised, we want you to find Nadzia's killers. The actual murderer is dead, of course, but there are many unanswered questions, and there is a probable link to this mysterious weapon."

I started to call her on a statement that was clearly nuts, but decided to go along, at least a little bit. Maybe there would be dessert. "I'm not an investigator."

No mistake. There was relief in her eyes. "We understand that. But you have had successes in the past. Also, based on what the murderer said before he died, your friend Walter Darlymple seems to be involved somehow. He will talk to you. We have faith in you." She ate another bite of sandwich. "And you're going to do it anyway. You know that. That's the reason you are here today, why you were willing to get on the helicopter. You're looking for all the information you can get." I sighed. Naturally, she was right, except she thought the Snake would talk to me and it didn't seem like he was interested.

"Okay, like you said, I'm looking for all the help I can get, and yes, I would like to find out what happened and why. That's what Elijah hired me for, although he never said so." Eddington looked miserable. "On top of that, the people looking for this weapon have made it clear that they will not leave me alone until they get it. So, okay, for now, okay. We need to talk about Roger Winters. He escaped from Biggin Hill and he's one of the most dangerous people on the planet." Harker started to speak, and again I cut him off. "Trust me on this. He is dangerous."

Agatha said, "We know nothing about that."

Harker looked pale. "Well, um, you see, that might not be entirely accurate."

I said, "Oh, boy. I can't wait to hear this."

He swallowed hard. "I keep the news on in my quarters, you see, and when I went to retrieve Mr. Macdonald's laptop I saw it. Hikers came across them in the hills above Temescal Canyon."

"Came across what?" Agatha asked. I was pretty sure I knew and, when I looked at her lined face I was pretty sure she knew, too. But we both wanted him to say it.

"Um, two, two bodies. The Drivers License of one—"

I finished for him. "Said, 'T. R. Macdonald.'"

Agatha looked at me. "You knew?" She licked her lips. "Did you perhaps—?"

"No. Why does everybody think I go around killing people? Never mind. I knew because Roger told me, or at least he tried to. When I visited him he said, 'I want out.'"

"And?"

"Biggin Hill is a crackerbox to somebody like Roger Winters. He could have knocked those orderlies' heads together and been over the wall any time he wanted. Once out, he'd never be found."

Ray-Ray spoke for the first time. "He's that good?"

"Better. Roger Winters is the single most dangerous human being I've ever met."

Ray-Ray said, "You captured him."

Harker said, hopefully, "That's right."

I smiled sourly. "I got lucky, very, very lucky. Okay, tell us the rest."

"Why, that's all, I—"

I stood up. "Agatha, thank you for a lovely lunch."

"Harker, if you know more, tell us. At once."

He licked his lips, fiddled with his ascot again. "Well, you see, actually, the dead man with your Driver's License? I'm not sure, but, well, I believe I might have recognized him. If he is who I believe, then he is, or was, part of a group, sort of a club, you see, a club that was under the leadership of my ex-assistant, Blondell Baines."

I sat back down. Agatha stood and started putting dishes in the sink. My Dad raised me right. I got up to help. She accepted a plate from me and said, "I believe we need to ask your Mr. Baines about this, don't you?"

Now Harker didn't look nervous; he looked afraid. "That's why I was gone so long. I was calling him and he didn't answer. But his key card shows him on the grounds of the winery."

Agatha looked at Edna and the sweet little old lady was gone. "Find Mr. Baines. Bring him to me." Edna was not helping us with the dishes because she was watching out the back window and cradling an Ithaca 12-gauge shotgun in her arms as if it were her baby. Ray-Ray had another one unobtrusively down by his leg as he spoke softly into a lapel microphone in a language I didn't recognize. A year ago I wouldn't have recognized the weapons, either. Things change fast.

I said, "My gun." RayRay looked at Agatha, who nodded, then handed it to me. I checked the loads, verified the safety was on, and holstered it. "All right, but I do it on my own terms. And the first thing I want is a word with you Agatha, in private."

Ray-Ray looked at his boss. "No."

She dried her hands, carefully hung the dish towel over a hook, and patted his arm. "We'll just walk out back for a bit.

I'll need my bonnet." Edna vanished out the back door. Ray-Ray started to object again. "It will be all right, won't it, T. R.?"

Ray-Ray draped his shotgun over his shoulder and held out his hand. "Gun."

"No." Agatha watched us for a moment, then patted his arm. He gave in and handed her the bonnet. But he never took his eyes off me.

We strolled into the vineyard, between precise rows of shoulder-high vines, old, with thick twisted trunks and branches, each meticulously attached to a cross-like wooden support. Ray-Ray trailed behind us. Edna stepped out from between rows ahead of us and paced in front, watching us over her shoulder. She had hung the shotgun over her back on its strap and now carried some kind of automatic weapon in addition to it. I felt like Michael Corleone. The soil was soft, the surface uneven and white PVC pipes crossed the path at intervals; I offered Agatha my arm and she took it. In the distance I could hear water splashing and the chug-chug of a diesel engine, some kind of farm machinery providing irrigation. The air was fresh, the sky was clear; soon the grape vines would put out new shoots to begin a new cycle of life and we were talking about death.

I said, "It's a good story, you know, holds together well. And a lot of it's true." She stopped walking and peered up at me with her keen little bird eyes. "But you don't really care about Nadzia," she started to speak but I raised my hand. From the corner of my eye I could see Ray-Ray take two quick steps toward us, kicking up little spurts of dust as he did. I dropped my hand. "At least, you don't care about her enough to go to all this trouble. No, you want me for something else. Bait."

"Go on, young man. It's your nickel."

"Our goals may overlap, but they are not identical. All I care about is whoever ordered that wire shoved into Nadzia Kamnik's ear. I don't care about this weapon, and I really don't care about your traitor."

For a moment she looked surprised, but she recovered quickly. "I should have known you would reach that conclusion."

"It took me a while, but I got it. If you just wanted the people behind Nadzia's killing, you'd have Eddington hire professional investigators, or you'd use your influence to make it a high priority with Homeland Security. You're not even that worried about this weapon. You're worried about somebody on the inside, a traitor. This weapon came to your attention at the same time somebody else found out, and they must have inside information. So you fly me here, have this long, highly-visible talk, and turn me loose, hoping whoever it is will make a try for me."

"Will you do it?"

"Hell yes. I wouldn't miss it for the world."

She kissed her fingertips and gently touched my cheek. "Bless you, young man."

Ray-Ray drove me back to the helicopter landing pad in one of the winery's golf carts. Looking at his coat, I said, "Lily Pulitzer?"

He glanced over at me. "Yes, sah, it sure is. It is the only kind of jacket I wear. You know your clothes."

"I had a wealthy client from Palm Beach and his father wore them. You really like Ms Plumlee, don't you?"

He paused, deciding what to say as the bare stalks of grape vines rolled past. In the distance we could see a tour group, about a dozen middle-aged people with cameras and baseball caps, being shepherded around by a slim dark-haired teenage girl in walking shorts and purple Polo shirt, before being taken in to the tasting room. At last he spoke. "There are not many things I would not do for that woman. She took Edna and me out of a very bad situation. Bad situation. You know Kingston?"

"No."

The girl waved as we rolled by the tour group and so did many of the people. We both waved back and I wondered who they thought we were. "Kingston's got lots of folks that ain't very nice. No, sah, some of them, they not very nice at all. We was both young and poor, and in that city, man, that is a bad thing to be, poor. My wife had a problem with a man, a bad man. We both were in jail after I fixed him, and we knew if we was released that bad man's friends would kill us both. Missus Plumlee, she rescued us. Saved us."

"How long ago was this?"

He didn't answer the question. Did not speak another word until I was walking to the helicopter, when he saluted and said, "Good luck, sah."

Chapter Fifteen   Shoebox

"So you agreed? You actually said 'Yes' to this?" Mary did not sound happy. In fact, she sounded totally pissed. It was afternoon. We were seated in my kitchen, back in Huntington Harbour, looking out over the channel and sipping cups of Starbuck's Christmas Blend while my brain struggled to catch up. Fast doesn't begin to describe how things had gone during the last twenty-four hours—first there was the party at Duke's, then the wild chase on the beach, then the helicopter rides and the meeting with Agatha Plumlee. Before I left Babbling Brook Winery Eddington had made a dozen calls and the result was that the cops were letting me off the hook. Completely. I was met by a thirty-something brunette who introduced herself as Special Agent Irene Morse and I dictated a statement to her in the limo that took me from the Long Beach heliport to the Harbour, and everybody was happy. I didn't even have to go in for questioning. It was impossible, but there it was. I wondered just how much pull it took to get that done.

I put down my mug and looked at Kandi. "Agatha Plumlee was right. I was going to do it anyway. At least now we have a budget, which seems to be pretty much unlimited."

"Yes, but, honey, what are you going to *do*?"

"Say again?"

"What are the next steps?"

"Oh. That." I looked at her blankly for a moment. "Well, in the movies I think the PI beats somebody up and makes them talk, you know, gives 'em the old knuckle sandwich till they spill the beans, see?" I waved my fist around. "Those dirty rats can't get away with this. They'll take it and like it."

"You need professional help. And I need to cancel your subscription to Netflix."

"Wanna meet my little friend?"

"I believe I have."

"He's been lonely."

"*Lots* of professional help."

So I turned off the coffee, carried her upstairs and, after getting reacquainted with my little friend, she murmured, "Top o' the world, Ma," and we slept.

The sun was setting when I made fresh coffee and we sat out back on my dock, my feet dangling in the water, Kandi's carefully folded under her, tailor-fashion. She will sail with me, but truthfully, doesn't like water very much. She's that rarity in southern California, a non-swimmer.

We had many important things to discuss, so of course we talked of trivialities—at least, at first I thought they were trivialities. "When you were folding my underwear, what were you thinking about?"

"You mean, other than the obvious? How there could be so many different kinds?"

"C'mon, I'm serious."

"So am I. It's like this endless variety. Not that I'm complaining."

She traced her index finger with its short, unpainted nail, around the rim of her coffee mug. "We're getting pretty domestic here."

So much for triviality. I slipped my arm around her waist. She leaned her head on my shoulder and we watched a small sportfisher rumble by. The guy at the wheel waved and I waved back. "I love you, Kandi."

"Me, too, Sailor."

"But, if you're asking where our relationship is going, I just don't know."

She sagged against me. "Thank God."

"Huh? You're not mad?"

"No. I don't know where we're going either and part of me felt like I should. Remember we were talking about life scripts? Well, the one I was raised on says I'm supposed to want to know, to want you to commit."

"Nadzia said that."

"What?"

"Never mind. You're happy?"

"Well, yes, as a matter of fact I'm happier than I've ever been in my life. Oh, my dissertation is taking longer than I wanted it to, but setting overly-high expectations is normal for me. How about you?"

"No. I mean, yes, oh hell. Kandi, I was supposed to keep her alive and I failed."

"Impossible. They both withheld information. As far as you knew you were just driving the SeaDoo."

I sighed. "I don't think Eddington knew. At least, not exactly."

"He knew more than he told you. Okay, I'll ask you again. What are the next steps?"

"For us, or finding out who wanted Zia killed? I'm not exactly sure in either case."

She said, "Put us on the back burner for a while. I have some things coming up that are going to make it harder. And, oh, shit, I didn't want to say that. Never mind."

"What?" Of course I knew.

"Let it go, please. Not now." I swished my feet around a little in the water, nodded. She sighed in relief, then said, "Well, in the movies the PI goes to some sleazy underworld contacts and asks questions."

"I think this is where we left off, only I said it and then—"

"Watch it, big guy."

"It could work. So, do you have any sleazy underworld contacts? You work in a bar."

"Nope. You?"

"Me either. The sleazy criminals I know are all corporate."

"Okay, then we just wait for somebody to try and kill you."

"You know how you say you don't like my plans? I have to consider that a fallback position. 'Ask the Snake.' The dead guy said it, just before he died, and I just keep coming back to it."

"And when you asked him Walter says there's nothing."

"And my friend is definitely holding out on me."

"How do you feel about that?"

"How I feel doesn't matter. Okay, let's work back. That day there's the party on the yacht."

"We meet a bunch of people."

"Yes." I got to my feet and started walking back and forth on the dock. She twisted her head around to watch me. "Snake's friends from Berkeley."

"The Jamie Lee Curtis lookalike lives in Belmont Shore. She tracked Walter down on Facebook. What were their names?"

"Henrietta Graveline, Brad Zucco, and Lisa June Culhane. All of them Berkeley in the sixties. Brad was a business major, Lisa June French lit, and Henrietta was microbiology."

"Wow, Sailor, I'm impressed."

"Parlor trick. Anybody can learn to remember names and basic information about people if they work at it. Graveline's the one that looks like Jamie Lee Curtis, Lisa June could have been a model. And I saw Brad and Henrietta for a beer at Perqs. In fact—" I called Chet. He was going over security videos from Nadzia's party.

"Pard, we got zero from the regular cameras—"

"I hear a 'But' coming."

"The kid, Kaylee, sent me something. Check your email. I think Kandi should see it, too."

It was less than fifteen seconds. Amazing that Kaylee found it out of all the videos. It showed Lisa June Culhane talking to Blondell Baines. Faith Valentine walked up, words were exchanged. Lisa June turned and walked away.

Kandi watched it three more times. Then she sat and stared out of my kitchen windows. "She asks him to dance. He laughs at her."

"Wow."

"Kaylee saw it, too. She understood."

I said, "They know each other, Culhane and Baines."

"That gown! Wow! Spectacular, flamboyant. Not many women could carry it off at any age. And I remember now. Lisa June *was* a model, in the seventies, she told me about it. Her claim to fame is she actually worked with Lauren Hutton. And Brad Zucco is holding on to his youth with a shaved head, goatee dyed brown, and board shorts."

"And he's piloting a yacht worth over four million dollars. Drives a Shelby Mustang, yellow with blue racing stripe. Told me all about it." That made me think of cars. I looked at my watch. Unfortunately, the New York office of Fields, Smith, and Barkman was still open. "Well, might as well get it over with. I'll have to tell them about the Porsche sooner or later."

Kandi snickered. "You could call Roger Winters' father. He still owns several dealerships."

"Right. 'Hey, Mr. Winters, your son went to the nut house, and you nearly went to prison because of me, so—how about a deal on a car?'"

"Don't forget he thinks you tried to seduce his wife. But, you didn't let his son die when you had the chance and a good reason."

"The seduction was the other way around." Something clicked. "You know, he went to Berkeley, too. Roger told me."

"Roger's father? Happy Winters is a Berkeley alum? Whoa, Sailor, mere coincidence or proof of ancient astronauts?"

Bernice, my boss's Executive Assistant, answered on the first ring. "Fields, Smith, and Barkman, Mr. Barkman's office."

"Quick, I just got a golden parachute and I'm looking for a hottie to run away with me to a tropic isle where we'll sit by the lagoon and I'll strum my ukulele."

"Would I have to wear one of those coconut-shell tops? They look uncomfortable."

"The sound you hear is me drooling on the phone."

"What, again? You need to talk to a physician about that. Sorry, no deal. Mac, I was just going to call you. Guess what?"

"You came back from lunch with Barkman and your underwear was on inside out—again."

"I told you about that?"

"Bernice, you tell me everything."

"That's what you think. Hey, you want to hear this or not? It's about your car."

Panic set in. "The Porsche? Right. Prize, Trader of the Year, that's me, and I know the lease is up soon and I'm supposed to return it, but there's been an accident—"

"You took it off-road chasing some bad guys and totaled it."

"Oh. You know."

"I know everything. Ervin says you get a new car, pick whatever you want, within reason."

"Bernice, that's not funny. Barkman hates me." Ervin Barkman is a senior partner in our boutique brokerage. He and I do not get along.

"True, but this afternoon we got a check by courier and he had me put it in your account."

"He's delusional, isn't he? Howling at the moon?"

"You wish. No—and, hey, you didn't hear this from me—he got a call from the Zurich holding company that owns the insurance company that covers the FSB vehicles. There was some shouting on his part, then it got quiet, and then he came out of his office and told me the courier was on his way with a cashier's check, what to do with the money, and to call you. He looked, uh, like he'd just swallowed something *really* nasty. Mac, are you going to tell me what's going on?"

"Are you going to wear the coconut-shell top?"

"You're a rat."

"Yes, but I'm a rat who gets a new car."

"Rat I said and rat I meant. Okay, I remembered you had a client, a car broker—"

"You know Donna Lee?"

"I told you I know everything."

Bernice may be having wild animal nooners with our mutual boss, but that doesn't mean she isn't extremely good at her job. A few months ago, when the call came in about Diana, asking for me but providing no information, she somehow knew it was important, and left her desk to drag me off the trading floor to talk to the Harrison Clinic, where my wife had just been delivered after a near-fatal overdose.

"Donna Lee is expecting your call. Ciao."

Kandi said, "What was that all about?"

"Hmmm? Oh, a new car. And, I'm pretty sure, a message from Agatha Plumlee."

They took me in the parking garage under Slam Dunk Management and they made it look easy.

Kandi had dropped me off on her way to work so I could pick up a car. Eddington was lending me one of his pearl-white Escalades until I could connect with Donna Lee and get wheels of my own. I went upstairs, picked up the key and said hello to Elijah, and when I stepped out of the elevator in the garage there was a messenger leaning his bicycle against the wall. He had the usual bike shorts, skin-tight shirt in day-glo green, helmet and delivery pouch. I held the door for him; he said, "Thanks, man," reached out and touched my arm with something. It was like sticking your tongue into a wall socket—just wham! Good night, Mac-boy.

When the world came back I was sitting in the passenger seat of a big car. I could see the pearl-white hood. Aha! I figured it was the Escalade, the one I was borrowing. My seat was reclined, my head was lolling back, and I didn't feel well. In fact, I felt like shit and I'd drooled on my Polo shirt. Faith Valentine, Chooch and Rod stood back a few feet. The messenger was next to them, straddling his bike. They pulled me out of the car, turned me around to face it and Rod sucker-punched me in the kidneys. The car window smacked me in the face. Faith stepped up and decked him, which was fine with me. Just like that, a blow to the side of his face that dropped him to the cement. I mumbled, "I was just going to do that." Rod struggled to his knees, head dangling and glared at her for a moment, then swallowed and said, "Sorry."

"Mr. Baines wants to talk to him." She rubbed her hand, smiling, bent and gently kissed her gloved knuckles. She took a cell phone out and spoke into it briefly.

Chooch leaned over, got in my face and whispered, "This close enough to the swing set, asshole?"

"New shoes?" I looked down and he stepped back quickly.

After that they didn't say anything, the four of them just watched me lean against the car, and since Faith had already decked Rod I didn't feel the need to attack them. The familiar black stretch limo came down the ramp, the messenger dismounted, leaned his bike against the wall and opened the door. Blondell Baines was in the back seat, talking on a cell phone. He put it away and said, "Please get in, Mr. Macdonald. I want to talk to you."

"Call my office. I can fit you in next year."

"Anybody ever tell you you're not as funny as you think you are?"

"Every now and then, yeah."

"You should listen. Okay, the point of this was to send a message, and, in case you missed it, the message is we can take you whenever we feel like it. We keep trying to communicate here, and you don't pay attention. Okay, this is done, over. Water under the dam, right? You can go if you want, but we can trade some intel if you get in the car. What do you say?" He smiled, his Boy Scout face breaking into a bland Boy Scout grin, as if to say, 'Aw, shucks, using the stun gun on you was just horseplay between us guys, maybe a little rough but really no worse than those buzzer things that you hide in your palm before you shake hands.'

I hauled myself off of the Escalade, only exaggerating how much I hurt a little when I tripped and went to one knee. The tall one stepped forward and helped me up—big mistake. I could have taken him with the edge of my hand to his throat or, if I'd been in a good mood, just laid him out with my pool cue handle which I could still feel strapped to my forearm under my jacket. Instead I stumbled into the back seat of the limo. Faith Valentine had shifted position slightly, bringing her purse closer to her right hand; okay that confirmed her as the pro. The messenger closed the limo door and it got quiet. Baines was silent a moment, looking out at his people. He pushed a button, the window next to me hissed down and he motioned her over. "Faith, have the guys spread out. And keep your eyes open." The window hissed up and it got quiet again. Baines had on black slacks, a lime green sport coat and a black t-shirt. His slicked-back hair glistened. He said, "Listen, sorry about roughing you up, but sometimes things like that just gotta happen. I wanted to send the message, and the stun gun made The Rod feel better. He was pretty pissed about getting buzzed at the skate park. Gotta keep the troops happy, right?"

I wondered how happy the Rod was after being punched by Faith. "Happy troops are—happy. Right." I finished lamely. I wasn't feeling very well.

Baines nodded enthusiastically, then stared over my shoulder at his troops. He frowned. "What do you think of those guys?"

"They're my new best friends. I feel like we've really bonded."

"They talk about me while you were waiting?"

"Baines, I was unconscious. Then Rod punched me and Faith decked him."

"She's the only one I trust. The others—I think they've got something in mind, except they ain't that smart." He rolled down the window again and waved his troops over. "What are you people talking about?"

They looked at each other. Chooch said, "Uh, nothiing."

"Nothing what?"

"Nothing, Boss."

"Get back to work."

"Yessir." But the window was already going up.

He shook himself. "Okay, listen up, pal, here's the deal. There's a weapon floating around out there, you know that, but what you don't know is I got a buyer for it. Help me get it and there's a nice piece of change in it for you." He twisted open a bottle of water and gulped some down. "And this is for a good cause. When I found my dynasty we'll do good works. Children's hospitals, shit like that."

"And if I don't?"

He looked pained. "Nobody cooperates, you know that? Nobody ever says, 'Sure, I'll help.' Why is that?"

"Well, in my case, it's because I don't like you."

"I knew we'd get to this, I just knew it. Everybody's out for themselves. You got plans of your own, right? Well, forget it. Listen, I coulda had those guys whack you but I didn't, okay?"

Yes, he actually said, "Whack."

"I don't suppose it makes any difference that I have no idea what you're talking about?"

Now he really looked pained. "For your sake, pal, I hope you don't mean that."

"Why did you kill Nadzia?"

"That was a mistake. I mean, I mean, whoever ordered it, you know, they made a mistake. Hey, you should be grateful, okay?"

"She was supposed to kill me, wasn't she? Only she changed her mind."

"Maybe. Maybe not. Anyway, you're alive, okay? So, do we have a deal here or what?"

The smart thing to do, of course, was play along and see what I could learn. I didn't feel like being smart, in fact I was sick of it. "So I ask myself, what's changed, why don't you want me dead anymore?"

"Just be grateful. Let it go."

"And the answer comes back that you're losing people. Nadzia—"

He licked his lips. "Pal, you really need to shut the fuck up here. I already said it was a mistake. You could be causing yourself some real problems."

"—the guy who killed her, the two people who broke Roger out, you practically admitted they were yours, and—most important—Roger Winters himself. You wanted him, you got him out, and you lost him."

"We'll find him."

I laughed in his face. "Roger Winters? Not likely. He likes weapons—hands, sticks, explosives, you name it. He killed your people because they became inconvenient. The only way you'll find him is if he wants you to and, trust me, you won't like it if he does." Baines leaned back and looked at me speculatively, drumming his fingers on his knee, and I had a very bad moment, wondering if I'd pushed too hard. True to form, I plowed ahead. "Working for you doesn't seem very healthy. I'll pass, but keep my application on file."

"Not working for me is less healthy. Maybe not just for you. We're done here. Get out, please."

"I know it's biologic, some kind of germ, but where did it come from?"

"Get out." When I didn't move, he lost it, just like at the skate park. His eyes widened until the whites showed all the way around the iris, his nostrils flared and an ugly red flush moved from his shirt collar to his hairline. "I said get out," he screamed, "and I want you to know that I've just about had it, right, yes, I've just about had it with people not doing what they're supposed to!"

"Baines, listen—"

"Shut up! Shut up! Shut up! *You* listen! I'm talking and when I talk people better listen, oh, yes, they better listen because I have had it with people ganging up on me and laughing behind my back and not listening. Those days are over, pal, you understand me, *over!*"

"I understand, I—"

"Over! Over! Over! Shut up! That's over!" He was panting for breath. Saliva flecked his lips and chin. All at once his fingers, which had been scrabbling at the upholstery, went limp. He took a deep breath, closed his eyes and when he opened them he smiled. Another deep breath. "I'm glad we could talk and that you understand. You're free to go. I'll give you two days."

There must have been some kind of a signal, a button maybe, because the door next to me was jerked open and this time I hopped right out of that car. As the fake bike messenger reached out to the door I called out, "Let's do lunch." Baines just stared. The messenger closed the door, the limo did a quick K-turn and hissed up the ramp.

I could have jumped the other ones, I mean, there were only four of them, right? Three men and Faith Valentine. But I wasn't feeling very good, and they were probably all tougher than me, so instead of beating them up I staggered to my borrowed Escalade and watched as the guy who had stunned me pedaled up the ramp to the street. The others got in an anonymous white Toyota and left. I sat for a moment, then went home.

Donna Lee called the next morning. I hadn't needed the Escalade after all. "Mac, you never call, you never tweet."

"Hey, Donna Lee. How's the car biz?"

"I get by, I get by. No tests to grade, you know? Say, did you hear John Holmes is selling real estate?" Donna Lee is a friend and a client. She taught high school Algebra for thirty years, until her feet got so bad from standing on a cement floor all day that she retired. About that time her husband ran off to Micronesia with a flight attendant named George; Donna Lee discovered that she hated retirement, and one day, when she went to lease a car, she thought, "I can do that." Now she's one of Orange County's most successful car brokers, specializing in what is known as "exotics." She has also become somewhat earthy. "I'd buy a house from John Holmes. Hell, yes. 'Prove it wasn't trick photography—flop that bad boy out and it's a deal.'" She cackled. "So, I hear you need a car, and this Bernice person—she sounds nice—says you practically have a blank check. What's the story? You have pictures of this guy Barkman in Central Park with his hog out?"

"What *is* it with you and male organs?"

"If you'd been married to Tuck," she said darkly, "Why, he—"

"Donna Lee, way too much detail! Just tell me about the car."

"Look at the pictures attached to the email I sent. I know you're a car guy, thought you might like something a little different. The owner's a woman who just joined my support group, and she wants to dump this car."

I opened the pictures and whistled. "Wow, she's beautiful, but old."

"Nope. Hubby had it built, and he spent a fortune. Steel body, built like a 1955 Shoebox Chevy, sits on a Corvette chassis, Chevy small block mill putting out three hundred horsepower. Mac, I have driven this little beauty and, believe me, she will pick up her skirts and *scoot*."

"I love it."

"I'll have it delivered this afternoon."

"If I'd known it would be this easy I could have saved myself a lot of trouble."

"How so?"

"Long story."

She was a two-tone, four-door hardtop, cream top over slate blue with mild pinstriping, a tan interior, bench seats, and an automatic shift mounted on the column to keep the stock appearance, but the mag rims and oversized tires were a giveaway. I signed the papers, arranged for Eddington to have somebody pick up the Escalade, and tooled around in my new hot rod for a while, picked up Alys Winters at school—as I idled at the curb waiting for her and keeping an eye out for her psycho brother Roger, the car drew an admiring crowd—and delivered her home safely. Then I went home and called Agatha Plumlee. After I related my encounter with Blondell Baines she said,

"T. R. I must say I'm just a bit disappointed. We expected this to happen, and that you would deliver Mr. Baines to me. So, I assume you have a plan?"

"A plan? Sure. Don't worry, this is all part of it. We've got him right where we want him."

"Young man, I worry about you."

"By the way, thanks for arranging for the car. Let me guess, you own the company."

"Lands sakes, no. Harker informs me one of my cousins owns a controlling interest in the banks that own the insurance company. And that is the most you will ever learn about our financial dealings. You are welcome; it was the least we could do. So, tell me your plan."

"I'm going surfing. Afternoon glass-off."

The fabled glass-off, when the wind dies and the surf get smooth, never materialized. It was choppy, blown out, cold and nasty. Suited my mood perfectly.

Chapter Sixteen Paddle-Out

A day went by when nothing happened, and it made both of us nervous. I had no idea how to proceed, except wait for someone to try to kill me. Oh, sure, we were doing the usual stuff. Chet was looking for Baines and Valentine electronically, I talked to The Snake, and Agatha's connections got me a copy of the police report on Nadzia's murder. Baines and Valentine didn't use credit cards that we knew about, Snake had nothing to add, and the kid who killed Nadzia had no record. We both kept guns handy and never went out alone. Then I got the text.

```
KAYLEE M
Mac U home? MUST see U!
Pick me up at school! 3:15.
```

So Kandi and I took my new-old Chevy out of the Harbour, up Warner to Bolsa and picked her up in front of Marina High, and drove back to the Harbour. Kaylee didn't talk, just huddled between us in the front seat clutching her pink-and-white backpack to her chest. Since the Chevy only looked retro, it came with air bags and a seat belt for the middle passenger.

Back at the house we sat around my kitchen table, with Kaylee still holding the backpack in front of her. I didn't bother hiding the fact that I had a gun stuffed into the small of my back, just took it out and carefully set it on top of the refrigerator. I got her a bottled water. She took a gulp, choked a little, and nodded thanks. "All right, I'm scared and I have to do something and I don't want to do it by myself, so thanks, okay, thanks."

Mary said, "Do your parents know you're here?"

"They think I'm at soccer practice."

Mary put her hand over hers, "Kaylee, you don't have to do anything you don't want to. We're here for you."

She glanced at Mary and muttered, "Shit, I'm all warm and tingly." Then she looked up at me. "Sorry." She laughed, only it was a sound more like a sob, pulling her laptop out of her backpack. "Sometimes you have to do it anyway don't you?" She looked at me. Kaylee was one of those kids you look at and see potential, enormous potential that she hid behind attitude. She had the brains and the drive, and she'd get over being chubby and grow into beautiful. Now she was truly frightened, perhaps for the first time in her life, and she didn't like it.

I said, "Yes. Sometimes you have to do it anyway."

Mary sniffed

Kaylee licked her lips, working her way up to saying it, then blurted, "I got an email from the girl. Today. Z set it up with a delayed send, and it's got this video attached, and she says to show it to you."

"And it scares you. What scares you about it?"

"She's *dead*, isn't she?" Her water was gone. "Can I have something else to drink? Got any Diet Mountain Dew?" Kandi got her a Diet Coke from the fridge. She stretched a point and took it, rolling the cold can across her forehead before she started. "The girl was into something bad, really bad, and you know, I thought the cops would find who killed her and then you killed him anyway and I thought it was over only it's not and—"

I looked out the windows at the still channel water, rippling with the typical afternoon breeze. Tomorrow was Nadzia's paddle out.

"First, you better read the email."

Kaylee if your reading this some very bad shit has happened and I have to tell you about it. Don't show the video to anybody but Mac. Do whatever he tells you. I'm really really sorry this happened. Be good. Do your homework and don't stay up too late. Z.

The video looked like it had been shot in a hotel room. Stationary camera, probably placed on a table or nightstand. We could see part of a bed, bland walls, bland paintings, a short hallway that probably led to the door. Nadzia was wearing a white terry cloth robe. She started out sitting on the bed, but got up and paced, sometimes moving out of the frame. This is what she said.

"Hey, Kaylee, hey, Mac. Um, well, shit. Shit. If you're watching this it means I messed up, bad. I'm probably, uh, probably dead. I saw this in one of the *Scream* movies, you know, where this guy gets killed but he sends a video to warn his friends." She moved out of the frame, came back in, sat on the bed. "Okay, look, this thing everybody's after is real, at least I think it is and I think it's bad. I just met these people at a reading, you know and they were talking and it sounded good." She paused, took a deep breath and faced the camera squarely. "I was mad, okay, totally, totally pissed. My parents had gone off to wait for the end of the world and left me behind and I was mad so I helped them. I mean I helped these people. I did it. I did it and I'm not going to say I'm sorry. Okay, they lied to me. The people who said if they got this germ thing we could use it to change the world, and they said it wouldn't kill people but they laughed at me when I found out what was really going on and told them it was wrong. Anyway, look, they showed me a lab and I was blindfolded but the van drove inside the building so it was big, like a warehouse. Test tubes and, oh, shit I'm so scared and I'm sorry I got all of you into this and I love—" She lunged at the camera, arm outstretched. The screen went dark. We never did learn who she loved. Everybody, I guess.

We watched it again. I copied it to my new laptop. Then we took Kaylee home. Her father was standing at the door when we drove up in the Chevy, so it seemed he had figured out that soccer practice wasn't happening.

Tomorrow was Nadzia's paddle-out.

A paddle-out is how surfers say goodbye to one of their own. As many as feel compelled to get on their boards and stroke out past the break line, usually in silence, sometimes with low conversations about the lost one. Once outside, they form a circle, the swells rock the boards up and down, and they share stories—times the lost one was locked in the tube, classic wipe-outs, beach parties, the good times. The stories go on as long as necessary. The surf always goes on, sliding endlessly toward the shore, toward those who will never understand what it is like to try to learn to surf and in the early stages to think, "I'll never get this," and then if you're persistent, to one day think, "I can do this," as you drop in and make your first turn.

Sometimes at Huntington there's a current that requires constant paddling to maintain position but today there was none.

I borrowed a nine-foot longboard, a classic, blue with a white stripe and a balsa stringer, and an O'Neill fullsuit for Kaylee, perched her on the nose and we paddled out on the north side of the Huntington Pier to say goodbye to Nadzia. Kandi watched from the Pier. It was late afternoon and the surf was small and glassy, so clear that as we bent low over the board the setting sun shone through the unbroken wave, a sight of incredible beauty that I never tire of.

Skateboards, along with bicycles, are not allowed on the Pier. If you break the rule, a lifeguard comes on the loudspeaker and tells you to walk your board or bike back to the street. Today was an exception. From the waterline to Ruby's the rail on our side was lined with Nadzia's people, shoulder to shoulder. Each skater stood silently, holding their plank against their side, one end grounded. As the line of surfers paddled out past them, hoodies were pushed back, knit caps were swept off, baseball caps removed.

There were so many of us on surfboards that we formed two concentric circles, about twenty boards in each. We held hands while we talked. Luke and a few others spoke. Kaylee tried to, choked, shook her head. Finally, staring down at a clump of kelp drifting past the nose of the longboard, she straightened and said clearly, "Nadzia Kamnik was my friend. I loved her. I still love her. She made me a better person. I'm glad she got to ride Maverick's." At that last I had to splash water on my face. Well, it was hot in my full suit and I had started to sweat and it was running into my eyes. We all threw our flowers into the circle, the petals rested on the swells. and that was it. Nadzia was gone.

They were waiting for me on the beach, standing on the sand, shading their eyes against the glare, obviously uncomfortable. He was tall, pushing seven feet, with sideburns and gray hair combed over a large bald spot. His suit was navy blue, looked like it had been expensive but now showed shiny spots at the knees and elbows. The woman next to him was tiny, 5' 2" at most. Her below-the-knee skirt was also navy, her white blouse frayed at the cuffs but clean, with a large bow at the throat Her hair, blonde with some gray at the temples, was pulled back into a bun at the nape of her neck. I knew who they were at once. Kaylee was struggling with her wetsuit zipper. I pulled it down for her and said I needed a few minutes with these people. I tucked the longboard under my arm and walked over to them.

He said, "Mrs. Kamnik, please wait in the car."

"Yes, Mr. Kamnik."

One of Elijah's seemingly limitless supply of tall black guys was waiting at the foot of the stairs, the same ones I had taken my Carrera down only a few nights ago. Nadzia's father watched until Mrs. Kamnik was next to the tall black man, with him holding her elbow as they trudged up to street level. When he was satisfied he turned to me and said, "I was tempted by

Mammon, and I was weak. The Almighty showed me the error of my ways and I repented."

We started walking up the beach, me carrying the longboard. He limped slightly on his left leg.

"Mr. Kamnik, I just don't know what to say, except that I am very sorry. Your daughter was a good person."

"No, sir, not yet she wasn't, but she might have repented in time. Now she has lost that opportunity. That opportunity is gone forever."

What do you say to that? He pulled a business-sized envelope out of his coat pocket and held it out to me. I saw a return address, "Surf Motel, Huntington Beach" carefully lined out. "This is two hundred and fifty-three dollars. I want you to find the man responsible. Bring him to man's justice before he faces The Lord's."

"Mr. Kamnik, I can't, I—"

"I know it's not enough, but we can send more. Mrs. Kamnik does alterations and I have a job."

Up on PCH a double line of Harleys roared by, smoke and lightning, the sound temporarily drowning the surf. He was looking at me with something close to desperation. I took the envelope. "No, sir, you don't need to send more. You've hired yourself a detective."

Later, on the beach, I talked to Kandi.

"I wanted to hate them, you know? They ditched their own daughter. But, you know what? Who am I to judge? I got that offer to move to the Manhattan office and I jumped at it; big promotion, big bonus, lots of money. I *jumped*. And I left Diana behind." Left unsaid was anything about Chicago. We hadn't mentioned it since her return from UCLA.

"Mac, it's not the same, really, it's—"

Kaylee came back from the Ladies. Sitting in the shoebox 55, with the salt water rinsed off and warm in dry clothes, Kandi and I in front, Kaylee in back, I turned and asked, "So, where did Nadzia hang out?"

"Frac."

"Exactly. 'Frac' sums it up."

Nobody laughed. It occurred to me that maybe I might not be as funny as I thought, but of course that was silly. Kaylee stuffed her pink tissue into her purse and said, "Cranial Fracture. It's a skate shop, but I know the cops have been there because it was a hot thread on KayleeTalks. Lots of kids got interviewed."

"Let's go."

Cranial Fracture, or 'Frac" as it was known to the in crowd, was located in a garage in old Huntington Beach, about a mile inland from Main Street. I don't mean a building where you parked your car; I mean where the business had been brake jobs and oil changes, and where the cement floor still had oil stains. The glass storefront was covered with stickers and posters of skate tricks; inside the walls were covered with planks—skateboard decks to the uninitiated—with a wide variety of designs, mostly drawings of skulls, snakes and guns, with the occasional hottie in a short skirt or a thong bikini for variety. Three huge circular clothes racks held shirts, all black or plaid, shorts, and had mounds of caps piled on top. Thrash metal blared while flat screens hanging from the ceiling showed clips of kids doing impossible things on snowboards, skateboards, scooters, and BMX bikes. A glass-topped counter ran across most of the rear, filled with brightly-colored skateboard wheels and silver trucks. The young woman who came out from behind the counter to greet us was in uniform—black tank top hacked off to show a lot of midriff, frayed cutoffs short enough for the bottom of the front pockets to stick out, and multi-colored bracelets from wrists halfway to her elbows. Her head had been shaved a few days ago, but the tattoo of a woman's hand holding a double-barreled shotgun showed clearly through the bleach-white stubble. However, instead of sullen we got a perky smile and, "Hi, I'm Bridget. Yes, sir, may I help you?"

"Hi, Bridget. My name is T. R. Macdonald and I was wondering—"

Her eyes widened. "I *knew* it was you, I did! I knew it!"

"I'm not Justin Bieber, despite the resemblance. I'm a friend of Nadzia Kamnik's."

She had her cell phone out and was frantically texting. "You're the guy who helped Z! And today was her paddle-out and I had to work but I watched it on YouTube and I cried. You drove the jet ski. And you chased those guys, right? The ones that, uh . . ."

"That was me. Yeah, I chased them."

For a moment she stopped texting and just stared. Then, softly, "Wow. Oh, wow."

"Bridget, I understand Nadzia hung out here, and—"

She was nodding before I could finish the sentence. "Yeah, yeah, she sure did. She'd come in and sign kids' decks and stuff, you know it was really cool. She never got pissy about it and she'd stay as long as they wanted. Are you like, investigating what happened? Wow. That's cool, that is *so* cool, but, you know, the cops have been here and asked everybody lots of stuff."

"I just wondered if maybe there was something else, anything at all."

"Can I see your gun?"

"No, but I have a sawed-off pool cue handle I'll show you." Kandi kicked me in the ankle. I wish she'd quit doing that. Bridget looked confused. We stood for a moment while I tried to think of another question. I couldn't so I turned to go.

"Wait, wait. Look, the cops talked to Ricky and I didn't get to hear what they said. He's out back and I guess you could talk to him."

"Let's do it."

Ricky was a skinny blond kid trying to grow a soul patch, wearing duct-taped tennies, tight plaid pants and a black Metallica tank top. He was doing verts off a homemade wooden half-pipe set up in the parking lot behind the shop, getting some pretty good air. We got his attention and he took a break. Bridget was watching the whole thing, alternating between whispering into her cell phone and using it to take pictures. We were going to be the topic at the Westminster Mall food court as soon as she got off work. Totally.

Ricky kicked the tail of his board up and caught the nose, spinning the wheels and listening to the bearings as he talked. "The van, man, that's what I don't get, you know. She got in the back of this van, like a delivery van, you know, and they drove off. Out back, here, you know."

I said, "Did you recognize the people she went with?"

"Nope. Old." That meant over thirty.

"Ever see the van before?"

He spun the wheels, thinking. "Maybe. Maybe once."

I was stumped. Kandi said, "But it must have struck you as odd because you remembered it. Why was that?"

Kandi he looked up at, dragging his attention away from his wheels, and smiled. Shrugged. "Dunno. Just did."

I said, "You said she got in the back. Did she open a door or did someone open it for her?"

"Dunno, I—wait, yeah, the back doors opened and she climbed in. And, whoa, I got it! Her board, she left her board here. I saw it over there against the wall so I took it inside and gave it to Bridget to hold. She never does that, man, *never*."

"Okay, thank you, Ricky. You've been a big help."

"Sure, glad to help. I took it inside for her, her board. I didn't want nobody to bag it, you know."

I looked at Bridget, who shook her head. "Video?"

"We had a camera back here but it got broken."

Ricky lowered his voice. "It was the old people next door. Betty's."

"Betty's Used Boards?"

He snorted, "Huh. Not just boards, man. They, like, hate us."

Bridget said, "Totally."

So we paid a visit to Betty's Used Board Plus.

Chapter Seventeen   Betty's Used Boards

When we opened the front door a little bell tinkled. They needed it—this was not exactly a bustling surf shop. In fact, we were the only customers, and looking at the dusty boards racked untidily against the wall I could see why—these sticks were all beaters, none without gray spots where serious dings had been patched, some with dings waiting for patch treatment. A glass-topped display case with cash register on top separated the rear quarter of the shop; behind it a doorway covered with strings of beads led to rear rooms. The first thing I noticed after the sad surfboards lining the walls was how much smaller this was than Cranial Fracture. There was a significant amount of floor space behind those beads. Signs over the counter advertised safe, economical, tanning beds and therapeutic massage for sports injuries. Betty's Used Boards seemed to offer a number of services.

A woman I judged to be in her late fifties came out of the back room. Kaylee suppressed a snort followed by a giggle and I could feel Kandi nudge her. I also felt like snorting and chuckling.

The woman had a head full of curly blonde hair that I devoutly hoped was a wig because it looked like a piece of somebody's shag carpet, sliced out and glued to her head. Under the carpet were brown eyes circled with black mascara, and brilliant red lips that looked like she'd put her lipstick on in the dark after six or seven shots of Johnny Walker. Her strapless slut shoes were topped with skin-tight calf-length pants that had a snakeskin pattern and were so low-cut that I *really* hoped she didn't drop anything on the floor. A guy could go blind. Her fetching ensemble was topped off, in more ways than one, by a shiny black leather bustier with cups the approximate size and shape of Cruise missile nose cones. This stylish item pushed her up, and up some more, and then out, way out, with the result that she displayed approximately a foot of cleavage so tanned and wrinkled that it looked like the leather purse my grandmother carried. In case anybody missed it, which was impossible, she had liberally sprinkled multicolored glitter all over her ample chest. Now, I like cleavage as much as the next guy, well, okay, more than some of the next guys, but this was way over the top and boy, do I need to work on that phrasing. She looked like if she sneezed she'd pop right out, glitter would go flying around the room, and I'd go blind. It took me a moment to notice, but she had a small tattoo of a goggle-eyed Mickey on her left breast. Mickey was looking a tad the worse for wear, what with the deep tan and the wrinkles, but he was still gamely waving the peace sign and saying, "I'm drunk." She looked like somebody's grandmother who'd spent too much time surfing porn sites, escaped from Leisure World, and turned into a dominatrix.

"Yeah? What? Help you?" She was glad to see us, too. I'm perceptive about these things.

Kandi and Kaylee were obviously speechless, so of course it fell to me to carry the ball and, ever-manly, I stepped right up to the plate. "Hi, uh, Betty, my name is Macdonald, and I have a couple of questions I'd like to ask you."

She put her hands (of course she had rings on each finger and a spoon ring on her left thumb) on her hips, glared at me, and shouted, "The freaks next door sent you, didn't they?"

Since shouting involved her taking a deep breath I sort of lost track of what I was saying as I desperately tried to look away, failing as I was drawn to Mickey writhing around and waving as if he wanted out. I couldn't blame him. After a moment my brain came back. "Cranial Fracture? Yes, and—"

"Beat it. I got nothing to say."

"Look, I just want to ask you—"

"Wait a minute." She vanished into the back. As she pushed through the beads separating the rear of the store I saw a young woman in a very short hot pink satin robe and high heels dart across the hall.

I whispered to Kandi, "Beat it, then wait a minute. We're making progress."

A moment later she reappeared, an unlit cigarette dangling from her lips, and said, "Yeah? Help you?"

Kandi whispered, "This is where we came in."

Hey, I interviewed CEOs for years, so I am nothing if not persistent, and for that matter used to a certain amount of craziness. "Yes. My name is Macdonald and—"

She came back. The first one, that is, and stood next to her double. "We're twins," the one without the cigarette in her mouth said.

"No shit," Kaylee muttered, then blushed.

A very large young guy in low-riding baggy jeans, a dirty wife-beater tank top that had probably been white in the early nineties, sporting tats up and down both arms as well as on his neck came out of the back, wiping his mouth with a paper towel and smearing whatever it was he'd been eating into his scraggly goatee. The yellowed shirt had a bumper sticker glued across the front that said, "Save a tree! Eat a beaver! Betty's Boards Plus, HB." His biceps showed a lot of hours at a weight machine; a guess on my part, but I didn't think he had it in him to do free weights. I also guessed that he had taken a minute before coming out to do a few push-ups to inflate his guns. His shaved head was so shiny it reflected the fluorescent tubes in the ceiling. I smiled at him, stepped forward and said, "So, you must be Betty?"

He kind of squinted his eyes, trying to figure out if that was an insult and, while he was cogitating, the twin without the smoke said, "I'm Perl and this is my sister Merl. And you're done here." She gestured to the big guy. Her sister Merl, snickered, causing Mickey to writhe around again.

The tattooed man belched discreetly into the napkin, wadded it up and threw it on the floor before he advanced on me confidently, grinning, put both hands on my chest and shoved.

Now here's the deal. Everybody has certain things that really piss them off and getting shoved is one of mine. In my defense I was also coming off a very, very bad few days, and I was not in a good mood. Okay, I was in a really crummy mood. I was pretty sure Mr. Tat was going to shove me and could have gotten out of the way, but, you know what? I just didn't feel like it; what I felt like was punching somebody and he was not only handy, he seemed to be offering. But, it's important to set a good example for the younger generation and Kaylee was standing next to me so I restrained myself. It didn't last long, the restraint.

As his palms pressed against my chest (note to self: throw this shirt away; these grease stains will never come out) I got both of his hands and bent his wrists back. He said, "Hey," tried to pull free and when he found that he couldn't and started to go to his knees to take the pressure off, I brought my left knee up into his forehead. There was a solid, satisfying *smack* and he was sprawled on the ground, flat on his back on the wadded-up paper towel he'd thrown down.

Always backing my play, Kandi had stepped to one side, pulling Kaylee behind her and had her hand in her purse where her Raven .25 lurked. Mr. Tat was trying to get his feet under him, holding his head. In a way he was lucky. If he'd shoved Kandi he wouldn't be getting up.

I turned to the twins. "Now, where were we?"

Perl shrugged. "What are you gonna do, punch out a couple of old ladies? We got nothin' to say to you. Beat it."

"The people at Cranial Fracture say you broke their security camera. The one in back."

"We got nothin' to say. Beat it."

It might have been satisfying to slap them around, but probably not—for one thing, they might like it. Their bouncer, or whatever he was, showed signs of sitting up. I dropped a card with my cell number on the counter.

As we were leaving one of the twins said, "Earl, you're fired."

He whined, "Aw, Mom—"

In the car Kaylee looked at me and said, "Um, those ladies? If I dress like that when I get old, shoot me."

"My pleasure."

I said, "Okay, we've got a car trip. Gone roughly an hour."

Kandi said, "And the police have this information, as well. Ricky said he told them."

Chet, Kandi, Kaylee and I were back for a strategy meeting, surrounded by the noise, warmth, and cooking smells of the kitchen at Fred's. I said, 'But we're pretty sure she went to a warehouse. I'm guessing this is the trip she talked about in the video."

My cell buzzed. When I picked it up a voice I recognized said, "This Macdonald?"

"Who's this?"

"Perl."

"Betty's Boards Perl?"

"How many Perls you know? Yeah, Betty's Boards Perl. Come back. Me an Merl wanna talk."

"On my way."

Driving by we saw there was a Closed sign in the window. When we parked in back the door opened at once and Earl ushered us in. For this trip I took Kandi but had Chet drive Kaylee home after making her promise not to go out alone, not even to take out the trash. She said she was freaked enough to do what I said.

Earl looked at me, then dropped his eyes. I noticed that he moved stiffly, and that he had two black eyes that I figured I was responsible for, and that his biceps were no longer pumped up. We passed down a hallway with small windowless rooms on each side. Each room had a single bed with clean pink or black silk sheets turned down, a small table with magazines on it, and a flat screen TV mounted on the wall.

There was no office, just a couple of stools set up in the front room behind the counter, with Perl and Merl in them, smoking and watching the street. A half-full quart of gin and a stack of little paper cups were on the counter. As I watched, Perl poured a cup three-quarters full and downed it.

"If Earl wants a rematch tell him to forget it."

They both turned and Kandi gasped. Both had black eyes, and one had a bandage across her nose. They both had given up the leather tops for loose pink sweatshirts, which they pulled up to show me taped ribs. Been there, done that, more than once. I knew how much it hurt. I'd slug some gin, too, if I was them.

"Somebody else paid you a visit."

"This is your fault."

"Merl, it ain't. You know it ain't." Perl sighed, dragged on her smoke, and said, "bout an hour after you left these people show up, asking what we'd told you. We tell 'em to beat it, just like we did you. Earl did his best, but there was two guys and this woman so they laid him out pretty good."

Merl took up the story. "So I say, 'What are you gonna do, beat up a couple of old ladies? And this woman says, 'Sure.' Worked us over pretty good. Want some gin?"

"I'll pass. What about the camera?"

"Your loss." She had a swig and gingerly touched the bruise under her eye. "Yeah, we busted out the camera. See, a lot of our clients come in the back way, you know, and some of our business is, um—"

"Of a delicate nature."

"And their camera had something?" Kandi said.

"No-o—, but . . ." The twins looked at each other.

"You have your own and it shows the van that Nadzia left in." Perl nodded and tossed me a CD. "One more question. Why are you helping us now?"

She paused and poured more gin into her cup. "My kid's got cracked ribs. Because it will piss that bitch off when she finds out." I glanced at Earl and saw that he was cradling a full-size shotgun, fancy carved stock, side-by-side barrels about a yard long.

He said, "Hope she comes back."

I shook my head. "These people are bad news. There is a very good chance that they killed a young woman a few days ago."

Earl said, "The skate bitch. We heard."

"Earl, I'm giving you a pass because you've been worked over twice today and because you don't know any better. But if you say that again, I'll hurt you."

Normally, on TV when the hero makes speeches like that I think they're stupid. In this case it just popped out. Oh, well. Like I said, I'd had a few very bad days and was not in the best of moods. I picked up the CD and we backed out.

We went next-door used the laptop at Frac to look at the video. It showed the van, but only the last digit of the license number, and that wasn't clear. Bridget said, "Could be a nine, or a one, or whatever."

Kandi said, "Yeah."

"Yeah, but check this out," Ricky said. "It's a late-2000's delivery van, white, looks like a Ford, I'm not sure, but Mango will know."

"Mango?"

"It's his name. Yeah, he hangs here and he's a total car freak when he's not boarding." And, sure thing, in less than fifteen minutes Mango had answered the email and ID'd the van as a 2006 or 7 Ford. And he had pointed out the primer spot by the left rear wheel well.

Kandi sighed. "Do you know how many vans and how many warehouses that could be?"

Ricky stood up and opened the back door, allowing about fifteen kids to troop in, all carrying skateboards.

Chet was in on this from his laptop in my spare room. He said, "Expanding the radius of the area we're considering to allow for error on Ricky's part with regard to the amount of time they were gone, and assuming a stay of thirty minutes once they were in the warehouse, and with a mid-range definition of 'warehouse' I make it about a hundred structures. More if she spent less time in the building."

"Well, we can't possibly check out that many warehouses in a reasonable length of time." I tossed down my pencil and walked over to inspect the rows of colorful boards on display.

Kaylee spoke up from her house. "If you could, what would you look for?"

"A white van with a primer spot on the back near the wheel well."

"Okay, I'll have my brother drive me to Westminster Mall and we're on it."

"The shopping center? Why?"

"Kids, of course. I'll get some of my buds looking for it. I don't want to ask on my blog because I think the people we're after are reading it, but I can tell a few kids in person, and each of them will tell a few more, and they skate and ride everywhere."

"Exponential growth," Chet said.

Ricky said, "We'll start from this end. I got some buds here already."

"Kaylee, Ricky, I'm not sure I'm comfortable with this. It could be dangerous."

Kaylee laughed. "Please. Kids on BMXs or boards? We're invisible to the adult world, either part of the scenery or somebody to run off."

Ricky said, "She's right. We can do this." They were all copying stills of the van to their cell phones.

"It might work, you know, it just might. But under no circumstances go inside the warehouse. And don't get caught."

Bridget giggled. 'Yes, Mom."

Back in the Chevy Kandi said, "Now what?"

I drummed my fingers on the dash, and dropped the car into Drive. "You know me—when in doubt, call a meeting. It's time to confront some people."

Henrietta Graveline's Belmont Shore home was on the water, a three-story mini-palace with common walls on each side. Her living room was mid-century modern, all spindly legs and sharp lines. We sat around a low table, sipping tea. The lady of the house, Brad Zucco, and Lisa June Culhane huddled on the couch.

"I've been expecting you," she said. "We're all very sorry about Nadzia. I only met her once but she seemed like a nice person."

"This all goes back to Berkeley, doesn't it?"

"Maybe. We're not sure."

"You really know a kid who wanted shirts?"

"Absolutely. And he really does ride a skimboard. He's quite good on it."

"He like the shirts?"

"Yes, and you really like to sneak up on the point, don't you?"

"Let's say I've done my share of interviews."

She put down her tea cup. "All right. I—we—want to help."

Lisa June spoke up. "I think someone is following me. What Henrietta told you was true. I didn't want her to tell you, but she did and it's true."

Henrietta said, "We think this goes back to a group called Five to One. In the Sixties, particularly at Berkeley, there was this enormous upwelling of—"

"Righteous indignation." Zucco snorted. "And it turned out to be a big joke."

Henrietta said, "Moral certitude. Yes. Missing from this foul time." Who else had talked about that?

Zucco shook his head. "Get on with it. I don't have all day."

Lisa June put her hand on Henrietta's. "Yes, please. Tell it."

"There were articles in an underground paper called the Berkeley Broccoli, about this radical group, like the Weathermen, only much less famous. Then there was a fire in a microbiology lab, and of course everybody thought it was the CIA, or that the lab was doing defense work and it was torched by Five to One. They wrote to the Broccoli and claimed responsibility, but who knows? Pick one."

"And now?"

She looked at the others and some unspoken signal passed. "Okay. Like I said, there were conspiracy theories going around after the fire, and one of them was that the lab was testing biologic weapons, and that some samples were never found." She shrugged. "In that time, forensic science was not what it is today."

"Tell me about Five to One."

Lisa June took up the story. "Not much to tell. One of the zillions of radical groups. They used noms de guerre when they wrote to the *Broccoli*, like Medea, and Cassandra, and, help me out here, Brad."

He said, "Moloch."

"Right. Anyway, there were rumors that what was in the lab was a germ and that Five had it. They wrote and said, no, but if they got it they'd give it to the school administration and force the government off campus."

Henrietta stood and walked over to the windows.

I said, "And Henrietta worked in the lab."

"Yes, I worked in the lab. The pigs questioned me, searched my apartment half-a-dozen times. Of course they found nothing. I had not removed any beakers, Petri dishes, whatever."

"And now, somebody thinks you have it. They probably left you messages, sent emails."

"Yes."

"How does this relate to me?" I said, even though I had a pretty good guess.

"We knew Walter, the Snake. When I read about him, and his connection with you, it seemed like maybe you could help us. So I arranged the meeting on Brad's boat."

"Tell me about your adventures."

She turned and faced me. "Yes! Yes! Only there was no chance to talk to you and then your home was invaded and we had a pretty good idea why. It was because you'd talked to us."

"But you still didn't say anything."

"What's to say?" Brad laughed. "This shit is forty years old. Man, I hardly remember those days. I said to leave you out of it because it made no sense. The emails are a joke, the home invasion had nothing to do with us because there's nobody after us." He stood up. "I gotta go. We're taking the boat out, me and some yacht club buddies for a raft-up in Two Harbors. You're welcome to come along."

I said, "Catalina actually might be a good idea, because I think Henrietta's right. And if somebody is watching Lisa June, being out of town sounds good."

The two women shook their heads. "No," Henrietta said, "I won't run. Forty years too late, but I won't run."

Lisa June swallowed, said, "I'm with you, m—my friend." Henrietta took her hand.

Kandi and I stood. "One more question. This stuff, this awful germ, what was it supposed to be?"

Henrietta stood too, and was showing us to the door when she said, "The first of its kind. A flesh-eating bacteria."

In the Chevy, cruising south on PCH, Kandi said, "What do you think?"

"You first."

"Well, I like them, all of them. And they're afraid, with reason. And it sounds like whoever this is, and of course my money is on Blondell Baines and Faith Valentine, they think somebody has this sample. So, Sailor, I ask again, what do you think?"

"I think we need the skate kids to find that warehouse." And they did.

Chapter Eighteen   Warehouse

That night we were parked across the street in a van we'd rented with one of Chet's anonymous credit cards.

"All right, Mac, the warehouse does most of its shipping between six pm and midnight."

"Ah. Suspicious, right?"

"Naw. Traffic's lighter then so the trucks are less disruptive. They got this chapel place next door."

"Oh."

Chet settled his black Stetson a bit lower on his head.

We saw the warehouse where the van had been spotted, "Interstate Distributors" on the door, and next to it something called, "The Chapel of Non-Denominational Rest." It had stained glass windows on each side of wooden double doors, white-painted walls that made it look like a church grafted on to a warehouse.

A tractor-trailer rig pulled up and Chet said, "Okay, now watch. This ol' boy's gonna get out with his cell phone in his hand, climb up onto the loading dock and enter a code into the keypad that's next to the door. The door rolls up, he uses a forklift that he brought in his trailer to do the loading. At no time does he go inside, at least not very far, and at no time does anybody from inside come out to meet him." Chet was right—the drill was exactly as he described it. The semi backed up to one of the dozen roll-up doors, the driver climbed down out of the cab with their cell phone, entered numbers in a keypad, the door rolled up, the driver backed a small forklift out of the semi, and loaded the trailer with pallets stacked with shrink-wrapped cardboard boxes.

"How do you know the shipping always stops at midnight? We just found this place."

"The security cameras record to an offsite server which stores seven files, each consisting of twenty-four hours worth of images. One still every fifteen seconds. Saves storage space and makes it easier to review."

"So, I take it you watched while one of the drivers put in his code."

"Yep, but it ain't gonna be that easy, pard. Remember the drivers always have their cell in hand when they go to open the barn door? Turns out they call a number after they back up to the dock. The person—or, more likely the machine—he calls gives him the code, probably a different code every time the door is opened. Pretty sophisticated security for a simple warehouse."

"Ah! Suspicious!"

He rolled his eyes, shifted a little on the car seat. "Never fear, ol' Marshal Chet is here. And I got me a plan."

Kandi muttered, "He's been around you too long."

Our urban cowboy watched as the driver walked around his rig, checking cables before he got in, the truck hissed as the air brakes released, lurched forward a little, then rolled slowly away from the loading dock. Chet looked at the time display on his cell phone, muttered, "And the bull's coming out of the chute." He pointed a strange object, sort of like a shotgun with a tiny TV screen and swept it back and forth. "FLIR. Forward-Looking Infrared Radar. Heat signature is low, so it's safe. Nobody's home that we care about. Let's go."

Walking quickly across the street to the warehouse parking lot, I said, "Chet, we've gone into places we weren't supposed to before, as cable guys and—"

"That dog won't hunt."

"Okay, so what are we this time?"

"Rustlers." He looked at us both. Kandi paused, then shrugged.

I sighed. "Rustlers. Just so long as we know."

"I've fixed their security snapshots to repeat, just show the same image over and over, but they'll pick it up sooner or later. Best I could do."

It was a good plan but it didn't work. We couldn't get in. Chet had the number, called it on a disposable cell, but the robot voice on the other end said it didn't recognize the caller and to please contact the district dispatcher. We couldn't hang around in plain sight too long, so we hustled back across the street to the van. And the clock was ticking on how long we could sit in the strip mall parking lot, before human security spotted us. Time for the direct approach.

I watched until another semi rumbled up, slowing for the right turn into the warehouse parking lot, and was across the street before it had completed the first part of the K-turn necessary to load, keeping the trailer between me and the cab. I bent low, darted out and jumped onto the passenger-side running board, crouching there holding my breath until he had backed in. As the rig gently bumped the dock I dropped off the running board and slid under the trailer, hiding there while the driver, a twenty-something with a oily red gimme cap and an eighties down vest on, climbed up on the dock and put the code in. Then I slipped into the shadows behind a huge tire while he backed his baby forklift out and tried to figure my next move. It had to be when he was loading the first of the boxes, so he would be inside the empty trailer, all the way at the front. He scooped up a loaded pallet, pulled the forklift into the trailer and I slithered up onto the dock and ducked into the building. I could hear him backing out for another load as I looked frantically left and right for a place to hide, finally at the last second diving under a large translucent sheet of discarded shrink-wrap that was piled in a corner. I buried myself and listened. If he had seen me, or if he looked closely, I was in trouble, but fortunately the warehouse was dimly lit. Most of it, including my corner, was in shadow.

The forklift approached, rolled on by. I watched as he drove back and forth with it a few more times, lifting shrink-wrapped bundles and loading them into the trailer; then footsteps came back and stopped. He grunted softly and settled down next to my hiding place, sitting with his back against the wall, a lighter flicked and a moment later I smelled fragrant dope. Perfect—he was smoking a joint before getting back on the road. He sighed and pulled his cap off, tossed it down next to my foot, which if he looked closely he could see through the plastic before plugging in ear buds and cranking up some tunes. I stayed absolutely motionless.

All at once I thought of my cell phone. Was it on vibrate? Chet would surely have the sense not to call me now, but what if somebody else called? As the driver sucked deeply and started humming under his breath, I slowly edged my hand into my jeans pocket until I touched the phone. Now what? I could try to turn it off blind, but if I pushed the wrong button it would beep and even if I figured out the right button I couldn't remember for sure if it made a noise as it powered down. If it beeped, would he hear it over the music? Sweat trickled down between my shoulder blades. His scuffed, booted toe started bopping back and forth in time to the humming. At last he finished his joint and stood up. A minute later I heard the trailer door roll down, followed by the warehouse door. I blew out the breath I'd been holding for it seemed like forever, and almost came out but realized that I hadn't heard the truck drive away. So I stayed buried for a minute, and was glad I did when the door rumbled up again, footsteps hurried in, stopped where he'd been sitting, and then hurried out. He must have left the roach. This time when the door rolled down the truck pulled out immediately.

I slid out from under my plastic sheet and pushed the button to raise the door a little bit and Chet bent low and rolled in. "Pard, you nearly gave this ol' boy a heart attack. Wait one,

I gotta call." He pulled a bandanna out of his hip pocket and mopped his face, then pushed a button on his phone and said, "He's okay. Hang tight." In the distant parts of the warehouse there were mechanical noises.

"Chet," I whispered, "there are people here. They're working."

He grinned. "No and yes."

"Have I mentioned I hate it when you're cryptic?"

"Have I mentioned how you frequently scare the crap out of me?" He looked around. "And I really don't like dark creepy places."

About ten yards away an odd-looking wheeled machine rolled past the aisles. It was square, about three feet on a side, painted Day-Glo orange, and looked like a large steel suitcase lying on its flat side. As we watched, it paused for a moment as if considering, before it rolled under a stack of shelves, settled itself and rotated 180 degrees Then it raised up, lifting the entire rack, before motoring swiftly toward us with its load. We stepped aside and let it pass. Chet said, "Working, yep. People, nope. This spread's fully automated." It stopped at an intersection to let another robot trundle by and we saw that it had a cheery nametag, the kind you get at conventions, pasted on its front—or what was most likely its front—saying "Hi! I'm Bella!" After the road was clear Bella rolled on with her load. "The robots don't mind the low light, since they navigate by bar codes in the floor. The humans they work with make friends with them, give 'em names."

"Like Bella."

"Sure. She'll probably send her favorite human a birthday card."

"Chet . . ."

"Really. We need to get to the other side of the building, where there's some space not accounted for in the blueprints. We'll follow Bella here and let her break trail."

We trailed our orange suitcase, dodging other robots, until we found an unmarked door with a keypad lock. Chet had it open in less than five minutes, and most of that time was spent making sure it wasn't wired to call the owners if opened. We passed through a second door into a large room filled with racks of equipment, and steel tables with more equipment.

"It's a lab of some kind," I said.

It took me back to invertebrate biology at CSULB. I recognized three centrifuges, two autoclaves, two small steel refrigerators, and, of course, metal workbenches with Bunsen burners, stacks of Petri dishes and racks of test tubes. A large industrial refrigerator stood against one wall.

Chet was walking around, snapping dozens of pictures with his cell phone. At one point he pulled a tissue out of a box and wiped a table top with it.

"Wait a minute," I said. "Chet, can Bella talk?"

"Nope. Uh-oh."

"Coming this way."

We turned out the lights and stepped out of the lab, quietly closing the door behind us. I caught a glimpse of a black-clad figure darting between the rows of shelves. My .45 was in my hand as I jumped and looked down the next aisle. The figure had come halfway down, but was pinned between two robots moving toward each other and between the two of them taking up every inch of space. Effortlessly, and without dislodging a single box, the figure leaped to the top of the shelves and silently dropped on the other side. I kept my gun out.

Chet said, "So, that's what made the noise?"

"No."

"*No?*"

I said grimly, "That wasn't what we heard. There's someone else in here, other than the one we just saw."

"How can you be so sure?"

"Because that was Roger Winters." Voices were approaching. 'Hide." We ducked into a shadow. Chet shivered and then settled down.

The Rod and Chooch came into view, guns out, followed by Blondell Baines and two Asians in identical gray suits, white shirts, black ties, and dark glasses at night. Baines had a machine gun on a strap over his shoulder. We both snapped pictures.

I whispered again "Hide."

Peering between shelves, we watched them stride down the aisle toward us. I looked at my cell phone and saw the ever-popular "No Service." I nudged Chet, showed him. He shrugged, whispered, "What's with the guns?"

"They're just trying to impress their guests." I hope. In one respect "No Service" was a relief since it meant an incoming call would not give us away. I put my lips close to his ear and whispered, "What's Kandi going to do when she sees that on her phone?"

"Oh, shit. She'll try to get in and see what's wrong. And she'll run into the guards these guys undoubtedly left outside."

"Faith Valentine. Or she'll run into Roger Winters, which would be much worse."

Chet said, "I don't think we can get out until they leave."

"Follow me." Baines and company led the Asian Blues Brothers into the lab and closed the door. We ducked down another aisle, pressing back as one of Bella's buddies trundles by with a stack of shelves. I saw another flicker of black ahead and nudged Chet. "That way."

As I'd hoped, Roger led us to his escape route, and we got lucky—he didn't spot us trailing along behind him. It was a rope ladder leading up to an open window. The flimsy corrugated metal wall rattled as we climbed up. Voices approaching told me we'd been heard. Chet hung for a moment, then dropped. I followed, pulling the ladder up after me. Now all we had to do was get by the guards outside.

When I peeked around the corner they were both slumped against the wall, unconscious. I hoped they were only unconscious.

Kandi saw us and drove by. We jumped into the van.

I was torn. Kandi—when she was Mary—would have said I was conflicted. I wanted to go after Roger Winters, and I wanted to get out of there before the gun-totin' psychos came back. Reality set in and I realized there was no chance of catching Roger, and there was an excellent chance of the gun-toters shooting us. Baines had not committed a crime that I could charge him with, let alone prove. It was not illegal to take guests into your lab in the middle of the night. I signaled Kandi and she drove our rented van away.

Chapter Nineteen   Parade of Lights

The next morning Kandi went to teach a class. Chet and I took the snapshots of the lab to Henrietta Graveline so maybe we could figure out what was going on; this time we met upstairs in the study of her Belmont Shore home surrounded by memorabilia. The famous psychedelic posters of John, Paul, George and Ringo hung in silver frames on one wall; a lava lamp bubbled on a bookshelf crammed with battered college texts. The furniture was five paisley beanbag chairs, a low glass-topped table and four chairs around a spool table.

I said, "This is great! All the stuff from my college days got trashed."

She laughed. "So did mine. About five years ago I started collecting. I bought almost all of this on eBay." We sat at the wooden table. Chet moved a hookah to one side, opened his laptop and she began scrolling through the pictures, moving slowly, occasionally going back to review one, lips pursed in concentration.

At last she leaned back and looked at us, puzzled. "And this is supposed to be a place where they're working on—what? This ancient flesh-eating bacteria?"

I said, "What does it look like they're working on?"

She scrolled through the pictures again. "Where's the containment?"

"Containment?"

"Okay, look. For this kind of work you need, well, if it's pharmaceuticals, you need to protect the product from the people, right?"

"Uh—"

Chet said, "Sure. You don't want to mess up your work."

"Exactly. For example, if you're manufacturing Tylenol, you don't want somebody with dirty fingernails to contaminate a batch."

"Got it."

"Okay. In this case you need to do that, but you *also* need to protect the people from the product. The workers can be contaminated easily, so they gown up before work." She turned away from the laptop, leaned back in her chair, lecturing. "You need three areas. Gowning—gowns, booties, head covering, mask, of course—and that's usually associated with an airlock, then you need an area to handle the product, and finally an area for analytical testing. These pictures show me a small room with gowns, a big room with lots of instruments, and that's mostly correct. But unless you missed it there's no real airlock. And there's no area for testing. Wet chemistry looks dramatic and might fool a lay person, but there's things wrong in these pictures. It's a hodgepodge of stuff; hell the only thing missing is that v-shaped spark thing from *Frankenstein*."

I said, "There were gowns. And those bootie things you wear over your shoes."

"Okay, but what about an airlock?"

"No." Chet scrolled back and I pointed to the screen. "They had these hanging strips of thick plastic."

"Not good enough for this."

"But it would look good," I mused.

"To an untrained eye? Sure."

"It's easy to get contaminated?"

"Oh, yes."

"Just by touching the wrong stuff?"

She hesitated. "Yes, it can happen, yes, sometimes just by skin contact. It's called colonization."

Driving south, I said to Chet, "I think last night we saw Baines' buyer for the bacteria."

"The Asians."

"He wants them to think he's developing this bug, but in reality he's stealing it."

Chet said, "Think you got it, pard. Think you got it. And by now it looks like he's figured out that you don't have it and that you don't know who does."

"He's been quiet for a day. You may be right. He may not need me anymore."

But we were both wrong.

If one of them hadn't been blond they would have had me. The rest of the day went by with no incidents—no more threats, no more phone calls, no more post-mortem toes delivered pinned to toy surfboards. Mary was at UCLA, defending her dissertation outline before her committee. Baines' deadline had come and gone without action on his part, probably because he knew so many people were looking for him, and in general it seemed like things were returning to some form of normalcy. The warehouse was being watched, and sooner or later Baines would surface. Agatha had used her influence to persuade the police to pull him in for questioning about Nadzia's death, and once they got him they would keep him on ice for a while. The mysterious weapon had not turned up and for all we knew Baines was taking his buyers to Disneyland to ride Space Mountain.

That evening I ran errands. Life does not stop just because people might want to kill you. Wait, that might be wrong.

Chet had gone to make a call on a client and I'd taken the Whaler across for Kung Pao shrimp, tied up at the dock behind Fred's Fine Mexican Food, and strolled three doors down to The Happy Fish. Marvin, owner of the Happy Fish, put a lot of pow in his Kung Pao shrimp, so I was forced to guzzle three Sapporos (the regular size, not the giant ones). When the last shrimp, the last cashew, and the last grain of rice was gone I declined green tea ice cream, left money on the table and waved to Marvin as I headed out the back exit. At ten p. m. Peter's Landing is quiet, only a small amount of traffic and voices in the distance.

A cement walkway runs between the channel and the restaurants and shops that make up Peter's Landing; floating wooden docks extend out at right angles from it. I strolled along toward Fred's dock, mostly in the shadows between the restaurants, not thinking about much except maybe I'd get my skateboard and catch some late-night cement tubes. Good thing I wasn't whistling. About ten yards from the Whaler, I saw a gleam of light reflect off blond hair. Someone was standing on the dock by my boat. I froze, then stepped quietly off the cement onto a floating dock and into the shadow of a forty-foot Mainship trawler. After a moment I could see not one, but two figures on the dock next to my little dinghy.

Before I could decide on a next step, three words came clearly across the water. ". . . here he comes."

Looking over my shoulder I saw a third person briefly, as he passed into and out of one of the overhead lights. Nobody I knew. He was moving slowly, peering into the shadows as he passed each dock, carefully checking the spaces around the boats. All right, call me paranoid, but I was pretty sure he was looking for me.

My other clue about his intentions was that he was holding a shiny chrome long-barreled revolver in his right hand, keeping it down low by his leg.

My guns were all locked up safe at home. Dumb, right? Hey, I had reasons. The trip was a spur-of-the-moment event—I'd taken the Whaler out to run the outboard (if you're an outboard owner you know it's important to stay on top of things like that), stopped at the gas dock for a fill-up, and decided on a quick stop for dinner. Of course my house was locked and Chet had fixed my smart phone so it talked to the security system and would tell me about intruders. Okay, they're really excuses but they're all I have. And I did have my trusty pool cue handle tucked into my belt.

As quietly as I could, I took out my wallet and cell phone, reached up and stashed them on the deck of the trawler, crouched, and slipped off the dock into the water.

In winter the sea temperature in Surf City, USA, drops into the low sixties, high fifties, definitely fullsuit time if you're surfing. Instantly the water found its way up the legs of my jeans, shriveling what sportscasters politely call the groin. In reality, my balls took refuge where it was warmer. The shivering didn't start for another minute.

I felt like I was fairly well-hidden until the guy walking toward me took out a small flashlight and started probing with it. "He down there?" he called to his buddies.

A voice I knew answered. "Yes, he is. We're hiding him because we like watching you wander around." Faith Valentine. The pro among Baines' helpers. I remembered her white leather gloves and the way she had kissed her knuckles after decking The Rod, and how she smiled as she did it. Faith gave me the creeps and I didn't mind admitting it.

"Well, he ain't in the restaurant."

"So do your job."

"Yeah, yeah. Bitch." But he was smart enough to mutter the last softly so I was the only one who heard. The searcher's pals said something but I couldn't make it out.

It was a longish swim, but I could make it across the channel to my house if I got rid of my Topsiders and Official Titanium Redhead sweatshirt. The thing is, I didn't want to go.

The searcher was moving down the wooden finger next to the one I was clinging to, taking it slow and careful.

Here's a tip: If you're sneaking around at night looking for somebody, the weapon of choice is not a shiny, nickel-plated revolver. I could see it clearly in his right hand, now crossed under the hand holding a flashlight, just like in all the cop shows. Well, so much for thoughts of leaping out of the water and beating him up. It was never much of a plan anyway.

He finished checking around two sport fishers and headed my way. Taking a gulp of air, I pushed myself under water.

I had a plan. There's about three inches of air space between the water and the boards, and that's where I thought I'd come up. It didn't work. First my questing fingers found nothing but air—that hand must not be under the dock—so I jerked them down quickly, stroked twice and when I reached up again I touched timber. No air pocket, just water, then wood. Desperate, I quit trying to find space with my hand and pressed my cheek against the wood. Nothing. At last, as I was gritting my teeth and fighting the urge to breathe, seriously considering sticking my head up next to the dock to see if the guy would shoot me with his shiny gun, my cheek passed through air and bumped against a barnacle-encrusted plank. The dock was old and must have been sagging under years of boaters, most carrying heavy ice chests full of beer, because there wasn't three or four inches of air space, it was more like one, none in places. I had to turn my head sideways to get my nostrils into the air. It reeked of rotting seaweed, tar, and dead fish and it smelled like heaven. The dock rocked side-to-side as the man with the gun walked toward my end and the light from his flashlight flickered through the cracks. Not wanting him to spot me, I took a breath and slipped beneath the surface again.

When I came up he was standing right over me. "Swear I heard a splash, but he ain't here." The answer was inaudible, but he must not have liked it. He muttered, "Bitch," again, and tromped off, rocking the dock, sending ripples of water up my nose and almost making me choke. But I got lucky—he walked right by them and didn't see my wallet and cell phone on the deck of the boat.

I slipped to the seaward end of the dock, where it was darkest, and raised my head. The three of them were standing next to the Whaler, talking. I really wanted to hear what they were saying; and maybe there was a way, as long as I didn't give myself too much time to think about it. Whatever they decided, the one with the gun out shrugged and started back toward my dock. "The one where you heard something? Check it again. And do a good job this time." Faith sounded unhappy. Now I had a problem. I could be seen if the guy looked closely, and there really wasn't enough time to get back to the air pocket and do it quietly. Inspiration struck.

It was the annual Christmas Parade of Lights in Huntington Harbour. What happens is that fifty or more boat owners decorate their boats with plastic Santas, lights, and small trees and whatever, load up on beer and wine and motor around the harbor so non-boat-owners can stand on shore and look and clap. Hey, it's tradition. The end of the parade came by in time for me to slip out and catch the dangling bumper of a passing motorsailer. I caught the rope and let it pull me toward the turning basin where the parade reversed its route. Over my shoulder I saw the flashlight moving back and forth. A dark-haired five-year-old wearing red and blue Spiderman pj's under a life jacket, and tethered to the handrail, clutched his action figure in a chubby, none-too-clean fist and looked somberly down at me. I held my finger to my lips and the Spidey nodded before the little brat shrieked, "Mommy, Mommy, there's a man on the boat!" I hoped his brother swiped his action figure. Before Mommy could come and raise the alarm, I let go and slid back into the water in time to see the blond with the gun looking at the next dock in the row.

It looked like he'd covered my dock so I quietly breast-stroked back to where I started.

I thought about my plan, the one I'd had to put on hold before swimming out to meet Spiderman's owner. It didn't seem any better, but, then it didn't seem any worse, either.

If I could work my way back down the wooden finger I was hiding under, and swim under the cement walk to the dock they were on, I could slip my head up into the air space and hear everything. The problem was swimming under the cement walk. Since it was on pilings it did not float, at high tide the water rose up the sides. The ramps leading down to the dock fingers floated up so they were level, and, of course, when the tide was high there was no air space between cement and sea. That meant a fifteen yard swim underwater, at night, with clothes dragging me down, and people who wanted to do bad things to me waiting at the end—like I said, it wasn't something I wanted to think about too much. I slipped off my shoes and, reaching around, set them on the dock in the shadow of the trawler. Then I pulled myself along the edge of the dock finger until it intersected the sidewalk. Taking a peek, I established that they were still in place, as if they expected me to walk up and say hello. And, okay, that little voice in the back of my head was disappointed since, if they'd been gone I wouldn't have to do this. No doubt it was the voice of reason.

The water in between my position and them was clear and well-lit; if I tried swimming over they'd see me and either laugh or shoot me, or both. As I'd feared I would have to go under the cement. I took three deep breaths, exhaling sharply after each one, held the fourth, and pushed myself under.

Finding my way turned out to be pretty easy—I just kept the lighted water to my left and breast-stroked along a few inches under cement. "Come to the dark side, Luke," a misquote from a movie from my childhood, popped into my head and it was hard not to laugh. I wondered if lack of oxygen was already making me goofy.

I had either underestimated the distance or overestimated my lung capacity, because I was about twenty feet short when I had to breathe. When I was in grade school I was slow and overweight and a real target for the class bully; once or twice we'd been "playing" in the public pool and he'd held me under long enough for it to be scary, for me to think, "He's gone crazy and is going to drown me." This was like that—real fear. Had to breathe, no choice, no, "I can make it," *had* to have air, but luck was with me—there was a clump of kelp carried in by the tide, silhouetted by the dock lights, floating a few feet out. Bracing my right arm against the dock, I stuck my left hand out and dragged it in next to the cement. Then, keeping my body hidden, I pushed my face into the leaves and sucked in air. Heaven.

"Did you hear something?" Faith asked.

"No."

"Well, don't just stand there, go look. Do what we're paying you for." She was one of those people who enjoy being in charge, and she liked making these guys do whatever she wanted, not really caring much if it made sense. She said 'frog' and they jumped, so of course she said, 'Frog' at every opportunity.

I could hear footsteps and, through my kelp mask, could see legs moving toward me. After another blessed breath of air I slowly, slowly, slipped my head under the surface. Once under the walk again I breast stroked along to the wooden dock finger where there was an inch of air between water and boards.

The first voice said, "He ain't around."

"Figured that out, did you? All by yourself?"

"Listen, bitch, I'm getting sick of you."

"This may surprise you, but I will be able to live with the pain of knowing that. Mr. Baines wants to interview this gentleman again, and to deliver a message. Do it one more time."

"Hey, Blondell don't—"

I never got to hear whatever it was Blondell don't because there was a solid, meaty *smack* and when I peeked he was down on his knees gasping for air and looking like he wanted to puke. He might have felt better if he had.

Faith rubbed her gloved knuckles gently and then raised them to her lips. "To you he is Mr. Baines. You are not one of the Five. We will wait for you."

After Voice Number One left, she said, "What an idiot."

The Rod said, "Yeah. Where does Baines get these goons? They're not really part of us."

"Hired muscle is all."

He said, "Does the boss have any candidates to fill the spot?"

"No. We stay at four."

"Yo, I'm down with that. Ms. Valentine, we can't find Macdonald so we can't deliver his message this way."

Faith sighed. "Agreed."

"Plan B?"

"Yes. Call Chooch before the genius gets back here. Remember we will need time to join the other team. And, Rod, I'm sorry. I know you guys were going clubbing tonight."

"Hey, thanks for saying that, Ms V, but when this is over me and Chooch are gonna par-tay." He paused then hesitantly asked, "What about you, Ms. Valentine? When this is done, I mean, you and Mr. Baines been together a long time. He wants start this uh,"

"Dynasty."

"Yeah, like those rich people."

"The Rockefellers, the Mellons." She laughed. "Me? This girl's going to ramble till they have to cut her down."

I didn't hear his response because all at once I realized I had a problem, maybe serious. My fingers and toes had lost all feeling, and, guess what? You can die of hypothermia in seventy-degree water and this was much colder. The underwater swim back to an unobserved dock where I might be able to crawl out was out of the question and so was the swim across the channel.

When things are bad, never think they can't get worse. Someone said, "Can I help you folks?" The voice belonged to Mario, just-hired chef at Fred's and creator of the new salad we'd sampled. No doubt out back for one of his little cigars. He's about 6' 3" and his day job is training fighters for their next UFC bout. And he looks more like Ultimate Fighter than chef.

Faith answered. "Is this Mr. Macdonald's boat?"

I heard a match strike. "Can I help you?"

"We're waiting for T. R. Macdonald. This *is* his boat, right?"

"Ma'am, I'll have to ask you to wait somewhere else. This is a private dock."

This was getting worse rapidly. Mario would feel, with some justification, that he could take both of these people, but he had no way of knowing they were thugs, that there was a third one prowling around somewhere, and that at least one of them was armed. I slipped out and got both hands over the edge without being seen—they all had their backs to me, watching Mario in his double-breasted white jacket and tall white chef's toque. The good news was that I was so cold that I didn't feel the splinters that the dock inserted into my palms. My plan was simple—if a fight broke out, lever myself out of the water, roll onto the dock and lay out as many of them as I could with my pool cue handle. Try to avoid getting shot. Take out Faith first. Wait, revise that. Make "Try to avoid getting shot" the first priority.

A burst of laughter, rapid Spanish cut off in mid-word. "Hola, Mario. Que pasa?" I had to think a moment then I connected the voice to a bus-person at Fred's, out for a break. In the silence that followed I could almost feel Faith assessing the situation, deciding what to do. At last she said, "If you see Mr. Macdonald, would you tell him that Ms. Valentine was looking for him? Mr. Baines would like to speak with him. Thank you."

Mario said nothing, not even acknowledging that he knew me. After a moment I could hear Mario and the other guy move away, low voices in Spanish. Faith said, "Make the call, Rod. Then have the genius go to Macdonald's house. Tell him to wait where he can see the dock and if Macdonald comes back, deliver the message. If we get it done first I'll call him. I'll be in the car." She left, not running but moving quickly.

I was feeling pretty smart as the other two hurried to their cars.

My wallet, cell phone and shoes were where I left them. Carrying them, I walked to the back door of Fred's where Mario looked at me, dripping, and said, "Come on in."

I said, "I'm going to drip everywhere," and he pointed down at the thick perforated rubber mats over the floor in the kitchen area. Everybody gathered around and somebody brought me some hot coffee, which probably saved my life, at least that's what it felt like.

Feeling pretty smart lasted less than an hour, just until I warmed up a bit and thought to check my voicemail.

Chapter Twenty Plan B

The message was from Kandi. Call her. Important. I called.

"Mac, Mac I want you to listen not get too upset."

I went cold all over, but my voice was steady as I said, "Tell me."

"I'm in the hospital. Long Beach Memorial. I—I was attacked. A little while ago, outside my apartment. Not, not sexually assaulted, just—just slapped around a little." She stopped and I could hear her swallow. For a moment I simply couldn't speak. I mean, I tried, you know, my brain sent messages to my throat to make words, but it just didn't happen. "Mac, are you there?"

I took a breath. "I'm here." My voice was steady.

"One of them, one of the people who beat me up, said, 'Tell your boyfriend time's up.' Look, I don't think you should drop everything and race up here. I think they'll release me as soon as the doctor looks at the x-rays and okays it. I'll probably be out in the morning."

"I'll be there. Something I have to do first." After the usual platitudes, don't worry, take care, follow the doctor's orders, drink a lot of fluids, blah, blah blah, just noises to let the other person know you care, I hung up and called Eddington. He was dismayed when I told him what had happened and said, yes, of course he'd take care of anything I needed. I had a list.

I was too wet to put my cell back in my pocket so I held on to it and handed the coffee mug back to Mario. Jesus bustled into the kitchen, towel over his shoulder, holding a white board and dry-erase markers, getting ready to print tomorrow's specials. Shrimp burrito. Bonita tacos. It was inconceivable to me that life could be going on as if nothing had happened. I told Jesus I needed his car. He took one look at my face and said "It's the mini-van out back; got Fred's painted on the side." and handed me the keys. Mario stopped me on my way out. "Man, let me go with you. Those people—" he shook his head.

I smiled and he stepped back. "Thanks, Mario. Not this time. Tell Jesus his van will be across the street from my house, keys on the driver's side tire." He nodded slowly, staring at my face. I realized I was still smiling and quit.

Faith's boy was exactly where I'd set up if I were going to watch the dock in back of my house, sitting cross-legged in the deep shadow of the flower bed where someday I'd plant something. It was the new guy, the 'hired muscle.' I came around the side of the house behind him. The fool had even smoked a cigarette; I could smell him out on the street.

Nothing subtle; I wasn't in a subtle mood. Not even trying to be quiet, I walked up behind him, stomped his hand when he put it down so he could turn, crouched and slammed my pool cue handle across his throat. I grabbed the end in what is known as the bar-arm choke hold, and pulled up hard. Most police departments have banned the bar-arm because it's too easy to kill somebody if you press on their windpipe too hard. "Go for it," I said conversationally. "Go for the shiny revolver. You can probably pick it up just as I crush your throat. You might even get a shot off, but they tell me it's an ugly way to go, no air, face turning blue, clawing at your throat. Maybe you can shoot me first. Want to find out? I'm game if you are." This chest-beating speech was mostly for effect, but as I said it I realized I meant every word. He was making really ugly noises and scrabbling at the wood of the pool cue handle, and he had not tried for his gun, so I let up a little. I left the gun next to him on the walk. If he went for it I'd bash his skull in. "It's a night for messages. I just got the one from Baines. Unless I kill you, I want you to deliver one for me. Can you do that? Nod if you think you can remember it. It's not a long message and if you won't deliver it I'll hit you on the head and dump you in the channel." He nodded frantically. "Good boy. Here's the message. I was telling the truth when I told your boss I knew nothing about this stupid comic book weapon. I still don't, but I'm going to find out. And when I do I'm going to make sure he doesn't get it. Got that?" I didn't wait for a nod. "Someone I care about very much is in the hospital. You're lucky, you weren't part of putting her there, because you were here, having a smoke and watching my dock. That's why you get to deliver the message." I realized that I had tightened up again and he was pulling feebly at my arm and let him go. I took his gun, emptied the cartridges. Then I dragged him to the dock and threw him in. I didn't bother to see if he could swim or not. I had things to do.

First up was a visit to Kandi in Long Beach Memorial. All the way up PCH to the traffic circle to the hospital I was driving carefully, signaling for lane changes, obeying all laws.

Ray-Ray was standing outside the door to her room, arms loose at his side, watching everything in the hall. He had on one of his flashy Lily Pulitzer sport coats and pressed jeans. He merely nodded as I went in.

She was in bed, with the back raised so she could work on the dissertation notes piled next to her, but she was reading a two-month-old copy of *Us* magazine. "Hey, Sailor," she said softly, and actually grinned. She had a black eye, a butterfly bandage across the bridge of her nose and a gauze square in front of her left ear. That one, the gauze in front of her ear, high on her smooth cheek, had a tiny brown stain where blood had seeped through. That has become another memory snapshot, like the petals from Nadzia's white gardenia corsage fluttering to the floor—that tiny little stain where blood had seeped through her bandage. Under the hospital gown I could see lumps where her ribs were wrapped. An IV on a chrome stand dripped something into her arm.

"I'll wait outside." Elijah Eddington III turned from where he'd been standing, looking out the window. I hadn't even noticed him. "Take all the time you want. But then we need to talk."

When the door closed after him she lost it. Her face crumpled, just came apart and tears started running down her cheeks. She dropped *Us* to the floor, sobbed and pounded her fists on the mattress, causing the IV tube to flop around wildly and the tall chrome rack to tip. I caught the rack, went to put my arms around her. She shoved me away. Without thinking I reached out again and she batted my arm aside, glared at me. "They made it look so easy. Just so damn *easy*. There were two, a man and a woman, they looked like a couple just walking down the street arm-in-arm so I didn't pay attention, and the woman punched me in the stomach, no warning, just this nice couple walking by and 'Wham' I'm doubled over and I can remember all the moves, I know what to do, I know exactly what I'm supposed to do, I just can't do it . . ."

"I think those gloves she wears have weights in them."

". . . went down, books everywhere, and as I rolled—I got that part right at least—I thought, 'So this is what it's like.' Then the man was behind me and he had my arms and he lifted me up and the woman hit me again, in the ribs. I tried to kick her but she was too quick. I got in a head butt, connected to her cheekbone, and she just laughed. Her hat came off and it was that woman, we saw a Nadzia's party, that Faith Valentine. The man grabbed my hair and pulled my head back and she got in my face and said, 'Tell your boyfriend time's up. Next time—we get serious.'"

Kandi punched the mattress again, then took a deep breath. I reached out and this time she let me hold her hand. We were quiet for a moment, the only sounds the muted hospital noises, carts rolling by and machines beeping rhythmically, announcements,

"Respiratory tech call 403. RT call 403," all filtering in from the hall as if life were going on normally. There was the ever-present hospital smell, made up of equal parts disinfectant, medications, pain, and fear. The sheets rustled as she shifted position. I buried my face in her blonde crimped curls and she pressed a hand to my back. *She* was comforting *me*.

"Mac, I want you to promise me something."

I kept my head buried in her hair. It smelled nice, better than the hospital. "What?"

"Don't do what you're thinking. Don't go after the people who did this."

"Right now that's not what I'm thinking about." Especially since I've already started.

She didn't understand. That was okay.

I trained in a very tough arena. Business believes so much in "Eat the weak" that it's an article of faith that doesn't even need to be articulated, and Wall Street, the laugh-a-minute world of stock manipulation, leveraged buy-outs, insider trading, and layoffs, makes the regular business world look like Disneyland. One lesson, perhaps the number one lesson, is 'Give in to emotion and lose.' Stephen Covey, who cares a lot about ethics and still makes money, says, 'First things first.'

So the incredible rage that clawed from my heart to my throat and back to my heart again, like a vicious animal inside me, that emotion was caged. It didn't like the cage, but for now I could keep it in there.

So, first things first. Assess Kandi's condition and make her feel, if not better, then less scared, alone, and hurt. Second, make it as hard as possible for these people to get to her again. Third, gather some information.

Then, why, then it might just be time to open that cage door.

"That's not what I'm thinking about."

"Promise me."

"I know what you want. I promise I'll be careful."

"I'm serious. You have limits, they don't."

A doctor bustled in, gave me a hard look before she turned to Kandi and said, "Your x-rays are negative. We'll have the lab work back in an hour or so. If it's okay we'll release you in the morning." She looked at me again. "Sir, would you mind waiting outside?"

I kissed Kandi's forehead and said, "You rest. There will be somebody here at all times. You're safe." She started to speak. I touched her lips with my fingertip.

At the door I thought *Limits? Of course. We just haven't found them yet.*

In the hall, Eddington said, "Mac, I'm sorry as hell I got ya'll into this I—" He paused, shook his head. "Shit. That ain't true. Nadzia's dead and that's connected to what happened here, ain't it? And you're my best chance at finding the people who did it. That's what you're gonna do."

"Yes."

He looked at me, shivered, dropped his eyes. "There's some things I didn't tell you. I should have."

"Like when Nadzia fired the first guy and insisted I drive the wet bike, you were all for it because you thought she was in trouble and I'd be a bodyguard."

"I thought you would figure it out. You knew and you did it anyway."

"You're my friend. She was my friend."

"Anything, anything you need—"

"Ray-Ray stays with Kandi. He was here in Huntington Beach already, wasn't he?"

"Yeah, it seemed like I might need him and Edna and there's other people who can take care of Agatha. Of course, he stays with Kandi. They both will. Where will you be?"

"Talking to another friend."

"Mac, wait, please. When I said, 'Anything you need' I meant it, of course—"

"Elijah, just say it."

"Nadzia was involved with the New Five to One. That's what the folks looking for this thing call themselves."

"Yes. They sent me a toe."

"Nadzia helped them, and some of the things she helped them with were bad."

"She didn't kill me. She was supposed to."

"What? How—Well, anyway, I just got off the phone with Agatha and Agatha thinks it may be time to let this go. Let the authorities handle it. She thinks it's getting out of hand."

"What do you think?"

He looked miserable. "She may be right."

I shook my head. "She is right. Okay, you've said what she wanted you to. But you don't fool me, Elijah. Is this the forward who took a shot to the throat, was carried off the court, and came back in the third quarter to level the guy who did it?"

He chuckled, remembering. "The T-wolves, that's who we was playin'. Romanian guy, big and mean, that fool clipped me a good one." He absently rubbed his throat. "I got called for a flagrant foul."

"So Nadzia got pushed around and decided to push back. They tried to get her, take her with them by force, didn't they? The parents."

"The first time they did get her. Two young guys from the church grabbed her, hustled her into a car." He grinned, unpleasantly. "My guess is they thought they was grabbing a teenage girl. What they got was full-on pissed-off skate bitch. She hit one in the face with her skateboard, broke the fool's nose, and bailed out of the car when the driver slowed to gape at the blood from his buddy's face. How did you guess?"

"She told me part of it. And it was just too pat—she tells them, 'I want to stay' and the parents say, 'Okay, sure.' And she was too angry. Also, that explains the level of security you kept around her. Guessing is a shocking habit, anyway." I paused. Our eyes met.

A range of emotions flashed across his face as we stood in the busy hospital corridor, listening to discreet, muted conversations from the nurse's station, aware of the impassive, alert Ray-Ray, now joined by Edna, standing on either side of Kandi's door—emotions ranging from misery to anger, to uncertainty, and finally settling on thin-lipped anger. He nodded. "Let's do it," he said. "Let's get the fuckers. I'll convince Agatha to keep paying the bills, and if she doesn't, I will. What's your next move?"

"Talk to an old friend. What he says will drive the next step."

Chet, of course, had heard the news and called.

"You had one of them and you let him go?" Chet sounded confused.

"I want Baines to know I'm coming. Makes him predictable."

"Whoa."

"I have a plan."

Chapter Twenty-One   Feed Your Head

I found the Snake once again sitting in the darkened living room of his tiny house. As I parked the Chevy in his driveway I saw that the drapes were open. It was almost six am, a hazy glow behind Saddleback mountain signaling a new day. He saw me coming up the cement walk. He didn't get up. I opened the screen door. I sat on the couch. He didn't turn his head. In profile he was round, bearded, and gray. And miserable. Well, there was a lot of that going around.

"How long has Cheryl been with them?"

He sighed. "I'm not sure exactly. How did you—"

"Poetry. Everybody talked about a poetry reading, she's the only poet I know, she has radical leanings. And she's gone, isn't she?"

"They've got Cheryl," he said. "Think how you'd feel if somebody had Kandi." I didn't have to imagine—I knew. A few months ago Kandi had, in fact, been kidnapped by Roger Winters, who was still out there somewhere, still crazy, and still a problem that I'd have to deal with sooner or later. Later. "I know about Kandi. I'm sorry." There was a lot of that going around, too.

"Snake—"

"Let's walk." He jammed his feet into sandals, stood up and stumbled out the front door. My friend was easy to catch as he ambled along Third Street toward Ocean Boulevard and the beach. The sun was almost all the way up. A group of five or six kids on BMX bikes rode by, all wearing wetsuits, and carrying short tri-fin surfboards under their arms. They checked us out and snickered.

"You might want to do something about that," I said, and nodded at the unlit bomber joint in his hand.

"Oh. Yeah. Raided Cheryl's stash. She says it's good shit." He casually dropped it in his shirt pocket.

"If you're gonna carry it around you should make it a blunt. Hollow out a cigar and stuff it in."

He snorted. "That's for the hip-hop crowd. I'll take mine straight, like a man. How much have you figured out?"

"It started with Cheryl. She met some old radicals, probably at one of her poetry readings, and they told her stories about the old days at Berkeley and a fire and some kind of biologic weapon. Now Blondell Baines and his crew, the New Five To One, want it."

"Yeah."

"Nadzia Kamnik was at the reading and hooked up with Baines and friends and she was looking for a way to hit back for what her parents did to her."

"Cheryl quoted her as saying, 'You want End of Days? I'll give you End of Days.'"

"Then, when it wasn't a game anymore, Nadzia changed her mind."

"They both did. At least, I'm pretty sure Cheryl wants out. They let her call me a little while ago."

"And she said she wants out?"

"No, no, of course not. I mean, people are listening, all the time." He looked over his shoulder, then went back to staring down at his sandals. Not me. My attention was on the quiet street around us, and on the gun in my shoulder holster. "Surveillance nation, man. No, according to her everything's fine, she can't tell me where she is, but she'll be home soon. Water her African violets."

"That's it?"

"Mac, we've been married forty years, come June. She wants out, I know it, I know it in my heart. When you came I was sitting there trying to think of a way to find her, or what to say to you when you showed up. She didn't mean this. I didn't mean this." He looked up at me and for a minute I was certain he would break into tears.

"Oh, really? You didn't intend for your wife of forty years to get kidnapped by a gang of vicious psychos?" He stared at me, open-mouthed. I grinned. "C'mon, you hippie degenerate, snap out of it." I punched him lightly on the shoulder. To do what needed to be done I needed Snake functional. What happened to our friendship was something that would come later.

He smiled weakly. "You're an asshole."

"So I've been told. We've been in trouble before, you and I."

"What am I gonna do?"

"We. What are we going to do. Get her back, of course. Tell me everything you know." He did. Unfortunately, it wasn't much.

"Tell me about Five To One." He looked at me. "If there's a 'New' there's probably an original. And keep in mind that I already know quite a bit."

"You're testing me." When I said nothing he nodded. "At Berkeley in the sixties there was an underground group, like the Weathermen or the SLA, called themselves Five to One, and they wrote to papers claiming responsibility for at least one fire. I was questioned and released and so was Cheryl. And that's all I know."

"And the fire in the lab?"

He swallowed, took the joint out of his pocket, looked at it, put it back. "Rumor had it they were doing government work on the side."

"Perfect."

I went home and slept for a few hours, with the house locked down and my .45 next to me. My sawed-off shotgun leaned against the headboard. When I woke up I took a shower and knew what to do.

First I called Henrietta Graveline. "My patience is at an end. I want the whole story. Now."

She didn't even bother trying to get out of it. "Brad didn't go to Catalina. Come to the harbor. We'll go out on the Waiting for the Sun. And, honey, I'm sorry, so, so sorry."

Brad Zucco's yacht was on autopilot, cruising slowly south, heading out of the Long Beach harbor toward Avalon. He brought me a Dos Equis Dark. It should have made me nervous that everybody knew my choice of beer but I was beyond that. They were all there: Henrietta, dressed in jeans and a long-sleeved gray sweater that matched her eyes, Lisa June Culhane in shorts and an orange t-shirt, Brad in his board shorts and black tee.

About a mile outside the breakwater he cut the diesels and the only sound was the sea lapping against the hull. "Okay, we can talk here."

Henrietta took the lead. Setting her wine goblet aside, she looked directly at me and said, "We killed a man."

"You were Five to One. The original." Henrietta just looked over my shoulder at the sea. Zucco's jaw dropped. Lisa June choked on her wine.

Brad figured it out. "You knew?" He choked. "Henrietta, you knew he'd identified us?"

Before she could answer, I said, "Brad, old buddy, if you're thinking maybe I should have a terrible accident, fall overboard, well, you're welcome to try." They were older than me, but there were three of them, they grew up in the drug generation, and that bottle of beer had been open when Zucco handed it to me.

Henrietta ignored my chest-beating act, which made me feel better. Maybe I hadn't been lured out here to get tossed overboard. "We want to tell you the story."

Lisa June blurted, "It was an accident and I'm sorry, oh, hell, I don't even know what I'm sorry for, all of it, I guess I'm sorry for all of it. Go on, you tell it, Medea." She drank the rest of her wine and held out her glass for Zucco to fill, focusing on the pale yellow liquid as it filled the glass, murmured, "Remember that Sangria we used to make? Red Mountain and oranges sliced up. And sometimes we had to shoplift the oranges?"

Brad, filling her glass, said, "Yeah, big whoops. Personally, I think the good old days sucked." He snorted. "Broke. All the time broke." He gestured at the cabin of the yacht, checked the course and radar, spoke without turning. "But, all right, I'm overruled."

Henrietta looked at me intently and said, "First you must understand, it was 1967, a different time. Moral certitude. Yes, moral certitude. We were Right, with a capital 'R.' There were five of us, at first. We all made up names that we used when we wrote to this underground paper called the Berkeley Broccoli. I was Medea, Lisa June is Anna, and Brad is Moloch."

"Medea, Moloch, and Anna?"

"She was reading Anna Karenina. Nadine was Cassandra, Mark was just Mark. He wouldn't play."

Brad—Moloch—chuckled. "They got the guns, we got the numbers. And we believed that shit."

Henrietta once again was the spokesperson. "We were undergrads at Berkeley. I said it was a different time. I wonder if I can make you understand just *how* different it was." She stared at her wine, slowly twirling the glass. "The world was changing, for the better, at least, that's what we believed. Morrison said it best. We went to a concert at the Fillmore, not The Doors, some other group. Oh, honey, it was so amazing, everybody wasted, dancing in the aisles, wherever and we knew it was the beginning of something wonderful. So we get back to our apartment—we had this place in the Castro and it had this Murphy bed, you know, the kind that pulls down out of the wall—and about three am we're sitting on the bed smoking some weed—"

"That great Thai stick." Zucco brought us fresh drinks. I decided, what the hell if they were going to throw me overboard another beer wouldn't matter. "I bought it off a black guy in my Federal Accounting class"

Henrietta looked out at the sea. "I knew him. He was killed, wasn't he? I saw his name on the Wall. I think it was him." Her breath caught. "Now I can't remember his name, but I saw it, I know I did." Zucco nodded. Henrietta got up, stood for a moment looking out. I wondered what she was seeing. She shook herself and picked up the wine bottle. While she was pouring for Lisa June the Sun hit some chop and the yacht corkscrewed, but she didn't spill a drop. Seeing that I had noticed, she shrugged and said, "Lots of lab work." She filled her own glass. "So many," she murmured. She tossed her head and I realized she was in the past, flipping long hair out of her face, long dark hair that I could almost see—parted in the middle and bangs, yeah, she'd have had bangs. It had been gone for probably more years than I'd been alive. "So, this kid, a dealer we called Pryboy, comes to the door of the apartment and he's totally stoned, screaming that Nadine owes him money for a lid she bought last week."

Lisa June took up the story. "It got hinky really fast because Nadine—Cassandra—says she paid him and the next thing we know he's got this gun out—a real gun, I know because back home one of my Daddy's friends was the Chief of Police and he used to come out to the house and he always had his gun—and Pryboy's waving it around and yelling that we're all narcs, but then he starts laughing and says it's okay because he's a narc too and he won't shoot us if Nadine pays for the lid."

Brad said, "He was pretty wasted."

Henrietta continued. "So he points the gun at Nadine and pulls the trigger, just like that, bang! He missed and Brad jumped him."

"We all did."

Lisa June patted his arm. "You were first, dear. You probably saved all of us."

I said, "So there was a struggle, the gun went off . . ."

Henrietta shook her head. "No, it wasn't like that. Our fifth friend, Mark, had eaten a whole blotter of acid—"

"Yeah," Zucco grinned. "Good shit. Had Donald Duck printed on it. I *told* him to just do half."

"It was Minnie Mouse flipping the bird. Anyway, he'd been sitting in the corner for an hour staring—"

Lisa June giggled, "Death by potato peeler." Her eyes got huge, "I can't believe I said that. Oh, God, I'm sorry." She drank the rest of her wine, muttered, "God, I keep saying that."

I looked back at the shoreline, slowly receding behind us as the tide carried us out. This was one of the places I'd trained with Nadzia, when we were doing offshore catches. "What next?"

"Mark just stared at the potato peeler for maybe an hour. Then he went into the bathroom, and he never turned the light on."

Lisa June, pouring herself more wine, killing that bottle, giggled. "He always called it pissing by sonar. He wanted to be a writer."

"And Pryboy comes in, and Mark comes out of the bathroom and he's still got the potato peeler, and he jumps on the pile with the rest of us. I'm not even sure he knew what was going on. So, all at once Pryboy's on the floor, just laying there, not moving and when we roll him over he's got this wood handle sticking out of his throat. And we're all going, 'Holy shit where did *that* come from?'"

Lisa June said, "He died really quick because it went up into his brain or something." Zucco looked out over the bow. "Death by potato peeler," she mumbled into her glass.

"What does this have to do with the bacteria?"

Henrietta said, "Oh, we'll get there, trust me on that. Nadine wanted to call the police."

Zucco shook his head. "Can you imagine bringing the pigs in? No, no, you can't. Think about it: we're so stoned we can't figure out how to fold up the Murphy bed, so we're sitting on it and now we got a dead guy on the floor, we killed him, and this is a time when, 'Outta the car, long-hair' was not a joke. We'd be getting out of jail just about now, maybe."

Lisa June picked up the wine bottle, found it empty. "And there were other complications. Like, two days before this happened, Pryboy beat up Nadine, and Mark said he'd kill him."

Henrietta nodded "Unfortunately, she really took chong—bad bruises, a black eye, he racked her up good, and Mark was upset and it was in the cafeteria when he said he'd kill Pryboy."

I said, "Witnesses."

"About a hundred, give or take."

"So you had this dead guy in your apartment. What then?"

Lisa June rummaged in her purse, took something out and dry-swallowed it. "Hmmm? Pryboy? Oh, we put him in the bathtub. Henrietta told us to. She figured it all out."

Brad took up the story "Then Henrietta had us go through his pockets. He had a hundred bucks in his wallet and a little over two thousand in his boots. So around four am we snuck him up the stairs to his apartment, and when we searched it we found ten grand in cash, almost three keys of weed, and a baggie full of reds. Mark says, 'We're fuckin' rich.'"

"And Henrietta says, 'No, but we could be.'"

"Get to the bacteria."

"Oh, I'm pretty sure it's a girus—a giant virus. So we sold the dope. We knew we didn't want to be dealers, even back then it was too scary and people were getting killed, but we had start-up money and we started Co-Ed Taxes."

Lisa June said, "It was great. I recruited girls from my modeling classes; Brad trained them. You got your taxes done by a cute co-ed in our uniform—white boots and a white micro-mini.

We let the girls could wear whatever color blouse they wanted. Most of our customers were men."

Henrietta patted her knee. "And we all got rich. Brad was a business major and he was good with money."

"What happened to the others?"

There was a pause. Lisa June said, "Mark got drafted."

Brad said, "MIA."

"Nadine?"

Henrietta sighed. "She couldn't handle it. Dropped out, drifted around. One morning they found her body on the rocks below The Cliff House restaurant."

"She was such a sweet girl. I wish . . ." Lisa June's voice trailed off.

I said, "Finish it, Henrietta. The flesh-eating whatever."

"Yes, there was a sample in the lab. It behaved like a flesh-eating bacteria, but mild, strictly non-lethal in all of our tests and then there was a fire. But it was a long, long time ago, and like I said, the stuff wasn't that bad, anyway. Hazardous, but not lethal. Anyway, it made a good story for the underground papers and so we became Five to One because then we could write to them and say Pryboy was a narc and we killed him and that threw everybody off our tracks, and when the paper said they thought we were responsible for the fire in the lab, well, we let it go. Then we sold the business and moved down here, I think it was 1975 or 76. Now somebody's heard about us, Five to One, and wants to imitate us. They think we have the sample."

Lisa June said, "And we always knew that someday we'd have to pay for what we did. It was wrong. Cassandra—Nadine—knew. We were too rich, it was too easy."

I said, "And Baines found out and wants it. He claims he wants to change the world. Help him or he'll expose you."

"It's not as bad as it seems."

"Well, Baines is willing to kill to get it."

"How did you figure it out?"

"Research is second nature to a broker-analyst. I noticed the name of Brad's boat."

Brad said, "Oops."

"'Waiting for the Sun' is a Doors album. Popped right up on Google. But registration shows this is the first boat you've owned with that name. The numbers at the end aren't roman numerals at all, and the eleventh song on that album is called 'Five to One.'"

Brad said, "One in five."

Henrietta finished. "No one here gets out alive."

Chapter Twenty-Two   Moving Target

Zucco started the diesels, turned us back toward shore. "The Doors were wrong. The Who nailed it."

Henrietta said, "Meet the new boss, same as the old boss. Will you help us?"

"I took your money, didn't I?"

My next step was to go to a party. Kandi had been released from Long Beach Memorial and was back in her apartment with Edna camped in her living room and Ray-Ray dropping in regularly. I called Chet and had him do some work at my house, then accepted the invite to the Al-Thani gala.

Harriet Ousvenskaya Al-Thani, one of my best friends in the LA office of Fields, Smith, and Barkman, was getting an award. She had invited me to the event at the spacey glass towers of the Bonaventure Hotel in downtown Los Angeles, and it suited my purposes to be away from the house and my usual hangouts for a while. I locked the .45 in the gun safe, stashed my pool cue handle in my sock drawer, and climbed into my best black suit. Since my Armani tux had not survived rolling around on the beach in tar and kelp, I'd told the butler at the Long Beach airport to give it to Good Will.

Tell me about your adventures.

The Bonaventure is the jewel of the LA Financial District. It features a six-story glass atrium; Jules Verne glass elevators slide up and down the lobby delivering people to their rooms and to the revolving bar at the top, the one with the spectacular view of downtown LA. In this case I was headed for a private party large enough to fill one of the special-purpose rooms on the third floor. The hotel boasts the largest hotel banquet room in LA, but Harriet had settled for a mid-sized room, expecting only a few hundred of her closest friends.

I pushed my way through the crowd, awash in the sounds of people drinking and eating. And talking, always talking. Mergers, acquisitions, new issues, predictions on what the Feds would do next to the interest rate, and of course who was banging who and why. One or two refugees from academia who felt impelled, after a few shots of pretentious tequila, to argue the merits, or lack thereof, of behavioral economics as if it were life-and-death. A small combo played easy-listening jazz but was mostly drowned out by the talk. According to the invitation they would be replaced by a DJ later and there would be dancing. I didn't plan to be around for it. The food was actually quite good for a buffet, and only a few people wanted to hear about my adventures since Bernice pulled me away from selling with the news about Diana, and I hung up the phone to walk off the trading floor at FSB. Diana's dead, Nadzia's dead, surf's up.

I waved to a few people I knew from the time I spent in the LA office. Of course my boss Ervin Barkman wasn't there. He'd come to the West Coast once and hated it and I could never make him understand about Orange County not being about a block south of LAX.

There were three new hires—Stanford, UCLA, and Harvard, the two young men aggressively casual in unstuffed white shirts under black $5,000 Armani suits, no ties, the woman in a severe long-sleeved black cocktail dress, Versace, high-necked in front and backless. All of them were determined to look cool, not like they had just moved out of a college apartment, living on Stouffer's and microwave popcorn, into a two-hundred-grand-a-year job, not counting bonus. Nadzia had had that look when she made her entrance at Duke's. 'I made it. I can't believe I made it,' and you know what? I probably had it once, myself.

I was the only guest whose coat was tailored to conceal a shoulder holster. I was the only guest with a fading black eye, a souvenir of a real-life car chase.

Harriet, a permanent fiftyish, going against the grain by wearing a red floor-length gown, plump and smiling, collared me at the bar sipping a club soda with a twist of lime. I said, "Congratulations. You look very nice, Harriet."

"Thanks, Mac, and thanks for coming. You look a little worse for wear. How's the shoulder?"

My left shoulder took some damage when I was wrestling, then I slammed it into the railing when Roger Winters shoved me down a flight of stairs. After I wrecked my Carrera on the beach it had been giving me some trouble. I'd made the mistake of mentioning it in an interview. Before I could answer she moved on.

"Okay, enough with the idle chit-chat. Meet Del." A tall, skinny blonde with short spiked hair, no make-up, wearing a lime green pantsuit stepped up and held out her hand. As we shook, Harriet said, "You need to walk Del to her car. Then if you want come back and we can have a nice chat." Harriet looked at me and I read urgency in her eyes. She nodded fractionally.

"My pleasure." I put my glass down.

I offered her my arm and she ignored it. "I could lose my job over this," Del said.

"Hey, I haven't assaulted a young woman in, oh, several hours," I said and at once regretted it for multiple reasons.

Harriet shrugged. "Yes, sweetie, you could. But if you don't tell him you'll more than irritate me, so make up your mind." She looked toward the doors where four large men in identical gray suits came in, surrounding an elderly man in flowing white burnoose. "The prince! Mac, take care." She gave me a quick hug and kiss on the cheek and turned to go. Then she turned back. "When I said, 'Take care' I meant it. You watch your back. And listen to what Del tells you." Then she was gone trailing a wave of Chanel.

Del muttered, "Fat bitch." All at once she had her cell phone out and was furiously thumbing the keys. She showed me the text before tapping Send. It was to Harriet. It said: I'm doing it because it's right. I'm not afraid of you.

"Harriet is my friend."

She sniffed. "That's not my fault. All right, let's get this over with."

Walking across the crowded, noisy ballroom, I said, "Look, she's a good person to have on your side."

Del flared, "I'm not one of the money honeys in their darling little black dresses at three grand a pop. I'm the assistant DBA for FSB West."

"Well, BFD."

After that the conversation sort of died and we rode the elevator down to the parking level in silence.

Striding along between two rows of parked cars, with her looking down at her shoes—green to match the pantsuit, one with a smudge on the toe—while I tried to look everywhere, she muttered, "Okay, I deserved that, I guess. But I'm scared. Oh shit, my car's right here and we still need to talk."

I bent and pretended to tie my shoe. "Don't look at me. Look around the area and tell me *at once* if you see anybody. And talk fast, because parking structures make me nervous."

"Oh, no. Oh no. I knew it. Oh, I *hate* this scary stuff."

On TV the hero says, 'You're safe with me.' I knew better. I looked up and met her eyes. "I said not to look at me. And talk fast. I know you're scared. It'll be all right. Deep breaths." Who else had I said that to? Alys Winters. Too much, too fast—I'd lost track. I had a bad feeling of events spinning out of control.

"Okay, okay. Yeah, deep breath. Okay, what happened was that Kevin, he's the Data Base Administrator and my boss, was out sick and I was on night duty when somebody started accessing personnel files and they're really restricted."

"And one of them was my personnel file."

"Yours was the *only* file they really cared about. It took them a while to find it because you're sort of on leave." At that she looked down at me, hoping I'd fill in the details, provide some gossip for the coffee room. I didn't oblige. "Anyway, I see the activity so I block them at once, and then I start running a trace and I text Kevin and an hour later the word came back down to me personally to stop. A text directly to me."

"And that's unusual."

"Yes, and that's when it gets weird. The text telling me to quit looking into the hack? *It* was a hack. Somebody was punking me." I must have looked blank. "The text telling me to stop said it was from Kevin but it wasn't. Kevin didn't know anything about it. I was punked." She was involved in the story now, treating it as an interesting problem to solve, and so she forgot to be scared. "So by now Kevin's come into the office and I tell Kevin all this and he's pissed that somebody's in the system and that they obviously read my text to him. We've been hacked three times, once to get your file, once to read my text to Kevin, and once to send me the fake message."

"And?"

"And nothing. It just dies. We do all kinds of stuff to tighten security, and, boy, did we get complaints! So I'm complaining, too, right? In the break room and the little princess from Harvard looks up from her tweets and says, 'Macdonald? I heard about him. He's Harriet's bud. You better tell her."

I stood up from pretending to tie my shoe. "I don't understand about the 'I might get fired.'"

"Now they've really clamped down. The big bosses are afraid that if clients find out we got hacked they'd get scared and pull their money. I'm not supposed to talk to anybody."

"They're right. Clients are funny about things like information leaks, but I think this will be all right. Okay, thanks." I looked at her in her green pantsuit that didn't quite match her shoes, unsuccessfully mingling at a party full of money honeys in darling little black dresses from Versace, knowing that what she did was far more intellectually challenging and difficult than moving piles of money around, and that it paid less than half of what they took home. Now she was scared again, looking over my shoulder, watching around. A quick study. A white sedan cruised by the end of our aisle and up the ramp to Figueroa Boulevard. "What else?"

"I heard about the girl, the one who got killed. I'm sorry. This is the same people, isn't it?"

"Maybe. We'll say it is for now." But somehow it didn't feel right. "What else?"

"You'll think I'm delusional. *I* think I'm delusional."

"Okay, you're nuts. Tell me anyway."

"You're a jerk." Well, that was a step up from asshole, I guess. "I think somebody's following me."

She probably was delusional, but probably wasn't good enough. "All right, listen to me. If things go bad and for any reason I can't help you, call New York, Barkman's office."

Her eyes widened. "Mr. Barkman, the partner?"

"Yeah. Talk to a woman named Bernice, and *only* to her. She's Barkman's assistant. Tell her everything, including this conversation and that I said to call. She'll help you."

"Barkman's office. Bernice."

I punched a number on my cell. "Fidel? Mac. Yeah, hey, I know, I know, I'm back in LA and I haven't called to collect that beer you owe me and don't claim it's the other way around, you Cuban welcher. Go ahead, tell me I'm a jerk." He did and I laughed. Now that the formalities had been observed, I went on. "I'll bet you and your stalwart minions are all over the Bonaventure event."

"Stalwart minions? What you been reading, amigo?" Fidel is in charge of security for FSB, an old beer buddy, good for talk that wasn't about money and a sucker for bad basketball bets.

"The master, of course. 221B Baker Street and the game is definitely afoot."

"Wish I was rich so I could smoke the good stuff. Yeah, we got us a real, live Saudi prince at the event in addition to the usual rich types, so I'm coordinating with Bonaventure security, Saudi security, the LAPD and I got two calls from Homeland Security. What's up? One of us is working here and it ain't you. And, by the way, this ain't your regular cell, it's a new number."

"Bonaventure parking structure, level three, young woman, FSB employee, needs an escort home. It's a long story, but it would be a good idea if you could provide that and an apartment check once you get her there."

"Wait one. Okay, I see you." I flipped the camera the bird. "Wrong one, pal. That one's just for show. To your left. She drunk? She need somebody to drive her?

"No, she can drive. Her name is Del—" I looked at the girl.

"Midler."

"Midler."

"Can't believe you don't know her last name. Yeah, that's her. Got her ID here. No problem; company wants us to take care of things like this."

"Thanks, man. I appreciate it."

"We even on that Lakers thing?"

"What's that? Double or nothing on the Stanley Cup?"

"Asshole." A short time later Fidel himself pulled up in a white Porsche Cayenne SUV, nodded to me and they left, the big car trailing her little green Beetle

Chapter Twenty-Three   In the Killing Jar

Back inside I spent another hour at the party, this time with coffee and chatter, figured that was enough time. Then I sent Chet a two-word text.

```
Let's rock.
```

This time they took me inside of my garage and I made it difficult. It was the guy from behind my house and another man I'd never seen before, crouching and rushing in before the door rolled down. They each grabbed one of my arms, high up on the bicep; I went limp at once, letting my weight pull them down with me. The smart one let go and, stepping aside quickly, kicked me hard high up on the meaty part of my thigh, just below the hip bone. Pain exploded up and down my leg and it decided to take some time off, refusing to support my weight. His buddy had foolishly held on, bending over with me as I went down; under other circumstances it would have looked like I'd stumbled and he was trying to help me up. As my numb leg folded under me, I head-butted him in the face, rolled on my back, slammed my knee up into his gut, and threw him over my shoulder into his pal. The fool still had my arm and as we tumbled onto the cold cement I let go of him and felt a stab of pain in my shoulder, followed by sudden flaring heat that radiated down to my elbow. My right thigh and left shoulder were on fire. My car keys—complete with alarm panic button—skittered across the floor and under the car.

I pushed with my elbow, rolled over, got some support from one arm and one leg, and started crabbing toward the door to the house. I wasn't too fast. Here's a laugh—what popped into my head as I crawled along, trying to get away from two guys who wanted to do me serious bodily harm, was, "First my tux, now my best black suit." Mary's right: the brain is a funny thing.

Two crab steps and a foot slammed down firmly into my back; my tweaked shoulder and aching hip couldn't take it and I was mashed face-down into the cement. A voice I recognized said, "I should let him get away from you clowns, or maybe I should beat the crap out of you myself."

Oops. There were three of them, not two. And one of them was somebody I really didn't want to tangle with unless I had to. The foot was removed; I rolled over on my back and saw Faith Valentine step back and lean casually against my car. She had on a short, black leather skirt, a white blouse and a black leather jacket.

"We had him. He just got lucky." The one who'd kicked me sounded sulky.

She pulled a compact and mirror out of her purse and touched up her lipstick as she said, "Bag him. You idiots think you can handle that while I get the car?" Perfect. Just what I wanted.

They dragged me to my feet and pushed me up against the Chevy. When they jerked my arms in back of me to wrap plastic cable-ties around my wrists, my shoulder hurt so much that waves of gray started occluding the edges of my vision and I nearly passed out. I swayed and—oh, joy—found what Faith Valentine meant by "Bag him" when a thick, plastic bag was pulled over my head and a cord tightened around my neck. The bag had a lot of dust in it and smelled funny; then I recognized the odor from a short stint taking care of a friend's pet in New York—my head was jammed inside an empty cat litter bag. The dust got to me. I sneezed explosively three times and heard the guys laugh. Then they started in on me.

Take my word for it, getting worked over is bad any time, but getting worked over when you can't see where the next blow is aimed really sucks. Stomach, face, ribs, kidneys, no pattern to the blows, just pain punctuated by grunts and once, "Ow!" as one of them hurt his hand. On my face. It's easy to break one of the small bones in your hand on somebody's face, and I sincerely hoped his was shattered. They kept it up, taking turns, grunting with effort. Every once in a while I'd lash out with my bad leg, (had to stand on the good one or fall down) just to keep them honest, but I never connected; after a while it just hurt too much to keep it up so I quit. Then I fell over (discovering that it's much harder to roll and break a fall when you can't see the floor).

I heard a car pull up; a car door thunked and they stopped beating on me. Maybe they were tired. I was pulled to my feet and dragged probably to the car. I made them drag me, making my leg look worse than it was, at least worse than I hoped it was. I'd find out when I had to use it. Something that might have been a bumper pressed into my shins.

Faith's voice said, "Can't you two do anything right? I said strip him."

One of them said, "Take your shoes off."

"What? Why?" That got me a punch in the gut. I waved my tied wrists, there was some muttered talk, then my hands were cut free. I bent painfully, only exaggerating a little, and pulled my shoes and socks off. Faith said, "Nice suit. Take it off." I just couldn't help myself. "I thought you'd never ask. To my surprise I didn't get punched. I pulled off my pants, coat, tie and shirt, harder than you might think with my head covered and stood shivering in my boxers while they conferred in low tones and then bound my hands again, behind my back.

Okay, on TV this never happens—not getting stuffed into the trunk of a car, that happens all the time—but when it does the hero or heroine never has the normal biologic problem. Not me. I'd had a Dos Equis Dark, a club soda, followed by three cups of passable French Roast before I left Harriet's party at the Bonaventure, followed by an hour cruising south on the 110 and 405 freeways. When they started pushing my head down preparatory to stuffing me into the trunk, I said, "I need to take a leak."

The one I'd thrown in the channel said, "Tough," while the other snickered.

"Here or in the car, pal. Your choice."

There was some muttering, then Faith said, "Mr. Baines would hate it in the limo, even in the trunk. Take him around to the side of the house."

The one I'd head-butted (he sounded very congested) said, "I ain't taggun it out. No fuggun way. Huh-uh."

"Do I have to figure out everything?"

I said, "Hey, Faith, honey, I can answer that," which got me a kidney punch, but on the whole I thought it was worth it even though it exacerbated my aforementioned problem.

The long-suffering Ms Valentine solved the problem. "Move his hands in front. Use another tie. And if you hit him again without orders from me you will be very, very sorry."

"Hey, baby, I just knew if it was that kind of problem it would be something you could handle, so to speak." I leered in her direction, but of course my face was hidden under my dusty, smelly, cat litter bag.

Things went, er, smoothly, at the side of the house. I did think for a moment about the conversation that would take place if my fussy neighbor, USC cheerleader-turned O. C. socialite Beth Applegate, happened to look out her side window and, as she did at every opportunity, called the cops.

"Yes, officer, I'm sure it was some kind of ritual. There were three of them and one of them was in his underwear and he had a hood over his head and he was *urinating*! Right there at the side of the house!"

Nasal-voice said, "What are you laughing at?"

"That's just relief."

"A word of friendly advice. You really don't want to piss her off."

"Nice choice of words, but thanks, I'll remember."

I finished; they led me back and forced me into the trunk, head first, then folding my legs in, a painful process. They threw some cloth in on top of me that might have been my suit, closed the lid and we drove for a while. Sherlock Holmes would have kept track of turns, taken note of sounds and smells along the way, and known exactly where he was at all times. Me? I knew we drove for a while. I knew I was in the trunk of a car, probably a limousine because it was a big trunk. Also, Faith had used the word, 'limo' and I was sure that was a clue.

In situations like this the thing to do is think about something else, something other than being locked in the trunk of a car with your hands tied, some pointy object digging into your side and a cat litter bag over your head. I thought about surfing. I listed favorite spots, starting with Trestles, then the Huntington Pier (north side of course) and moving up the coast, there was Fifth Street, Seventeenth Street, Dog Beach, Thalia Street in Redondo Beach, and D&W, aka Isidore B. Dockweiler State Beach at the foot of Imperial Highway and thus right under the take-off from LAX. I'd worked my way as far north as County Line, almost to Santa Barbara, before the car stopped.

When they got their hands under my arms and dragged me out, scraping my back against the bumper, my legs cramped after being folded and I would have fallen if they hadn't held me up. My arms were numb but my shoulder was on fire and every place I'd been punched hurt, and I'd been punched just about everywhere. Well, it was what I'd been expecting. After all, I'd caused them a lot of trouble. And it was worth it, since I'd gone to a fair amount of trouble to get here.

They led me for a short distance. I tried to shuffle my feet in case there were steps. Falling down a flight of stairs was not part of the plan. We walked twenty-six steps, stopped, and I stood shivering in my boxers for a minute while they used a cell phone to consult with someone. Then they shoved me a few more steps forward. The consulting detective in me took note that the floor was hard, smooth, and cold under my bare feet. Probably cement. I wasn't sure what good the information would do, but you never know. They untied the cord and jerked the bag off my head. I sneezed again and blinked at bright fluorescent light. I was standing in the doorway to a room that was three-fourths full of oblong wooden crates stacked up to the ceiling with one corner given over to a stained white counter with a coffeemaker minus the pot, drawers and cupboard below. "Got you now," I mumbled. "Cement floor." They said nothing, obviously because they were so amazed they were speechless. They also didn't punch me, which I counted as a victory.

They shoved me into the room; just for laughs one tripped me as I went forward, but I fooled him. I twisted, took the fall on my good shoulder, and rolled to a sitting position. I didn't wrestle Varsity in high school and college for nothing.

My boxers had been pulled down almost past the decent zone and before I could tug them up Faith Valentine followed us in, put a high heel into my chest and pushed me flat on my back. She smiled down at me;. "Like my shoes?"

"Red soles, which makes them either Louboutin or Yves St. Laurent."

"Impressive. Fetish?"

"You wish." Her lips tightened. She looked at me and after a moment her mouth relaxed into a smile, curious, interested, like I was a new bug she'd just captured and was examining closely before dropping into the killing jar. "I follow the fashion biz and there was a lawsuit. Come a little closer so I can look up your skirt."

"Are you trying to provoke me? If so, why? Surely you can't think I'll do something stupid so you can escape, so I can only conclude that you just have a big mouth."

"So I've been told. And don't call me Shirley." She looked utterly blank. I sighed. "Old movie. My Dad loves it." Some people have no culture. She dug her stiletto heel in a little more and not only did it really hurt, it also made me think again of bugs pinned in a collection; of course that thought led to the toe pinned to the little plastic surfboard and that kind of freaked me out, so I scooted back a little and my boxers moved a little farther south; hip-hop territory now. Faith was able to control herself.

Smiling, pink tip of her tongue showing between red lips, she took her foot off my chest, straightened up and pushed her hair back from her face. I pulled my shorts up. "Mr. Baines wishes to inform you that you will survive this experience if you behave. Otherwise he has promised to turn you over to me." She smoothed her skirt over her hips. "You probably wouldn't like that."

"Something to live for," I muttered.

She shook her head, nodded to her boys and they all left, locking the door behind them.

A moment later she came back, checked my wrist tie, and started double-checking the cupboards. Without turning, she said, "It doesn't have to be like this. You could join us."

"I have noticed that your hiring practices could stand some improvement."

"The ones from your garage? Rent-a-thugs." Faith smiled. "You'd be surprised at how many athletic young men find the prospect of life in an office cubicle intolerably boring." She looked at me. 'Or maybe you wouldn't. You escaped the nine-to-five same-old, same-old." I figured she'd expect me to subtly test my bonds while she talked, so that's what I did. "The ones who count are Rodney, Chooch, me, and of course Mr. Baines. We have room for a fifth."

"Have you noticed your boss is crazy?"

"He likes to ramble. So do I."

"Well, Faith, thanks, but I don't think Baines likes me very much. You might say he hates my guts. Wait, come to think of it, so does my boss at FSB. There's a pattern here!"

"Don't deny that you like the life, the action. We have a great deal to offer someone like you. I can handle Baines."

"Yes, but can you handle the ancient astronauts when they come back, led by the Cigarette Smoking Man? Counteroffer. Get out now. This can't work, Faith, and it's time to cut your losses."

She turned. "I'm going to ramble till they have to cut me down." The room seemed to get colder. She meant it. "Last chance. I disabled the camera at your house. No one knows we have you."

"And both of their names begin with 'B.' Baines, Barkman. I see it now."

She looked at me for a moment, then left. There was nothing I needed to do at the moment so I took a nap. When I opened my eyes and rolled to my left I was staring at the other end of the women's shoe spectrum—a worn pair of brown leather Birkenstock sandals exposing toes that could use a good scrubbing, beneath the frayed hem of an ankle-length faded green skirt that I knew was pure organic cotton made in clean, brightly-lit shops by cheerful, well-paid workers. "Hey, Cheryl," I said.

"What are you doing here?"

"Rescuing you, of course." I looked up and there she was. Cheryl Darlymple, Snake's wife, is tall, about 5' 11," tan from work in her organic garden and toned because she doesn't own a car and walks or bikes almost everywhere. Her long hair, formerly brown but now mostly gray, is parted in the middle and hangs down to her waist. Her faded skirt was topped off by a white cotton pullover blouse. Naturally she wore no make-up whatsoever.

She sniffed, "Off to a good start, aren't you?"

"Snake said you wanted out. I couldn't figure out how to find you, so I thought I'd have them bring me to you."

"What makes you think I'm a prisoner? I'm not a prisoner, am I? Well, I'm not, not exactly. Quit saying that I'm a prisoner." Despite her strict vegetarian diet and herb tea, Cheryl tends to get a little overwrought sometimes. I once told Snake that I'd like to get her stoned and feed her an extra-large mocha grande, just to see if her head would spin around; he was not amused. I'd like to say that underneath it all she's really a nice person, but since I've heard her poetry I can't. She does volunteer at an animal shelter so she's not all bad.

"Uh-huh. Is that door unlocked?"

"Well, of course not. They don't trust *you*, now do they?"

"And very perceptive of them, too. How about you? Do they trust you?"

"Yes, certainly, of course they trust me, why wouldn't they? I have their complete trust. We have had some issues recently, relatively minor philosophic differences, but we're engaged in meaningful dialog and are moving toward resolution."

"Can you go home?"

"Home? At the moment, well, not, not exactly." She licked her lips. "You wouldn't understand, they are desperate, and they have a Cause and—"

"And these desperate people who have a Cause with a capital 'C' have locked you up. I guess they figure that will help facilitate the conflict resolution." I was looking around the room, without spotting anything that I could make into a weapon that would allow me to open the door and deal with Faith and four or five guys with guns who didn't like me. I looked again and it was the same. They did have a Mr. Coffee but it looked like they could have been culturing the bio-weapon on the burner. There was no pot.

Cheryl licked her lips. "Perhaps, perhaps it would be more uh, comfortable to continue the dialog, um, in another setting."

Yeah, like a police station with Baines and Valentine in a cell or, better yet, on the other side of those thick glass windows with built-in speakers you see in old movies where the gun moll visits Vito in the big house. But I didn't say it.

The door slammed open; the man himself marched in, hands down behind his back, chin down on his chest, followed by a grinning Faith Valentine and the new guys. Her grin made me nervous. I read somewhere that if you cut a roach's head off the body lives for a week or more. Is the body still alive when it comes out of the killing jar and the steel pin is pushed through it? Better question: Why do I think of stuff like that? He slapped his meaty hands together and said, "All right, meeting in session. One item on the agenda: I need that sample. You'll tell me where it is."

I winked at Faith. "I could listen to him all night." I thought I saw her mouth twitch in the start of a smile.

He gestured to the new guys. "Slap him around a little, just for openers." And they did just that—open hand slaps to the face that were noisy and dramatic, but that did little real damage. Oh, they split my lip early on and I bled, but in general it wasn't too bad.

I was literally saved by the bell. Baines' cell phone played the love theme from "The Godfather," he listened for a while, grunted and slipped the phone back into his pants pocket. "Gotta go. The meeting I am on my way to take may solve our mutual problem, and if, as I hope, that is the outcome, you will both be released." He smiled, an unpleasant twisting of his lips in his mannequin face that did not reach his eyes. Sure, and I've got a deal on some Enron securities.

Baines dropped his head to his chest, gestured at the door which was snatched open for him, and they left. I heard the lock click behind them, but that didn't worry me too much—I had other problems. I struggled to my feet, stumbled over to the door and listened. Standing next to me, Cheryl clasped her hands at her waist and said, "I wrote a poem while I was here, which I will now share with you." Remember I was locked up and unable to run. She focused on a point over my head, possibly somewhere in Mexico or the Andromeda galaxy, before taking a breath and reciting,

"I saw a weed out in the street
I saw it down there by my feet
It doesn't know that it's a weed
Sun and water are all it needs
The Gardener is coming."

I was listening for activity outside the door, heard none. "Very nice." Compared to some of the works in *Geranium Joy*, her most recent collection, it was.

"It is about death. All art is about death, don't you think?"

"Sure." The plastic tie around my wrists wasn't too much trouble—I just bit through it. Cheryl frowned as I stumbled over to the coffee counter and searched. Of course they had removed all the silverware from the drawers when they took the glass coffee pot and there were no ceramic cups, nothing but half a roll of paper towels in a cupboard and a single Styrofoam cup that had been crumpled and tossed in the trash can. A memory surfaced. Bingo. Worth a try. I filled the sink with cold water, put in the stopper and fished the cup out of the trash. I rubbed it rapidly back and forth against the metal wall until friction had heated and softened the foam, burned my fingers a little as I shaped it into a cylinder, rubbed it some more for more heat and to sharpen it to a point then quickly dunked it in cold water in the sink. When I was done I tested the point; I had a crude weapon.

The author of *Geranium Joy* said, "What in the world are you doing?"

"Saw it on one of those reality shows, *Life in the Big House* or something. The trick is you heat the Styrofoam cup and form it into a pointed cone when it's soft, then you warm it again and dunk it into cold water, like case-hardening metal. Pretty neat, huh? Instant shiv."

"You're out of your mind. Wait, you're not going to hurt them, are you?" Before I could think of an answer to that one we heard footsteps.

Chapter Twenty-Four Your Friend, Mr. Forklift

I got lucky. The whole group didn't come back, only the new guys.

They got all the way into the room before stopping and gaping at the space where I'd been tied. For a moment they were frozen. I was behind the door and slammed it into the second one, sending him back into the wall.

If Kandi had been with me she would have taken out one or both of them, grinning as she leveled them with spin kicks. Cheryl actually fluttered her hands like the heroine in a bad fifties movie. Her contribution as I lunged to stab the first one was to scream, "Look out!" Wonderful. But these things work out sometimes—as the first one turned to see what she was yelling about, I jammed my makeshift blade into his side. It slid right in between two ribs, requiring only about as much pressure as pushing a dull knife into a thick-skinned orange. The one I'd hit with the door had gotten to his feet was fumbling to get his gun out of his pocket. I stepped back and let the first one fall, clutching his side looking surprised as he said, "You *hurt* me!" as if he could beat me up, stuff me in the trunk of a car and not expect me to do something about it. I tackled the other one, a memory of my brief, undistinguished high school football career surfacing. I crouched, launched, and planted my hairline just above his belt buckle before he could shoot me. If you do it right, the impact is transferred straight along your spine and you don't hurt yourself. Most of the fight and wind went out of him at the first impact, but to make sure, I slid off to the left, got my shoulder into his midsection, and drove him into the counter with the coffee service, then down to the floor, where he landed with his feet splayed out and slid back into the wall. His eyelids were fluttering, so I grabbed his hair and banged his head against the wall. The metal wall gave a satisfying 'bong.' He wouldn't bother us for a while. Yeah, since he was one of the thugs who worked me over when my head was in the bag, I sort of liked it. Okay, strike the "sort of." Mary would shake her head and tell me I have anger management issues; Kandi would bang his head again.

I was the one who was bleeding, after having been worked over, stuffed in a car trunk, then worked over some more, but did the woman I was rescuing care? No. Cheryl was bending over the guy I'd stabbed a little, fluttering uselessly as he held his side, with blood leaking out between his fingers. "You hurt him!" she shrilled at me. The poor injured fellow pulled a gun out with the obvious intention of shooting me, so I kicked his wrist as hard as I could. The gun skittered across the floor, bounced against one of the crates and fortunately didn't go off. I went to the coffee counter, got the roll of paper towels and tossed it to Cheryl. "Make a pad and give it to him. You, push, press it hard against your wound. You'll be all right." Of course, I had no idea how serious his wound was and if he'd be fine or not, and didn't care much one way or the other, but I needed to reassure Cheryl.

"You can't just leave them! Can you? Can you? Two human beings who may be seriously injured? I suppose I can believe it of you, but *I* will not compromise my ethics, now will I?"

My response to this speech was to grab her arm and start dragging her toward the door, with her batting ineffectually at my face. Her non-violence apparently didn't extend to me. "Cheryl, three points. One, when their friends come back and see this, they're going to be very upset, and they will probably take it out on whoever they find handy. Two, if we get out of here we can send those poor, possibly seriously injured people help." Well, it was sort of true—cops have first aid training, right? Close enough. We were almost at the door, with her still struggling. "And, three, points one and two don't matter because

I'm taking you whether you like it or not. I told Snake I'd bring you back."

"Pig." She was dragging her sandaled feet and trying to pull my hand off her elbow; when that didn't work she returned to feebly slapping me.

I opened the door and peeked out. She slapped again, catching me behind the ear and drawing blood, so I turned and shook her a little, well, okay, her teeth rattled. "Cheryl, this is the second team. Chooch and Rod don't seem to be here and that worries me, a lot" I shook her again. "Kandi was supposed to call me and she hadn't before they took my phone." She started to say something so I gave her another shake. "Roses are red, violets are blue. You're coming with me no matter what you do. Deal with it." I realized what I was missing, dragged her across the room to where both guns had come to rest against the cabinet. I hid the little automatic under some towels and took the revolver with me. "Cheryl, they will kill you. *Geranium Joy, The Second Sprout* will be posthumous."

"No, they wouldn't." She stopped batting at my face. "Uh, you really think so? Kill me?"

"Yes, I really think so. And so do you."

If she licked her lips any more they were going to bleed. "Perhaps we should hurry?"

We slipped out the door into a hallway. Opposite us there was a door that said, "Client Preparation Room." I opened it and saw steel tables and tubes, bottles labeled Formaldehyde. It looked like the Chapel of Non-Denominational Rest was a full-service mortuary. I muttered, "Guess I know where the toe came from." Cheryl looked at me oddly but had the sense to keep her mouth shut. There was no other way out of the embalming room so we went back into the hall. At the end we pushed open a door and found ourselves in a warehouse.

This warehouse was full of identical oblong wooden crates, arranged on metal racks reaching to the ceiling. Rows of fluorescent lights under white reflectors hung down, but of the four tubes per reflector only one was lit, no doubt conserving energy when the place wasn't in use, or maybe it was robot-run like the warehouse next door. Deep shadows filled spaces the light didn't reach. The number of crates explained why extras had to be stacked in the coffee room—the place was crammed literally to the rafters. Gripping Cheryl's arm with one hand and holding the gun in the other, I led us down a narrow path between shelves. It was just like a movie except instead of a gorgeous, deadly blonde I had a cranky senior citizen. And I was in my boxer shorts.

All at once we heard a rumbling like a garage door—a really big garage door—going up and the rest of the lights came on. Car doors slammed, the door rumbled down.

"Now you've done it," Cheryl whispered. "They're going to be mad, aren't they?"

"Gee, you think?" She didn't need encouragement to run with me down an aisle until we could see a clear area by the doors. The limo was there, parked next to a huge yellow forklift. Baines, Valentine, The Rod and Chooch were standing next to the car, talking. Then Faith beeped the limo locked and they walked off in the direction of the room we'd been confined in.

"Well, that does it," I said. "Stay here for a minute, and when I call you come running." I could see the look in her eyes. "Never mind." I dragged her out, over to the nearest wall where I slapped a fire alarm and was rewarded with a siren, flashing lights, and a downpour from the ceiling sprinklers.

I got very lucky—the keys were in the forklift and I got it started just as we heard yelling behind us. "Can you drive one of these?" Cheryl screamed. I dragged her up next to me and scooted over so she had part of the single seat. She clutched at the rollbar—the first sensible thing she'd done all night.

"Sure! I watched a guy do it just the other day." I said and backed into a stack of crates that tipped over, spilling out coffins. The Chapel of Non-Denominational Rest was a warehouse for coffins. The impact knocked the gun off my lap and it vanished into the darkness. That was all right—I didn't really want to get into a firefight anyway. But that gave me an idea that, if I do say so myself, was one of my better ones. Baines and crew were running down an aisle toward us, slipping on the wet floor, waving their arms, waving guns and yelling, but they weren't shooting, yet. Faith stopped running, assumed a textbook Weaver shooting stance with her right hand gripping the Ruger and her left wrapped around it. Baines chopped her arm and yelled, "No!" Wanting us alive placed them at a tactical disadvantage, but they did seem to be seriously upset, so I drove our forklift in a circle, clipping stacks of coffin boxes as I did, scattering crates and coffins everywhere, slowing down our pursuers. For some unknown reason the forks went down and we scooped up two coffins, both bronze with ornate handles, one on top of the other along with parts of their crates, and then again for reasons of its own the fork went back up, making it hard to see. Chooch jumped out and waved a gun at us, but he lost interest after I aimed our forklift at him and mashed the pedal to the floor. He barely made it clear. I shouted, "Hold on"—utterly useless but that's just what you do in that kind of situation, peered around the coffins on the fork, and drove straight at the wall next to the closed roll-up doors, aiming at a spot under a row of windows. Big steel doors, like the ones in front of us, are usually reinforced and sturdy, but a warehouse wall is flimsy and under windows there aren't load-bearing struts. I saw it on TV.

On TV it works the first time; you just crash out with parts of the obstruction, no matter what it was, flying everywhere

dramatically. Sometimes they throw in an explosion. We must
have gotten a bad script or something, because the first time
we smashed in and the wall just bent. The forks punched holes
in it and the coffin crates crumpled, then the forks screeched,
pulling free as I backed up and hit the wall again, and this time
we punched right through. Metal fragments scraped up and over
the roll cage and we were free, except we were on the raised
platform where trailers were backed up for loading or unloading
and there was a trailer parked there with the doors open. I sort
of lost control for a moment because Cheryl covered my eyes,
we swerved and all at once when I slapped her hands away all I
could see was the black mouth of the trailer. Fortunately, it was
empty, because I couldn't stop—I had figured out steering, but
was still working on brakes—and we skidded into the dark box,
stopping when the forks bumped against the end of the trailer.
The coffins were mashed back against the roll cage.

Behind us, Baines yelled, "Come out of there!"

I shouted, "Okay." Cheryl clutched my arm. "Hold on," I said
again, uselessly, and jammed it into reverse. I backed us out at
full speed, careening off first one side of the trailer, then the other,
losing the coffins in the process, until we were on the platform
again, with our pursuers, who had foolishly stood waiting for us
to come out, jumping for their lives—except for The Rod, who
leapt and landed on the back of the forklift. He fell off when I
lost control and we went off the edge backwards. It was about
a three-foot drop, bone-jarring, slamming the seat up into me
and snapping my head back. Something must have broken, or
jammed, in our sturdy vehicle, because I couldn't get it into
a forward gear, so was forced to back wildly in circles while I
regained some control, but it did discourage our pursuers.

I was looking over my shoulder, backing down the middle of
Bolsa Chica Avenue at full speed when the limo raced by and the
police and fire department arrived, followed by the Huntington

Beach Police helicopter and Chet Shaw in a Space Floozies Enterprises van. I got Mr. Forklift to stop. Car doors opened and a large number of people in uniform jumped out of their vehicles and started running around. Many of them had guns. Some people started toward us, some headed for the warehouse, some just seemed to be staring at the forklift. All of them seemed very excited. There was a great deal of arm-waving. Radios crackled and said incomprehensible things that seemed to be mostly numbers. The helicopter, uncertain where to focus the spotlight, moved it from warehouse to forklift to Space Floozy van and back. I thought about waving to it but decided not to since they might misinterpret the gesture and shoot me. Cheryl crouched next to me, fists clenched, eyes wide. Her lips were moving; she might have been reciting poetry or she might have been praying.

Chet, followed by a fireman, and a motorcycle officer approached, Chet hurrying, the uniforms trailing behind cautiously. Wide-eyed, cowboy shirt half-unstuffed, Chet said, "Mac, are you all right?"

The firefighter said, "There's no fire, is there?"

"No, sir."

The policemen took off his helmet so he could get a better look. He smiled. "Good evening, sir." He held up a black-gloved hand. "Wait, wait, don't tell me, let me guess. Your name is Macdonald?" I nodded. "Well, Mr. Macdonald, I'd ask for your license, but you appear to be in your underwear."

I looked down. "Oh."

Several other police and firefighters strolled up. A lot of the urgency was gone. They seemed to be having a good time.

"You might want to do something there." I looked down at my lap again and made the appropriate adjustment. "I just can't tell you how much I'm looking forward to this explanation, but, first, do you by any chance know where your pants are?"

I waved in the direction of the warehouse. He nodded and a uniform trotted away. "I don't suppose this is your forklift?"

"No, sir."

"I see. May we have it back now?"

I nodded. "It's broken, anyway. Only goes in reverse."

Cheryl stopped staring at Andromeda and chose that moment to speak up. "He backed it off a cliff." She bobbed her head solemnly. "I told him not to. It hurt my bottom a lot when we landed. I write poetry." Again with the head bob. The officer was understandably at a loss. "I saw a weed—" then, mercifully, she fainted. I caught her before she fell out of the seat. Two white-coated paramedics bustled up, gently pushed her gray hair out of her face before reviving her with an ammonia capsule under the nose, and helping her down.

I climbed down off the forklift, gave it a pat to say thanks. A news van screeched to a stop and a very pretty dark-haired reporter in a short skirt and a blue blazer with the station logo embroidered on the pocket and a microphone in her hand jumped out and started asking questions of anybody who looked official while a cameraman filmed her.

While all of this was going on Chet, of course, had been sending texts. He asked me again, "Are you okay?"

"Where's Kandi? She was supposed to call."

He hesitated. "Not sure. She's not answering texts."

"I'm okay. What took you so long?"

"Camera two didn't get all the license number. Took a while to track the limo to this address."

"Thanks, pard. It all worked out." He mumbled something, pulled out a blue bandanna and wiped his forehead.

Suddenly it was very bright. The reporter in the short skirt had noticed the guy sitting on the forklift wearing soggy boxer shorts and the cameraman had me in his lights. For a moment she was at a loss for words. Fortunately the cops took me away before she could think of a question.

Somebody found my pants. Paramedics wrapped Cheryl in a blanket and led her to an ambulance; cops put me in the back of a police car. I told them that I'd get the upholstery wet, but they said it was ok.

Instead of a jail cell they took me to the Huntington Beach Hyatt Regency. The night had been so strange that the weird-o-meter in my head had long since gone into the red. Picked up driving a stolen forklift in your underwear after setting a false fire alarm and stabbing some guy with a Styrofoam cup and instead of a jail cell, they take you to the best hotel in the city? Sure, why not? Three officers, two holding my elbows and the third following behind, escorted me through the lobby, down a corridor and to the double doors to the Mellon Family Suite. The one in back stepped in front of us, knocked softly, and opened the door. The other two gently ushered me in.

The suite was on the ground floor. Floor-to-ceiling windows looked out on the pool. Elijah Eddington III tried to hand me something—later I realized it was a Dos Equis Dark—but I didn't see him because Kandi was off the couch and running to me and then I was holding her and somebody was talking but I was burying my face in her hair so I couldn't hear them. Then we were both talking and it boiled down to "Are you all right?" and "Yes," and we were both laughing and everything was all right.

"I was locked up by some Federal agency."

"Let me guess. It wasn't Special Agent Irene Morse."

"No, somebody else. I thought you never guessed."

With one arm around Kandi's waist, I took the beer from Elijah, who was waiting patiently. "I'm dripping all over."

Agatha Plumlee said, "It's all right," standing in the door to what was probably the master bedroom.

"You own the hotel."

She smiled. "And now—"

Roger Winters walked in from the other bedroom.

I couldn't help it All at once it was just too much and the rigid control I'd maintained ever since I'd seen Kandi in that hospital bed, looking small and afraid but brave while others were there, and I'd had to stay sane and cold, all that control was gone. I dropped the bottle and launched myself at him. Whirling him around I got my forearm across his throat and my hand on my wrist in a chokehold. He just stood quietly with his arms at his sides. As I started to apply pressure I felt a gentle hand on my shoulder. It was Ray-Ray. "No, man, ya'll don't want to be doin' that. You don't want to be carryin' that around. You listen to me now 'cause I know."

It wasn't the fact that Roger wasn't struggling. It was Ray-Ray. I looked at his sad, knowing eyes and let go. Collapsed on the couch. Kandi sat next to me and held my hand. Ray-Ray nodded slowly and went to stand next to Edna. Roger just stood there.

Agatha said, "Meet your new partner."

"I need a shower and some dry clothes."

She said, "Ray-Ray."

"Right through there, Sah." He pointed. "After Ms Plumlee was able to get her released, we had Ms Shaw get some clothes from your closet."

Agatha said, "Yes, dry clothes, perhaps a sandwich, then we'll talk."

"Kandi comes with me. In the bedroom." Closing the barn door after the horse is over the horizon? Protecting her when it's too late? You bet. Made me feel better. Her, too. She sat on the bed, said nothing about my multiple abrasions and bruises, just watched with eyes that were too big and too still. When we came out, holding hands, I had on jeans and one of my Aloha shirts. They were all waiting.

Agatha said, "Harker is dead."

"I'm sorry. How?"

Agatha glanced his way; Ray-Ray took up the story. "Two shots to the back of the head. I found him this morning, but he'd been dead a while."

"Where?"

"Babbling Brook. His apartment."

"Gun?"

"Cops haven't said, but there were no exit wounds so I'd guess small-caliber, maybe a .22."

"Faith Valentine."

"What about him?" I indicated Roger, who was sitting quietly on a stool at the kitchen counter.

"Baines sent the people who got him out of Biggin Hill. They had weapons, said if he didn't come with them they would take him by force and people would be hurt. When he went with them but refused to help, they got orders to eliminate him." Ray-Ray's voice was flat, unemotional.

Roger smiled and spoke for the first time. "I think I knew they were going to kill me before they did."

"So Roger killed them."

Agatha frowned. "This is not what we wanted. I'm afraid it's out of control."

"Can't argue with that," I said.

"So, we need to end it. We need to prevent Baines from selling the sample."

"I thought he didn't have it."

"We believe he is getting close. What I don't understand is why he is willing to go to such extreme lengths."

"For a cup of coffee I'll explain." Ray-Ray produced one quickly, in a gold-rimmed cup with matching saucer. I drained it and held it out. Next time he came back with a normal mug.

"Thanks. Baines is in trouble, big trouble. He took the money." Agatha pursed her lips, nodded understanding.

"That explains his behavior." Mary nodded from the leather couch. I sat down next to her.

"His clients, the Asian men you saw at the robot warehouse. they offered him, no he probably asked for, money up front and he took it. Lands' sakes, yes, he probably is afraid. I should have seen that, yes, I really should have." Agatha sounded sad. "Money. He wanted more. We paid him well, but I suppose it wasn't enough."

I finished my coffee. "Never would have been."

Edna picked up he sawed-off and said, "I'll take a walk, check around the hotel."

Chapter Twenty-Five   "... Is Not a Crime"

Despite, or maybe because of, the events of the last few hours, I woke up early. Around me the Mellon Family Suite was quiet. I slipped out of bed carefully, so as not to wake Kandi, and stood for a moment looking down at her. I understand there are people who are not cute when they sleep, often because they snore or drool. And, to be honest, there were occasions when my wife Diana had been a drooler. Not my Kandi; she was as beautiful sleeping as awake, lying on her back with blond lashes feathered on her cheeks, lips slightly parted, and with a small half-smile as if she might be having a pleasant dream. I brushed a lock of hair back off her forehead and the she sighed, rolled over and stuck her hand under her cheek. We tend to sleep nude, but considering the circumstances we both wore sweatpants and tees to bed. I tugged the sheet up over her shoulder.

I knew I would not be able to get back to sleep so I wandered out to the living room thinking I'd make some coffee, but then I had a much better idea. It was almost dawn and the beach would be empty except for a few joggers and bicyclists, and of course the Dawn Patrol out for some early waves, and some skaters. My short Rip Curl tri-fin was on its rack in my garage, but when Kandi had packed some clothes for the night at the Hyatt along with weapons she brought my new skateboard; now it was leaning against the wall on my side of the bed, wheels out, Titanium Redhead calling to me. All at once it seemed like more than a good idea—it seemed *essential*. Cross the bridge over PCH and roll north for a half-hour or so, to get my head together, as Henrietta might say. I threw on jeans and a gray hoodie sweatshirt, got my .45 off the nightstand, checked the loads and safety, stuffed it in the back of my pants, scribbled a short note to Kandi and left it on the bathroom counter, and was out the bedroom door. In the living room Ray-Ray was dozing on the floor next to Edna on the couch. He raised his head and waved. Roger was off looking for some things I'd asked him about, supplies from his days as a nutcase bomber, and also because I didn't want to sleep in the same suite as him.

Outside the fancy carved wooden double doors, the carpeted hall opened on the pool. The flagstone path was empty at this hour; the only other person I saw was an early maid struggling with a large, chest-high cart loaded with cleaning stuff and trying hard to keep it quiet and not disturb the suite-dwellers. I had the hood of my sweatshirt up and was carrying my board, looking like any skater out for some early morning cement tubes. The maid bobbed her blonde head as I went by, and continued to drag the heavy cart down the hall. Something red, like the toes of shoes, stuck out from under the piles of towels on the top shelf. The bottom shelf was enclosed, silver doors covering whatever supplies she needed. I strolled past the pool, through the lobby and down to street level, heading for the pedestrian overpass that led to the beach.

Before I got to the bridge it hit me, what was wrong with the maid. No, not the maid, what was wrong about the cart—there were shoes sticking out from under the stack of towels on the top shelf, red, very expensive red-soled shoes by Louboutin. Knowing and running were simultaneous; as I pounded up the steps to the main entrance I was very glad for all the training I'd done with Nadzia. I slowed, pushed open the doors.

The blonde maid had her back to me, bending as if to get something out of the bottom of her cart, and I knew who she was at once, in spite of the wig, and she wasn't getting something out of her cart because it was Faith Valentine and she had Edna in a headlock. I almost shouted, but she obviously had been into the suite and she was just as obviously armed; I couldn't shoot because I might hit Edna, so surprise was my best weapon. I ran for a couple of steps before I dropped my skateboard, stepped on and started that long leg swing good skateboarders use to get up to speed. I must have been going nearly twenty miles an hour, completely silent on the carpeted floor, when Faith turned and saw me and as long as I live I will remember the open-mouthed gape on her face as I took one more push, launched myself off the board and slammed into her. Faith went flying—I probably outweighed her by fifty pounds—and bounced off the wall. Edna clutched her throat and dropped to her knees. My board flew off on its own and I fell, rolling and trying to reach behind me to get my gun out, coming to rest sitting against the wall opposite Faith. Then I saw what she had been pulling out of the cart's bottom cabinet. It was Rodney. As I watched he unfolded and stood up. I got my feet under me and lunged at Faith, knocking her gun aside.

The Rod looked pissed as he grabbed Edna and threw her aside and bent down, reaching for me. I had my hands full of a struggling Faith Valentine and had no chance of getting my gun out. Rod pulled Faith aside, and shot at me as I rolled, but he missed and as I pulled my .45 out he fired again and I felt a tug at the sleeve of my sweatshirt. Faith was on her feet with her long-barreled pistol in her hand as Ray-Ray threw open the doors of the suite. She ignored him, turned and shot Edna between the eyes. Then Blondell Baines was stepping out of the stairwell door and he had a submachine gun that he used to spray the hall as Ray-Ray and I dove for cover, through the open door to the suite. As I looked back to see who was going to kill me, Faith ran for the door but before she pushed the crash bar she turned and shot The Rod. He looked surprised as he slapped a hand to his chest and toppled to the floor.

Baines and Valentine disappeared out the door to the pool and a minute later we heard shouts, then silence.

Kandi stepped quickly into the hall, scanned both ways, and when she found no threat stared at me, wide-eyed, little

Raven .25 held carefully, pointing down. The .45 was heavy, so I stuffed it into the back of my jeans. Over Kandi's shoulder I saw Ray-Ray blocking Agatha. She clutched her robe to her throat and for the first time looked really old. They all looked at me for an explanation and for once I had one.

I picked myself up, waved everybody into the suite. "They're cleaning house. Tying up loose ends, and I'm pretty sure Harker was the first, which means Baines and company are planning an escape, one they are pretty sure will work. And we need to warn people." Ray-Ray then went out into the hall.

I said, "Agatha, we have less than five minutes before hotel security, then the cops get here, and Kandi and I need to leave. Can you hold them off?"

From the hall The Rod yelled "I'm bleeding here, man. I need help!"

Ray-Ray said something that didn't sound friendly and he shut up. A moment later the tall black man came back in, cradling his wife in his arms. He laid her gently on the couch, got a blanket and covered her. Once again I heard sirens in the distance. I was getting used to it.

Agatha said, "Police, yes. The people who had Kandi may be problematic, however, I have some friends working on ways to influence them. You young people need to exercise a certain amount of haste."

As we ran for the Chevy, Kandi said, said, "What do you mean, 'They're cleaning house?' Why did Faith, Baines, and The Rod come to the Hyatt?"

"By now they know we don't have the bacteria."

"Then why? Revenge?"

"I called Henrietta so she knows some of it. We need to get them all out of the line of fire."

In the car Kandi said, "I know that look, Sailor. You think you've got something, don't you? There's more to it."

"Maybe, just maybe."

"And I don't suppose you're willing to share that information?"

"Soon. First things first."

When I pulled up Henrietta and Brad were waiting at the curb in front of her house. She was standing next to his yellow Shelby Mustang; he was behind the wheel. Henrietta ran up before we could get out, leaned in my window and said, "I'm freaking out here." She tossed her head. "We can't get in touch with Lisa June. Follow us." She ran to the car and we trailed them to Ocean Boulevard and the huge circular high-rise where Lisa June lived. Henrietta had a keycard; we took the Residents Only elevator from the parking garage to one of the upper floors.

The door to Lisa June's condo was locked, but Henrietta's keycard opened it. Short entryway, large living room with a curved wall. Floor-to-ceiling windows on the left looked out over the cylindrical convention center with its Wyland whale mural. The windows opened onto a balcony, the breeze billowing gauzy white curtains. It was very quiet. I had my gun out and so did Kandi. We immediately separated. I motioned the two civilians to stay put while I looked on the balcony and Kandi checked the kitchen. We looked like TV cops, guns pointed at the ceiling, fingers carefully extended along the gun barrel as we moved carefully from room to room, and not feeling a bit silly or self-conscious doing it. We found her in the bedroom.

She was arranged neatly on the enormous antique four-poster.

Her hair was tied back in a ponytail. She was wearing the spectacular gown she'd worn to Nadzia's party. Her feet were bare. It was hard to tell much about her face and hair because there was a plastic bag over her head. An open bottle of pills stood on the walnut nightstand next to her. It had tipped over, spilling large white tablets. I yanked the bag off her head while

Kandi felt for a pulse and Brad called 911. Kandi said, "I've got a pulse but not much. I don't think she's breathing."

Rescue breathing is two breaths followed by fifteen chest compressions. It's hard work; even a trained paramedic can't do it for long, but by taking turns Henrietta, Brad, Kandi and I kept it up until Lisa June choked and started sucking in air on her own.

She recovered enough that we got her story before they took her away.

A half-case of Babbling Brook white wine had been delivered the day before, with a note saying that it was compliments of the winery, since she'd liked it so much at Nadzia's party. She had been at home, pretty ripped, almost ready to start on her second bottle of the wine and watching a movie in the den, when someone grabbed her from behind. They—she was sure it was more than one—had poured pills into her, washed it down with more wine, then dressed her, arranged her on the bed, and taped the bag over her head. She got a finger up under the tape enough to loosen it before she passed out and that saved her life.

This time we got a double dose of questions and answers from Special Agent Morse and Long Beach police. There were two solid-looking men with buzzed hair and gray suits who stood discretely off to the side and just watched. We waived protective custody and went home, that is, Kandi and I went back to my house in Huntington Harbour. Henrietta and Brad went to the hospital with their friend. The security system at home said the defenses hadn't been broached and the cameras didn't show anybody lurking outside.

Chet came downstairs with a new cell phone for me and went back to the guest room to work. Kandi was on the couch answering emails. I needed to do laundry and I should probably at least look at the hundreds of tweets that had piled up. Laundry was out of the question and I was afraid that answering the tweeters would be like feeding pigeons—I'd never get rid of them. Instead, I took a mug of coffee and my .45 and sat on the deck staring at the round burned spot and listening to the gentle wavelets lap against the dock.

Chapter Twenty-Six   Play With Fire

When in doubt, try to get more information, right? I called Homeland Security and got Irene Morse. "Ms Morse, hello."

"You can call me Special Agent." She paused. "Sorry. FBI humor."

"I get it, har de har har."

"Jackie Gleason, right? I just love the classics, like, remember when Alice had a phone installed and Ralph just flipped out? Phones were big deals then, and everybody had a party line. My grandmother had one, and she was convinced one of her neighbors was always listening." Her voice had a sense of urgency. I got it. Two things were clear: she wanted to talk, but not now, not on the phone.

"I loved that one, too. My wi—I mean, Diana, gave me the DVDs."

She laughed. "Mac, I'm glad you called. Remember you said you'd give me a ride to John Wayne when I needed to fly out?"

"My pleasure. I can show you my new wheels. When?" I'm proud to say I didn't miss a beat, even though I'd made no such promise.

"Well, that's my problem. Soon, like I need to be there in an hour. I'm at the Surf Motel—"

"On Pacific Coast Highway? I know where it is."

"Room 16."

The Surf is only ten minutes from the Harbour, across the highway from the ocean, three blocks north of the Pier. You can stand in the parking lot and see beach, waves, the offshore drillings rigs Emmy and Eva (they all have women's names) and ultimately Catalina. When I pulled in past the sign begging guests to hose off sand before entering the rooms or going in the pool she was standing on the walk in front of the room, hair pulled back in a stubby brown ponytail, wearing a businesslike gray pantsuit with a small green suitcase next to her and looking at her cell phone, not the view. She checked out the hot rod Chevy as I rumbled in with the twin glasspacks bubbling, and whistled appreciatively as I opened the enormous trunk and put her suitcase in.

"This is a *fabulous* car. Wow."

"Wait till I tell you about it. Custom-built; there's not one original part on the whole vehicle."

She reached out as if to touch it, pulled her hand back. "Let me say again, Wow."

The moment we were in the car heading north she turned serious. "Thank you, Mr. Macdonald. I was pretty sure you'd understand the potential eavesdropping and play along. We need to talk, but first, is this vehicle wired? If there are any recording or transmitting devices you are required to tell me or anything they record is inadmissible."

From where we were starting it was just as good to take surface streets to get to John Wayne airport, so I made a u-turn at 17th. And this way I got to check out the surf. I pointed the car south and said, "It's clean."

"All right." She fiddled with her purse on her lap. "I'm taking a serious career risk here. But, what the hell. It's true that I've been recalled. We're off the case."

"You personally?"

"Not just me, the FBI and Homeland. Everybody."

"Oh, boy, it's falling into place. You were pushed out by another agency."

"How did you know?"

"They questioned Kandi, probably saving her from Baines' merry men, and they hacked into my personnel file at Fields, Smith, and Barkman."

"They're some spook shop out of—probably—CIA. Let me tell you, my boss was *pissed*. But it's theirs now; these Black Ops jerks are in charge and we're out. 'Thank you for your fine work but we will assume responsibility from this point on as there are national security issues involved.'"

"You ID'd the Asians from the lab, sent that information up the line."

"They always wave that 'National Security' flag. All right. The men you photographed are North Korean, but they're not government. If their boss back home is who we think he is, he wants to replace the son, wants to be top man."

"That's what got you shut down. There's more, or you wouldn't be telling me this."

"You know the perp Rodney is alive? He's in the hospital under guard."

"Take your time, John Wayne's about half an hour from here."

She gave me a dirty look. "When they shut us down, two spooks came to the room we were using as an office. I overheard one side of a cell phone conversation to which I was not supposed to be privy and as a result I know at least part of what they are planning." I grinned at her. She blushed. "The spook took the call outside the front door, but the walls are thin."

"And you only had to press your lovely shell-like ear to the door a little bit."

That got me another dirty look. Then she grinned. "The spooks don't want Baines and Valentine, well, not exactly. They think there's a small helicopter hidden locally, and Baines can fly it. They plan to use it to get offshore where they will rendezvous with a freighter of Liberian registry, really North Korean. This spook group is going to find the location and there's going to be a terrible accident the moment they lift off. No survivors."

"Rod told them about the helicopter?"

"I just don't understand why they want them dead bad enough to risk it."

"It's a favor. Our government, or some part of it, possibly rogue, is helping out the North Korean government. This solves everybody's problems—there's no coup in North Korea, and there's no trial in the US, no bad press."

"Well, at least they don't know where the helicopter is."

"I think I do. And if I can figure it out, so can they."

"The warehouse?"

"Look out there, the surf's great today." And it was, nice shoulder-high waves with the excellent shape and glassy faces that Huntington gets in the winter. I belonged out there. But, you know what? I belonged here, too. "So poor Rodney is in the hospital?"

"Yeah, the big one on Beach Boulevard. He's expected to make a full recovery. That little target pistol didn't do much damage."

"Under guard?"

"Yeah, but they're not too serious. Only one guy."

She didn't press me for more information, so I didn't have to lie. There was too much of that already, and more to come if I was right. At the Departures level at John Wayne, I dragged her suitcase out of the trunk, pulled the handle up and we looked at each other. She said, "Thanks for the ride in the great car. You've got my number, call me if anything comes up. I'm interested."

"My pleasure." She turned. "Hey, Special."

She looked back, grinned. "Hey, yourself."

I didn't exactly burn rubber after she rolled her suitcase into the building, but I was tempted. I had things to do, but as it turned out, they had to wait.

I got a text.

```
Luke
Mac, go to Frac URGENT.
```

The skinny kid with the scraggly beard was waiting outside Cranial Fracture when I drove up and jumped in the passenger side as soon as I stopped.

"Oh, man, oh, man, I was right. She's not with you, is she?"

"Who?" But a sick feeling in my stomach told me I probably knew.

"I came here because I couldn't think of anyplace safe. At least I'd be in public on the street."

"Luke, *who?*"

"Kaylee. They got her." I said nothing, just felt ill. "Kaylee. She got punked, man. A text from you saying to go meet that Henrietta woman and they could fix everything, find Nadzia's killer. Save the day, you know."

My mind went on vacation for a moment. "They cloned my old cell. Or . . ." Or she knew it was fake and did it anyway. Next door I could see one of the leather twins from Betty's Boards peering out at us. As I watched she turned the sign from Open to Closed.

Luke said, "Oh, man, this is bad."

Naturally, it got worse. We needed firepower and influence. Agatha Plumlee had both, and she was glad when I called. Unfortunately she was glad for the wrong reason. She said, "Mr. Macdonald? First, I want to thank you for all you have done." I could guess what was coming next and saved her the trouble.

"And now you want me to stop."

Without missing a beat she said, "Mr. Macdonald, my involvement, and yours, are now at an end. An agency of our government will take care of everything. They say there are national security issues involved."

"Henrietta Graveline and possibly Kaylee Miraflores are with Baines now, against their will."

"Oh my, that is a shame. But we must no longer interfere. I can no longer assist you. Do you understand?"

"That's unacceptable, and—"

"I'm telling you, Matt—"

"Matt?"

"Oh, I'm so sorry. Lands sakes, I'm an old lady and sometimes I get confused, and I have a great-nephew named Matt. I mean Mr. Macdonald, dear. You must desist. I cannot help. Under no circumstances should you try to interfere. Do you understand?"

"Yes, I hear what you're saying, but this is just wrong."

"Why don't you come back to the hotel and get your things. Then go home. Mr. Macdonald, it's over. I have instructed Ray-Ray to come to the hotel to escort me back to Babbling Brook. Before all this happened he and poor Edna were going to have lunch at that Mexican restaurant, oh, I forget—"

"I know where you mean."

"Just come back here and everything will be all right."

"Yeah, I get it. Come to the hotel, then go home. Okay, you win." I hung up.

Kandi picked on the first ring. "Kandi, Mac."

"The game is afoot." My phone was only hours old. Chet was in residence so my house was safe. I told her what had happened. "Chet's got a company van out front, doesn't he?"

"Yes."

"Have him drive it into the garage then you drive it out. He stays in the house, then you meet me."

"Moving."

Luke grabbed my arm. "That's it? You quit? Just like that? Well I'm not quitting, I'm, I'm gonna—I—I don't know, I don't know what I can do. I'll put it on her blog, that's what. I'll tell everybody."

"Luke, it will be just one more conspiracy theory. No proof. And the people we'd be trying to prove something about are very good at covering their tracks."

He looked out the window at two girls walking by with short tri-fins under their arms. Luke sniffed, wiped his nose on his arm. "Well, what do we do?"

I removed his hand from my arm. "You need to send some text messages for me. Then you and some of your friends need to get arrested."

I made some calls, told Luke what he needed to do and went up Main to Beach to visit a sick friend.

She came into my arms as soon as I walked into the hospital lobby. I brought her up to date.

"Oh, Mac, I'm so sorry," she was almost, not quite, in tears. She was in a short red skirt and retro paisley blouse, long-sleeved to hide her most recent bruises, worn like a jacket over a black tank top. "What is going on? Baines and Valentine have Kaylee? Why?"

"Let's talk to The Rod. I need to be sure I'm right because we'll only get one chance at this."

On the fourteenth floor, I slipped into a room. After a brief, hopeful, look the patients went back to TV and paid no attention as I watched through the crack as Kandi walked by Rod's room, pushing a wheelchair we'd appropriated along the way and managed to drop her purse. The guy in the suit standing outside the door looked exactly like what he was—an ex-military, plainclothes gunman.

She grinned at him and bent to pick it up. He didn't move from the door but, being human, could not help but watch. As she straightened with her bag all hell broke loose—there was a loud clack-clack noise like many wheels on the tile floor, shouts and yells and all at once there were people coming toward us, fast. Six kids on skateboards jammed down the hall, swerving to dodge carts, wheelchairs, and gurneys, jumping their boards into the air and in general having a great time. One kid flexed his board, banked it off a wall, stuck the landing and was rewarded with hoots of appreciation. Luke, bringing up the rear, gave us a thumbs-up as he sped by, pursued by red-faced orderlies and uniformed security, all of whom were yelling. Those patients who were able stuck their heads out to see what was happening, and, after they got over their surprise, most of them started laughing and cheering. It broke the monotony, totally, and the guard was as open-mouthed as anyone, staring at the show. A moment later we heard an alarm as the marauders escaped through an emergency exit. Maybe some would get away.

That's when Kandi shot the guard with Nadzia's stun gun.

He went down like a sack of sand. We dragged him into Rod's room. The blond thug was reclining in bed, IV connected to a needle in his arm, dropping his copy of *Hustler* and staring as we dragged the unconscious guard in. He reached for the call button but I beat him to it and moved it out of his reach. I said, "Hey, Rod, how's it hangin'? Listen we probably don't have long before this guy wakes up. Before that happens you're going to tell us where Baines has his helicopter and when he's leaving."

"Bite me."

"Faith shot you."

"Bite me. It was a mistake."

"Rod, we're not kidding around here. Your boss Baines has two women. I'm going to get them back and to do that I need you to tell me where the helicopter is."

"Oooh, I'm *so scared*! Listen, pal, you're not gonna do nothin' to me and you know it. It just ain't in you, so fuck off. The Rod's telling you nothing. We're changing the world."

"Baines is in it for the money."

"Figured it out, did you? Well, bite me. You're doing nothing, so get out of here."

Unfortunately, he was right. He was a bully, probably capable of murder, but he wasn't murdering anybody at the moment, in fact, he was flat on his back with large dressing over a bullet hole in his chest and he looked bad. I wasn't prepared to torture him, let alone really kill him and he knew it. Next to me I could feel Kandi tensing, clenching her fists.

"Dude, when you go, leave the skank, she's got a great rack. The Rod likes a good rack."

All at once Kandi bent over him and got about an inch from his face. She began to talk and she didn't sound angry. She sounded insane. "Listen to me you social misfit. I have a major paper to defend in three days, my committee wants me to read three more articles and they're in German, I've got a class to proctor the day after tomorrow, and I've got a weasel plagiarizer who not only wants to steal my work but also is accusing me of stealing his and I'm behind schedule because your friends assaulted me." She paused for breath.

I said slowly, "You were one of the people who beat her up?"

She held his free arm down with one hand and pinched his nostrils shut with the other. Insane. That's how she looked as she continued her rant. "I have had a very bad week, hell I've had a bad couple of weeks, and I am sick of this. I was a victim of bullying as a child, but no more. I'm done with that, do you understand? Finished. Can you grasp that, you hostile, maladjusted, useless, oxygen-waster? Is this getting through to you?" She spoke slowly and clearly, enunciating every word. Her eyes were wide, her nostrils dilated. In between sentences I could hear her teeth grinding. "And those are comparatively minor issues. Your friends have kidnapped a fourteen-year-old girl. We want her back. We. Want. Her. Back."

I started to say something and she turned on me. At least she let go of his nostrils. He opened his mouth, I think to scream for help. He lost interest when I wrapped my hand around his throat and he saw my face. "You were one of—"

"Be quiet, Mac! I'm sick of their methods, their belief in violence as a first resort, their utter lack of anything approaching human values, do you understand? I have so much hostility built up it keeps me awake at night, for the first time since high school I am carrying grudges, and I am unable to let even the slightest insult, real or imagined, go. I have become unable to connect with my feelings in a healthy manner; the people I am counseling are asking me what's wrong, and I am *pissed*! Do you understand?"

I didn't take my eyes off the Rod. "You were one of the people who beat her up." My hand was tightening on his throat.

The guard we'd dragged into the room showed signs of reviving. Kandi leaned over him, smiled asked, "Sir? Sir? Are you all right?"

"Uh. Uh." He sounded very groggy.

"Do you have a history of fainting?"

"Huh? No, I—"

"Good." She hit him with the stun gun again, and watched critically while he twitched and flopped.

I let go of his throat so I wouldn't kill him, at least until he told us what we needed to know. Rod looked at me, eyes wide. "Dude, I feel sorry for you. I bet she goes on the rag like this all the time. And you still won't do shit, so shut the fuck up, bitch. Get me some water. Or come over here and sit on my lap." He laughed and slapped the sheet with his free arm, pleased at his wit. He was tougher than I thought, but he was also really dumb.

It was the wrong thing to say. In fact, on a Top Ten list of Wrong Things to Say, this would be near the top, right under, "Sure, I'll wrestle that hungry alligator." She closed her eyes and I could feel her counting to ten in Latin, then German, then French. When she opened them she smiled and it was not pretty, more like one time when I'd been on vacation in Maui, and I was swimming from Canoe Beach to Black Rock, following the reef that runs off the Ka'anapali coast, and all at once a Moray eel

299

stuck its head out of a hole in the reef about three feet below my face and opened its jaws wide. Scared the crap out of me; my legs must have looked like something out of Roadrunner cartoon as I kicked away. "You are *so* wrong," she said softly. She went to the dispenser on the wall and snatched out a pair of latex gloves.

"Whoa, all right, I knew you was kinky. C'mon, bring that rack over here, baby. You're gettin' The Rod all worked up." This guy just didn't know when to shut up. "The Rod loves kinky shit."

"How kinky?" she said softly. He didn't answer. Maybe he was getting smart.

Snap. First glove on. "See that?" She pointed at the red trash can labeled Hazardous Waste. He looked and shrugged. *Snap*. Second glove. She yanked a handful of tissues out of the box on his nightstand, flipped back the lid on the Hazardous Waste can, grimaced, and wiped up some of whatever nasty shit was living in there. The tissues came out mostly yellow, dripping with brown and red stuff. She studied it critically, wiped it again and it came out worse. "You know what an infection in an open wound feels like? You're in a hospital so I don't think it will kill you but it will be extremely painful, and there is always the possibility of HIV, remote, but possible." She ripped the dressing off his bullet wound. He opened his mouth to scream but I clamped down on his throat. He closed it quickly. "Kandi, um . . ."

She turned on me again. "Be quiet! I have had a bad week and I am sick of this bully. I realize he has stunted emotional growth, in all probability resulting from traumatic childhood experiences, and almost certainly he would benefit from counseling, but right now, you know what? I just don't give a rat's ass. He's one of the ones who beat me up."

The Rod looked at me. "Dude, help, she's gone nuts. Please, man, help."

I said, "My pleasure," and held his shoulders down. I turned to Kandi and said, "Don't get any on me."

She did the eel smile again and turned back to The Rod, who was as pale as the sheet under him. "Pay attention. If you open your mouth I will shove this in it. We already know with some degree of certainty, but we need to be sure, so Mac is going to say where it is and you will confirm or deny. Nod if we have it right. And, if you lie, one of my friends will come back and do much, much worse than this." His wound was stitched, red and raw where Mary had ripped off the gauze. It started to ooze blood. His eyes, wide and bulging, were fixed on the dripping tissues in her hand. "Oooh, look, a drop got on your arm, but not in the wound. Want to do something about it?" He nodded frantically. With her free hand she yanked out several of his stitches. He whimpered.

I said, "Aminoil." He nodded. "Tonight?" Another nod. Kandi wiped him with the gauze anyway, but beside the wound, not in it. His bladder let go, then The Rod fainted.

While Kandi scrubbed her hands, I helped myself to the guard's weapon, a fine 13-shot Glock, two extra clips in his pocket, a small revolver in an ankle holster, and a pocket knife. The guy was a walking armory.

On the way out we stopped a harried-looking Hispanic in scrubs. I said, "Nurse, that guard in front of 14D was chasing those crazy kids on skateboards and he fell and I think he hit his head. We got him inside the room but that's all we could do for him. Oh, and the patient in that room had a little, uh, well a little accident. Bedpan."

He muttered, "I love my job," and hurried to help.

Chet, Kandi, Roger, Alys, and I met at Fred's one more time. The restaurant was closed. Shadows enveloped the corners of the spotless kitchen. Before we got started Ray-Ray walked in, carrying a gym bag that looked heavy. I was guessing it didn't hold an extra pair of sweatpants. He set it down, nodded at us and stood next to where Roger Winters was leaning against a wall, unmoving and alert. On my instructions, Snake had taken Cheryl and left for an undisclosed location.

I said, "Remember they were cleaning house? That's why they killed Edna and shot Rod. Part of that is punishing me."

Kandi said, "Now Baines has Henrietta and Kaylee. Henrietta went on her own, to make things right. She even said she wanted to when we were on the yacht." I sighed. "She's who picked up Kaylee."

I said, "What is this guy, a chick magnet?" Kandi poked me. "But that's not all of it. Henrietta's making it better, all right, by delivering the sample to Baines."

Kandi said, "You mean she had it all along?" I nodded. "And now Agatha Plumlee says she won't help and to go home."

"That call? It was a message all right, but that wasn't what she wanted to say. She wants me to finish this. These black ops people were watching my house and they were listening to her so she warned me to stay away. She's staying at the Hyatt until the end."

Chet got it first. "It was backwards. Everything she said should be reversed. Clever."

"The key was when she called me Matt and said she was a forgetful old woman. She's about as forgetful as a Jeopardy champ."

"Pard, what are we gonna do?"

"First, we need to get the attention of this black ops group, give them something to think about." I explained in detail what we needed to do.

Then I ditched my friends. I lied to them, sent them all off on useless errands and I ditched them. I had something to do.

I parked the Chevy blatantly in front of the robot warehouse, not seeing the black ops watchers, but knowing there were cameras on me and not caring. I took the wooden box out of the trunk, opened it and from behind me Chet said, "Is that, whoa, pardner, is that what I think it is?"

I whirled. They were all there—Chet, Ray-Ray, Alys, and of course Kandi. I said, "You all are supposed to be waiting at Fred's. You can't, you can't help here. I want you to go."

"Yeah, right, like we're going to let you do this alone."

"Chet, I—"

Kandi said, "Don't make me get tough, Sailor. We're not leaving, so get on with it."

"Is at least Roger doing what I asked?"

"Prowling around the perimeter of the oil field. He'll call when he finds a way in."

"Look, I appreciate this, really, but . . ."

Kandi put her hand on my shoulder, gently, because it was the sore one. "We're your friends. Let us help."

Chet said, "Damn straight."

I looked at them and could only nod.

In the box was a tube about three and a half feet long, five inches in diameter, and painted matte green as if the maker had wanted it to look like Army issue. Folding out the handle and raising the site I said, "And just what do you think this is, Tex?"

He swallowed. "LAW. Light Anti-tank Weapon."

I twisted the set screw and opened the hatch covering the compartment in the base. "Kandi, you and the others need to wait in the van." She shook her head. "Look, when he built this Roger branched out and didn't use his typical solid explosives.

The propellant's solid, I think, but this thing's got a binary liquid warhead. It's like epoxy glue, you mix the liquids and instead of turning into a solid, it explodes. See? That's the two liquids and the partition through this glass. Fifteen years ago it was cutting edge, now not so much."

"You *think* the propellant is solid?" Chet sounded nervous.

"Sure, Roger told me all about it when he gave it to me. It's what I sent him to get when Faith came to the Hyatt and—"

"Killed Edna." Ray-Ray's voice was flat, unemotional.

"And I made some notes but they're in the car and it looks pretty straightforward."

At that moment Chet's cell chirped and the display said it was Roger. Chet handed me the phone. "They have a camera on the Tidal Inlet, so we can't get in by sea, and your house is still being watched, so we can't get the SeaDoos anyway."

"But you've come up with something, right?"

"Yeah, put Chet on." I handed it to Chet, who held it so we could all hear. "I've got a house just off Gothard that I think is vacant, with a backyard that backs up to the wetlands. We can get in that way. I just need you to make sure it's listed for sale and that the people have moved out."

"I'll get somebody on it and call you." Chet pushed his cowboy hat back on his head. "Mac, what, uh, what are you going to do with the Light Anti-Tank Weapon? I don't see any tanks."

"This thing will smash the door to the warehouse, alarms will go off, people will respond, and our black ops boys, who are undoubtedly monitoring police channels, and who know about this place—"

Kandi snickered. "Next door to the site of The Great Forklift Escape. In your underwear."

"—will think something's happening here. They'll show up and that will give me a chance to get into the oil field. There's only robots inside the warehouse and they're not working close to the door anyway."

"Are you sure?"

"Would I do it otherwise?"

"You don't really want me to answer that, do you?"

The damn thing was heavy. I hoisted it to my shoulder but my arm couldn't support the weight; it had just taken too much abuse. First Kandi, then Chet stepped up and steadied it. Our eyes met; she winked. He muttered, "And the Brahma bull is in the chute. Do it, Pard, do it."

I lined up the site, said, "Duck, Bella," and pulled the trigger. The fuse lit and the barrier between the liquids dropped. The red liquid began to seep into the clear liquid and it was actually kind of pretty. Then the solid propellant ignited, there was a soft *whoosh*, fire spewed out the back and the missile left the tube like a, well, like a rocket.

My aim was good, except it didn't knock down the door—instead it punched right through, doing remarkably little damage other than blasting a hole about two feet in diameter. There was no explosion, so it looked like the warhead part of the missile hadn't gone off. Maybe it was a dud. Kandi grabbed my arm and we waited. For a heartbeat nothing happened and all right, I admit it, I was kind of relieved, a little disappointed, but mostly relieved. Then the missile punched through the other wall of the warehouse, zoomed straight and level across the parking lot on a streak of smoke and fire, smashed through a stained glass window and exploded.

Kandi said, "Congratulations. I believe you blew up the Non-Denominational Chapel of Rest." We heard several alarms go off, there was a second explosion, and the chapel was on fire almost immediately. I hoped my friend Mr. Forklift escaped the fire.

I exhaled the breath I'd been holding. "Lousy cheap warehouse construction. Time to go."

Chapter Twenty-Seven   Invasion

Kandi, Alys, and I took my Chevy, Ray-Ray and Chet were in the van; we drove quickly but legally down Springdale, past Garfield and into the winding streets of the upscale tract that backed up to the oil field. We parked a block away from the house and walked openly down the street, chatting about nothing—which is the best way to do it if you want to be unnoticed. It was one of those mini-mansions built when times were great and everybody thought they'd go on forever, and shows like, "Flip Your House" had through-the-roof ratings. It was obvious this two-story ranch-style had been vacant for a while—minimal maintenance on the front yard, less on the side. That and the "For Sale—Bank Owned" sign tipped me off. If it looked sad and lonely it had company; its neighbor on the left was in the same shape. Alys slipped into the shadows next to the garage to act as lookout. When we made our way into the back yard luck was with us—an optimistic owner had built a redwood playhouse complete with child-sized porch, making it easy to step across from the railing and climb down the simple chain-link fence. We found ourselves on a dirt service road; on the other side of it we found the real fence—twelve feet high, topped with razorwire. "Don't jump down," we heard Roger whisper from the other side. "The ground's uneven, and further in there's pipes everywhere." We carefully climbed up, slid through a gap Roger had cut in the razorwire, and climbed down into the wetlands. Roger appeared out of nowhere and gestured for us to follow. We carefully made our way through the ankle-deep water about a quarter of a mile to the maze of pipes and odd-looking devices that made up the field.

In the night we could hear pumps moving up and down. Occasionally a bobbing pump head would show against the clouds. "How long have you known?" Ray-Ray said softly from my left.

"About Edna? Almost as soon as I found out Harker sent you two after my laptop. *You* wouldn't have done it for Mr. Ascot, but if your wife asked you to . . ."

"Begged. That girl, she just begged me. It was a lot of money." He sighed. "Never had a bed of her own, you know what that's like? Growin' up, three sisters in one bed, two little brothers on the couch." I almost commented that it would put a crimp in bringing dates home, but for once exercised restraint. "When she ran away because her folks just couldn't feed all the kids, she slept wherever she could. Then her and me, we're gettin' married and we love each other, man, love like that you do anythin' for, only she says all she wants is a bed of her own." For once I kept my mouth shut. "It just ate at her, you know, bein' afraid of goin' back to poor and she don't want that, no sir, she don't."

"Baines offers her money."

He walked on silently for a moment. Then, "You gonna tell Ms. Plumlee?"

"Edna's dead, Ray-Ray. What good would it do?"

I heard him sigh again. "You think we can do this thing tonight? Take care of these bad people?"

"Yeah, Ray-Ray. We're gonna take care of these bad people."

Chet stepped over to us, face lit from below by the light from his cell, like at summer camp when you hold a flashlight under your chin and tell scary stories. He whispered, "It worked. Lots of activity at the warehouses. Nothing here." He reached up to adjust his Stetson realized it was in the van, and shoved his hand in his pocket.

"Hey, Tex, I thought for a minute there you were going to tell us when they got home the couple found a hook hanging on the car door. You okay?"

"Yessiree, Bob. Rarin' to go. Get this over with." He paused. He looked down at his phone and sucked his breath in sharply before he showed me. No service. "They're here."

"Good."

Next to me I heard Ray-Ray ratchet his shotgun.

Things started to go wrong almost as soon as we went into the oil field proper. The moon, only half-full anyway, went behind clouds and all at once it was totally dark. We all froze for a moment, waiting for our eyes to adjust. I closed my eyes and counted to ten. When I opened them it got better, but not by much. Chet whispered, "Please leave the light on Mommy, I'm scared of the dark," and laughed, a laugh had a nasty edge I didn't like. We were feeling our way across rows of pipes, listening to the pumps moving the rigs up and down, watching where we put our feet, watching for Blondell Baines, Faith Valentine, Chooch, or some Reat-a-Thug—any of the long list of folks who wanted to shoot us—when Ray-Ray stepped on a pipe instead of over it. It was slick and oily and he fell. The vague silhouette just vanished down into the space between the pipes, up to the hip; he pitched forward, reflexively throwing his hands out. There was a thud, his shotgun went flying off into the darkness and we heard him gasp.

I whispered, "Nobody move." I could hear him grunting in pain as he tried to free himself. Shuffling my feet—I didn't want to drop into a hole like Ray-Ray—I crept slowly, cautiously, in the direction of his pain.

Deciding I had to risk it, I covered the lens with my hand and turned on my flashlight. More summer camp—I could see dark bone silhouettes down the center of my fingers. Cautiously, I spread two fingers and moved a sliver of light across the surface. What was amazing was that we hadn't all slipped and broken bones. Pipes ran along the ground, rose to form metal arches, vanished into pits, climbed into complex structures. And there were pits everywhere. I switched off my flashlight and thought. In addition to Ray-Ray's soft noises I could hear Chet's ragged breathing. That decided me.

I turned on the light again, and found Ray-Ray. He was dragging himself out of the space between two pipes by sheer will. One of the first things they teach you in First Aid is to assess the situation before you try to help someone—it does no one any good if you rush in and become a casualty yourself. So I took it slow as I made my way over to him.

I crouched next to him, turned the flashlight off and tucked it in my belt, got my hands under his arms and eased him the rest of the way out. If you've had the same First Responder training I got at FSB Manhattan, you're saying, "Don't move him! Possible spinal injury!" You're right, but they weren't talking about a situation where he was also faced with the possibility of being shot by the people we were here to stop, so he had to be moved. Once again covering most of the lens, I used the flashlight again and got my first good look at him. It was bad. Blood ran down his face from a scalp wound but that was not the big problem. His leg was twisted at an impossible angle.

Softly, I said, "Chet, use your light, but cover it. Come over here, but watch your step." A minute later he picked his way over to me, followed by Kandi. "Tex, I need you to stay with him. Somebody's got to."

Kandi said, "He needs medical attention. We can't leave him."

Ray-Ray's arm shot out, grabbed my hand. "No! Please."

"Mac, neither of you is thinking clearly, and—"

"Find them!"

He couldn't squeeze anymore, so I squeezed for him. "Count on it."

As Chet was easing Ray-Ray into a more comfortable position, Kandi whispered, "All right, I guess I can accept it. I don't like it, but I'll accept it. So I know you have a plan—how do we find them?"

"No idea.'

Roger appeared out of the gloom holding oily rags and scraps of lumber. He squatted next to Ray-Ray and began wrapping his leg in a crude splint. I said, "Roger? Chet? Any thoughts?" They both shook their heads.

"It's a big place," Roger said.

Chet had his phone out. "I've got a satellite image saved that will get us to the helicopter landing pads. There's three." So he gave me his phone and we moved off, watching for our quarry, looking out for jutting pipes, some of which looked old and rusty. Around us the working pumps moved up and down, patiently extracting the black gold. Behind us Chet did one of the bravest things I've ever had the privilege to witness: he turned his light out.

The first two pads were not only empty, they were clearly not in use. Debris covered most of the tarmac in both cases. I muttered, "Third time's the charm."

We approached the third pad very carefully, Roger going first without a word, simply vanishing into the dark as if he'd never been there. Kandi was on my right. I took a deep breath and started to edge forward on my stomach, peering at the shadows that covered everything. Beside me I could dimly see Kandi sliding carefully around a loose coil of chain. I heard a noise and froze. Kandi pressed herself into the oily dirt. We held our positions for what seemed to be an eternity, but the noise was not repeated. The clouds over us were the only thing that moved. The noise came again. Kandi stiffened, then clutched my arm. The clouds parted and a rat the size of a Chihuahua trotted purposefully into a patch of moonlight and stopped to look at us eyeball to eyeball. He had a lizard in his mouth, drooping down on each side like a Fu Manchu moustache. Completely unafraid,

Mr. Rat stood about a yard from my face, peering from side to side, twitching his nose and giving us a close look, either to see if we were a threat or to size us up as possible food. He reached up with a pink rat foot to scratch, then, still curious, he waddled closer. If he touched my face with his rat nose I wasn't sure what I'd do. The moustache wiggled and Mr. Rat bit down, switched his scaly tail and trundled on to have dinner, eclipsing a light in the distance as he did.

All at once I knew what to do. I got to my feet and stood quietly, waiting. It didn't take long. The clouds moved across the moon again and in about five minutes I saw one of the few lights eclipsed—blink—at ground level as someone walked by. No, wait, I'd almost fooled myself. The blink was wrong, single instead of the two blinks from legs going by. Another rat or maybe a possum. The next time it was blink-blink. Then we caught a flicker of movement to our left and glimpsed a group of figures moving through the machinery.

A group of five shadowy figures passed us. Baines was dragging Kaylee; Faith was at his side. Chooch was behind them, walking holding the arm of a shadowy figure. They were moving slowly, using flashlights with taped lenses; they were better prepared than we were. As I watched Kaylee kicked Baines in the ankle and he stumbled. Bad luck—he didn't slip and break a leg. He shook her hard enough to rattle her teeth and I added another reason to dislike him to my list. Not that I needed it.

The shadowy figure stumbled and Chooch turned his light on her face. Henrietta Graveline.

Tell me about your adventures.

I whispered, "Freeze." If they looked our way when the moon came out they would see us. I felt something on my foot. I looked down and Mr. Rat was back, and he was standing on my shoe. I could move my foot and he'd get scared and run away, or maybe he'd get mad and bite me and I'd die of some horrible rat disease. I choose not to move. After a moment, ignoring me, he waddled across my other shoe and vanished into the darkness.

They stopped in the moonshadow cast by a pump. Baines said, "Okay, we need to wait a while to make the rendezvous." He pushed Kaylee down. "Listen up. Macdonald is a pain in the butt, hell, this would have worked so slick without him. So—"

"You want to get to a verb here? This is *so* boring."

"You're insurance, okay? He won't do anything as long as I've got you. Everything goes like it should, we leave you behind."

Faith said, "And if it doesn't I get to kill you both. Are we clear?"

Henrietta said, "Please, I just want to make this right."

Kaylee said, "Should I be taking notes? Is there going to be a quiz?" Faith backhanded her.

Chooch said, "What about Rod?"

Faith kissed her knuckles. "Tie the kid up."

"What about Rod? He was one of us. One of the Five." Faith stepped toward him, smiling. Baines put out a hand, stopped her.

"Okay. Okay, pal, you asked. I didn't trust him and I was right not to." He was getting worked up, his eyes narrowing, voice going up an octave. Faith watched him, expressionless. "The little shit didn't listen. He was trying to make a deal on the side. So he's out, understand? Out. He didn't listen to me and he's out." Baines brooded, chin down on his chest.

Faith nodded at Chooch. "Do your job."

"But . . ." He nodded.

While Chooch tied her up they moved off about ten yards, taking Henrietta with them. Chooch finished and went to join them but he turned so Kaylee was always in sight.

But he had taken his light with him and it was totally dark. I crept close and cut Kaylee's tie. When she felt me behind her she didn't make a sound. "When I give the word, run straight behind us. Kandi's waiting."

I knew Chooch would see it as soon as Kaylee ran. I figured I'd shoot him or Roger would leap out of the darkness and do a Jackie Chan on him. If Henrietta could get away from Baines, great, if not at least he'd only have one hostage. And I had reason to believe he wouldn't hurt her.

Okay, it was a terrible plan. But, it almost worked. I yelled, "Now!" Kaylee jumped to her feet and sprinted into the dark. Being fourteen made it easier to jump from one pipe to the next. Then Baines said, "Come back here or I blow her brains out. She doesn't have to be alive for this to work." He held the gun to Henrietta's head. Faith was in a perfect shooting stance, pointing the Ruger at my head. All three of us raised our hands.

They took our guns. There was no sign of Roger. I wondered if he had made it out safely. Couldn't blame him for taking a shot at freedom.

And there it was right next to him, covered with a tarp. A small helicopter, small, but big enough to get them out to the freighter.

"If you take that tarp off and start the engine, the people watching will shoot you down."

Baines said, "I don't believe you." Faith held the gun on me, steady.

"Believe it. It's over. Some part of the US government has struck a deal with the North Koreans. Part of the deal is you don't get out alive."

"Bullshit." Baines looked at his Tag Heuer.

"Let Kaylee and Henrietta go. At least do that."

"Not a chance. I need Henrietta for the sample, and Kaylee is insurance and payback. You caused me a lot of trouble. Even if they're out there, and they're not, they won't shoot if she's on the helicopter."

"These guys will."

Let me say again, whenever you think things can't get any worse, they do. "Mac, Mac—" Chet stumbled out of the darkness. There was blood down the front of his shirt.

"Hi, pal," Baines grinned.

Chet ignored him. "Mac, he's worse. I think he's going into shock or something." He took a step toward the edge of our little clearing. "You gotta come. I can't move him by myself."

"Hey, pal, I'm talking to you." Baines' voice was soft. "You need to listen when I talk."

Faith was watching everything carefully, keeping her gun pointed between me and Chet.

All at once she said, "Change of plans. Chooch."

That worthy pointed his gun at his Baines.

It looked like something out of a Tarantino movie—Faith pointing her Ruger between me and Chet, Baines pointing his Steyr machine pistol at me, and Chooch pointing his automatic at Baines.

Faith said, "We talked about it and decided we didn't want to live in North Korea."

Chooch snickered. "Yeah. I hear it ain't very nice. Me and the Rod are gonna party. Party hearty, man."

Baines' expression was comical, or at least it would have been if he hadn't been pointing a gun at me. Chooch laughed out loud. "You're always thinking people are out to get you, hell, it had to be true sooner or later." It started to sink in. If I'd been a better person I might have felt sorry for Baines, betrayed by the one person he trusted. Nah.

I said, "That's why Rod's alive. Faith's too good a shot to miss at that range, unless it's on purpose."

Chet was on a mission. "Listen, we can deal with this later. Ray-Ray needs a doctor, and he needs one now." He was still backing up. Faith was occupied taking her former boss's gun. All at once I got it.

Chooch walked over to Chet, close to the edge and raised his gun. Suddenly Chet dropped flat. Chooch fired twice through the space he'd occupied and then Roger was on him. He simply flew out of the dark as if the night itself had come to malignant life. It was no contest. Roger chopped Chooch's wrist, kicked the side of his knee, and clipped him in the head as he went down. He was smiling as he did it, not even breathing hard.

Kandi sprinted in from the other side, snatched Kaylee and was gone in an instant. Unfortunately Faith never took her eyes off me.

She had me.

Close range, no chance of missing.

Faith Valentine shot me.

On TV the bad guy always makes a speech, "I'm gonna kill you because . . ." Blah, blah, blah. Faith just shot me. At the last second I twisted to the side and the bullet took me in the back. She steadied the Ruger with her left hand and fired again. Roger Winters stepped in front and took the bullet. Mine was a graze but Roger's was worse.

Ray-Ray stumbled out from behind a stack of pipes, dragging his splinted leg, and slapped her gun aside. She lashed out and caught him in the ribs with a spin kick that would have done Kandi proud. He grunted, staggered, but didn't go down. Then he had one hand around her neck, lifting her off the ground as she brought the gun around. He slammed her head into the pipes and still she hit at him with one hand and tried to bring the Ruger around with the other. He smashed her head into the pipes again and she went limp. Blood was trickling from her nose, mouth, and ears, dark, almost black, in the moonlight. He picked her up and threw her into a row of pipes that arced up out of the soil. She landed on her back. We all heard the sickening crunch as her spine snapped.

"Baines, it's not too late. Nadzia's murderer is dead. Faith's dead. It's not too late. There will be legal consequences, but at least you'll be alive."

He pushed is glasses up and said, "I have things to do, a dynasty to found, great things to do." In the confusion he'd picked up his Steyr. He held the machine pistol on us.

"Faith did the actual killings. She's dead, it's too late for her but you can still let Henrietta go."

Kandi said, "And you don't have the sample, so your buyers will be very unhappy, to say the least." He smiled, tightened his grip on Henrietta's arm.

Looking at her, I said, "Do you want to tell them or shall I?"

"What?" Kandi said.

"Henrietta *is* the sample. At some point she colonized her own skin and it's been living there ever since."

She said, "We believed. Moral certitude, you know. Gone now, all gone. It was wrong for this to only be in government hands and we knew they would misuse it, so I took it. It was easy. I had taken a rather bad fall on my bicycle and had a scrape on my calf. I just pulled off the dressing and swabbed the wound with some of the culture. Then I, I took a sample from it and kept the culture alive in Petri dishes."

"They burned the lab to cover their tracks."

"In part. Mostly they burned it because the experiment was a failure, non-lethal, like I've said all along." She looked at Baines. He just grinned, tightened his grip on her arm and looked at his watch again. I didn't like that. It meant he had a back-up plan. "All of this because Lisa June talked too much. When this started I knew I had to destroy the culture dishes, but the organism, well, I wanted it to live. As long as I had it I had something to bargain with. So, I scraped my leg and put it back—re-colonized it. It's really not all that bad." She pulled up her pant leg, jerked off the bandage and in the moonlight we could see the sores, many over an inch across, penetrating her skin in red-rimmed, oozing craters.

"That is so *gross*." Kaylee said.

"So, you see now, don't you? She is how I will keep it alive until we reach our destination." Baines smiled.

"You still can't get away, Baines, they're watching."

"I think I can, pal."

Henrietta said, "But it won't do you any good. Like I've said all along, the bacteria is non-lethal. It makes old people sick and people who are already sick worse, but it's not some kind of bio-weapon. Your buyers will be very disappointed."

I said, "They'll be delighted. It's just what they want."

Kandi said, "I don't get it."

"They're going to use it on their own people. They spread it in the North, blame the South, and, presto, a new government." I looked at Baines. He shrugged.

Baines nodded. "Doesn't matter what they do with it, just that they pay. And I can get out of here, with her. We'll be going now. Don't follow us and you won't get shot." He ignored the helicopter and dragged Henrietta into the darkness.

I yelled, "Down!" and pushed Kandi down and covered her body with mine, a moment before bullets sprayed out, sparks flying as they ricocheted off pumps and pipes. Just his way of discouraging us from following him. See what I mean about lack of trust being a good thing?

"Kaylee, take care of Chet and Ray-Ray. Kandi, take the gun. If Baines comes back, shoot him."

"But—" Then she nodded. "How will you catch him?"

"I won't. He'll catch me."

I ran into the dark after Baines.

His real plan, hidden even from Faith, was to launch the black inflatable from Dog Beach. All he had to do was get across, or under, Pacific Coast Highway. It turned out to be under. He headed for a storm drain.

Suddenly, lights appeared on the beach and the police helicopter rose above the cliffs and started sweeping its spotlight back and forth. Special Agent Morse had gotten my message.

He gave up dragging Henrietta and threw her aside, smashing her into a large pump. "Take care of her." I yelled to Kandi, and then it was just the two of us. He fired and I ran. He yelled, "You can run but you can't hide." Of course, I didn't bother correcting him, just made sure to make just enough noise to lead him deeper back into the maze of pipes and pumps.

He must have heard me because he shot twice more, but in the dark, aiming at a moving target he had little chance of hitting me. I ducked behind a large machine with gears and belts and heard a shot ricochet off it. He was better than I thought. My back was on fire and I knew I was losing blood.

We dodged around dusty piles of equipment; I lost him. Running in the direction I'd last seen him go, I cursed under my breath, slowed to a walk. Then I heard a crunch of gravel behind me, turned and there he was. He pointed his gun at me and I ran, ducking around a storage shed, rolling under a truck and freezing. The truck was the last one in a row of similar vehicles. Baines was moving carefully, purposefully checking under each one. We were far enough from the people I wanted to protect. He turned and went the wrong way. I made some noise to draw him back. It was time—whether I liked it or not. I rolled out from under and darted over to an arch of pipe. He'd flipped out, given up on escape. He wanted to find me, shoot me, then go back and shoot my friends. Well, it was what I'd expected. What I hadn't taken into account was getting shot. He had a light and a gun, and he was patient. Without giving myself time to think about how insane it was, I slithered up the ladder, crawled out and clung to the underside of the crosspiece like a human bat. Baines walked by about ten feet away and, even though he looked up, he was shining his light at the tops of the structures and under vehicles, not on the bottom in the deep shadows cast by the moonlight.

A moment after he went by I dropped quietly to the ground and followed.

Then he stopped under an arch of pipe. This was what I'd been waiting for. I crawled up and out over him.

It was higher than I liked, but I pulled myself from my knees up to my feet, crouched and dropped on him anyway. In the last second he must have sensed something because he turned and looked up and I swear I saw the reflection of my white-soled Vans in his glasses. I landed on him, one foot squarely on each shoulder and most people would have had all the fight knocked out of them, at least I was expecting that Baines would be down, either unconscious, winded, or—my personal favorite—in agony with two broken collarbones; unfortunately what I got was a very pissed off psychopath who wanted nothing more than to beat me to a pulp, kill me, and then kill my friends. I landed on my butt and then flopped to my back. He staggered, but stayed on his feet, kicked me once and then tried to drag me up so he could punch me. I held him off with one hand and groped with the other till I found something to hit him with. It was only a piece of wood so he batted it away easily. He stood, found his Steyr machine pistol, pointed it at my face. I kicked his feet out for under him; he went down but held onto the gun. The world was slipping into and out of focus. Blood was running into my eyes from a scalp would I hadn't noticed I got to my feet, swayed.

He pulled the trigger again and, when the gun clicked empty, threw it at my head; this guy had *definitely* watched too much

TV. By pure reflex I caught it, left-handed. He swung at me, I blocked it with my right forearm and clocked him a good one in the side of his face with my left. And I put him down with one punch.

That's right—one punch. Okay, I had two pounds of metal in my hand, but it was still one punch. Blood exploded out of the area around his nose, a couple of white specks that I hoped were teeth flew out of his mouth, he spun in a circle and went down hard, landing on his back. Baines had left the building.

I got his feet and dragged him back to the others. Henrietta, Medea in another time, was sitting up, holding her head.

I dropped Baines' feet and swayed as the world narrowed to a tunnel and a surf-like roaring filled my ears. Dimly, I knew that he was crawling away, but I didn't seem to be able to do anything about it.

Kaylee stepped up and kicked him in the balls, hard. He didn't exactly scream; it was more like the screech of a teakettle at full boil. Then he curled into a fetal position and I figured Mr. Baines wouldn't give us any more trouble. She turned to me and shrugged. "Two years of AYSO. I'm not a total nerd." Baines' teakettle screech had brought me back to life.

I nudged him with my toe. "Just not your day, is it, pal?"

I led Roger a short distance away, made sure he had somebody's shirt wrapped tightly around his flesh wound. I found the rope Chooch had used to tie Kaylee and tied him to a pipe. He was, after all, an escaped mental patient wanted for two murders. He didn't resist as I tugged the knot tight, nodded at him and walked away.

I went back to the others. We heard sirens in the distance and settled down to wait.

A moment later I smelled the orange fragrance of Constant Comment tea and saw her in the shadows. Brown leather mini, matching boots, beige long-sleeved silk blouse with a big floppy collar buttoned to her throat. Beads around her neck. "Hello, Diana."

She took my hand, squeezed it. I could feel the pressure, her smooth palm. "Nadzia says to work on your grinder."

"I wish—"

"Shhh. It's all right." She touched a fingertip to my lips. I could feel it, gentle, cool, and loving. Then she was gone.

I turned back to the others, who of course were going on as if nothing had happened. Around us the night would soon be filled with lights and people with guns, but for the moment it was still and quiet.

Then Kaylee was next to me, touching my hand and looking up at me shyly. "Who was that woman?"

As the paramedics were hooking me up to an IV, the cop said, "So, how much head start did you give him?"

"What do you mean? I tied him right there."

The ropes where Roger had been secured to the drill rig were empty. "Mr. Macdonald, you have been a sailor most of your life. You want to convince me you couldn't tie a knot that would hold him?" I declined to answer.

He'd been shot, the oil field was surrounded by police, and several helicopters circled the area, shining spotlights everywhere. Of course they never found him.

Kandi

After another trip to the ER, the rest of our day was spent with various government agencies. Most of the people we talked to carried guns, but they didn't seem interested in shooting us, so it was all right.

That night we sat in my Jacuzzi, Kandi with a glass of white wine, me with my usual Dos Equis Dark. I was sitting up on the ledge to keep my dressing dry. The water bubbled, the channel behind us was quiet. She poked me with her toe. "What are you smiling at?"

"I thought I could do something and I found out I couldn't." I set the beer down and took her in my arms.

"No. You decided you didn't want to. Big difference." She snuggled close to me and murmured, "Sailor, I believe the game is afoot."

"That's not my foot."

A few minutes later, she whispered, "You realize we could be under surveillance?"

"Well, we better make it good."

We did.

Text on Mary's iPhone:

```
Mary U think I'll let you make me go away. LOL & GL.
K
```

The End

Mac and Kandi will return in *Correction*.

Author Bio

James R. Preston spends most of his time at the keyboard, writing the award-winning Surf City Mysteries—think "beach noir." Pennies For Her Eyes is the fourth novel in this series and was preceded by Leave A Good-Looking Corpse, Read 'Em And Weep, and The Road To Hell. You can read the opening chapter of each book at JamesRPreston.com.

Away from the keyboard, James likes reading, films (especially 1950's SF like Them and The Crawling Eye), sailing. bodyboarding, and Texas Hold'Em Poker. James played in one of the 2011 World Series tournaments and sadly busted out early. This year will be different.

www.JamesRPreston.com

Other Surf City Mysteries

Leave A Good-Looking Corpse

From the journals of T.R. Macdonald:

It isn't every night that a wet, bleeding man leads the hostess into her party at gunpoint . . . not even in Hollywood and this was Orange county, home of Disneyland, Knott's Berry Farm and the Crystal Cathedral. Hell, even our baseball team is the Angels. A drop of blood ran down the side of my face. I let it drip off my chin, figuring it made me look tough.

That wet, bleeding gun-waver is me, T.R. Macdonald, and I'm a broker/analyst based in NYNY, or I was until I got a phone call about my wife. I walked off the trading floor, packed a bag and started driving for the left coast. After I got there things turned weird, then weirder. Some the weirdness was ok, but a lot of it was very nasty; for example, right after the party I had to shoot a kid.

Read 'Em And Weep

From the journals of T.R. Macdonald:

I was sort of hiding from two guys who either thought we were in business together or who wanted to kill me.

"Sort of hiding" because I could have left town and been relatively safe, but Las Vegas, NV, has so many wonderful things to see and do that I decided to go to a topless rollerskating show instead.

"Sort of hiding" because I was fairly sure that the guys in question would take Door Number Two and try to shoot me, a lot.

Why me? I'm T. R. Macdonald, a sort-of unemployed broker/analyst from the boutique—we handle a small number of very rich clients—firm of Fields, Smith, and Barkman. My sort-of girlfriend, Kandi, had asked me to go to Vegas to see if we could talk to her cousin Chet, because she thinks his adoptive father, Dr. Woodrow Shaw, may be nuts. Are you getting all this? There will be a quiz. Dr. Shaw asked me to go, too, and he offered to pay.

It sounded like easy money.

So I went.

I must be nuts.

The Road To Hell

From the journals of T.R. Macdonald:

I was standing in the desert, in the sun, outside of a semi-abandoned church, and I had a gun. My girlfriend, the lovely blonde Kandi Shaw, and I were registered in the Maiden's Blush Suite, one of the finest in Las Vegas' lavish Bromeliad Resort and Spa. Unfortunately, I wasn't in the suite. I was standing in the sun, waiting for my brains to finish boiling.

I'm T. R. Macdonald, a semi-unemployed broker-anaylst from Huntington Beach, California—Surf City, USA. And I was here instead of sitting on my short tri-fin outside the break line at the Huntington Pier because the casino offered me money to assist in security for WillieFest One, the richest slot tournament in history.

But so far I'd been mainly a moving target or punching bag—I was run off the road, chased by pit bulls, mixed it up with a vicious pimp, and was nearly trampled in a club stampede. Not to mention the part where I was poked in the nose. With a sawed-off shotgun. All of that led to the church, and my gun, and Kandi standing next to me with her gun in her hand—and she wanted to shoot somebody.

And if the two men inside the church didn't listen to reason, I was very much afraid she was right—I'd have to shoot them.

CPSIA information can be obtained
at www.ICGtesting.com
Printed in the USA
BVHW032249221219
567526BV00001B/4/P